Lena Diaz was born in ~~California, Louisiana an~~ with her husband and two children. ~~romantic suspense~~ author, she was a computer programmer. A Romance Writers of America Golden Heart® Award finalist, she has also won the prestigious Daphne du Maurier Award for Excellence in Mystery/ Suspense. To get the latest news about Lena, please visit her website, www.lenadiaz.com.

Janie Crouch has loved to read romance her whole life. This *USA TODAY* bestselling author cut her teeth on Mills & Boon Romance novels as a preteen, then moved on to a passion for romantic suspense as an adult. Janie lives with her husband and four children overseas. She enjoys traveling, long-distance running, movie watching, knitting and adventure/ obstacle racing. You can find out more about her at www.janiecrouch.com.

This story is dedicated to the *Tennessee Takedown* readers who demanded that I make it a series. I've absolutely *loved* writing these stories about the Destiny, Tennessee, SWAT team. I hope readers love *SWAT Standoff*, the exciting conclusion to this thrilling ride.

SWAT
STANDOFF

LENA DIAZ

MAJOR CRIMES

JANIE CROUCH

MILLS & BOON

First Published in Great Britain 2018
by Mills & Boon, an imprint of HarperCollins*Publishers*
1 London Bridge Street, London, SE1 9GF

Swat Standoff © 2018 Lena Diaz
Major Crimes © 2018 Janie Crouch

ISBN: 978-0-263-26581-1

39-0718

MIX
Paper from
responsible sources
FSC™ C007454

This book is produced from independently certified FSC™ paper to ensure responsible forest management.

For more information visit: www.harpercollins.co.uk/green

Printed and bound in Spain
by CPI, Barcelona

SWAT STANDOFF

LENA DIAZ

Chapter One

SWAT Officer Blake Sullivan crouched behind some honeysuckle-vine-covered logs and peered at the weathered gray barn through his rifle scope. His target was little more than a shadow in the second-story window that had probably lost its glass long before Blake was born. How the suspect had managed to get up that high without crashing through the rotten stairs or floorboards was a mystery. The dilapidated building should have collapsed long ago in the violent winds that sometimes blew down from the nearby Smoky Mountains. Blake imagined the only reason that it hadn't fallen down yet was that it was sheltered from the elements by a thick stand of Tennessee sugar maples and white flowering dogwoods.

With the early morning sun slanting through the trees behind him, and a lull in the light spring breeze that had been blowing moments before, conditions were perfect to take the shot. He eased his finger from the cold frame of his rifle to the smooth, welcoming cradle of the trigger.

Two chirps followed by a high-pitched whistle sounded off to his left. It sounded just like a bobwhite bird, common here at Hawkins Ridge and Tennessee in general. But Blake knew better. That was the SWAT team leader, Dillon Gray, signaling him. But if Blake looked away, he might lose the perpetrator. Dillon would have to wait.

Ignoring a second, more insistent whistle, he edged the barrel of the rifle down a fraction, exhaled slowly and squeezed.

Pop.

Red bloomed across the suspect's chest. He cartwheeled backward, disappearing from sight.

Blake grinned. One down; one to go. Now he could see what Dillon wanted.

He looked over his left shoulder. The team leader stood a good twenty yards away, talking to Donna Waters, the only female member of their team. Dressed in green camouflage, they both would've completely blended into their surroundings if it wasn't for the white S-W-A-T letters across Dillon's back. Neither of them seemed to notice Blake. Whatever Dillon had wanted earlier must not have been that important.

Blake turned his attention back to the barn. Had the suspects split up? Initially, they'd worked as a team, staying close together. If they stuck to that plan, the second one had to be somewhere close by.

Nearly a full minute later, his patience was rewarded. A dark shadow moved near some trees to the right of the building. The man furtively looked around as if to see whether anyone had spotted him. Destiny, Tennessee's entire seven-member SWAT team, plus their chief, was out here somewhere. Correction, *six*-member team, now that Colby had taken a new job a couple hours' drive from Blount County.

Blake glanced back to signal Dillon and Donna. But,

either they were blending in with the trees so well that he couldn't see them now, or they were gone. He considered radioing the team to let them know he'd gotten one of the suspects and had eyes on the second. But he worried there might be static or that the sound of his voice would spook his prey.

He scanned the front of the barn again. The suspect took off, sprinting across the clearing toward the woods. Blake jerked up his rifle. The man looked right at him, his eyes wide with panic. He lunged for the cover of some pine trees.

Pop, pop.

Missed. The man disappeared into the dark gloom of tree cover.

Blake cursed and straightened, knees popping from crouching so long, and took off in pursuit. When he reached where the man had entered the woods, he shook his head. The guy was about five foot five and probably weighed a buck thirty, if that. He should have been light on his feet, easily weaving his way through the thin early-spring vegetation without leaving much of a trace. Instead, he'd plowed through like a linebacker, heedless of breaking small branches and leaving clear footprints in the dew-laden grass. He might as well have put out a sign saying Bad Guy Went This Way. Either the guy was an idiot, or he was extremely clever, trying to lead Blake into an ambush.

Another birdcall chirped behind him, this one the not-so-convincing squawk of a blue jay. There was no mistaking SWAT team member Randy Carter's signal. Blake rolled his eyes. He doubted even a novice in the woods would think that was a real bird. He paused and glanced over his shoulder. Sure enough, Randy stood in the same copse that Blake had left just moments ago. Randy motioned for him to come back and made another motion toward his left.

Blake shook his head, held up one finger and pointed down the path where the suspect had disappeared.

Randy insistently pointed to his left again.

Blake tightened his hand on his rifle in frustration. If Randy couldn't understand a simple signal, then that was his problem. Blake refused to put the team in danger by breaking off pursuit. The suspect could circle back around and sneak up on one of them, or he could escape altogether. Ignoring Randy, Blake headed into the woods.

Ten minutes later, he found the suspect. The man was holding his rifle above his head to keep it dry as he waded across a waist-deep stream.

Blake brought his rifle up and stepped from the cover of trees. "Police. Freeze."

The suspect whipped around.

Blake squeezed the trigger. *Pop.*

The suspect let out a blistering curse. A dark red stain covered his right shoulder. Blake took another shot, giving the man a matching stain on the left.

"I give up! Stop shooting!" The man held his gun over his head and glared at Blake.

Blake kept his rifle trained on him. "Work your way back to this side of the river. If you make any sudden movements, I'll pop you again."

The man's eyes narrowed with the promise of retribution, but he started forward as ordered.

After taking the man's gun, Blake pulled a set of handcuffs from the holder on the back of his belt.

The man's brows shot up. "Really? You're going to cuff me?"

"It's all part of the game, my friend. Turn around."

"You don't play fair. That second shot was completely unnecessary."

"I play to win. That's all that matters." He clicked the cuffs into place, slung the straps of both rifles over his shoulder and marched the man back toward the barn. Now that it was safe to break radio silence, he pulled the two-way off his belt and opened a channel.

"Blake to base. SWAT two, suspects zero. I got both of them. The first one in the barn, the second at the river. I'm on my way back with the second one."

His prisoner glanced over his shoulder, aiming a frown his way.

"Keep moving."

The man gave him a look that should have made him burst into flames.

The radio remained quiet as they strode toward the barn. No one answered Blake's call. He pressed the button again.

"Blake to base. Copy?"

No answer. Maybe they were in a communication dead zone. Cell phones were virtually useless out here. He supposed the same thing could happen even with their powerful radios. Or the equipment could be malfunctioning. Destiny was a small town with an equally small law-enforcement budget. Their equipment wasn't exactly top of the line and was rarely purchased new. The only reason that Destiny could even afford to have their detectives operate in a dual role as a SWAT team was that neighboring townships augmented the Destiny Police Department's budget. In return, Destiny

SWAT responded to calls across several counties, when needed. But even the extra money never seemed to be enough.

When they moved into the clearing by the barn, Blake jerked to a halt and drew in a sharp breath. There, lying on the ground, were his teammates—everyone except their leader, Dillon. They were all dressed in green camouflage uniforms, covered with red splotches.

Chapter Two

Blake's prisoner started laughing. He was tempted to shoot the man again.

"I see you got your suspect," someone snarled close by.

He whirled around to see Dillon Gray striding toward him. Beside him, Chief Thornton's white puff of hair lifted and fell with every step he made. Both of them looked mad enough to wrestle hornets.

A sinking feeling settled in Blake's gut. What had he done wrong this time? He looked to his teammates for support. But they were all lying motionless on the ground. He cleared his throat and straightened his shoulders as Dillon stopped directly in front of him, the chief a few steps back.

"What happened?" Blake waved toward the team. "I don't understand. I took out the first suspect in the barn. I know he didn't get off any shots. And I followed this guy to the river."

"There were *three* suspects," Dillon snapped. "While you were off gallivanting alone, the third suspect ambushed the rest of the team."

Blake's gaze dropped to the red splotches on Dillon's chest that added weight to his accusation.

"But our intel said there were only two." Blake motioned toward his prisoner, who was still laughing, but was now sitting on top of a rotting log. "This guy took off, so I—"

Bam. White-hot pain exploded through Blake's jaw and he slammed back onto the ground. He glared up at Dillon, whose fist was still clenched as if he were ready to punch him again.

"What the hell was that for?" Blake snarled. "I got two of the bad guys."

"Yeah. You did. But you ignored the signals from both Randy and me and went all Rambo on your own." Dillon waved toward the bodies on the ground. "You weren't here when the team needed you."

Blake shoved to his feet. "I don't know what has you so fired up. If an entire team can't handle one bad guy without my help, you should be mad at them, not me."

"You idiot." Dillon took another step toward him.

The chief grabbed his shoulder. "Easy," Thornton said. Then he let Dillon's shoulder go and moved back, making it clear that he trusted his most senior officer to handle the situation. But he'd rather it not devolve into a fistfight.

Blake wanted to punch both of them. He'd done his job. It was the rest of the team who'd failed.

Dillon's jaw clenched and unclenched several times before he spoke again. "You can get up now," he told the team. "Everybody reload your paint guns and get fresh camo. We're doing this again until we get it right."

A chorus of grumbles sounded from the others as they stood. But they dutifully headed toward the stacks of supplies on the other side of the clearing, where their gear was laid out for the day's training exercises.

"Tim, you okay?" Dillon asked the man who'd played the suspect that Blake had "killed" in the river.

"A bit bruised. He shot me *twice*. That second one was out of pure meanness."

"Oh, for Pete's sake. You didn't go down," Blake said. "I had to make sure you were dead."

"I was in the water. What was I supposed to do? Go under?"

"It might have been more convincing."

The man swore.

Dillon waved Tim toward the other SWAT team members. "Have one of the others uncuff you. If you don't want to stay for round two, I understand. You'll get paid either way."

"Nah, that's fine. As long as *he* isn't part of the next exercise." He angled his chin toward Blake.

Blake rolled his eyes. The man was being melodramatic. But then Dillon stepped closer, blocking his view of their pretend-perpetrator.

"That won't be a problem," Dillon said. "Blake's not participating in any more training."

Blake frowned. "Why not?"

"Seeing your teammates lying dead on the ground isn't answer enough?"

He barely refrained from rolling his eyes. "You obviously staged that for effect."

"You're right. We did catch the third suspect. But it was a close thing. None of us knew there was a third one out here. The chief surprised us with that element, which just proves how important it is to always be alert and operate as a team, watching each other's backs." He poked Blake in the chest as if for emphasis. "You were supposed to watch your partner's back. But Donna said you took off without her halfway through the scenario. What was that about?"

Blake felt his face flush with heat. He glanced toward the trucks. Donna had already changed into fresh camo and was retying her blond hair into a ponytail. She was also the only member of the team not paying attention to him and Dillon. Had he upset her? Did she feel that he'd let her down?

She'd been training him for several months, teaching him the Destiny Police Department's way of doing things, which wasn't the way he'd been trained in Knoxville. He was supposed to stick with her today. But when he'd seen the suspect racing through the woods, he'd taken off in pursuit, without waiting for his partner.

"I screwed up," he admitted. "I didn't want the suspect to get away, so I chased him to the barn. I assumed Donna would follow. But I lost her."

"No kidding. She was scanning the woods, searching for the suspects, and when she turned around, you were gone. Not exactly a team move."

Blake clenched his hands into fists at his sides. Not that he'd use them. He and Dillon were both a couple of inches over six feet and equally brawny. No doubt a fight between them would be long, bloody and painful. But that wasn't why Blake wouldn't hit him. Blake respected Dillon, even if the sentiment wasn't returned. He'd never raise his fists against him.

Too bad Dillon didn't share the same compulsion.

Blake waggled his jaw to ease the ache. "I had no reason to believe that Donna was in jeopardy. I would have come back to look for her, but the suspect holed up in the barn, giving me the perfect opportunity to pursue him. Once I took him out, the other suspect appeared. What was I supposed to do? Ignore him? Let him go?"

"What you're supposed to do, always, is follow orders. Your primary objective today was to stick with your partner. I made that crystal clear this morning. Failing that, when I signaled for you to report to me, you ignored my signal."

"I couldn't turn around. I would have missed my shot."

"You could have responded to me over the radio if you were worried about losing your sight line of the suspect. But you didn't."

"Not at first, no. I couldn't risk the noise alerting him. I did call later, after—"

"After the rest of the team was ambushed? And killed?"

Blake clamped his jaw shut. Why was he even trying to explain? As usual, Dillon refused to listen. He was a great leader and friend—to the *rest* of the team. But he'd disliked Blake from day one and made no secret about it. The only thing Blake could figure was that Dillon resented him because the chief had hired him without asking for his input.

If Chief Thornton hadn't offered him a job when he'd run into Blake at the Knoxville Police Station and gotten a taste of the drama going on there, Blake would be unemployed by now, with no prospects for another law-enforcement job. He owed a lot to the chief, including his silence about Blake's past. Blake hadn't wanted to share the details of what had happened, because he didn't want to prejudice his new team against him in case they didn't agree with his side of the story. But on days like today, he wondered if they'd both made a mistake. Their pact of silence meant that both of them had to lie to the team in answer to their questions about Blake's past. And lies were the worst sort of foundation on which to build trust. Which was why he always felt as though he were running in quicksand around here, never gaining traction no matter how hard he tried to fit in.

Except with Donna.

Beautiful and smart, she was the one bright spot in his life in Destiny, the one person who treated him as if he mattered. And he'd gone and screwed up with her, too. He'd run off after a suspect when he should have stuck by her side, training exercise or not. She probably despised him just as much as Dillon now.

He raised his hands in surrender, trying to defuse the situation. "Look, I'm sorry. I shouldn't have gone after the suspect on my own. I see that now."

"Gone off on your own? It's not that simple. You risked your partner's *life*. And don't you dare tell me it was *just* a paint-ball fight. This weekend's exercises are designed to test our instincts and improve our reactions, just as if this was the real thing. If this *was* the real thing, you just proved you can't be trusted to watch over your partner or follow instructions."

"You're overreacting. If this had been a true SWAT situation, I would have stayed with Donna."

Dillon shook his head. "You still don't get it. You can't act one way in training and plan on acting another way on an actual call. Training is supposed to make things second nature, so you'll react on muscle memory, without having to think about it. You have to treat every exercise like the real thing. Didn't they teach you that in the military?"

Blake stiffened and glanced at Thornton. But there was no help from that quarter. Thornton wouldn't even look him in the eye.

"Are we done here?" Blake demanded, his patience gone. There was only so much lecturing a grown man could take with his entire team a stone's throw away, witnessing his humiliation.

"Yeah. We're definitely done. Because you're toxic—always have been. You're a lone wolf, a rogue who has to do things his own way. People like you get people like me killed. The chief saw something in you when he hired you. I'll admit that I never did. But I worked with you, gave you every opportunity to prove my doubts wrong, to figure out how to be a member of this team. But all you've managed to do is prove me right. And I'm not willing to risk the lives of everyone here for your ego." He motioned toward Chief Thornton. "And neither is he. We both agree on this. It's over. Go home, Blake. You can turn in your equipment Monday morning. You won't need it anymore. You're fired."

Chapter Three

Donna entered the sleazy establishment that passed as a bar in this corner of Sevier County. Back in Destiny, this place would have been condemned and torn down, deemed unfit for even pigs to slop around in.

There was a plus side, though. It was quiet, too early in the evening to have more than a handful of patrons. And none of them had felt inclined to feed any money into the old-fashioned jukebox in the corner of the room.

Wrinkling her nose at the smell of urine and stale beer, she forced herself to step all the way inside, even though she was tempted to make an emergency run for a can of Lysol first.

A familiar figure sat on a bar stool at the far end, accepting what she hoped was his first drink of the night from the bartender. If Blake Sullivan was plastered, that was going to make her little crusade that much more difficult.

When he lifted the shot glass to his mouth, his hand shook and he sloshed some over the side.

So much for hoping that he wasn't plastered.

He downed the amber liquid in one swallow and wiped the back of his hand across his mouth. Donna flexed her hand against the pistol holstered at her waist.

If it had been loaded with paint balls instead of nine-millimeter slugs, she'd have already shot him. She was that ticked.

"Hey, lady," the bartender called out. "No guns allowed in here."

Blake slowly looked at her, his reflexes obviously dulled by the liquor. A sober cop would have jerked around to assess the danger as soon as the bartender mentioned a gun.

She pulled her badge out of the pocket of her jeans and flashed it. "Cop."

The bartender's expression turned frosty, his eyes as dark and deadly looking as the ones on the cobra tattoo snaking up his neck. "Makes no difference to me. No guns."

"Don't worry. I'm not staying." She put her badge away and strode across the room, her boots echoing on the scarred hardwood floor. Stopping beside Blake's stool, she motioned toward the door. "Let's go."

He scowled at her. "Another whiskey." His words were slurred, his face ruddy.

The bartender stepped toward him with a bottle of Jack Daniel's. Before he could refill the shot glass, Donna slapped her hand over it. "He's done."

"No. He's not." Blake yanked the glass away from her and held it out toward the bartender. "Fill 'er up."

The bartender lifted the bottle.

"He's drunk," Donna warned. "You pour that, and he gets behind the wheel, I'll arrest both of you."

He hesitated, shrugged and moved down the bar to a patron who promised to be less trouble.

Blake glared at her through bleary eyes. "This isn't Blount County. You can't arrest anyone here."

"He doesn't know that." She jerked her thumb toward the bartender.

Blake swiveled around and slouched back against the bar. "How did you find me?"

"Call tree."

He frowned. "Call what?"

She sighed. "One of many things you've failed to learn, even though I've told you about it before. Destiny's a very small town, so—"

He snorted. "No kidding."

She wanted to punch him. Instead, she forced a smile. "Unlike you, I consider Destiny's cozy size to be one of its many assets. Case in point, the call tree. Someone goes missing, I can make one call, and pretty soon, half the people in the county are looking out their windows. It's more efficient than a big city's AMBER Alert system."

His mouth quirked up. "You put out an AMBER Alert on me? I had no idea you cared so much."

"There are a lot of things you don't know," she grumbled. "Maybe you should pay more attention."

His brow crinkled in confusion, but his inebriated brain couldn't seem to grasp what she meant. Thank goodness. Admitting she cared about the brute while in a bar that smelled like pee wasn't something she wanted sober Blake to remember.

"My point is that one of the benefits of living in Destiny is that we watch out for each other. After a few calls, I knew you'd left town and what road you'd taken. Unfortunately, just like with my jurisdiction, my useful contacts end at the county line. So I had to do a bit of searching on my own after that."

He picked up his empty shot glass, frowned and

thunked it back onto the bar. When he looked at her again, he blinked as if surprised that she was still there.

"What do you want?" he slurred.

She eyed the few people in the room, noting how closely they were paying attention to the exchange. It was bad enough that they were witness to Blake being drunk. If word got back to Chief Thornton or Dillon, there was no way she could fix what was probably already an unfixable situation and get them to rehire him.

"We need to talk. Alone."

He shook his head. "I'm not going anywhere. I like it here."

She snorted. "Yeah. It's real nice. Great ambience. You could mark your territory right where you're sitting, and I bet no one would bat an eyelash."

His brow wrinkled again. "Huh?"

She counted to ten and tried to remember all the reasons she liked this man enough not to shoot him with real bullets. But she couldn't seem to think of even one at the moment. "Just step outside so we can talk. You can drink yourself under the table later."

"Bar."

It was her time to frown in confusion. "What?"

"Drink myself under the bar." He thumped the polished surface for emphasis. "You called it a table."

"No, I…" She drew a deep breath. "Whatever. Let's go."

"Nope. You have something to say to me, say it right here. Then you can skedaddle on home and let me drink in peace." He waved toward the bartender and held out his glass.

The bartender took one look at Donna and shook his head. "Sorry, man. No can do."

She snatched the shot glass from him and set it out of his reach. When he opened his mouth to complain, she stepped closer, sandwiching her hips between his open thighs. The way his breath caught when she leaned in close would have been satisfying if she thought he was reacting to her as a woman. But as drunk as he was, there had to be another explanation. Like maybe the smell of shampoo and soap from her recent shower was too startling a contrast to the odor of urine and stale cigarettes he'd been basking in this afternoon.

She whispered in his ear. "You smell like a brewery, so I'm betting your bladder is full. I'm also betting you'd rather not wet yourself in front of all your lovely friends—which is exactly what you'll do if I have to come back in here with my Taser and take you on a five-second ride." She stepped back and shrugged. "Your choice. Walk out of here on your own with me. Or wait here for my Taser."

Her threat carried the weight of sincerity. She wasn't bluffing. He mumbled some coarse words and threw a few bills on the counter. But he didn't argue anymore as he stumbled after her to the parking lot outside.

When they reached her *previously* white Ford Escape, courtesy of the muddy back roads she'd slogged through to find him, she leaned against the front passenger door. A raindrop splatted on the top of her head.

She glanced up at the dark, ominous-looking clouds. The weatherman had predicted more thunderstorms tonight, which was why Dillon had cut their training exercise short. He'd wanted them to have enough time to thoroughly clean and stow their equipment, real guns or not, before it started to pour.

Normally Donna would have been right there with

her teammates, helping out. But she'd been so upset over Blake getting fired that she couldn't focus and started making mistakes. Dillon had finally told her to go home and come back fresh in the morning for the second part of the training.

After a hot shower failed to make her feel any better, she'd done the only thing she could think to do. She'd called Blake. A lot. And texted. When that failed to get a response, she'd started to worry. That was when she'd put out a few feelers, trying to figure out where he might have gone.

Now, watching him sway on his feet in front of her, she was questioning her sanity in thinking she could undo the damage that he'd done today. After all, he'd accomplished what no one else had ever done.

He'd made Dillon Gray give up.

For goodness' sake, Dillon lived on a horse rescue ranch. He and his wife ran horse clinics every summer to help disabled and underprivileged children. He believed every living being could be helped or rehabilitated if given enough trust and support. For him to wash his hands of Blake was a shock that still had Donna reeling. But even if Dillon was ready to give up on him, she wasn't.

Not yet, anyway.

"I'll make this quick before we get soaked," she said. "I think Dillon overreacted. Calling you toxic, staging our fake deaths in that exercise to try to shock you and make his point, then firing you anyway, was a bit extreme."

"No kidding," he drawled, a note of bitterness creeping into his voice.

"But," she continued, "I do agree that you're not a

team player. And he had every right to kick your butt after the stunts you pulled today."

Thunder sounded overhead. But it was nothing compared to the dark look in Blake's eyes as he stared down at her.

"I got two of the perpetrators all by myself. *Two*."

"Whoop-de-do. Any one of us could have done what you did. But that wasn't the point of the training."

He arched a brow. "Seriously? Catching the bad guys wasn't the point?"

"Well, yes, of course it was. But not on your own. The purpose was to teach us how to operate together, to have each other's backs."

"I need another drink." He started back toward the building.

She jumped in front of him, boots crunching on gravel as she shoved him against her car. "I drove halfway across this county looking for you. It was only through dumb luck that I drove past this place and saw your truck out front. The least you can do is listen to what I have to say."

He arched his brows. "Call tree didn't work the way you'd hoped, huh?" he mocked.

"You fool." She shoved him again. "I wouldn't have even known that you'd driven out this direction if it *hadn't* worked." Another raindrop plopped onto her cheek. She wiped it off and glared up at him.

"I never asked you to come after me," he said. "What the heck do you want, anyway?"

"What I want is to know that I didn't waste the last four months of my life trying to turn your sorry butt into a decent detective and SWAT team member. I've been showing you everything that I know—"

"Stuff I *already know*." He thumped his chest for emphasis. "This whole *teach me how to do things the Destiny way* is an insult. I was in the military before I became a cop. Surprisingly, I never once needed a babysitter. And I wasn't too shabby a detective in Knoxville after that. And yet you people all treat me like I'm a rookie. I've been putting away criminals just as long as any of you—longer than some. But you ignore any suggestions I make and criticize every little thing I do. You feel like you've wasted your time with me for the past four months? Welcome to my world, lady. I'm not exactly feeling like coming to Destiny was my smartest move either."

She blinked up at him, surprised at both his words and the hurt and resentment in his tone. Did he really feel that way? Or was it the liquor talking? He sure sounded coherent, even if his words were slurred. More important, could he be right? In their zeal to help him fit into the team, had they done just the opposite? Pushed him away?

"Blake, I don't know what to—"

He waved his hand in the air as if to erase their conversation and stepped to the side, forcing her to turn to face him.

"Forget it," he said, sounding angry and weary. "You wanna light me up with fifty-thousand volts? Be my guest. It won't be the first time I've been on that ride. But I'm not hanging around to listen to another lecture. I'm done." He started toward the bar.

"Blake, wait." When he didn't stop, she added, "Please."

He stiffened and halted in his tracks. But he didn't turn around.

She hurried over and stood in front of him. The defeated look on his face had guilt curling inside her even more. All along, she'd never once considered that the problem might be on both sides—maybe because blaming him was easier than facing her own failures.

"I'm sorry. Really, I am. I never meant to make you feel like you weren't a valued member of the team. It never occurred to me that—"

He shook his head. "Don't. Don't apologize, Donna. You've been the one good thing in my life since coming here. But it was a mistake coming here to begin with. *My* mistake. I was in a tough spot with…my career in Knoxville. And I took the easy way out, or thought I did, when the chief approached me about working for him. I should have known it was too good to be true."

She frowned. "A tough spot? The chief? Are you saying that he recruited you? I don't understand. Your file says you came here for a change in pace, to get away from the city grind. There wasn't any mention of the chief asking you to come here."

"My file." He laughed, sounding bitter again. "I wonder what else Thornton invented to cover for me."

"Blake, you're not making sense. What are you talking about? Were you in trouble? Why would he have to cover for you?"

He squeezed his eyes shut as if in pain and scrubbed his hands over the stubble on his jaw. "I'm drunk. Not making sense. Forget what I said." He dropped his hands to his sides. "Look, I appreciate you checking on me, making sure I was okay—assuming that's why you're here. But I'm a big boy. And it's time I started taking care of myself."

She stood in confusion, his little speech sparking all kinds of questions as he circled around the front of her car and headed toward his truck. All this time, she'd never once questioned his decision to leave his position on a large team in Knoxville to come here, probably because of her own bias in thinking that Destiny was the better choice. But to someone like Blake, who definitely didn't seem to care for small-town life, could the move have been considered a step down?

The pay had to be less, no question. But she'd figured the benefits of a smaller, more intimate team would have made up for it. To someone like her, it would. But now that she looked at it with fresh eyes, it really didn't make sense. Not for a guy who made no secret of his preference for cities over small towns. Then why had he come here? And what role had the chief played in his decision? More important, where would he go from here?

It wasn't until he wobbled and missed a step, nearly falling on top of the car next to his truck, that it dawned on her that she needed to intervene. She hurried after him, reaching his side just as he fit his key into the lock. Or tried to. He missed and scraped about six inches off the paint. She grimaced in sympathy. But before he could try again and do more damage, she swiped his keys.

"Hey, give those back." He grabbed for them, but she whirled around and ran for her car.

In spite of his wobbly gait, he caught her in three strides. He grabbed her with one arm around her waist and whirled her around to face him. Good grief, he was strong. She pushed her hands against his chest but couldn't budge his viselike grip.

"Let me go."

"After you give me my keys." He held out his free hand, palm up.

She should have been angry. But she was still feeling guilty and confused over everything he'd said. And there was the distraction of how darn good his hard body felt against hers, and how wonderfully masculine he smelled. Even the whiskey on his breath didn't deter her ridiculous, unwanted response to being this close to him. Instead of pushing him away, she wanted to slide her hands up his chest and lock them behind his neck. Which was why she had to make him let her go. Now. Before she made a fool of herself.

She pinched his arm. Hard.

He snatched his arm back and rubbed where her nails had formed indentations on his skin. "What'd you do that for?"

"You're drunk."

"No kidding."

A drop of rain landed on her head. Then another. "Look, I just want to talk some sense into you. I came here to ask you to come back. You're a good cop, a solid detective. You—"

"Was," he interrupted. "I was a good cop. Past tense. Dillon fired me. Remember?" He squinted at her through the smattering of raindrops that were starting to fall faster.

"Maybe we can fix that. Dillon has scheduled another training exercise at nine tomorrow morning. If you show up in your gear, like you're ready to try again, you can talk to him, apologize—"

"Apologize? You're kidding, right? He said I was *toxic.* You think an apology is going to change his opinion?"

"I think it would be a great start."

He shook his head. "There's no point in talking to Dillon. His mind is made up."

"So, that's it?" she said. "You're just going to quit?"

"I...was...fired." He enunciated each word slowly and concisely, as if she were hard of hearing. "I don't have a choice. My career in Destiny is over. Finished. There's nothing I can do." He held his hand out again. "We're about to get soaked. Give me my keys, and I'm out of your life forever."

His words took the breath right out of her. Did he really not care about her at all? What was she to him? Not even a friend whom he would miss? More angry than concerned about his welfare at this point, she whirled around and dashed toward her car.

This time, the element of surprise was on her side. Or maybe the rain slowed him down. She'd just gotten her driver's door closed and locked when he reached her. His shoes slid across the gravel as he tried to stop. But he ended up slamming against her door and grabbing her side mirror to keep from falling on his face.

He swore and straightened. Then he yanked her door handle a few times before leaning down to glare at her through the window. The clouds chose that moment to open up. Rain pelted down on him in sheets, drenching him in seconds. He hunched his shoulders against the onslaught, his dark eyes promising retribution through the glass.

"I need my keys," he yelled to be heard over the thunder and rain. He rapped his knuckles on the window. "Keys."

"You're drunk," she yelled back. "You have no business driving. Walk home." She dropped his keys onto the seat beside her and started the engine.

He slammed his hand against the roof of her car, making her jump. "My house is over twenty miles away."

"I can give you a ride home. But your truck stays here."

"No."

They glared at each other through the window. Him probably hating her. Her hating herself for having wasted so much time on him, both personally and professionally. Maybe she should give up on men entirely. They weren't worth the trouble.

She put her foot on the brake and shifted into drive.

His eyes narrowed. "Donna, don't you dare—"

She slammed the accelerator and zoomed out of the parking lot.

Chapter Four

Where was Blake, and was he okay? Those two questions had been worrying Donna all evening, ever since she'd left him standing in the rain, yelling after her.

She sat in her recliner, her legs tucked underneath her, while she cradled a cup of hot chocolate in her hands. It wasn't that the house was cold. Outside, it was only mildly chilly, and then only when the winds blew down from the nearby mountains. But she didn't need cold weather as an excuse to have hot chocolate. It was her poison of choice when she needed soothing.

Tonight, she definitely needed soothing.

Across the room, the TV screen hung over the fireplace, dark and quiet. Typically, unless her mom or one of her mom's well-meaning klatch of friends had set her up on yet another disastrous blind date, she would spend Saturday nights binge-watching recorded cop shows. The ones with the fake forensics and technology were the most entertaining. Where an investigator could search a single database and come up with a person's entire life history in seconds—like what books that person had checked out of the library in kindergarten and never returned. Nothing could make her laugh harder than their implausible, ridiculous storylines. But tonight, instead, she stared at the set of keys on the coffee table. Blake's keys.

And she wasn't laughing.

Guilt was riding her hard. Not for taking his keys. She'd probably saved his life, or someone else's, by not letting him drive. But she shouldn't have left him in that parking lot with no way home. She should have argued with him until he agreed to get in her car. She could have taken him back later—once he was sober— to get his truck.

Where was he now? What was he doing? She had absolutely no clue. When she left him, she'd driven away for all of fifteen minutes before guilt had sent her back to that rancid-smelling bar. But even though his black pickup was still sitting in the gravel right where she'd left it, Blake wasn't.

The bartender had only shrugged when she asked him where Blake had gone. She suspected he knew the answer. But he had no inclination to tell her. Four hours later, with the clock edging close to midnight, Blake still hadn't responded to any of her calls or texts.

Not that she could blame him.

If he'd left her in that parking lot, she'd be furious. For days. Maybe longer. Mama always said her temper ran hotter than a busted radiator and cooled just as slowly.

She let out a heavy sigh and set her still-full cup on the side table. There was no use delaying the inevitable any longer. No amount of chocolate or silly cop shows were going to make her relax. And there was no point in trying to sleep. How could she even try to close her eyes when he could be lying hurt somewhere, maybe passed out in a ditch?

That lovely image had crossed her mind so many times that she'd called the emergency room in Maryville to see if he'd been brought in. The state police and the dispatch operators for both Blount and Sevier Counties had no reports on him either. She should have been relieved. Instead, she was more worried than ever. It was as if he'd vanished.

Okay—that was it. She absolutely couldn't sit here any longer, waiting for a call that was never going to come. She would have to head back out and find him herself. Again. And this time, she wasn't leaving until he was safe and sound at home.

After retrieving her holster and pistol from the floor beside her chair, she went into her bedroom to change out of her nightshirt. A few minutes later, dressed in jeans and a simple button-up blouse, she headed toward the front door.

A loud knock had her whipping out her pistol and flattening herself against the wall beside the door. Her pulse rushed in her ears. Who would be pounding on her door this late? Or even at all? Saying that she lived in the boonies was an understatement. Visitors willing to drive out this far from town, this far from *anything*, were extremely rare. Even her own family was loath to make the trip and bounce down the pothole-filled street in front of her house. Donna was the one who usually made the long trek to see them instead.

The knock sounded again. "Donna?" Blake's deep voice bellowed. "I know you're up. I saw you through the front window."

Blake. He was okay. *Thank God.* Her shoulders dropped, the tension draining out of her as she holstered her gun and reached for the dead bolt. Then his words sank in. She hesitated, without opening the door. "Why were you peeping in my window?"

"I wasn't *peeping.*"

She could practically hear him roll his eyes.

"Your lights are on, and the blinds are open," he continued. "I could see you from halfway down that death trap out front that you call a road. The suspension on my truck is probably shot now. What'd you do? Tick the mayor off, and now he won't send the city out to maintain your street?"

She flipped the dead bolt and pulled open the door. "Actually, it's his wife. She sped through a school zone, so I radioed for a patrol unit and followed her to city hall. She didn't appreciate me detaining her until the uniformed officer got there. And she especially didn't like the two-hundred-fifty-dollar ticket."

His brows rose as he stepped inside. "Did you know who she was when you saw her speeding?"

"Yep. Honestly, I probably wouldn't have bothered if she'd blown by me out on the highway. It's not like we have enough traffic around here to worry about her causing an accident. But she could have run someone's kid over. That's an unforgivable sin in my book. So if the price of making her stop and think next time is a bumpy ride home every day, I'll pay it." She winced. "But I do need to get a four-wheel drive if this vendetta goes on much longer. My little SUV isn't designed for that kind of punishment. It's already starting to rattle, and it's only a few years old."

He smiled. "I didn't know you had a soft spot for kids. Why haven't I heard this story before?"

She cocked her head. "Why haven't you ever visited my house before? And why haven't you invited me to yours? We're partners. We should kick back together after work sometimes, or on weekends."

His smile faded. "The answer to those questions are irrelevant, since I'm not a cop anymore."

She shook her head. "Once a cop, always a cop. And as far as I'm concerned, this current situation with Dillon is temporary."

"That's actually why I'm here. Partly, anyway." He waved toward the two leather couches and recliner a few feet away. "Mind if we talk for a few minutes? Or is the open door an unsubtle social signal that I should leave?"

She blinked, surprised to realize that she was still holding on to the doorknob. "Sorry. Go on, have a seat." She shut the door behind him and followed him into the part of the house that functioned as a family room.

He perched on the edge of one of the two couches, resting his forearms on his thighs with his hands clasped together. She didn't think she'd ever seen him look so unsure of himself. His confidence in everything that he did was one of the things that had always bugged Dillon, because he took it as arrogance. He expected the new guy to show more humility and work harder to fit in. Until Blake's little speech in the parking lot earlier, she'd thought pretty much the same thing. Now she wasn't sure what she thought.

"Nice place," he said as she sat beside him on the couch. "It looks a lot bigger inside than it does from the outside."

"It's the vaulted ceiling and the open concept. My dad helped me with the remodel. Took a couple of years. That was a long time ago, though. It's about ready for another update—new lights, new plumbing fixtures. The floors could use refinishing. But I don't have the free time I used to, before I added part-time SWAT officer to my full-time detective duties."

"You and your dad did all the work?"

"Most of it. We rooked my three sisters' husbands into helping with the heavy lifting. But for the most part, it was me and Dad. With Mom supervising, of course. She's a worse back seat renovator than any back seat driver." She waved toward the kitchen, which was separated from the rest of the room by a butcher block island. "You want a beer or something?"

His brows arched again. "I think we both know I had more than my quota of alcohol earlier today. But thanks."

"Right." She rubbed her hands on her jeans, hating the awkwardness that had settled between them. "I see you have your—"

"I wanted to ask you—"

They both stopped and smiled.

He waved at her. "You first."

She cleared her throat. "I was just going to ask how you got here. Since I, um, have your keys."

"My neighbor. I called him and he was just a few miles away, running an errand. We both have spare sets of each other's keys in case we lock ourselves out of our homes or cars. He and his son picked me up at the bar. His son drove my truck home while I slept off the liquor. In case you were wondering how I got my truck back."

"I tried to call—"

He pulled his phone out of his pocket and tapped the glass before turning it around. "I noticed."

The home screen showed fifteen missed calls.

Her face flamed hot. "Are all of those from me?"

"Every one."

"Wow. I didn't realize I'd been that big a pest."

"You texted even more than you called." He smiled and put the phone away. "I came over here for a couple of reasons. The first was to apologize."

She frowned. "What would you apologize for? I'm the one who left you stranded, in the rain, at a horrible, smelly bar. In my defense, I did eventually turn around and go back. But you were gone."

"Yeah, this is the part where I have to admit that I hid in the men's room when you came back into the bar looking for me. Not one of my prouder moments. But I was still angry and didn't want to talk to you."

"I *knew* that snake-tattooed bartender was lying. Well, at least you're okay. And you didn't end up with your truck in a ditch somewhere."

His jaw tightened. "Believe it or not, I'm not the bad guy everyone seems to think I am. And unlike the mayor's wife, I care about the other people out on the road. I would never drink and drive, in spite of how I acted earlier. The fact that you thought I would only contributed to my foul mood, so I didn't bother to tell you that all I was going to do was lie down in my truck and sleep it off."

"Blake, I didn't mean that the way it—"

He held up his hand again. "Please, let me get all this out before you think I'm blaming you for my own actions. I'm not. I was a jerk to you today. You were worried about me." He patted his pocket where he'd put his cell phone. "Obviously. And I didn't have the decency to answer even one of your calls or texts to let you know that I was okay. I'm really sorry, Donna. And even though I'd argue it wasn't necessary to take my keys, and it wasn't fun being left standing in the rain, it *was* a wake-up call. The whole day was a wake-up call, in a lot of ways. I hope you can accept my deepest, heartfelt apology. Can you forgive me?"

He startled her by taking one of her hands between his, while he watched her and waited for her reply. She swallowed hard, trying to remember what he'd even said. It was hard to focus when his large, warm hands held hers and he was staring at her with such intensity.

The man had definitely missed his calling. Instead of law enforcement, he should have been a sexy leading man in Hollywood, making all the women swoon and throw themselves at his feet. All it would take was one look from those intense, dark blue eyes to make the rest of the world fade away. She didn't think he'd ever looked at her this way before. It was doing funny things to her belly, and her pulse was racing so fast, it was a wonder he didn't say something about it.

He'd showered recently. His short, nearly black hair was still damp. And he was wearing fresh clothes—jeans, boots and a blue pullover shirt that made his eyes look an even darker blue than usual.

Not that any of that mattered.

She shouldn't care how gorgeous he looked, or how incredibly wonderful his warm skin felt against hers. But he'd never focused the full force of his attention on her before, not like this, as if the only thing that mattered in the world was her.

"Donna? Help me out here. I have no idea what that sharp mind of yours is thinking right now. Are you about to forgive me, or should I run for my truck before you pull out your gun?" His mouth quirked up in a half grin that had her toes curling against the floor.

Good grief, what was wrong with her? She was obviously more tired than she'd thought. And the day's events had made her emotions raw. Blake the police officer she could handle. Blake the sexy, nice, attentive man sitting across from her—holding her hand—was draining her IQ points by the second. If she didn't do something fast, she'd start stuttering and batting her eyelashes at him. Or worse, lunge across the couch and find out once and for all if he was the excellent kisser that she'd always fantasized that he would be.

His brows crinkled with concern. "Donna? Are you okay? You look flushed." He reached toward her face as if to check her for a fever.

She jerked back and yanked her hand free. Popping up from the couch, she said the first thing that flashed into her mind. "I have to pee."

His eyes widened.

She groaned and sprinted from the room.

WHAT HAD JUST HAPPENED? Blake stared at the empty spot on the couch beside him where Donna had been sitting just seconds earlier. Obviously he'd upset her, or she wouldn't have run out of the room like that. But other than an apology, he couldn't figure out how he'd managed to make things worse.

He blew out a frustrated breath and stood. He was too agitated to keep sitting on the couch, so he paced back and forth in front of the fireplace. Now that he'd delivered his pathetic apology, with disastrous results, he wasn't even sure whether he should hang around to tell her the other reason that he was here. After all, there were dozens of explanations for his concerns—all of which seemed valid and far more likely than the insane scenario that kept running through his head. Maybe he should have started with the scenario and skipped the apology part. But he'd been worried that she'd be too angry to listen if he didn't smooth things over first.

A lot of good that had done.

He checked his watch. Thirty minutes to midnight on a Saturday. This was silly. He should just go home and try to sleep off the aftereffects of a very nasty hangover that was already making his head pound in spite of the aspirin he'd taken. Everything was bound to look different in the morning. His concerns would be proven false, and everyone would go about their lives like normal.

Except for him.

Nothing had been normal in his life for a very long time.

"Blake."

He turned to see Donna standing by the recliner, her brow lined with worry. He cleared his throat and stepped over to her. "Whatever I did, if my apology somehow offended you, I'm truly sorry. I didn't mean to—"

"What? No, no. You did nothing wrong. It was just…" She shook her head. "Forget it. It was something stupid. Nothing to worry about. I'm just glad you're okay."

"Then we're good? You're not upset with me?"

"I'm upset that you got yourself fired. And I'll be really upset if you don't try to talk to Dillon to get your job back. Maybe if you just apologize to him, explain your side—"

"That's why I'm here. I mean, other than trying to fix things between you and me. I came here because I did try to contact Dillon. I wanted to meet with him, just the two of us, and talk this thing out."

"Oh, well, that's great. We're supposed to go back to Hawkins Ridge for another exercise in the morning, around nine. Maybe you could go up there and talk to him then, while the rest of us are getting everything set up." She frowned. "Why are you giving me a funny look? What's wrong?"

"It could be nothing."

"Tell me."

Lightning flashed off in the distance, illuminating the front windows. A distant boom of thunder followed. And still, he couldn't seem to force the words out. The longer he stood there, the more he felt like he'd jumped the gun. The whiskey and his hangover were dulling his brain, not to mention the lateness of the hour.

"Well?" she prompted.

"Forget it. It's stupid. I'll do what you said, try to catch Dillon in the morning before your training session. Sorry I bothered you so late." He circled around her and headed for the door. He'd just flipped the dead bolt and was reaching for the doorknob when she grabbed it instead. He looked at her in question.

"You're not leaving yet. Something bothered you enough to come over here close to midnight to talk to me. It wasn't just to tell me you were sorry. What's going on? Talk to me."

He dropped his hand and shook his head. "Forget it. I'm sure it's just the storm interfering with signals. Or maybe they're all too ticked at me to answer. I ignored dozens of texts and calls from you, and it didn't mean I needed help."

"Blake, if you don't start making sense, I swear I'm going to shoot you."

By the irritated look on her face, he didn't doubt that she would. He let out a deep breath and prepared himself for her laughter. "Dillon's missing."

She blinked. Then blinked again.

"See?" he said. "Told you it was stupid. It's nonsense. I went off half-cocked and still half-drunk and imagined all sorts of crazy things. I'm sure he's fine." He reached for the doorknob, motioning for her to move her hand.

She suddenly stood on her tiptoes, leaned in close and sniffed.

He jerked back. "What are you doing?"

"Seeing if I can smell whiskey on your breath."

He gritted his teeth. "I'm not drunk. I haven't touched a drop since you left me at the bar."

"And yet you said that Dillon's missing. What does that mean?"

The smile hovering on her lips had him feeling even more ridiculous. "I wanted to talk to him, like I said. So as soon as I sobered up, I called, both cell phone and radio. He didn't answer."

She shrugged. "Why would he? He fired you. I doubt he ever wants to talk to you again. Which is why you need to go see him in person—"

"I did. I went to his horse ranch. He wasn't there. Neither was his wife and daughter. The guy who oversees the operations—"

"Griffin."

He nodded. "Griffin. He said Mrs. Gray and her daughter had gone off on some cruise. But he didn't know where Dillon was. He figured he was still in the woods, conducting training exercises."

"What time was this?"

"Close to nine, I imagine."

She glanced past him, probably to the wall clock that he'd noticed over the TV earlier. "It's way too late to try calling him again. I'm sure he's okay, though. Dillon's one of the most capable men I know. He—"

"I called Randy, too."

"Okay. What did he say about Dillon?"

"Nothing. Randy didn't answer his phone either."

Her brow furrowed. "That's not like him. Even if he was upset, which is a rare thing for him, he wouldn't have ignored your call."

"That was my thought, too. So I called Max. Then Chris. I even tried the chief, on his home phone. No one answered any of my calls. I would have at least expected the chief's wife to answer."

She shook her head. "She's on the cruise with Ashley. All the team's wives went—Dillon's wife, Ashley, and their baby, the chief's wife, Claire, Max's wife, Bex, and Chris's wife, Julie. It's a law-enforcement family cruise some charity put together, a getaway for the families who do so much to support their law-enforcement loved ones. That's how it was advertised, anyway. That's why Dillon scheduled the training this weekend. I could have sworn you knew all this. Scenic Cruises? Out of Miami? It was organized by some charity group out of Knoxville. I'm sure Dillon mentioned it."

"I'm sure he mentions lots of things to you. He and I rarely speak unless he's ordering me around or telling me I screwed up." He waved his hand in the air. "Forget it. That's not the point. I tried calling all of them tonight. No one answered. It's highly likely that they're ignoring me because of what happened today, and I overreacted. But I couldn't ignore it without letting you know. Just in case."

"Just in case what?"

He fisted his hands at his sides, feeling like an idiot.

But he'd gone this far. He might as well go all in. "In case the entire SWAT team was abducted. Minus you and me, of course."

She blinked again. Then she started laughing.

He endured her laughter for a full minute. He couldn't take more than that. He brushed her hand off the doorknob and yanked open the door.

"Blake, wait. I'm sorry. Please don't go. I shouldn't have laughed at you. But you know cell service around here is awful. Your calls probably didn't even go through."

Since her voice was still laced with laughter, he didn't bother to reply. He strode out of the house and took the porch steps two at a time.

"Blake?"

He hopped into his truck and took off down the road, punching the gas to give free rein to his sour mood and temper. That was when he hit the first huge pothole. The front right tire slammed into the hole, and the entire truck lurched at a sickening angle before the tire popped out again. He cursed and was forced to slow to a near crawl. It took him a good ten minutes just to reach the end of the street-from-hell.

A flash of white zoomed at him from the left. He jerked around to see Donna's white Ford Escape barreling onto the road from an overgrown field. He swore and slammed his brakes, skidding and coming to a bouncing halt just a few feet from her driver's side door.

She stopped too, her face looking pale and drawn as she stared at him through her driver's side window, illuminated by his headlights. Before he could even unbuckle his seat belt, she was out of her SUV and running to his passenger door. He pushed the button to roll down the window.

"What the hell was that for?" he demanded. "You almost made me run right into you."

"I called them," she said. "The whole team. No one answered. I sent a group text. Nothing." She swallowed, looking visibly shaken. "I even tried the radio. All I got was static. It's not raining anymore. We can't blame the storm now. I can see them not answering your calls. But they wouldn't worry me like this. My God, Blake. What's going on?"

He popped open the passenger door. "Get in."

Chapter Five

Blake slowed his truck to turn down a gravel road that would lead them to the wooded area where they'd conducted the paintball exercise that morning. Beside him, Donna clutched a flashlight in her hands, anxiously staring through the windshield.

"What happened after I left Hawkins Ridge?" he asked. "Did Dillon take the team to another training site, maybe in one of those communication dead zones? Since you didn't have a partner at that point, I would guess he sent you home early. Maybe they decided to stay late, or came back for round two long after you were gone." He steered around a rut in the road.

"No. I mean, yes. Both." She swiped at her bangs, something she rarely did unless she was upset. "After Dillon…ordered you to leave, I…uh…went home early. Like you said. You know, because I didn't have a partner."

"Okay. He continued the training without you, then. Like I said, the communications might not be working. Or maybe the storm caught them by surprise, and they had to wait it out. A rain-swollen creek could have prevented them crossing, and they're sitting it out until it goes down."

"No. That's not it. He *did* send me home early. But training was over for the day. All that was left was for the team to clean the equipment and stow it in their trunks for next time. You know what a stickler Dillon is about maintaining equipment, even fake guns. Cleaning them and prepping the gear for the trip back would have taken a good half hour, maybe forty-five minutes. But he wouldn't have kept anyone longer than that. He kept up with the weather reports, knew a storm was moving in. No way would he risk anyone's safety by having them out in the middle of it. I'm telling you, they're not training."

The gravel ended, and the remaining fifty yards of road was dirt. The truck bounced around the last curve, and the clearing was revealed up ahead. But it wasn't empty. Five trucks sat parked side by side, exactly as they'd been that morning. Blake gave Donna a puzzled glance as he parked beside them. He killed the engine and looked over at the obviously empty vehicles.

"Why would they still be up here?" he asked. "It doesn't look like the vehicles have moved at all. I thought you said Dillon wanted everyone home, safe, with the storm coming in."

"He did." Her voice was quiet and strained, her face pale with worry for her friends. She opened her door.

"Wait. Did you call the station when you were making all those calls earlier?"

"Yes. The chief and the team hadn't checked in. But I was careful not to alarm the skeleton night staff. I was blasé in how I asked the question."

"Fair enough," he said. "Let's see if there's a reasonable explanation, or whether we need to raise the alarm after all."

He left the engine running with the headlights on to help them see better. But even with that, and a bright moon overhead, it was difficult to see much beyond the beams of their flashlights.

They took turns shouting out to the team. But no one answered. After a few minutes of searching, they were back at the parking area, with no clue about where their friends had gone.

Or, rather, where Donna's friends had gone.

To Blake, they'd always been just coworkers. Now, after he'd been fired, they weren't even that. But they all bled blue. If something had happened, he was darn well going to do everything he could to help them.

Whether they wanted him to or not.

"Maybe there was a medical emergency," Blake theorized. "If they stayed up here awhile after you left— maybe to do another training exercise—and they got caught in the storm—"

"Dillon wouldn't let that happen. He would have gotten them out of here before the storm let loose."

Her steadfast trust in Dillon was a little irritating. Blake didn't think the man could walk on water the way Donna did. "He's not a meteorologist. Let's assume for a moment that he misjudged the storm, that after you left he decided they should train a little longer, and they got caught out here. They took shelter somewhere, maybe in the old barn, where our fake perpetrator was hiding during the paint ball exercise. They could have holed up inside to wait out the storm. After the lightning stopped, something else happened. Maybe the chief had a heart attack, or one of them got cut or something. So they needed to take him back down the mountain to get him help."

He pointed to the puddles still in the dirt, the wet spots on the trunks of the trees closest to the clearing.

"Judging by the way the slope runs here, this parking lot is probably like a bowl in the rain. It could have been a small lake by the time the storm passed, and they couldn't get to their vehicles."

"So they just, what, trekked through the woods and got lost? Even if someone was hurt and they had to hoof it down the mountain, where are they now? They grew up around here. Getting lost isn't something that would happen."

"What else could have happened? I don't see any tire tracks or footprints. No signs of anyone else coming up here. In spite of my fears earlier, foul play against an entire SWAT team seems hard to believe."

"A SWAT team with fake guns," she said, her voice quiet. "Dillon was all about safety. He made us lock up our real guns and ammo while we did the exercises. He didn't want to risk an accidental shooting."

He studied her. "What are you saying? That instead of accepting that they could be lost in the woods, you think someone came up here and…what? What did he do with them?"

"No, I'm not saying that at all. I'm just throwing out the facts as we know them. The team drove up but didn't drive back down. They aren't answering their phones, radios or us yelling at the top of our lungs. Something bad must have happened."

Her voice was barely above a whisper the next time she spoke. "I think we may be in over our heads. We should call the station, get some volunteers out here to help us conduct a more thorough search. Even if they're not lost, they could be stranded somewhere, maybe in a cell phone and radio dead zone. Obviously something happened to them or their vehicles wouldn't still be here."

"Agreed. We need to get some help out here."

He raised his flashlight beam, training it straight ahead, slicing a path of light through the darkness of trees and bushes about twenty feet away. "While you make that call, I'm going to go deeper in to check that barn and the clearing in front of it. There have to be some footprints there, maybe a piece of torn fabric caught on a branch. I'd like to find some tangible proof that might show us where the team was last. The trackers will want to start from the last known position."

She shoved her cell phone back into her pocket. "We're not splitting up. I'm your partner. We'll check it out together. *Then* I'll call this in."

The wobble in her voice had him hesitating. He looked down at her, noted the intensity in her expression, the shine of unshed tears sparkling in her eyes. He'd been with Destiny P.D. since late fall of the previous year and had been her partner for over four months. In all that time, she'd always been decisive, in control, never breaking down no matter how tough things got. He'd never once seen her rattled. But right now she seemed… fragile, vulnerable. And he'd bet it wasn't just because she was worried about her friends. There was something else going on here. And he thought he knew what it was.

"Donna?"

"Yeah?"

"It's not your fault."

She frowned. "What's not my fault?"

"Whatever happened, whatever is going on with the team. I think you're second-guessing yourself, feeling guilty. But if anyone's to blame, it's me. If I'd been a good partner to you, we'd have both been here with them when—"

"When what? When aliens beamed them up to the mother ship? Come on, Blake. This is crazy. Four highly trained SWAT team members and the chief of police don't just disappear off the face of the earth. You know what I'm starting to think is going on? Group hysteria, or mass hysteria, or whatever psychologists call it. We're both feeding off each other's fears and making this into something it's not."

"I honestly hope you're right."

"But you don't think I am."

"I didn't say that." Before she could interrogate him about what he really thought, he said, "How about we finish our due diligence and get this over with? This whole place is giving me the creeps."

"You won't get any argument from me about that," she mumbled, scanning left and right with her flashlight, before training it in front of her again.

They headed into the woods, side by side. The truck's headlights didn't penetrate more than a dozen feet in, because trees blocked the light. Forced to rely solely on their flashlights and the moonlight overhead, they studied the ground, the branches and the bark of trees they passed.

When they stopped by a tree with red and blue paint splotches on it, Donna gave a small smile. "So much for Dillon's claim that our biodegradable paint will fade in the first rain. He's not going to be happy about that. He'll probably drop the vendor and start researching a new one." Her smile died a quick death as fears for her friends obviously invaded her thoughts. She stalked past the tree, and he rushed to catch up.

"Why didn't you tell me about the law-enforcement family cruise?" he asked, trying to steer her thoughts to more innocuous ones while they performed their search.

She hesitated, then continued forward, sweeping her flashlight across the ground. "Honestly, I guess it never occurred to me to bring it up in conversation. It's not like you ever socialize with the rest of us after work. Not very often, anyway. I'm not even sure you've ever met Chris's wife, Julie. And you probably only know Max's wife, Bex, from your first real case with us last year, when someone was trying to kill her. Dillon's wife, Ashley, of course, everyone knows. The station would probably riot if she ever stopped dropping off her homemade treats."

"She does bake a mean oatmeal raisin cookie."

"Banana nut bread. That's my favorite. Her recipe is to die for, and she refuses to share it. Trust me, I've asked. Many times. That stuff is amazing." She pressed a hand to her heart as if paying homage.

"Yuck on bananas," he said. "Not my thing."

"No banana pudding?"

He wrinkled his nose. "Not even if I was starving."

"No wonder you don't fit in with the team," she teased. "Banana pudding is a staple of any well-balanced diet. Especially in the South."

"And yet somehow I've survived all these years without it." He stopped and looked around. "This is about where I first spotted the guy I ended up shooting in the second floor of the barn."

"Larry. The second guy, the one you caught at the river, was Tim. Mike was the third guy. I don't think you ever saw him though."

He supposed he should have known the first two men's names. Maybe she and Dillon were right, and he really wasn't making enough of an effort to fit in. He'd really never accepted the blame for how things were going, always thinking it was everyone else's fault that they refused to accept an outsider. The truth, as with most things, was probably somewhere in the middle.

"Were Larry, Tim and Mike with the team when you left?"

She put her hand on his arm, her eyes widening as she pulled him to a stop. "Mike had to leave early. But Larry and Tim were still there. I didn't even think about calling them. If one of them answers, maybe they know where the guys went. Or, heck, maybe for some reason, they all piled into Tim and Larry's trucks and went to a bar somewhere, and it's too loud to hear their phones. With the wives out of town, it makes sense. They're having a guys' night out. Why didn't I think about that? Maybe Tim and Larry are the designated drivers. I bet we're going to feel really silly in about one minute. I just know it."

"I'm all for silly. It beats the alternative."

She checked her watch and winced. "If they're not in a bar, if they're back at Larry or Tim's house, sleeping off a binge, someone's not going to be happy about being woken up at one in the morning. But no way am I waiting until a decent hour to call. Which unlucky soul gets woken up? Larry or Tim?"

"I think Tim suffered enough being shot twice. I vote for Larry."

"Larry it is." After tucking her flashlight under her arm, she scrolled through her contact list and punched the send button.

A few seconds later, she crossed her fingers in the air and spoke into the phone. "Larry? Yeah, hi. This is Detective Waters. Donna, that's right. Hey, I'm really sorry to call so late, but it's important. What? Oh, yes. I'm fine. Sorry. You?"

She made an impatient rolling motion with her hand as she waited for Larry to finish whatever he was babbling about.

Blake didn't wait. If it was taking this long to get anything out of Larry, and she had to call Tim, too, he could at least check the barn out, since it was visible through a gap in the trees up ahead. He motioned toward the gap, and she gave him a helpless gesture, pointing at the phone. He smiled and headed toward the barn, sweeping his flashlight back and forth.

The dilapidated structure was just as he remembered it—a sagging collection of warped gray boards, which were partially covered in vines that should have given up the ghost a long time ago. He figured it was similar to many other old structures throughout the Smokies, like those found near Cades Cove. It was a relic of another century. But unlike its cousins that were protected because they were in the Smoky Mountains National Park, this one was clearly suffering from a lack of historical society preservation.

If the building could talk, he imagined it would have some amazing stories to tell, the same way old men liked to rock on front porches, reliving the glory days with anyone who would listen. He smiled at that thought and pulled one of the large double doors open.

And froze.

Footsteps sounded behind him.

"Blake? Larry wasn't out in a bar with them. And Tim—"

He whirled around to stop her, but it was too late.

She'd already seen inside. Her eyes widened with horror at what was visible in the beam of her flashlight.

"Oh, no. No, no, no. Oh, please, God. *No.*"

She dropped to her knees beside the bullet-riddled body of SWAT officer and fellow detective Randy Carter.

Chapter Six

Donna tried to peel Blake's hands off her arms. He was crouched beside her and wouldn't let her touch Randy.

"Let me go," she pleaded. "I have to check for a pulse. Maybe we can still save him."

"It's way too late for that. The blood's already starting to dry. He's gone." He gave her a light shake. "Donna, look in my eyes, not at him. Trust me, you don't want this to be the last image of your friend burned into your brain. You don't want to remember him this way for the rest of your life."

She was still trying to pry his fingers off her, but the anguish in his voice cut through her own haze of grief and despair and made her pause. Part of her had known that Randy was beyond help. But part of her was in denial, or had been. Blake's tone had snapped that second part back to reality.

She shifted her gaze to his. The hollowness and pain in his dark eyes nearly stole her breath. What was he remembering from his own past? What kind of tragedy would put those shadows in someone's eyes? Without even thinking about it, she cupped his cheek.

He ducked away, forcing her to drop her hand.

"Come on," he said, his voice gentle but strained, all

signs of whatever he'd been thinking about erased from his expression. "Let's make that call to the station."

"But—"

"But nothing. Randy was your friend. You shouldn't be here, cop or not. The best way to help him now is to leave the crime scene to others to process."

He didn't give her a chance to argue. He scooped her up in his arms and carried her out of the barn. She was so surprised that she didn't think to protest until he was lowering her back to standing.

She smoothed her shirt down and straightened her shoulders. "I'm a police officer first, a woman second. And I've spent half of my life working hard to ensure that I'm treated with the same respect that my male peers are treated. So don't you dare ever try to carry me like that again unless we're lovers and you're carrying me to bed. Got it?"

His eyes widened, and she could feel her face flaming over her poor choice of words. But in that one moment, with him carrying her from a crime scene, all her struggles, the fights to be treated with respect in a profession dominated by men, came boiling to the surface. She would grieve, bitterly, for her longtime friend later. But right now she needed to be the best cop—the best detective—she could be so they could catch the killer and find the rest of the team.

"Got it?" she repeated.

"Got it."

She nodded, feeling a little silly but glad that she'd set some boundaries. It made her feel more confident, more in control.

"What all did Larry and Tim say?"

The earlier disappointment that she'd felt after speaking to them settled over her again like a dark cloud. "Larry had definitely been drinking. At first, I thought that was a good sign, that I was right and he'd been at the bar with the others. That maybe Tim ended up being the DD for everyone. But once I cut through his slurring, he admitted he'd left shortly after I had. Tim said much the same thing. They were both supposed to come up here, to Hawkins Ridge, in the morning, to do another exercise. The same exercise Dillon told me about before I left."

"Okay. Donna? Give me a minute alone inside, okay? I just want to have a quick look around while you phone this in."

"You think there could be more bodies, don't you? We were so focused on Randy that we didn't look around."

He was shaking his head before she finished. "No. It's a small barn. I don't think we could have missed another body, even in our peripheral vision. But I still want to see whether there are any obvious signs that anyone else was in there earlier. Okay? Will you wait right here?"

She nodded, even though she had no intention of waiting. She understood his concern for her welfare, for her peace of mind. After all, these people were her friends. But as she watched him head into the barn, sweeping his flashlight back and forth across the floor, she also understood that she couldn't cower away from her duty as a police officer. And there was something she needed to check out before the barn was turned over to the crime scene techs.

After calling the station, she hurried inside and was kneeling beside Randy's body when Blake finished his inspection and saw her. He rushed over, stopping just short of touching her this time.

"Donna. Don't. Please."

She had already pulled on a pair of latex gloves. Like most detectives she knew, she always kept a pair in her pocket for emergencies. This definitely qualified.

"I've already called the station," she assured him while she finished adjusting the gloves. "One of the patrolmen is going to come up here to secure the scene until the techs arrive. Another will call Maryville to borrow their M.E., or get old Doc Brookes to play medical examiner if the Maryville one isn't available. I didn't say who the victim was, though. I didn't want that to get out until I can notify Randy's mom. This is going to devastate her. He's single, an only child. And she's a widow. I'll probably get my mom to go over there and sit with her."

"That sounds like a wonderful idea, having your mom help out. I wouldn't have thought of that. Donna, what are you doing?"

"Checking something really quick before we go. Did you see any signs that the others were in here?"

"No. What exactly do you think you have to check?"

She was about to answer him, but her breath caught in her throat when she finally, for the first time since entering the barn, looked fully at Randy's body splayed out across the floor. A deep sadness welled up inside her. She was the oldest of three sisters, but had never felt deprived over not having any brothers. Her fellow detectives, her SWAT teammates, were her brothers. Randy more so, because he was so sweet-natured. But she couldn't give in to her grief. Not yet. Once she started crying, she might never stop. The best thing she could do for him right now was to engage her brain, not her emotions. She needed to study him objectively, as a victim, and soak in all the information she could glean from his injuries, which were, sadly, extensive.

"Donna."

"He didn't go quietly, did he?"

His gaze shifted to the body. "No. He didn't. He put up a good fight."

Randy lay on his back, his arms and legs akimbo, his unseeing eyes staring up at the rafters. Green eyes, the color of spring, she'd always teased him. They were his best feature. She couldn't believe she'd never look into those smiling eyes again.

His shirt was saturated with what had to be blood. It was reddish bronze, definitely not the bright red from their paintball guns. Blood had pooled faintly beneath the skin just below his eyes, revealing cellular damage, probably from being hit with a fist. If he'd survived long enough for bruises to fully form, the shadows would be black and purple shiners.

"Let's hope that he scraped a boatload of DNA off the bastard and their profile is in the system already," she said. "From the looks of his shirt, I'd say he's been cut somehow—not necessarily stabbed—in addition to being shot. I count four bullet holes."

"Five. There's one on his leg, too. His right calf."

She had to fight to keep her breathing steady as she noted the fifth hole. His pants were soaked around the entry point, like his shirt. He'd been shot in the leg before his heart stopped pumping. Which meant he'd suffered.

Oh, Randy. Sweet, sweet Randy. How did this happen to you?

"Now can we go?" Blake asked, respecting her earlier insistence that he not pick her up again, even though it looked like it was killing him not to. He was a take-charge kind of man, probably not used to having to restrain his protective instincts.

"Soon. Did you bring your phone?"

He frowned. "Yes. Why?"

"I need you to photograph Randy's right hand before I pull that piece of paper out of it."

She'd laid her flashlight down on the ground, aimed toward Randy's hand. Blake looked down, his face mirroring surprise. He must not have noticed the paper earlier.

She could see the conflicting emotions in his expression. They both knew they shouldn't touch the body, or anything around it. They should leave the evidence collection to the crime scene techs and the medical examiner. But there was a lot more at stake here than just bringing Randy's killer to justice. There were four more missing people who needed to be found before it was too late.

If it wasn't too late already.

The piece of paper clutched in Randy's hand could be the clue they needed to save their friends' lives. And the hours they'd have to wait for the techs and M.E. before they learned what was on that piece of paper were hours they couldn't afford to wait.

He glanced toward the barn doors, in the direction of the parking area. Then he pulled out his phone. "All right." He didn't sound happy with his decision as he raised the phone to snap the first picture. "But as soon as we see what he's holding, we put it back, exactly the way we found it."

"Agreed."

After snapping half a dozen pictures of Randy's hand from different angles, he nodded.

She leaned forward and carefully uncurled his fingers, while Blake continued to snap more pictures of the body.

"Full rigor hasn't set in yet," she told him. "He hasn't been dead very long."

They both glanced toward the open barn doors.

"We're excellent targets in here with our flashlights lighting us up for a shooter," he said. "Proverbial sitting ducks."

"I was thinking the same thing. I'll hurry."

After gently working the paper free, she unfolded it. Blue cursive writing was scrawled across the white square, about a third the size of a typical sheet of notebook paper. There were only two sentences, neat and precise, as if the author had taken a painstaking amount of time to get them just so.

This wasn't a spur-of-the-moment murder. It was planned.

"What's it say?" Blake asked. "I can't make it out."

Her hand shook as she held it up in the air.

His jaw tightening was the only indication that he'd read it. He snapped several more pictures. "You know what this means, don't you?"

She nodded. "We need the cavalry on this. But they won't help us without knowing the special circumstances. And that means revealing that we read the note. We're trapped in a catch-22."

"It's only a trap if we try to wiggle out of it. Fold the paper and put it back exactly the way we found it. We'll come clean, admit that we touched it, but that we used gloves and tried to leave it the same way that we found it so we could maintain the integrity of the evidence. Then we'll face the consequences."

"The consequences are that we'll be removed from the case. No way am I going to let that happen. After reading what that note said, are you seriously going to stand there judging me and say that you wished we had waited hours for a medical examiner to give us a report? Really?"

He blew out a deep breath. "Okay, okay. You're right. In this instance, it's good that we read it. But covering it up after the fact—"

"Is exactly what we *both* agreed to do *before* we read it. You aren't exactly pristine in this little endeavor. So, are we in this together or not?"

Without waiting for his reply, she refolded the note, leaving both sentences clearly visible instead of hidden like they were before. Then she slid the edge between Randy's thumb and pointer finger to keep the paper from falling. "There. Anyone looking at the body can clearly see what the killer wrote. There's no reason to admit that's not how it looked when we got here."

"What if the way the killer folded and staged the presentation is significant to the crime? It could be an important clue to figuring out his identity."

"We'll pursue that angle on our own. If we find it's truly significant, we'll figure out a way to let others know."

Disapproval seemed to seep from every pore as he frowned down at her like an archangel ready to release his wrath.

"Let it go, Blake. I'm not going to screw up this investigation. But I'm not going to be kicked off it either."

He looked like he wanted to argue more, but the

sound of a siren in the distance had him swearing beneath his breath instead. "We need to get out of here. Respected police officer or not, you're about to be tossed over my shoulder and hauled out of this barn if you don't get moving."

"Meaning you're going to let this go?"

He gave her a curt nod and offered a hand to help her up.

Relieved that he'd given in, she took his hand and climbed to her feet.

"Don't forget the gloves." He motioned toward her hands.

She rolled the latex down her wrists, turning them inside out before shoving them into her back pocket.

He shook his head. "They're lumpy now. Someone might notice and ask about it. I don't want you to get fired, too. I'll put them in *my* pocket. If anyone finds out, it won't matter. They can't fire me twice."

"No." She grabbed the gloves and shoved them down her bra. "No one's getting fired. Including you."

His eyes had widened as he watched her hide the gloves. Now he cleared his throat and seemed to have difficulty lifting his gaze to look her in the eye again. "What do you mean, that includes me?"

"Detective Waters? Detective Sullivan?" The words were muted, coming from a considerable distance away. The uniformed patrolman she'd spoken to on the phone must have arrived and was looking for them.

"I'm saying," she said, lowering her voice, "that the only other person here who knows that Dillon fired you is me. And I sure don't want to work this case by myself. I need your help. You can't help me if you're a civilian."

He pulled her to a halt. "In addition to tampering with evidence—"

"I wouldn't call it tampering, exactly. We discovered something extremely important and made sure it can be shared and acted upon quickly."

"In addition to tampering," he repeated, "now you want me to lie and pretend I wasn't fired?"

"If that's what it takes to save our friends, our co-workers, then absolutely, yes. Lie."

She was all about having a conscience. But this was a heck of a time for him to be wrestling with it. Again.

She put her hands on her hips. "Seriously? You *really* have to think about this one?"

Her phone buzzed against her hip. She blew out an impatient breath and took the call. "Detective Waters." She listened for a moment, then said, "Yes, I heard you calling to us, Officer Lynch. We're heading toward the parking area now."

She ended the call and shoved her phone back into her pocket. "Well, Blake? You've had time to think about it. Not that you should need it."

He cursed viciously. "Okay. I'll do it. But I don't like it."

"That much is obvious." She narrowed her eyes in warning. "I can't believe you even hesitated."

They started off again toward where Officer Lynch was waiting.

"We're heading down a slippery slope," he gritted out. "One lie always leads to another. This could get really complicated, really fast, and jeopardize the court case later on. It might blow up in our faces and have all kinds of unforeseen repercussions."

"I'm not worried about a court case or repercussions. I'm worried about my friends' lives."

"Your *friend* Dillon wanted me off the force. I'm trying to do right by him."

"Yeah, well. Do right by helping me save his life. You can ask him to forgive you later."

He rolled his eyes.

A few minutes later, they stepped out of the woods beside Chris's blue pickup. She motioned for the patrolman who was standing by his car, bar lights flashing red and blue.

"There's one more thing we have to decide," she whispered.

"Wonderful." Sarcasm practically dripped off his words. "Can't wait to hear it."

She pressed the flat of her hand against his chest, her throat suddenly tight. "How are we going to break the news that a lunatic murdered Randy and is holding three more members of our team and the police chief hostage?"

Chapter Seven

Blake headed up the long concrete walkway beside Donna, his flashlight off even though it was close to two in the morning. The outside of Mrs. Carter's cottage was lit up like midday, with security lights framing both sides of the path and carriage lamps all across the wall of the front porch. Motion sensors had flooded the front and side yards with light the moment he parked his truck in the gravel out front.

Even now he could see lights coming on inside, probably because the motion sensors were hooked up to some kind of alert that had awakened the owner. Knowing cops in general and their intense need to protect their loved ones from the evil they encountered on a daily basis, Blake figured it was a safe bet that Randy was the one who was responsible for all these gadgets at his mother's home.

"How long before your mother gets here to sit with Mrs. Carter?" he asked.

"Probably five or ten minutes." She stopped. "We should wait. What was I thinking? I can't do this on my own. I can't tell her… I can't do this."

She turned back toward the truck, but he grasped her shoulders and gently forced her to face him. "Donna, you can do this. You're not alone. I'm with you, and I'm not going anywhere."

She shook her head. "You don't understand. Randy was like a brother to me. I've known him my whole life. We went to school together, from pre-K on. We went to prom together because neither of us had dates. It was one of the best nights of my life, because we were two friends just having fun, you know? No pressure. No weird goodnight kiss or worries that someone was going to want more than I wanted to give. He lived in this house his whole life. When...when we were little, we played in the backyard. He'd steal my dolls, and I'd steal his Matchbox cars." She sniffed, her eyes sparkling with unshed tears. "How do I tell her he's gone? I have to wait, let my mother tell her."

He slowly shook his head. "We can't wait. Mrs. Carter is standing in the doorway right now, watching us through the storm door."

Her eyes widened, and she shot a quick look toward the house. "Blake, you have to tell her. I'm sorry. Let me go. I—"

The creak of the storm door shattered the quiet. "Donna? Sweetie? Is that you?" Mrs. Carter stepped out onto the porch, tying the sash around her blue terry cloth robe. Matching blue fuzzy slippers protected her feet.

Donna gave Blake a pleading look.

He squeezed her shoulders. "It will be better coming from someone who knows her, who loves her, who loved her son."

"Donna? Who's that with you, dear?"

She drew a deep breath. Then another.

"Donna?" Blake asked.

"Okay. Okay. I can do this."

He dropped his hands from her shoulders.

When she turned to face the house, she pasted a smile on her face. "Mrs. Carter, so sorry to bother you at this insane hour of the morning." She hurried up onto the porch and took Randy's mother's hands in hers.

Blake climbed the steps and stood a few feet back, waiting.

Mrs. Carter stared up into Donna's eyes, her faded blue eyes searching Donna's. Like all law-enforcement family members, this woman was no stranger to the police life and had to know that a 2:00 a.m. visit from the police—without her son present—wasn't a social visit.

"Hurt or dead?" Mrs. Carter's voice shook as she waited for Donna's reply.

Donna slowly shook her head. "Oh, Mrs. Carter. I'm so, so sorry."

The elderly woman let out a small cry and started to crumple. Blake rushed forward and caught her in his arms before she could fall. Donna pulled open the door, tears freely rolling down her cheeks now as Blake carried the woman inside.

After settling her onto a baby-blue flower-patterned couch, he tucked one of the throw pillows beneath her head. Donna covered her with a cream-colored afghan that she'd grabbed from a side chair.

The old woman's eyes were closed, but she wasn't asleep. Tears streamed down her face, and her shoulders shook with silent sobs. Donna settled on the floor in front of the couch, holding one of the woman's hands while she gently stroked her hair and whispered soothing words.

Not sure how to help, Blake glanced around the small room. It was neat as a pin, as was the kitchen, visible through an arched opening.

"Tea. You should make her some tea," a feminine voice called out from somewhere behind him.

He turned to see a woman standing on the porch with gray-streaked blond hair cut to frame a face that could have been a twin to Donna's, except for the twenty or so years separating them.

Blake hurried to open the door for her. "Mrs. Waters, pleasure to meet you. I'm Detective—"

"I know who you are." She smiled as if to soften her words. "Call me Miranda, Blake. Do you know how to make hot tea?"

"Yes, ma'am."

Her brows arched up.

"Yes, Miranda," he corrected.

She smiled and patted the side of his face. "She takes two sugar cubes and a dash of cream. I take mine black." She gave him a shooing motion and hurried to the couch, where she hugged Donna. She then took a seat on the coffee table and took Mrs. Carter's other hand in her own.

Feeling relieved to have something to do, Blake went into the kitchen and tried to remember how to make hot tea. It had been years since he'd seen his mom make it, and thankfully it was as easy as he remembered. Randy's mother was obviously quite fond of the stuff. She had a teakettle on the stove, which he filled with water and turned on to boil. A teapot and service sat on the counter, along with an assortment of tea bags, sugar cubes in a delicate bowl and a tiny empty pitcher that he guessed was for the cream.

After searching through the refrigerator, he gave up figuring out what container might hold cream and went for the milk instead.

"Need any help?"

He turned with the quart of milk poised to pour into the little pitcher. Donna stood in the opening, shaking her head when she saw the milk.

"Half-and-half," she said, taking the milk from him and heading to the refrigerator. After exchanging the quart of milk for a pint-size container that looked like a miniature milk carton, she filled up the little pitcher. "There. All ready, except for the water."

"Thanks," he said as she replaced the container of half-and-half in the refrigerator.

"You did great on your own," she said. "Just figured I'd check on you. I don't recall you being a tea drinker."

"Not my thing," he admitted. "But I've suffered through a few cups in my day. Mom laced tea with whiskey and honey when we had sore throats. The only reason I gave in was the whiskey."

She smiled. "I would have done the same thing. I never liked tea either."

The kettle on the stove started to whistle. Blake moved toward it, but Donna gently pushed him out of the way. "I've got this." She turned off the stove and poured hot water into the teapot. She added a second cup to the tray. "There. Mom and Mrs. Carter can exchange stories about Randy over an entire pot of tea. They're already talking about the silly things he used to do as a kid. Mom's a miracle worker. I'm glad she came."

He glanced past her, relieved to see that Randy's mom was sitting up now, beside Donna's mom on the couch. Their heads were close together as they talked, and Donna's mom was holding the other woman's hand.

"She seems like a no-nonsense lady, your mom," he said. "Strong and kind. Like you."

"I don't know how strong I am right now. I'm barely holding it together." She waved toward the tea tray. "Want to carry that for me? Not that I can't do it. But I'm not so much a feminist that I'm threatened by letting a guy do the heavy lifting if one's around."

In answer, he carried the tray into the other room.

The two women on the couch barely seemed to notice him as he left the tray on the coffee table. They spoke in low whispers, and he distinctly heard Mrs. Carter mention Randy's name while smiling through her tears.

"We're going to head out, Mom, Mrs. Carter." Donna hugged both women, whispered something to Randy's mom, then nodded at Blake.

They quietly made their way outside and down the steps. Blake waited until they were at his truck before he asked, "Are you sure you don't want to stay here with your mom? I can handle things back at the station."

She shook her head but didn't say anything as she climbed into the passenger side.

They'd just rounded a corner, the cottage disappearing from sight in the rearview mirror, when she grabbed her door handle. "Pull over."

He looked through the windshield but didn't see whatever had her alarmed. "I don't see anything. What's the—"

"Pull over. Now."

He yanked the steering wheel and jerked the truck to a stop on the shoulder of the road. "Donna—"

She threw the passenger door open and barely made it into the bushes before she started retching.

Blake jumped out of the truck, leaving the engine running and the headlights on to light the way as he rushed toward her.

"Don't," she gasped. "Leave me alone." Her whole body shuddered as she retched again.

Ignoring her order, he crouched behind her and pulled her hair back from her face.

Apparently too sick to yell at him again, she threw up over and over, until she started to dry heave. When the storm finally passed, she shook her head and pushed his hands back, letting her hair fall around her face.

Blake moved to the side and gently tilted her chin to look at him. "Is it Randy? Or are you sick?"

She jerked her head back, forcing him to lower his hand. She blinked several times, drawing quick, shallow breaths. "Sh-she... Mrs. Carter, she asked me..." She shook her head and swiped at the tears now flowing down her cheeks. "I knew he was dead. I mean, I saw his broken body, saw the blood. But I didn't... I don't think it hit me that he's really gone, that he's...dead... until his mother asked me to help her plan his funeral."

Her shoulders shook as sobs suddenly racked her body, even worse than the dry heaves from moments earlier.

Blake swore and scooped her onto his lap. She stiffened at first, but then threw her arms around him and buried her head against his chest. His heart seemed to crack as he listened to her crying, felt her hot wet tears soak into his shirt. If her friend's murderer had appeared in front of him right then, Blake would have ripped the man's throat out with his bare hands for causing Donna such pain.

He rocked her against him, gently rubbing her back until she quieted. Then, as if she'd suddenly realized where she was, she shoved at his chest.

"What are you doing?" Her eyes widened. Then she

jerked her face to the side and cupped a hand over her mouth. "Oh, my gosh. I have to smell terrible."

"I don't care how you smell." He lifted her in his arms and stood.

Still keeping one hand cupped over her mouth, she said, "I told you not to carry me. I can walk perfectly fine."

"Your whole body is shaking, and you're way too stubborn to admit when you need help."

In spite of her protests, she didn't try to push herself out of his arms; she let him carry her the rest of the way to the truck. After settling her in the passenger side, he reached for the seat belt.

She tried to grab it out of his hand, but he simply finished clicking it into place. Then he snagged a clean rag and a bottle of water from the box of supplies he kept behind the seat.

He held them out to her without a word.

"Thank you," she said grudgingly as she took them.

"You're welcome."

He slowly walked around the back of the truck, giving her privacy and enough time to rinse out her mouth. When he hopped into the cab and shut his door, she pulled hers shut, too, and looked straight ahead through the windshield. Her cheeks were flushed, and he knew her well enough to realize that she was probably embarrassed that he'd been there to witness her being sick. Which of course was silly. She could be sick in front of him a hundred times, and it wouldn't bother him. What would bother him was if she needed him and he couldn't be there to help her.

He shook his head at himself.

Ever since Donna had walked into that bar, braving the stink and the worst dregs of humanity because she cared enough about him to try to save his job, he'd been off-kilter. The feelings he'd worked so hard to ignore were boiling too close to the surface—especially after finding Randy murdered. He kept picturing what might have happened if he hadn't gotten fired, if Donna hadn't come after him. Would she have been the one who had been killed? Would the killer have chosen her as his victim instead of Randy? Just imagining her lying there, broken, bleeding, sent a cold chill straight through him.

"Blake? Are *you* okay?"

Her question had him forcing a smile. "Of course." Since she was staring at him so intensely, as if trying to figure out what he was thinking, he threw her a curveball. "I'll have to take a rain check on taking you to bed. Maybe until all this is over. You know, since I went against your dictate and carried you again." He gave her an outrageous wink.

Her eyes widened. Then she started laughing. The delightful sound was like a balm to his soul, somehow giving him the strength he needed to lock away his ridiculous emotions and face the task ahead—the investigation, and the search for their friends.

He put the truck into drive and headed down the road. A few minutes later, he stopped at an intersection. "Back to the station? Or do you want me to drop you off at your house to get some sleep?"

She shook her head. "I can't sleep. Not yet. Not until I know…something, anything, that can shed some light on what's going on."

A half hour passed before they pulled into the empty parking lot of the stand-alone building that was several miles outside town, surrounded by woods. According to what the chief had told him, the idea when the police station was built was that the town would eventually grow out this far and surround it. So, rather than use the more expensive land back in Destiny, the station had been constructed pretty much in the middle of nowhere. That was a decade ago. And Destiny, Tennessee, showed no signs of growing outside its current boundaries.

They were heading up the walkway to the front glass doors when she stopped him with a hand on his arm.

"You never saw me cry," she said. "And you sure never saw me throw up."

"I don't even know what you're talking about."

Her expression mirrored relief. "Thank you."

They headed up the walk again. When they reached the doors, he pulled one of them open for her. "Donna?"

She hesitated and looked up at him. "Yes?"

"Crying, or being sick with grief over a loved one, neither of those makes you weak. They make you human. You're one of the strongest people I know. Nothing that happened today changed that."

She blinked, then cleared her throat and stepped inside. They'd only gone a few feet when she glanced at him over her shoulder. "Blake?"

"Yes?"

"Thank you. For everything." Without waiting for his reply, she strode through the squad room, grabbed a small toiletry bag out of her desk and hurried down the back hallway to the bathroom.

Chapter Eight

At 4:00 a.m. on a typical Sunday, there were one, maybe two, Destiny, Tennessee, police officers on duty. This Sunday, there were ten, plus a dozen state police. Every law-enforcement officer in the county who wasn't already on assignment had shown up in answer to Donna's calls, eager to help their fellow officers. Even some local civilians, awakened by her infamous call tree, were pitching in any way they could.

But only Blake and Donna were at the police station.

Everyone else was either helping collect evidence at Hawkins Ridge or scouring the county for potential witnesses.

Blake rubbed the stubble on his jaw and leaned back in his desk chair, looking around the nearly empty squad room. The freestanding building had only one entrance and exit that opened directly into this room. A kitchenette ran along the wall to the right of the entrance. Past that was the police chief's office and private bathroom. Along the back was a short hallway with two holding cells and the restroom the officers used. And to the left of the entrance was an interview room. The place was small, but efficient, and very quiet.

Too quiet.

He longed to be outside with everyone else, searching for clues. But since he and Donna were the only detectives left, here they sat, hunched over their keyboards in the last row of desks.

He rubbed his bleary eyes. One desk over, Donna was squinting at the computer monitor as if trying to focus.

Her shoulder-length blond hair was cut into a straight bob that gently curved around her face, giving her what Blake had always thought of as a pixie look, like a tiny magical fairy sent down to dwell among mortals. Or, at least, normally it curved around her face. Right now her hair was sticking up all around her head. The blouse she'd so carefully tucked into her jeans before they went up to Hawkins Ridge was hanging out in the back now, severely wrinkled. What little eye makeup she'd had on hours ago was now smeared, reminding him of a raccoon.

He didn't think she'd ever looked more beautiful. Too bad they were coworkers and the chief frowned on dating among coworkers. Apparently Max had been a ladies' man around the station at one time, dating interns and wreaking havoc whenever the relationships eventually ended. Now that he was caught for good by his wife, Bex, things had settled down. But he'd pretty much ruined it for the rest of them. Which meant Blake had to work extra hard at not letting Donna know that he'd grown to care about her a whole lot more than he should over the past few months. As smart and beautiful and fun as she was to be around, it wasn't easy.

He silently cursed himself for even thinking about something so unimportant in light of the case they were working on. He must be more tired than he'd realized, sitting here, mooning over Donna when he should be trying to find their missing coworkers. Looking at her now, seeing how pale and drawn her face was, he realized she had to be just as worn out as he felt. Maybe they both needed a break, so they could refocus on the case.

"You're exhausted," he announced, rolling his chair next to hers. "We both are. We should go home and get some sleep."

She blinked as if coming out of a trance, her fingers growing still on the keyboard. "What time is it?"

"A little after four."

"A little after four," she repeated, staring at the screen with a haunted look in her eyes. "Did you know that most people who are abducted are killed within the first three hours? We've failed them, Blake. They've been out there for far longer than that."

"That statistic applies to juveniles, not adults. And it typically involves pedophiles. We're dealing with something entirely different here. Let's focus on solving Randy's murder. We're well within the golden forty-eight-hour window, where most homicides are solved. Focus on that. We find his killer, we find the others alive and well and bring them home."

She shook her head. "I'm doing everything I can, but it doesn't feel like enough."

"You're forgetting something really important here."

She finally turned her head and met his gaze. "What's that?"

"This killer didn't kidnap just anyone. He kidnapped some of the most well-trained, intelligent, savvy cops I've ever met. I've worked with a lot of officers, so that's saying something. We're still a team here. You and I are working this case from the outside. But Dillon, Chris, Max and the chief are working it from the inside. That's an impressive group. Together, there's no telling what they'll get done. It wouldn't surprise me if they came walking in here in the next few hours with their kidnapper in handcuffs."

The corner of her mouth lifted in a smile. "I can totally picture that."

"Good. Hold on to that image and don't get discouraged. We're going to find this guy and bring our team home."

"Guy. One killer. I don't see it. You said yourself, Dillon and the others are an impressive team, formidable even. There's no way that one person could have killed Randy and taken the rest of them hostage. We're looking at a group of bad guys here."

"I won't argue with you there. I've been thinking the same thing."

She swiveled her chair toward him and started ticking off salient points on her fingers. "There's a lack of tire tracks. A meticulous note that had to be written ahead of time and brought to the scene. Transportation. Someone had to work that out ahead of time—a truck or van, something that could hold all our guys. And they sure as heck had to have a lot of firepower and manpower to make our men get into that vehicle without fighting them. A fight would have left obvious signs of a struggle at the scene, which there wasn't. All of that speaks to this being a large, well-planned operation."

Crossing her arms, she leaned back in her chair. "When you hear about criminals being highly organized, well planned, well resourced and willing to go after cops—a SWAT team for goodness' sake— what does that make you think?"

He didn't even have to think about it. "Drugs."

She nodded. "Exactly. That's what I'm thinking, too. But we haven't had any major drug cases in this county in years. The worst we've had is a few farmers growing pot plants out in their tobacco fields, hoping no one would notice a few Mary Janes mixed in here and there. But that was for personal use. This is way bigger than that."

"You're thinking methamphetamines."

"Possibly. Or some new exotic drug being manufactured in a homegrown lab. There's always something new out on the streets in big cities. You worked in Knoxville. Did you see any of that?"

"I worked homicides, so I didn't have much firsthand exposure to the drug operations going on. But there was enough crossover in the murder cases I worked to get a feel for it. I've still got a few contacts there. I can call them up in a few hours when they're in and put out some feelers, see if there are some groups looking to spread out into a rural county that might be behind this. But that doesn't feel right either. A major drug-running operation wouldn't want to draw attention by taking police officers captive. If the cops came across their lab or something like that, sure, there could be a bloodbath, a shoot-out. But that's not what we have here."

"The note," she said.

"The note. If this is drugs, why kidnap cops and leave a ransom note? That's the complete opposite of lying low and trying not to be caught. Whoever is behind this wants attention."

She shook her head and fisted her hands in frustration. "Not drugs, then. So what is it?"

"I didn't say it wasn't drugs. That still fits the well-funded, well-resourced side of this. But maybe the goal isn't to hide something. Maybe the goal is to send a message."

"What's the message? We don't have any ongoing drug investigations right now. So it's not like someone needs to threaten us to back off." She grabbed a small stack of manila folders from the far corner of her desk and plopped them on the corner closest to Blake. "We have three open investigations in Destiny. Two are typical local stuff—petty theft—and we know who's responsible. It's just a matter of gathering enough evidence to go to court. The third is the only serious one—"

"Our John Doe murder last month."

She nodded. "A stranger, a hitchhiker found shot multiple times, his body left lying in a ditch. He was in a remote section of the county near a two-lane highway that mostly only locals use. No witnesses. No tire tracks. No clues other than the bullet Doc Brookes dug out of the body—nine-millimeter. The backpack the hiker wore had typical hiker stuff in it. Best we can figure, he was hiking in the Smokies and decided to go off-trail and ended up here. Until we figure out who he is or find someone who actually saw him before he was killed, we're at an impasse. But no matter how I look at it, there's nothing about his murder that makes me think it could be part of what's going on here."

It was Blake's turn to count off points on his fingers. "Shot multiple times. No witnesses. No tire tracks. Left dead in a remote area. Sound familiar?"

Her eyes widened. "Randy."

He shrugged. "Maybe. Maybe not. But at the very

least, I'm thinking a fresh look at John Doe's murder is warranted."

"Agreed." She flipped open the folder.

Blake flipped it closed.

"What are you doing?" She frowned at him.

"It's almost four thirty. Neither of us has slept in almost twenty-four hours. We're running on empty. This—" he tapped the folder "—can wait. We won't be any good to anyone if we don't get at least a couple of hours of shut-eye."

Her shoulders slumped. "You're right. I can barely see straight. But until someone comes back to hold down the fort, we can't just leave."

"We're not doing anyone any good in our current conditions."

She shook her head, her mouth drawn into a mutinous line. "I'm not ready to stop. Not yet. I can't bear the idea of no one working the investigation while we lie around and do nothing."

"It's not nothing. It's recharging our batteries so we can be useful again."

Her silence was his answer. The only way he was getting her out of here right now was if he picked her up and carried her. And he'd already learned what she thought about that plan. Unless he was her lover carrying her to bed, of course. He swallowed and forced his tired, out-of-control thoughts not to wander in that direction again.

"What time is the cavalry supposed to get here?" he asked.

"They didn't say. But with an officer down, and four missing, I sure expected they'd be here by now. Especially since the Knoxville FBI field office is less than an hour away."

He picked up the folder. "Tell you what. While we wait for them, let me poke around a little more on the John Doe case. I'll expand the cross-check against missing persons to within a hundred-mile radius, see if something new pops up. You're working on the time-lines for our team, right? How close are they to being done?"

"I could use a few more hours to close some gaps."

"All right," he allowed. "We'll give it a few more hours. If they're not here by six—"

"Seven. We'll give them until seven."

He blew out a long breath. "Okay. Seven. If they're not here by seven, we get one of your call-tree buddies to man the phones while we go home and get at least a few hours of sleep before coming back. Agreed?"

She looked reluctant, but even sitting here, talking to him, she was struggling to keep her eyes open. He wasn't even sure she could make it until seven, but he was trying to placate her. Finally, she nodded and turned back to her keyboard.

"I'm going to need some coffee." She started typing and arched a brow. "It's your turn."

He smiled. "Black as always?"

"Cream and sugar to cut the bitterness, unless you're making a fresh pot?"

Her hopeful look had him smiling again. "One fresh pot of coffee coming up."

He crossed to the left of the glass-walled entrance, with its double doors, to where the long counter boasted a microwave, a coffeepot and an assortment of snacks, since they didn't have a vending machine. The mini fridge underneath the counter held sodas and water. The mini freezer beside it held an assortment of baked goods that Dillon's wife, Ashley, restocked every now and then, so they'd always have something good to nibble on. He set a couple of trays of muffins on the counter, figuring they'd be thawed out around breakfast time for whoever was in the station come sunup.

As he went through the motions of putting a fresh filter and grounds in the coffee maker, he called over his shoulder, "When will Ashley and the others be back from the cruise? We're going to have to notify them about what's going on. And interview them, too, in case they can contribute to the timeline."

"The ship docks in Miami today, around five in the afternoon. They're going shopping and taking in the sights. Then they'll fly into Nashville International Airport tomorrow. From there, they'll take a puddle-jumper to McGhee Tyson. I figure they'll get there close to noon. Since it's just a few minutes down the road, you and I could meet them when they get off the plane. I don't want to risk them hearing about this from any well-meaning friends in Destiny who don't realize they haven't heard the news yet. And I don't see the point of calling them now, ruining the end of their vacation just to tell them we don't have any leads. I'd rather hope and pray we find our team, safe and sound, before we even have to tell their families what happened."

Blake wasn't so sure that he agreed with her plan. He'd rather wake them and see if they knew anything that could help build the timeline. But since Donna was the one working on that timeline, he'd trust her to know if there were any gaps, anything she needed to corroborate. There were plenty of avenues of investigation they could explore right now. He was itching to get his hands on any information from the crime scene. And the autopsy might give them a DNA link to their killer. Hopefully Doc Brookes or the Maryville M.E. had the body at his office by now and was busy looking for clues.

He leaned against the counter, resting his eyes while listening to the tapping of Donna's fingers on her keyboard and the soothing sound of coffee pouring into the pot. It seemed like only a few seconds had passed when the machine beeped, letting him know the pot was full, ten cups ready for consumption. He must have dozed off standing up. He shook his head and poured them both cups before returning to their desks at the back of the room.

Donna murmured her thanks and took a deep, appreciative sniff before drinking some down.

Blake sipped his then set it aside as he noted what was beside Donna's keyboard. "The chief's planner? Where did you find that?"

She yawned and set her cup down. "In his office, of course. I grabbed it while you were snoozing by the counter. You snore, by the way."

Since no one had ever told him that before, he figured she was teasing. He sure hoped so, anyway. "I searched his office when we first got here. I didn't see a planner."

"Did you check his wall safe?"

"Wall safe?"

"Behind his desk, to the left of the window, hidden by that hideous deer head he hung up last summer. Not that he even hunts. I think his nephew gave it to him. You've never seen him use the safe?"

"I'm not exactly his confidant."

Her mouth tightened. "Yeah, sorry about that. When this is over, maybe we can all have a kumbaya moment together and become a real team."

He didn't bother to remind her that he'd been fired and would never be part of her team again. Their current pretense was only until they could find their missing peers. As soon as Dillon was back—and Blake refused to believe that he wouldn't be back—Dillon would tell him to get out. Which was yet another reason not to allow himself to pursue his attraction to Donna. There was no sense in trying to start a relationship when he'd soon be moving to another county, maybe even another state if that was what it took to find a job.

"The combination is the chief's wife's birthday, by the way. Two digits each for the month, day and year, just in case you ever need to get in there. The main reason he has the thing is to keep his spare gun locked up. He doesn't like to stow it in the gun cabinet with our rifles."

He gave her a curt nod and returned to his desk, coffee in hand. He didn't bother to remind her that he didn't know Claire Thornton's birth date, or that the chief wouldn't want him knowing the combination. That last part was a no-brainer, since he'd never even told Blake that he had a safe.

They worked in silence, taking turns getting each other coffee refills, desperately needing the caffeine to stay awake.

"How's the timeline coming?" he asked, when the wall clock above the front doors had inched past six thirty.

"It's about ready to review, actually." She motioned for him to join her.

He rolled his chair over, and she explained the setup of her worksheet, with a tab for each of the team members—including one for Randy.

Sounds from outside had both of them looking up. A group of seven men and women in dark-colored business suits, with crisp white button-up dress shirts and ties, headed up the walkway toward the front doors. Every one of them was holding a briefcase.

"Looks like the cavalry has finally arrived." Blake stood. "Only the feds know how to match their business suits so well that you can't tell them apart."

Donna let out a sigh and walked with him toward the front. "The chief would hate that I called the feds for help. Things didn't turn out so well the last time an FBI agent came out here to work with us on a case."

"Really? What happened?"

"He was murdered."

Chapter Nine

Donna tried not to let it bother her, or at least not let it show that it bothered her, when she let Supervisory Special Agent Richard Grant into the chief's office. Once the fellow FBI agents that Grant had brought with him were all there at the same time as the Destiny P.D. officers and the state police, the place would be over-flowing. It only made sense to give Grant this office. But it still felt like she was being a traitor to her boss.

He *really* didn't like the feds.

She glanced at Blake, standing next to the door as if he couldn't wait to get back to his desk. She couldn't blame him. Even taking time to give a tour of their tiny police station meant taking time away from the investigation, time they couldn't afford to waste. And in spite of the fact that they were both asleep on their feet, there were things they wanted to wrap up before being forced to get some shut-eye.

Grant set his briefcase on the desk and looked around the rather large office with its private bathroom. "Thank you for offering your chief's office for the duration. Looks like we could fit a few small tables in here and some folding chairs to accommodate my direct reports."

He indicated the three special agents who'd come inside with him. She'd already forgotten their names.

"Do you have anything like that?" he asked. "Folding tables? Chairs?"

She motioned toward the window behind the desk. "There's a storage building out back where the maintenance guys keep their tools and lawn equipment for when they make trips out here. There might be some folding tables and chairs too, not sure. But the chief never throws anything away. Every time we get a new piece of furniture or equipment, the old one goes out there, broken or not. Key's in the top desk drawer. Help yourself. Any office supplies you need—paper, pens, that sort of thing—should be in the file cabinets that run along the wall by the interview room. Those aren't locked."

He opened the top drawer, rummaged through it and pulled out the key she'd indicated. "Joel, Colin, why don't you see if there's anything out back we can use? It's going to be tight quarters around here, and it would be nice if everyone at least has somewhere to sit."

"Will do."

The one he'd called Colin—his name was Colin Lopez, she remembered now—took the key and headed to the door with Joel in tow. Blake opened the door for them and nodded as they stepped out of the office.

"Stacy," Grant said, indicating the remaining agent. "Can you give me a few moments alone with Detective Waters and Detective Sullivan please?"

"Of course." She paused beside Donna. "I'm terribly sorry for your loss, Detective. I'm Special Agent Stacy Bell, in case you forgot. If there's anything I can do for you, please let me know. We've both got the same goal. Catch the bad guys and save the good guys."

"Um, thank you." Donna shook the agent's hand, surprised at her little speech.

Stacy paused beside Blake and offered her condolences to him, as well, before leaving the office.

Blake shrugged when Donna looked at him. He obviously didn't know what to make of that speech either.

Grant sat behind the desk and motioned toward the two chairs in front of it.

"Detectives, won't you both sit down so we can discuss things more in-depth than the earlier summary you gave me?"

Donna slowly lowered herself into one of the chairs, feeling as confused as Blake looked as he closed the door. He settled into the chair beside hers. They hadn't given Grant a *summary* when he arrived. They'd told him every single detail they could remember. Well, except for two details that she had no intention of sharing—that she'd touched the note in Randy's hand and that Blake was technically a civilian.

"I'm not really sure what else you want to discuss," she said. "I think we told you everything. Unfortunately, we don't know very much yet. Which is why Blake and I would both like to get back to our desks to work on the investigation."

"Let's talk about the note that brought me and my team here."

He pulled a piece of paper out of his pocket and smoothed it out on top of the desk. It was a full sheet of paper, obviously a copy of the original that Randy had been holding. He read the words out loud.

"Instructions for ransom will follow. If you don't obey the instructions, the remaining members of your SWAT team will end up like this one."

"What's your take on the writing?" he asked.

Donna swallowed at the tightness in her throat. Her emotions were still too raw. She was barely holding herself together. "I'm not sure why you're asking me. I'm no handwriting expert. Isn't that the sort of thing you guys do?"

He smiled. "Yes, one of many things that we do. I have the original with an expert now, as a matter of fact. But time is critical. And I'm not from this area. I thought perhaps your instincts might be valuable in helping ferret out any clues about the author of the note."

She cleared her throat. "I see your point. Sorry. I'm running on empty, not thinking as clearly as usual. May I?"

"Please."

She took the note from him and leaned toward Blake so they could both study it. But her eyes felt like they were crossing trying to read the script and make out the letters. It was now seven thirty in the morning, which meant she was coming up on twenty-five hours without sleep.

"I can't even make the words focus." She handed the note to Blake. "What about you?"

He frowned down at the paper. "The obvious of course is that someone probably wrote this ahead of time. It's too perfect to have been scribbled at the scene. It's dirty and wet up on Hawkins Ridge from the storms that blew through yesterday afternoon. I remember the original paper was clean, crisp. Or at least, it looked crisp."

"Go on."

"It's not written in colloquial terms. It's formal— perfect grammar, punctuation. Almost too perfect."

Richard sat forward in his chair. "Too perfect?"

Blake handed him back the note. "It's as if someone is trying too hard not to make a mistake. I wonder if English might be their second language, so they referred to a grammar guide to get it just so. At any rate, I doubt they're from around here. That's not how we talk."

Donna smiled at him, but he wasn't sure why.

"Interesting angle. Anything else?" Richard asked.

"It refers to the SWAT team, but the chief isn't part of the SWAT team and he was taken, too. Plus, Donna and I are on the team and weren't there at the time the others were kidnapped. So any leads we pursue should be based on the intent, not what actually happened. I think the intent was to kidnap just the SWAT team, not the chief. Which takes him out of the equation as far as victimology is concerned." He shrugged. "Like Donna's, my mind isn't firing on all synapses right now. We've both been up all night. So I'm not sure what anything I just said really means, or if it matters in the investigation. I'll have to look at it fresh later."

Richard tapped the chief's favorite pen on top of the desk blotter. Donna wanted to snatch it away, tell him not to touch the chief's things. She had to curl her fingers against her palms to resist the juvenile impulse.

In the window behind Grant, she could see the two agents that he'd sent outside pulling things out of the storage building. She wanted to stop them, too. They were rummaging around in the chief's things, invading his privacy. And none of it was helping anyone find him, or the others.

"You mentioned that neither of you was on the ridge when the team disappeared," Grant said, breaking through her thoughts. "Why not?"

She blinked. Suddenly she realized that neither she nor Blake had discussed a cover story for this before the agents got here. The only reason that she wasn't there was that she wanted to find Blake and try to get him to apologize to Dillon and get his job back. If she admitted that, Blake would have to leave and quit working the case. What would happen to her? Did the FBI have any authority over her? She didn't think so.

"Detective Waters?"

Blake put his hand on hers and squeezed. "You probably haven't been up this late since college, huh?"

His words might have been teasing, but she read the seriousness in his eyes. He was trying to cover her hesitation, help her through it. But nothing was coming to her. Her mind had gone completely blank.

"It's my fault," Blake said, filling the awkward silence. He let her hand go and sat forward in his chair. "I screwed up. I didn't follow the rules of the training exercise. Actually, I pissed Dillon off."

"Dillon? The SWAT commander?"

"SWAT lead, yes. He slugged me, and I—"

"He hit you?" The agent sounded shocked.

Blake frowned. "It's no big deal. In his position, I'd have probably done the same thing. Haven't you ever punched someone?"

"Someone who was working for me? Never."

"Well, you're a better man than me. I've gotten in fights plenty of times."

"So I've heard. You had a bit of an anger management problem when you worked homicide out of Knoxville. Isn't that why you left? It was either quit or be fired? I believe there was concern over a grudge another officer had against you, maybe even a concern for your life if you stayed?"

Donna tensed. Could the agent be telling the truth? Was this why Blake had come to Destiny? Had the chief done him a favor, gotten him out before he could be fired? Or hurt? A light flush of red was creeping up his neck, which seemed answer enough.

"Reading someone's personnel files without a warrant is a crime," he said. "And I can't think of a single reason for a judge to give you one."

"I didn't have to read your files. All I had to do was make some calls to some friends on the force."

"I bet those friends enjoyed being woken up at, what, five or six in the morning, to spread gossip and innuendo that are entirely irrelevant to this case. Is that why it took you and your team so long to get here? You were wasting time digging into my past—for no good reason?"

Blake's voice hadn't risen during the exchange. Instead, it had grown steady, deeper than usual and deadly calm. She could practically feel the anger seeping out of his pores. And if she didn't know him as well as she did, she'd probably be scared right now. Then again, if he had these kinds of secrets he'd never shared, did she really know him at all?

Grant certainly didn't look impressed or intimidated. He arched a brow as if amused. "That's the real reason your SWAT team lead punched you, isn't it? Because you couldn't control your anger and punched him first. Is that what happened?"

"No," Donna interrupted, starting to get just as agitated on Blake's behalf as he appeared to be. She'd deal with his secrets later, in private. But they were a team, and he deserved her loyalty in front of others—especially a stranger who came in supposedly to help them and was wasting their time with pettiness.

Both men had looked at her in surprise when she spoke, and they seemed to be waiting to see what else she wanted to say. She straightened her shoulders. "The truth is that Blake showed remarkable restraint when Dillon started accusing him of not being a team player. Blake had just captured two of three fake bad guys in the exercise, all by himself, and was proud of that. It caught him by surprise to realize that Dillon was furious over the whole thing. But Blake handled it well. Dillon's the one who didn't. Looking back, with the gift of hindsight, they both could have handled it a whole lot better. Both of them made mistakes. But the real mystery here is how any of this is helping us solve the case."

Blake, oblivious of the SSA watching, took her hand again and squeezed. He nodded his thanks and let her hand go.

The agent frowned at both of them. He directed his next question to Blake. "Your lead was angry enough over your performance to punch you. Did he do anything else after that?"

Blake grew very still, his gaze locked on the agent. "Like what?"

"Like, I don't know, suspend you? Fire you?"

"Of course not," Donna intervened. "That would be

overreacting. Dillon dismissed him, from the exercise. That's it."

His gaze slowly moved back to her. As she tried not to squirm beneath his scrutiny, she couldn't help thinking that Blake had been one hundred percent right up on the ridge when he'd argued about whether they should lie. He'd warned her that one lie would always lead to another and that things could get really complicated, really fast.

Things were definitely getting complicated.

She cleared her throat, which kept seeming to want to close up. "Again, I don't understand why you're wasting time questioning us. Everything you need to know about the case is in the reports that Blake and I spent the last few hours working up. We offered you free access to everything when you arrived. Even now your agents are out there reading those reports. All of this is in them."

Something akin to skepticism, maybe even disappointment, flashed across the agent's face as he folded his hands on top of the desk. "Since you both keep questioning my motives in asking these questions, I'll skip to the heart of the issue and be perfectly blunt. Does the name Jason Kent ring any bells?"

She sucked in a breath. Her stomach fluttered like a whole field of butterflies had just taken off inside.

"Jason Kent?" Blake asked. "Who's that?"

"The special agent I mentioned earlier," she said. "The one who was killed."

"Murdered, you mean," Grant snapped. "Because your team lead, Dillon Gray, along with your chief and your entire police force, misled Kent and gave him the runaround when he was here working on an embezzlement case. While you all tried to protect the woman that Dillon eventually married—"

"Of course we protected her. Ashley was innocent, and the FBI was trying to railroad her. Kent didn't give us a choice. The men behind the embezzlement, the people who were framing her, would have killed her if we'd let Kent lock her up."

"No need to review the details. I'm quite familiar with all the excuses given during the investigation that followed." He drew a deep breath before continuing. "That history between the Destiny Police Department and the bureau warns me to take everything anyone here tells me with a great deal of caution. I'm sure you've heard the mantra, trust but verify? That's what I'm doing here. Which means that I need to hear your alibis for where you were when Detective Carter was killed and the rest of the team disappeared. And I assure you my team will verify whatever stories you give me. So choose your words carefully."

Donna was too shocked and angry to speak. Thankfully Blake was the calm, measured one this time. He smoothly explained that after his altercation with Dillon, he left, and that Donna left her team shortly after because she was upset over what had happened. He detailed what had happened at the bar, and him trying to call Dillon and the team later on, before finally stopping at her house. The only time she had to jump in was to explain the time gap after she left the woods to when she found Blake at the bar. She'd been home, alone, showering, changing and trying to talk herself out of going after him. Which meant she might or might not have an alibi, depending on when Randy was killed.

"Well?" she asked, when she and Blake were finished. "I'm assuming if you're asking for alibis that you've already read the autopsy report, even though neither of us has seen it yet. What was the time of death?"

"I prefer not to disclose that information until after we check out your claims—just in case you remember something else and change your stories."

Her mouth literally fell open. She couldn't believe he was acting this way. "You do realize that we can call Doc Brookes ourselves and ask him the T.O.D., don't you?"

"What I realize is that if you do, it could seriously jeopardize the investigation into your alibis. I strongly suggest that you not speak to anyone about the autopsy until you're cleared. If you're cleared."

She exchanged another stunned look with Blake. "Cleared? Really? We invited you here, thinking you could help us find the killer and bring back our team. But if you're going to waste your time going after us, consider yourself fired. You and your team can go back to Knoxville. We'll handle this on our own." She jumped up and headed toward the door.

"Donna," Blake called out. "Wait."

She stiffened, her hand on the doorknob. "Why? He's wasting our time."

"We invited him here to help us," Blake said. "You and I don't have experience with kidnappings and ransom demands. Like it or not, we need to work together and park our hurt feelings at the door to get the job done." He waved toward the chair. "Please."

Grant clicked open the briefcase sitting on his desk. "Excellent points. But I'm afraid there's a lot more to it than that, Detectives. You've asked what took us so long to get here." He pulled some papers out of the briefcase and plopped them in front of him. "I think you'll both want to stick around and find out the answer to that question."

She turned and leaned back against the door, arms crossed. She refused to look at Blake. She didn't want to see the disappointment that was probably on his face. The professionalism she normally prided herself on had disintegrated long ago, probably around the twenty-hour mark of being up with no sleep.

Everything she was saying would probably come back to haunt her later. But at the moment, she just couldn't bring herself to care. She was too angry, too upset over Randy and the others, to bother with diplomacy at this point. And she wasn't sure they did need the help from the feds. The state police were happy to help them. And they'd worked kidnappings before. She was starting to understand why Chief Thornton disliked the FBI so much.

"Go ahead." She waved toward the papers in front of him. "Enlighten us. What took you close to seven hours to get here even though your field office is, what, forty-five minutes away? Go ahead. Explain. I'm all ears."

His brows rose. "Other than the fact that my immediate team and I were in the middle of the prosecution of an important, multi-year, multi-million-dollar case and had to wake a judge to postpone the trial so we could help save your teammates? Is that what you mean about delays? I'm sure you've heard of the Sanchez case."

Scorn dripped from his every word, and Donna couldn't help feeling chagrined. She *had* heard of the Sanchez case. Who hadn't? Sanchez was a reputed Colombian drug lord with a stranglehold over organized crime from Knoxville to Nashville. But she couldn't pull back on what she'd said now. She'd stepped in this with both feet. The only way out was to go forward. So she kept her mouth shut.

He shuffled through the papers as if searching for one in particular. Then he turned one facedown on top of the rest. "As I said before, due to our history, I was wary about working with the Destiny police. So I took some necessary protective precautions, just in case things didn't pass the smell test when I got here."

"What kind of precautions?" Blake asked.

Donna didn't ask. She'd glimpsed the letterhead on the paper he'd turned over. She already knew exactly what was coming. The only reason she didn't jump up right now and storm out was the off chance that she could be wrong.

She really, really hoped she was wrong.

"I'll answer that question with another. With your chief of police missing, who do you both report to?"

Blake looked at Donna, perhaps surprised she wasn't saying anything. "I imagine the mayor will have to appoint a temporary chief."

Grant nodded. "Correct. I stopped at his home on the way in to settle that issue." He flipped the paper over. "He was upset that no one had notified him about the murder and the kidnapping, or told him the FBI had been called in."

"Yes, well." Donna cleared her throat. "Honestly, I didn't even think about calling him. I'm sure I would have, sometime today, maybe after a nap to clear my head." She really was embarrassed that she hadn't notified the mayor. That should have been the first thing she did after returning to the station from the crime scene. But the chief was the one who always talked to the mayor. It hadn't even occurred to her.

"I'm sure you would have." Grant sounded as if he believed her on that score, at least. "But when we discussed who in the department should become the acting chief, imagine my surprise when he made me acting chief, even though Detective Waters was available and has nearly fifteen years on the force." He frowned. "By the way, the mayor's wife said to send you her regards. Is that significant for some reason?"

Any guilt she'd had over not being truthful with him evaporated. He obviously knew exactly what the significance was, or at least had to suspect the woman held a grudge against Donna. She was so angry right now, her whole body had tensed up. Her hands were balled into fists at her sides, and she was actually wondering what the penalties might be if she punched SSA Grant, and whether the satisfaction would be worth it.

"Good to know we've got you to take care of all the administrative stuff," Blake said hurriedly, as if to cut off anything she might say, or do. "That leaves us to do what we do best, investigate. Come on, Donna. Let's get back to work." He jumped up from his chair and motioned for her to go with him.

"Not so fast. Did I mention that the mayor was familiar with the training exercises you do up there on Hawkins Ridge? Apparently he had to approve the extra expense of paying three civilians to help in the exercise. He gave me their names and phone numbers so I could get their statements about what they saw up there. One of them lives one street over from the mayor. In the interest of getting as much information as I could, as quickly as possible, we stopped and spoke to him. Any guesses as to what the gentleman named Tim Nealy said really happened in the altercation with Dillon Gray? You know, as opposed to what you both told me?"

He pulled another piece of paper from the stack. It was a typed statement, with Tim's signature boldly scrawled across the bottom.

Donna's stomach seemed to drop to her feet as she glanced at Blake. He was standing stock-still, his face red, his mouth drawn into a tight line. But he wasn't looking at the agent. He was staring at her. Because of the lies she'd made him tell. It was collapsing all around them. And it was all her fault.

"SSA Grant," she said. "I can explain—"

"Explain what? That SWAT team leader and senior detective Dillon Gray fired Detective Sullivan, and yet he's still here, pretending to be employed, working an active investigation? Or explain that you both lied about it to cover it up? Not exactly the ethical actions I'd expect of a police officer. Then again..." He waved his hands as if to encompass the entire station. "This is the Destiny Police Department. Color me *not* surprised."

She took a step toward the desk.

Blake grabbed her. "Don't. He's not worth it."

His gravelly voice had her looking at him in surprise. He was livid, but not at her. His anger was now directed at the agent.

"Go on." Grant motioned toward the door. "You're both fired. Hand over any remaining files or access codes my team needs. Then get out. I'll be generous and give you ten minutes. If you're still in the station after that, I'll have you both arrested."

Blake had to practically drag Donna out of the office. She couldn't seem to make her feet move. She was vacillating between anger and disbelief and horror that her actions were responsible for both her and Blake being dismissed, banned from the case. It was her worst nightmare come true—her friends were in trouble, but she had no way to help them.

Blake pulled the door shut behind them. "Breathe," he whispered in her ear. "You look like you're about to pass out."

"I can't believe that just happened. I've ruined everything. How are we going to save them now?"

"The same way we were going to save them in the first place. With solid detective work. We're just going to have to do it without anyone else's help." He motioned to the big round clock on the wall above the front door. "We've got nine minutes left. We need to get as much information from his team as we can before our time is up. I say we hit up his leads for whatever intel they can share. They don't know we're off the case yet. They've got no reason not to be straight with us. I'll take the guys—Special Agents Joel Lawrence and Colin Lopez." He waved toward the first row of desks, where the two agents were both talking to another agent. "You take the woman—Special Agent Stacy Bell."

Stacy was sitting at a desk in the back row. She smiled at them, oblivious of the drama that had just happened with her boss.

Donna smiled back.

"Go." Blake gave her a little push toward Stacy as he headed toward Joel and Colin.

Donna was breathless by the time she and Blake hopped into his truck and shut the doors. She plopped a thin folder onto the bench seat between them, and Blake added two more folders to the stack, equally thin.

"You first," he said.

"I spoke to Officer Lynch before I left. He's going to try to feed us information, keep us updated without letting anyone else know."

"Good thinking."

"I thought so. I also put my gloves in an evidence bag and slipped them to Lynch. I asked him if he could send them to a private lab to get DNA profiles on my dime, no questions asked. But that he needed to run those profiles against CODIS to see if we get a match on anyone's DNA in the system. If so, he's to call me immediately."

"Go, you," he said. "I forgot about the gloves. Hopefully it will pan out. What else?"

"Doc Brookes didn't conduct the autopsy. An M.E. from Maryville did, with Brookes assisting. That's fine and good. But other than to give a time of death—which is exactly when you and I were in the bar, thankfully, so we're in the clear there—the report is sketchy on details. I got a copy." She tapped the stack of folders. "I figure if we have questions, we can at least call Brookes. He won't care if we're fired or not. He'll see through that as bull. Cause of death is the obvious—gunshot. But get this. All of the samples taken during the autopsy were sent to the FBI lab, not our state lab. Seems to me that will take way more time and could delay the investigation."

"Agreed. That's odd. Did Stacy say why they did that?"

"Grant's orders, something about needing to cross every *t* and dot every *i* for this one because officers are the victims in this case."

"It's also a kidnapping case, with speed more important than anything else." Blake shook his head. "I don't get it."

"Me either. I have a copy of the crime scene report, too. It was pretty thorough. They found footprints that seemed inconsistent with the kinds of boots our team wears. And a ton of fingerprints in the barn. It'll take a while to see whether any of those prints belong to a viable suspect, though. They took blood samples from the body and inside the barn. But, again, instead of sending them to our lab, they're on their way to Quantico. Yet another delay. What did the guys tell you?"

"They were concerned about notifying the families of the deceased and the kidnap victims. I told them the contact information is all in that spreadsheet you put together, but that we'd already notified Randy's mom. They appreciated that. I didn't tell them that the wives were on a cruise."

She blinked in surprise. "You withheld information?"

"Yeah, well. Once you start down the path…" He shrugged. "I was going to tell them, but one of the other agents came up to ask a question, a really simple question. And it got me talking to Colin Lopez about the team that came in with him. He admitted that other than him, Special Agent Joel Lawrence and SA Stacy Bell, the others are pretty green, without a lot of experience. He said, normally, on a case like this, he would have expected more senior agents to be brought along. But they were all stretched pretty thin by this Sanchez thing. Even with a court delay, a lot of them were told to remain in Knoxville to try to gather more evidence to strengthen the case. Even though the case is supposed to be locked up tight. Seems strange to me."

"So, let me get this straight," she said. "The top investigator thinks our kidnapping is so important that he postpones a major case to lend us his expertise. He brings his top three leads, who were all working the Sanchez case before this. But then he chooses green new recruits for the rest of his team? We got the A team at the top and the D team at the bottom. That doesn't make sense."

"I agree. Without saying it that way, I did hint around about Grant being uptight. One of the agents, Lawrence, laughed and said they'd all noticed the same thing and were walking on eggshells around him this morning. Normally, he's supposedly this polite, nice guy, who's super family-oriented and a great person to work with. For the past few weeks, he's been a real bear. None of them seemed to understand why."

"Did you ask if it was the pressure of the Sanchez case?" she asked.

"I did. But they said the case has been going on for years. There hasn't been anything recently that would explain it. His wife and kids headed off on vacation last week—without him. They figure that might be it. That maybe he and his wife had a fight or something and she left him. He hasn't said one word about his family since."

She nodded. "Trouble at home could explain a lot, not that I want to give the jerk an excuse for how he's acting. So what do we do now? We have to get some sleep. Willpower alone isn't going to keep my eyes open. But I hate the thought of not doing something to keep the investigation moving forward. Trusting Grant to take care of it doesn't sit well with me. But what bothers me more than anything is the idea of him notifying Ashley and the others about what has happened. I sure wish we could talk to them before any feds do."

"Maybe we can. When does the ship dock again?"

"Today, about five o'clock, in Miami. The feds have a field office there. I guarantee they'll send some agents to interview them. All I know to do is try to call Ashley once they dock and hope I reach her before the feds. I hate telling her news like that over the phone, though."

"I agree. And I want to interview all of them, anyway, to augment your timeline and look for any evidence that any of this is personal—that maybe one member of the SWAT team, or even the chief, was targeted. That's hard to do over the phone."

She lifted her hands in a helpless gesture. "I don't see what choice we have."

He tapped the steering wheel, as if deep in thought. "Too bad we don't have access to a private plane. We could skip security, avoid the wait for a scheduled flight and go straight to Miami without any stops in between. We could sleep on the way and make it to the port long before the agents felt they needed to be at the dock, giving us a chance to, I don't know, get in position somewhere and somehow intercept the wives before the agents locate them."

He shook his head again. "I don't even know how we'd manage that, even if we did have access to a private plane. I don't know anyone with enough money to own one, let alone have a pilot available to fly it even if they'd agree to take us."

"I do."

He frowned. "What are you talking about?"

"The Carroll family. Remember, we saved their daughter from drowning last summer? They were tourists, taking the scenic route home to Nashville, passing through Maryville after vacationing in the Smoky Mountains. Remember?"

He slowly nodded. "Yeah, yeah, I do. We were investigating a robbery, and it led us to a hotel in Maryville. We were walking by the pool, and their little girl had somehow gotten out of their hotel room and jumped in the water. She couldn't swim, and you saved her life."

"Well, we both saved her is how I remember it. I dragged her out, and you gave her CPR. Regardless, the father is a commercial pilot, and the mom is one of those society ladies, comes from money. They have private planes in airports all over Tennessee. And they flat-out told us if we ever needed anything to give them a call. I can't personally think of anything I've needed more right this minute."

"Me either. And the worst they can do is say no. Let's do it."

Chapter Ten

Donna glared at the two FBI agents waiting at the other end of the terminal, right where the cruise ship passengers were about to disembark.

"So much for our grand plan to beat the feds here. This place is locked up tighter than an airport, and those two agents have the security team's ear."

With their dark suits and black ties, they were hard to miss. Especially since one of them was holding up a sign with Destiny, Tennessee, written on it, and the other had a sign with the last names of the SWAT team members' wives. Security was letting them stand right at the gangplank exit, several yards ahead of everyone else who was waiting for their loved ones.

"Did you try Ashley's phone again?" Blake asked.

"Are you kidding? I've texted and called her and the others more than when I was searching for you the day of that stupid paintball exercise. They must have all turned their phones off, unplugged from the world, while they enjoyed their cruise. There's no way we'll be able to get their attention first. Everyone from their ship will come down that same walkway, like hamsters through a tunnel. And we can't exactly shove our way in front of the agents."

Blake turned in a slow circle, looking around. "Maybe we don't have to. I've got an idea."

Donna glanced over her shoulder. Other than the restrooms, all she saw was a busy ticket counter, probably checking in passengers for the cruise ship that shared this terminal. The electronic board above the counter showed that the other ship was due to leave for a seven-day cruise to the Bahamas in a little over an hour.

"What's your idea?" she asked. "Pull the fire alarm?"

He winked. "That would be highly illegal, not to mention dangerous for anyone in the terminal. I prefer a more subtle approach. Keep an eye on the walkway. Call me know when you see our party."

She was so surprised by that playful wink that she stood frozen in place as he walked toward the ticket counter. He looked back and motioned toward the gangplank, reminding her she had a job to do. Clearing her throat, she nodded and turned back to watch for Ashley and the others.

A full minute passed, and she was about to turn around again to check on him, when the noise level inside the terminal changed. Passengers from the ship that she and Blake were waiting for were visible in the distance now, colorful shirts and Bermuda shorts filling the tunnel as the crowd hurried through.

Donna edged around several people in the crowd, craning her neck to see. A puff of white hair caught her attention. She squinted, trying to bring the woman into focus, and couldn't help wondering if a trip to the eye doctor was in her future. She'd been squinting a lot lately. A few seconds later, the woman's face came into focus—Claire Thornton, the chief's wife. To her right, Ashley Gray was pushing a baby stroller. To her left,

Chris's and Max's wives—Julie and Bex—were smiling and gesturing with their hands as they spoke animatedly about something.

A quick glance at the two FBI agents revealed they were still standing the same as before, looking bored as they held up their signs. They must not have spotted the women yet among the crowd. But it wouldn't be long now—assuming they knew what the wives looked like. Maybe they didn't, and were relying completely on the signs? The problem, of course, was that it really didn't matter. As soon as the wives saw the signs, they'd stop and ask what was going on.

She and Blake really should have come up with a better plan. Or, at least, a plan at all. They'd been so certain when they arrived that they'd be able to get past security and onto the top of the gangplank to intercept their friends. But that hadn't happened. Even flashing their badges—which they'd snuck out with them after being fired—hadn't bought them any extra consideration from the security staff. They were told to wait with the families, something about causing a dangerous situation on the small gangplank if they tried to intercept someone there. Supposedly waiting out here was safer and would accomplish the same goal.

So what were they supposed to do now?

She whirled around looking for Blake. His height made him easy to see above the crowd. He was grinning and passing something to a buxom blonde behind the ticket counter. The light flush on her cheeks and the flirty smile had Donna's hands coiling into fists. She was about to whirl around in disgust—and more than a little jealousy—when the woman picked up a desk phone and punched some buttons. The intercom speakers crackled overhead.

"Attention, there's been a change in terminals for the packages from Destiny, Tennessee. Packages are arriving now at Terminal D. Repeat, packages from Destiny, Tennessee, are arriving now at Terminal D. Thank you."

Packages? Terminal D? That terminal was on the opposite side of the concourse. Blake caught her gaze and gave her a thumbs-up sign, a big Cheshire Cat grin curving his lips as he started toward her. Was that his big plan? Flirt with the ticket agent to make her announce that silly message that wouldn't fool anyone? Blake motioned toward something behind her.

She spun around just in time to see the two FBI agents sprinting past her, a panicked look on their faces as they raced down the concourse—*away* from Ashley and the other wives, who had just stopped beside the security guards, perplexed looks on their faces. They'd probably seen the signs the agents were holding and heard the bizarre announcement over the intercom. It had worked. Blake's crazy, ridiculous plan had worked.

"Come on." His voice was suddenly by her ear. "Let's grab our friends before the agents realize what happened."

"I can't believe they fell for that. It was…brilliant," she admitted as they hurried forward.

"Cost me twenty bucks and a dinner date. Too bad I won't be here when she gets off her shift. She seemed like a nice woman. I hated lying to her."

Donna's hands were curling into fists again. "I'm sure she'll survive the disappointment."

"Donna, what are you doing here?" It was Bex who made that exclamation as she and the others rushed past the security guards to meet them. True to form for law-enforcement families, it was alarm, rather than pleasure, in Bex's and the others' expressions.

"Well?" Ashley said from beside Bex, her brow furrowing with concern as she glanced from Blake to Donna. "What's going on? And what was that announcement over the intercom about packages from Destiny? Is Dillon okay?"

"What about Chris?" Julie insisted, her face pale with worry.

"Ladies, we'll answer all your questions in a few minutes," Blake said while Donna was still struggling to speak past the sudden lump in her throat. "First, there's a security issue that has us concerned for your safety. We need to get out of here. Now."

Again, their experience as the wives of police officers kicked in. Even though they all looked worried, they didn't hesitate. They moved as one toward the exit, where Blake was directing them. Donna took up the lead, heading toward the nearest doors, while Blake moved beside Bex and took the handle of one of the two suitcases she'd been pulling along. Next to her, like a mother hen, Claire Thornton was shooing everyone forward, having picked up on the urgency in Blake's voice.

"Do you have any other bags to get?" Donna asked.

Ashley shook her head. "Bex has mine, or did." She nodded her thanks to Blake, her hands on the stroller with her little daughter inside, thankfully sleeping through everything.

The doors whooshed open, and the group of six adults and a stroller headed outside as one.

"Where to?" Claire asked, sounding like a drill sergeant.

"Over there." Blake motioned toward a spot at the curb. Then he waved his hand in the air.

Similar to the airport, no one was allowed to idle in a vehicle out front. Security guards patrolled up and down the now-crowded walkway to enforce that rule. But the limo Donna and Blake had hired was already zipping out of the parking lot across from the terminal and weaving around a line of cabs, ignoring their honking horns. A moment later, the limo screeched to a halt in front of them, and the trunk popped open.

Blake and the driver met at the trunk and began stashing the women's luggage inside.

"Wait," Ashley said. "The car seat for Letha, it's in my suitcase."

"There's a car seat in the back of the limo for her," Donna said.

Ashley gave her a grateful look and lifted her sleeping daughter out of the stroller. While everyone was piling into the car, Donna glanced around. The two agents who'd taken Blake's bait and had run toward the other terminal burst out of the building, chests heaving with exertion as they scanned the crowds.

"Hurry," Donna urged. "Everyone get in."

Blake looked past her, his jaw tightening. "I've got this one," he told the driver, and grabbed the last suitcase.

The driver hurried to get into the car and started the engine. Blake slammed the trunk and he and Donna hopped in with the others.

"Go, go, go," Blake said.

The agents were rushing toward them, looking around, as if they hadn't spotted them yet.

The limo sped away from the curb.

"Slow down," Blake cautioned. "We don't want to attract any attention."

The driver nodded and slowed.

Donna watched the agents stop at the curb where they'd just been, still looking around.

"They didn't see us," she said.

"It won't take them long to figure it out," Blake warned. "How far to the next car?"

"It's on the other side of the terminal. Two minutes away in this traffic." The driver weaved around a slow-moving cab.

"Would someone please tell us what's going on?" Ashley demanded, her voice firm but quiet so as not to wake her daughter. "Who is it? Who's hurt? Or…just tell us who it is. Please."

"Let's focus on getting away from the port first," Blake said. "When we reach the plane, we'll explain everything."

"You'll explain everything right now, Detective Sullivan," Claire ordered, sounding just like the chief. "You're worrying these ladies and me. We have a right to know what's going on."

"It's Max, isn't it?" Bex's face was drawn as she lowered her cell phone. "I just tried to call him. He's not answering."

"Neither is Chris." Julie exchanged a nervous glance with Bex and turned her phone around toward Donna. "I just turned this one on, and you've called me ten times today. Come on, Donna. What happened? Has there been an accident? What?"

The limo turned the corner and swerved into a parking lot beside another limo, this one white instead of black.

"As far as we know, your husbands are fine," Donna said, when Blake seemed to be struggling for words. "But we believe you're in danger. Please. Let's switch to the other car before we answer your questions. You're being followed."

"Those agents in the terminal?" Ashley asked. "They had to be feds. FBI maybe? They stuck out like a sore thumb. But before we reached them, they took off."

Donna nodded as the car stopped and both the driver and Blake hopped out. "Yes."

"Why are we running from FBI agents?" Ashley demanded. "And don't tell me to shut up and get in the other car. I'm not going anywhere until you give us something. The driver is moving the luggage to the other limo now, in case you were worried about him overhearing. Out with it, Donna. What's going on?"

She realized they had a mutiny on their hands if she didn't tell them. She cleared her throat and gave them all an apologetic look. "I wanted to break this to you more gently, but there's no easy way to tell you. Yesterday, Randy Carter was murdered."

A collective gasp went up from the women. Ashley's hand was suddenly grasping Donna's. "I'm so sorry. I know you and Randy were especially close. Was it in the line of duty?"

"Yes." Her voice cracked. "Yes, it was. I'm sure he was very brave."

Ashley's brow furrowed, and she exchanged a puzzled look with Bex. "You're *sure*? It sounds like you're guessing. You weren't there?"

She shook her head.

As if sensing her mother's tension, Ashley's little girl began to cry in the car seat next to her. But rather than comfort her as she would normally do, Ashley stared intently at Donna.

"Then what happened?" Her voice shook with a mixture of anger and fear. "We went dark on the cruise—no phones, no social media, no internet. It was all part of unplugging, relaxing, really getting away from the world. But now you've got me borderline terrified, because ever since we docked and turned our phones back on, none of us have been able to reach our families. And you just told us that Randy has been killed. And apparently we're on the run from the FBI. For God's sake, Donna. Tell us what's going on. Please, please tell us that Dillon and the others are okay."

The pleading look in her friend's eyes ripped another piece from Donna's heart, adding a new fissure on top of the gaping hole that Randy's death had created. She took both of Ashley's hands in hers, and Ashley held on to her like a lifeline, her whole body shaking as she waited for Donna to destroy her world.

"Try not to panic. Blake and I believe they're okay. There's still hope. But Dillon, Max, Chris, even the chief, they've all been kidnapped."

Chapter Eleven

It wasn't the type of hotel that Blake would have chosen for the next phase in their plan. One, because he couldn't afford it. And two, he wouldn't have chosen to stop at a hotel at all. The private plane was waiting to take all of them back to McGhee Tyson Airport, just down the road from Destiny, and he was anxious to continue the investigation. But Chris's wife, Julie, had plenty of money, courtesy of a wealthy grandmother, and had insisted on getting them a large suite in a five-star hotel to regroup and discuss what was going on. And the other wives had pretty much refused to get on a plane until they'd heard everything Blake and Donna could tell them about their husbands.

He sat beside Donna on one of the couches, his arm around her shoulders, offering his support. Right now he didn't care one whit what the others might think. What mattered was that Donna had looked so bleak and fragile as she began to recite the tale about finding Randy and the note. And when he'd tentatively put his arm around her, instead of pulling away, she settled into the curve of his body and gave him a smile of gratitude.

"That's it," Donna said, spreading her hands out in a helpless gesture. "We really don't know much at this point. But the fact that whoever kidnapped them left a ransom note is encouraging. It gives us hope that they're still okay."

"I'll pay it," Julie said. "Whatever the amount. How much are they asking? I can write a check right now."

Donna gave Blake a worried glance.

He gently massaged her shoulder and answered Julie's question. "Rodney Lynch, one of the uniformed officers back in Destiny, agreed to give us updates and said he'd call as soon as a ransom demand was made. But so far, there's been no contact from the kidnappers."

The four women exchanged worried glances, before Ashley once again took the lead as if they'd secretly nominated her as their spokesperson. "It's what, seven o'clock now? That means over twenty-four hours have passed since they…since they killed Randy and left the note. Is that normal for kidnappers to wait that long before stating their terms?"

"Honestly," Blake said, "I don't know. I've never worked a kidnapping case before. But the FBI certainly has. I'm sure they're doing everything they can to resolve this without anyone else getting hurt."

Ashley rolled her eyes. "Spare me the faith in the FBI speech. I was almost railroaded into prison by them. And they can't have brought their top team down here if their poor decision-making skills meant cutting you two out of the investigation. That's the most idiotic thing I've heard so far. You're the locals. You know everything about Destiny and the surrounding area. It makes sense that you should be in the thick of this, evaluating the evidence. Not sitting on the sidelines."

"Well," Donna said, "to be fair, we did try to cover up that Blake was fired. It's understandable that the

SSA thought he needed to cut us loose. I can't imagine what would happen if he found out about us touching the note."

"Thank goodness you did, or we might not even know the others had been kidnapped. At least this way, we can hope, as you said before," Ashley said. "So what can we do to help? What do you want from us?"

"Victimology," Blake said. "It's when you study the victims to find out—"

"Everything you can about them to build a timeline and try to identify suspects who might have targeted them," Ashley finished. "We're cops' wives. We know all about how investigations work. I'm sure all of us will be happy to fill in any gaps in your timeline and tell you anything you want to know. Right, ladies?"

A collective murmur of agreement went up from the group. A cry sounded from the bedroom. Ashley started to get up, but Claire waved her back down.

"I'll check on her," she said. "You all keep talking. From the sounds of that note and everything else, I don't think anyone targeted my Bill. They were after the team. The only reason Bill was on that exercise at all was that..." She gave Blake an apologetic look. "Sorry, sweetie. Cops do talk to their wives, and I've heard there have been some...issues with you and how you haven't been gelling with the team. Dillon asked him to be there. I think he expected something might happen—with you, not the rest of this."

"No apology necessary," Blake said to her. "Thank you for being candid."

She gave him a sad smile and headed into the bedroom.

Nearly an hour later, Donna set her notes on the

end table by the couch and sat back. "I don't get it. The timelines are complete. Every gap is filled in. And yet we don't have one single new clue about who could be behind this."

"Sure we do," Blake said. "The person behind this isn't interested in anyone on the SWAT team, or the chief, as Claire said." He nodded to her. She nodded back from the chair where she was rocking the baby.

"What, then?" Ashley asked. "Was it about Randy? And the rest of them just..." She swallowed hard. "The rest of them got caught up in it, and the ransom note is a diversion? The bad guys want to get out of town while the police are waiting for a ransom phone call?" Her last word was a broken whisper that barely made it past her lips before she burst into tears.

Donna gave Blake a look of pure misery before joining Bex and Julie in an effort to comfort Ashley. Many tears were shed before they all seemed to gather themselves.

Bex rubbed Ashley's back and put her arm around her waist. "Is there anything else you needed from us? I think we're all ready to head back home now." She frowned. "Or, I guess we should contact the local FBI? Since they wanted to talk to us? I know you two wanted to talk to us first because, otherwise, you wouldn't have been able to get your timeline information. But since the FBI is actively working the case, seems to me we should go ahead and make contact instead of hiding."

"I agree," Blake said. "That's probably better than just hopping on the plane with Donna and me. There's no point in not talking to them now. I can't thank you enough for speaking to us, though. You never know what will matter in a case, what little piece of information might eventually make all the puzzle pieces fit together. I just wish we could have resolved all of this before you came back from your law-enforcement family cruise."

Bex snorted. "Law-enforcement family cruise? That's a joke if I ever heard one. I don't know what happened. Some kind of mix-up, I guess. That cruise was a singles cruise. We were the only married ones on board. And there weren't any other police family members that I saw. Let me just say, we didn't exactly fit in."

Blake frowned. "You were the only law-enforcement family members on the whole ship? Are you sure?"

"Well, as sure as we can be," Bex said. "When there weren't any police-themed dinners or announcements or anything, we thought it was odd, and we started asking around. None of the staff seemed to have a clue what we were talking about when we mentioned the charity that funded our cruise." She glanced back and forth between Donna and Blake. "Why? Is that significant?"

Blake shook his head. "Probably not. Mix-ups like that happen all the time. Still, I'll note it and follow up, just to make sure it's not related. What was the name of the charity?"

Bex looked to Julie for help. "Do you remember the name? It was something really simple like *Fun for Families*. Was that it?"

Julie was nodding as she pulled a business card out of her purse and handed it to Blake. "It was completely arranged from beginning to end, all prepaid. Even if they ended up accidentally putting us on the wrong boat from the rest of the law-enforcement families, as far as I'm concerned, the cruise was great. We really had a good time." Her bottom lip trembled, but she drew a deep breath and held it together.

"We're all exhausted," Ashley said, once again speaking for the group. "I think we should freshen up, check out and head to the FBI field office to answer their questions. You two don't have to wait your plane on us. We've got commercial airline tickets already. We'll just switch to a morning flight so we have time to talk to the feds today."

Blake left Donna to help them make arrangements for the FBI to pick them up at the hotel while he headed into the kitchenette, where it was more quiet. He made a call to one of his contacts back in Knoxville to get more information on the charity. By the time he finished the call, his stomach was churning, and his blood running cold. He rushed into the main part of the suite.

"What time are the feds getting here?"

Donna rose from the couch. "What's wrong?"

"What time?"

She checked her watch. "About thirty minutes. Why? What are you—"

"Grab your things. We have to get out of here. Now."

"Blake—"

"No time, Donna. We have to get out of here before the feds get here. Trust me on this." He made a quick call to the limo driver, telling him to bring the car around, while the others grabbed their things, and Ashley put the baby in the stroller.

Blake could say one thing about these ladies. They were as well trained as their husbands. He didn't know anyone else who could have gotten things together and been in the limo, being whisked away from the hotel, in under six minutes.

"Okay, yet again, we're running from the very men who are trying to find our husbands," Ashley complained as she patted her daughter in the car seat beside her, trying to keep her whimpering from turning into a full-fledged tantrum. "Why?"

"A friend of mine did a quick trace on that charity," Blake said. "It was set up as a one-time thing and traced back to a shell company—basically a fake company like criminals use to cover their tracks. If they were a true charity, there wouldn't be any problem tracing it back. Because the supposed donors would want to be able to claim their contributions on their taxes. My friend also said that they'd been looking into the charity because one of the wives in Knoxville complained that the charity never announced the winners of the cruise tickets. It's as if the charity was set up for one purpose—to give just you ladies tickets. I called the cruise line, too. They didn't know anything at all about the charity or a law-enforcement family cruise on any of their ships."

Donna stared at him. "So a fake charity just happens to send the wives of our now missing officers out of town for a week. And no one else? Quite the coincidence, which means no way is it a coincidence. Why would they do that? What do they stand to gain? And what does this have to do with the FBI?"

"As to why and what they gain, I have no idea. But regarding the FBI, I have one name for you—Lopez."

"Lopez. As in SSA Grant's assistant, Lopez?"

"One and the same. The city balked at issuing a permit for the charity event. Guess who intervened and basically sweet-talked the city into granting the permit?"

"Lopez." Donna's brow furrowed in confusion. "But the FBI has no authority over something like that, unless…unless it has to do with white-collar crime or cyber-crime. Maybe they were investigating the charity and needed the event to move forward to help them gather more evidence? That could explain Lopez's involvement."

"Excuse me." This time it was Julie who had a question. "Who are Grant and Lopez?"

"They're both part of the FBI team in Destiny investigating Randy's murder and your husbands' kidnappings. Supervisory Special Agent Richard Grant is in charge. Colin Lopez, Stacy Bell and Joel Lawrence are his leads, basically his assistants, his right-hand, top investigators. All four of them were handling a high-profile case—the Sanchez drug kingpin case—before getting the judge to grant a delay so they could help in Destiny. Apparently they're supposed to be top guys from the Knoxville field office, and the bureau thought they were their best chance at getting the Destiny case resolved as quickly and safely as possible. There are some other FBI guys they brought with them, too. But Lopez is one of the top dogs."

"Okay, so you think, what, he's dirty? This Lopez guy? Just because his name comes up in support of the charity and he's working the Destiny case?" Julie continued.

"If it was just those two things, I probably wouldn't. But his boss, Grant, seemed way over the top to me in how he went after the two of us—almost as if that was his goal from the start. Each thing by itself seems okay, has a perfectly reasonable explanation. But, together, it starts to pile up and look suspicious."

"Each thing. Is there more you haven't told us?"

The suspicions swirling through his mind had made

perfect sense back in the hotel, with the FBI on the way. But now he wasn't so sure. Saying it out loud would just emphasize how little they knew and would make his doubts seem even more far-fetched.

"It's an ongoing investigation," Donna said. "We can't go into everything right now. Just suffice it to say, at this point, there are too many questions around Grant, Lopez and potentially others for us to feel comfortable with you being around them. We can pass the timeline information from you to Grant through one of the Destiny officers. That way, if our fears prove to be wrong, no harm done to their investigation. And if you can all lie low somewhere for a few days, or until we find the team, that would take a huge weight of worry off Blake's and my shoulders, knowing for sure that you're safe. Is that something you would consider doing?"

Julie looked at the others. One by one, they each nodded their agreement. She turned back to Blake and Donna. "Okay. We'll do it. But only if you follow through on the timeline data, like you said. I know I'd never forgive myself if something happened to Chris because I didn't speak to the FBI over a hunch that ended up proving false. I want them to have that information. And I don't see being able to stay away more than a couple of days, tops. I want to be out there, searching for Chris and the others, not holed up in a hotel room wringing my hands."

Alarmed, Blake said, "Please don't do that. Until we know the goal behind the kidnapping, I implore you to stay off the radar. Maybe you can hire some personal security guys for the duration, too. Couldn't hurt. I know my mind would be more at ease if you did."

Julie nodded. "I think that's a great idea. I'll take

care of that. We'll stay gone as long as we can, but if it's more than a few days, I can't promise you won't see every one of us back in Destiny, demanding an update from the FBI. Put yourself in our place, Blake. If Donna was missing, I suspect you'd move heaven and earth to be involved in the case and find her."

He blinked, not sure what to say to that. But Julie was already huddling with the others, speaking in low tones as they discussed something. He chanced a quick look at Donna. She was staring at him, her brow furrowed as if she was thinking about Julie's statement. He swallowed and looked away. Was he that transparent? Were his feelings for her out for everyone to see? Or had Julie just assumed he'd be that invested in trying to protect her because they were partners?

"All right." Julie turned back around. "We've agreed on a location, where we're going to stay for now. We'll—"

"No." Blake held up a hand to stop her. "It's better if we don't know the details. That way, if we end up being interviewed by Grant or the others, we can honestly tell them that we don't know where you are. The limo driver can drop Donna and me off at a car rental place. We'll get to the airport on our own from there. I wouldn't want you ladies with us, again, in case the FBI is watching the airport. I imagine they'll be watching the terminal for your commercial flight you scheduled, waiting for you to show up. So you'll need to drive wherever you go. They don't know about Donna and me taking the private plane, or even that we're here. So we should be able to catch our flight with none the wiser."

"Okay. Anything else we should know?" Ashley

spoke up this time, glancing from him to Donna and back again.

"Burner phones," Donna suggested.

"Right. Good idea," Blake said. "You can stop at one of those postal stores in a strip mall and mail your personal phones back home. They can be traced, so keeping them with you isn't a good idea, just in case someone really is going to try to find you. Make one stop, and one stop only, at a bank and draw out enough cash to get you by for at least a week. Purchase a prepaid phone without a plan of any kind to keep your name out of it. That's what Donna means by a burner phone—something that can't be traced back to you. After that, don't go to the bank or an ATM and don't use any of your credit cards anywhere. You need to go all cash and leave no electronic trace."

Ashley frowned at him. "We'll need a credit card to rent a hotel room."

"A five-star hotel, sure. But if you keep a low profile, you should be able to pay a cash deposit up front to convince someone to rent to you. I'm not saying you need to stay in a dive. Just pick a clean, modern hotel off one of the interstate exits, and you should be okay."

None of them looked happy with his plan, but to give them credit, they didn't argue. Half an hour later, Blake was driving with Donna to the airport in a fairly generic four-door sedan, after watching the wives head in the opposite direction, down the highway, in the limo.

"I hope we did the right thing back there," Donna said.

"Me, too. You know there's more to this than what I told them, don't you?" He steered around a slow-moving car, before moving back into the right lane.

She nodded. "I'm starting to feel that way, yes. Nothing about how the case is being handled feels right. The way the evidence was delayed by being sent to the FBI lab instead of a local one that's more than capable of processing everything, that alone raises questions in my mind. Added with everything else, the doubts are definitely piling up. Something is way off here."

"Remember what Ashley said earlier, asking whether the ransom note was just a diversion? No one has made contact with details about how to pay. That really struck me. Not that it was a diversion as much as a delay tactic. It puts things on hold while we wait to hear from the kidnappers. And that's not the only delay that has come up."

"You're talking about the Sanchez trial," she said. "Which was literally delayed because the main FBI guys were needed for our Destiny investigation?"

"Yes. I wouldn't think much of it, except that Officer Lynch updated us on the way here saying there wasn't any progress that he could tell with the investigation. Kind of surprising if the FBI's best guys out of the Knoxville field office were diverted specifically because they're so good. Wouldn't you expect more from them?"

Again, he passed a few cars before moving back to the right. A sign up ahead showed they were just a couple of exits from the airport. Blake had already called ahead to notify the pilot to be ready.

She nodded slowly. "I would expect more from the FBI, normally. You're right. Time is supposedly of the essence in a kidnapping situation. But instead of being proactive and pounding the pavement, trying to find our guys, it would seem that they're sitting back, waiting for first contact—or second, if you count the note. And like Ashley said earlier, it doesn't make sense to remove you and me from the case if the main goal is to find the missing cops. Who better to help navigate the local scene than the only two remaining detectives, two detectives who could have given them a lot more information about their missing peers to help them zero in on potential grudges, suspects who might have an ax to grind against Dillon and the others?"

Blake shook his head. "The more I think about it, the more all of this seems horribly wrong. If we assume our FBI guys are dirty, then what's the motive? Why kill Randy? Why kidnap the others?"

"Maybe the kidnappers know that Chris's wife is wealthy," Donna said. "Maybe that's why the note talks about a ransom—because they know Julie can pay."

"Except that no one has given instructions for how to deliver the money. The note didn't even list a specific amount so the families could gather the funds. The longer we go without a specific demand, the thinner the idea of kidnapping for ransom seems."

"Then why kidnap our team?" she asked.

He tapped his hands on the steering wheel as he reasoned it out. "Okay, how about this. What's the one consistent thread that keeps coming up as we talk this through?"

"Delays. No question," she said.

He nodded. "What if the delay in the Sanchez trial is the only delay that matters? What if everything else is secondary, and all of this is intended to divert the FBI's attention to Destiny and put a stop to the criminal case?"

She shook her head. "That doesn't make sense,

though, does it? From what I've heard on the news channels, the Sanchez case is wrapped up tight. A delay won't change the outcome. Sanchez's empire is about to come crashing down around him. He's going to go to prison for the rest of his life."

He put his blinker on for the airport exit. "Look at it from another angle. Our FBI guys went from high-profile case to high-profile case. Kidnapping an entire SWAT team is a big deal. And yet, they've managed to keep it out of the news so far. So it seems unlikely that the person behind this cares about media attention. If they did, they'd have leaked information and it would have already hit all the major networks."

"Okay," she said. "I'm with you so far."

"All the kidnapping has accomplished at this point is that it diverted resources and put the law-enforcement community's attention on Destiny instead of Knoxville."

Blake steered the car down the exit ramp and followed the signs to the car rental company's parking lot.

"All right." Donna picked up the line of reasoning. "We have kidnappers who don't seem to be in a hurry to get any money. And we have a case that diverted resources from another case. No matter how we look at this, it circles back to the FBI and the Sanchez case. Assuming that Sanchez's goons are responsible for Randy's death and the kidnappings—which seems like a logical leap—we need to figure out how this helps Sanchez."

Blake parked the car. "As soon as we land at McGhee Tyson Airport, I think we should head to where all of this—whatever this is—seems to have started."

She nodded. "We're going to Knoxville."

Chapter Twelve

Even though they'd both dozed on the plane to and from Miami, it hadn't been what Donna thought of as "quality" sleep. She was so exhausted, she fell asleep the moment she leaned back in the passenger seat of the little blue Ford Focus they rented at the McGhee Tyson Airport. And she didn't wake up until Blake shook her awake in a hotel parking lot somewhere in Knoxville.

She rubbed her bleary eyes, a flush of guilt heating her face when she saw how tired he looked. "I'm sorry. I know you're just as wiped out as I am. I should have offered to drive."

He gave her a sleepy, incredibly sexy grin. "We'd have been in a ditch just a few blocks down the road from the airport when you fell into a coma. You sure do fall asleep fast."

He leaned over the back of the seat and grabbed their satchels that contained just a few days' worth of clothes and toiletries—plus their pistols and ammo, of course.

"Where are we?" she asked.

"The neon lights spelling out *Embassy Suites* doesn't give it away?"

"Ha ha."

He smiled again. She noticed he smiled more when

he was tired, as if it was the only time he ever truly let his guard down. It did incredible things to his already handsome face, making her stomach tighten with want.

If she wasn't so tired, she might have jumped him just to finally get that crazy desire out of her system—and find out once and for all if he wanted her, too. But as tired as they both were, she knew that wasn't even on the radar.

As they walked under the portico to the front doors, she asked, "Seriously. Where are we?"

"Knoxville West, just off I-40. I've been here before, so I knew it was decent and clean. I called on the way and made a reservation. They only had a few rooms left. Since I couldn't get two on the same floor, I settled for a suite. Hope that's okay. It's got a separate bedroom and a sectional couch with a pullout sofa bed."

"I wouldn't care if we had to share the same bed at this point. I could probably sleep on the floor in the lobby right now."

His eyes had widened when she mentioned sharing a bed, but he recovered quickly, with another one of those sexy grins. "I think they frown on people camping in the lobby here. Let's at least get up to the room before you sink into your coma again."

She couldn't help wondering why he'd been to this hotel before. He'd lived in Knoxville, so why would he stay in a hotel instead of his house? Or apartment? Or wherever he lived? Had he brought a date here rather than take her back to his place? And why did that thought make her feel so pathetically jealous? It wasn't like they'd ever dated. And even though she'd been mooning after him for months, he'd always been the perfect gentleman—much to her dismay.

"Earth to Donna. You in there somewhere?" He was waving his hand in front of her face.

She blinked and realized they were standing in front of an open elevator, and he was holding the door for her. "Sorry," she mumbled as she stepped inside.

When the door shut, and he pressed the button for the fourth floor, she realized she'd zombied out at the registration desk and hadn't even remembered him getting the room keys.

"We'll have to keep up with our expenses so I can pay you my half," she said. "You've been buying everything. Heck, I should pay *all* of our expenses. You need to conserve your funds in case this doesn't end the way I hope it will and you don't get your job back."

"No worries. I've got plenty in savings. I'm not the live-paycheck-to-paycheck type."

She snorted. "I sure am. Most people I know are."

"All the more reason that I'm the one footing the bill. Seriously, don't worry about it." He waved the key card over the sensor on the lock and pushed the door open to let her go inside first.

THE SUITE WAS CLEAN, as he'd predicted, with a kitchenette, a desk, a decent-sized living room with a cream-colored sectional and what had to be at least a 42-inch TV on the opposite wall. As he stepped in behind her, she checked out the bathroom, which was thankfully just as clean as the rest of the place. And the bedroom had two queen beds. That, at least, made her feel less guilty. Neither of them would get stuck on an uncomfortable pullout.

"It's nice," she said, turning around in the bedroom. "Oh." She had to take a step back, surprised to find him so close behind her.

"Sorry." He hefted her bag in the air in explanation. "I was going to set this on one of the beds so you can shower, if you want, and get ready for bed. I'll get ready after you."

She frowned. "Thanks. Where's your bag?"

He motioned toward the living room.

"No way." She pushed past him and grabbed his bag off the floor of the main room. "There are two perfectly good beds in this suite. You are not going to toss and turn all night on a lumpy pullout mattress." She headed back into the bedroom and plopped his bag on the second bed.

He spread his hands in surrender. "If you're sure."

"Of course I am. But I'll take you up on the offer to take a shower first. Do you need to use the bathroom before I hop in?"

"I'm fine. Go ahead. Want anything from room service? I'm going to order a hamburger or something."

Until he'd mentioned food, she hadn't realized just how hungry she was. She couldn't remember the last time she'd eaten something that hadn't come out of a vending machine.

"What time is it?" she asked, even as she reached in her pocket to check her phone.

"A little after one. I know it's way too late to eat, but I'm starving. I won't be able to sleep if I don't get something in my stomach besides potato chips and a candy bar."

She tossed her phone on the bed. "You read my mind. I'll have whatever you're having. Wait, do you think the hotel restaurant is even open this late? I bet room service is closed."

"If it is, I'll order pizza delivery. Pepperoni okay?"

"Sounds great. But a cheeseburger and fries would

be way better. I hope room service is still open." With that, she disappeared into the bathroom with her bag.

She showered as quickly as she could, since it was already so late. She didn't bother to do more than towel dry her hair and comb it, and she figured there was no point in bothering with makeup. She'd just have to take it off to go to bed, anyway. It wasn't like Blake cared. Getting fully dressed seemed like too much effort, as well. And she didn't have that many clean outfits. So she decided to wear what she normally wore—a long nightshirt that fell to her knees and underwear.

The one concession she made was to keep a bra on. Not because she thought he'd even notice if she didn't wear one. But she didn't think she could take the embarrassment of him *not* noticing. A girl could only be ignored by the man she was half in love with for so long before dying of humiliation.

The delicious smell of cheeseburgers when she opened the bathroom door nearly made her weep. She hurried into the living room and pressed her hand over her heart when she saw the two trays on the table—fully loaded cheeseburgers and thick steak fries, with two cans of Diet Coke.

"I think I've died and gone to heaven," she said. "How did you get these? I saw a notice on the bathroom door about checkout and room service times. They closed hours ago." She turned around then froze.

Blake must have risen from the couch when she stepped into the room, but that was as far as he'd gotten. His mouth had fallen open, and his gaze had fallen, too—from her lips to her breasts, lower, and lower still, until he was staring at her legs. His Adam's apple bobbed in his throat, but no sound emerged.

Fearing she'd done something stupid—like leaving

the end of her shirt tucked into the top of her panties, she looked down, turning left and right to make sure the back was okay, too. Nope, thankfully, everything was covered. So what was his problem? She glanced up, then sucked in a sharp breath.

He'd crossed the room and was standing directly in front of her, looking so hungry it had her pulse rushing in her ears. She licked her lips and watched his eyes track the movement.

"Blake?" Her voice was hoarse. She thought she was reading the signs right, that he'd finally noticed she was a woman. But she was afraid to make any moves without being sure. "Are you hungry for the cheeseburger? Or...me?"

His gaze shot to hers. "What cheeseburger?"

"Oh, thank God," she whispered, just before he swooped down and pressed his lips to hers.

If the smell of the cheeseburger had been heaven, the feel of Blake's lips on hers was in a whole other dimension. He kissed her deeply, thoroughly, masterfully, until she was groaning against him, her fingers curling in his shirt, and her legs somehow curled around his waist, pulling him tightly against her. She didn't even remember him picking her up, but he must have. One of his hands cupped her bottom. The other clasped the back of her head as he pressed her against the wall beside the table.

They were both gasping for air when he broke the kiss. But he didn't stop, didn't even slow down his assault on her senses. He lightly nipped her neck, worshiped the top swells of her breasts with his lips and tongue. She threw her head back, and her lips parted on a sigh as she moved restlessly against him.

She'd wanted this—wanted him—for so long. She'd

dreamed of being held in his arms. But even in her fantasies, actually being touched by him, feeling his warm hand roam beneath her shirt and against her skin, made her fantasies seem like black-and-white Polaroids compared to high-definition color. Blake the man was so much better than Blake the dream.

"Donna?"

The sound of her name whispered in deep, husky tones next to her ear sent shivers up her spine. She arched against him, reveling in the feel of his hard chest pressed to hers. He shuddered and tightened his hand on her bottom. Then he swiveled his hips in a sinfully delicious way that had her breath catching in her throat.

"Do that again," she urged.

He did, and she almost climaxed right there in his arms, both of them still dressed. Or, at least, he was. Her night shirt and bra had both been pushed up above her breasts, leaving them exposed to his wandering hands and lips.

"I want to feel your skin against mine," she whispered. "You have too many clothes on."

He swallowed and rested his forehead against hers. A shaky breath stuttered between his lips. "Are you sure you want this?"

For the first time since he'd kissed her, she opened her eyes. He'd pulled back just enough to meet her gaze, and the intensity of his hungry stare nearly made her weep with joy. Finally, finally, he was as desperate for her as she'd been for him for so very, very long.

"If you stop right now, I'm going to shoot you. How's that for being sure?"

His mouth tilted in a devastating smile. Then he was kissing her again, and she was kissing him back, their tongues tangling against each other in perfect rhythm, giving and taking, sharing, enjoying, until she wanted to weep from the beauty of it.

She was vaguely aware of him lifting his thigh to support her bottom dropping his hands from around her. Then crackling, like the wrapper on a pack of crackers. A tug, the sound of a zipper.

Her eyes flew open, and she looked down. She realized what he was doing, and was shocked that she'd never even thought of protection. Thank goodness he had. He must have had a condom in his wallet. And he'd cared enough about her to ensure that he didn't forget, even when she did.

She kissed him again and rolled the condom onto him. He shuddered and thrust his tongue deep inside her mouth, as he thrust his length between her hands. A very impressive length. By the time she'd finished, they were both panting and sweating and so eager that she helped him fit himself to her without even worrying about trying to stumble to the bed.

Then he was inside her, filling her, loving her. And she was loving him back, giving and taking, her entire body straining to get as close as possible to this handsome, strong, brave, intelligent man, who had finally had the sense to realize they could be great together—in every way.

Just when she thought it couldn't feel any better, he'd do something wicked with his mouth, his hands, his hips, and take her to a new height. She tried to give him as much pleasure as he was giving her, but he was a master at this, like he'd been created with the express purpose of giving a woman pleasure.

"Blake," she moaned, raking her nails across his neck. "Please."

He didn't have to ask what she was begging for. He

knew. And he delivered. His hand moved between them and he stroked her, caressed her as he thrust in and out of her, making her gasp and make all kinds of strange, mewling noises she'd never known she could make. When her climax came, she would have shouted loud enough to wake the entire floor if his mouth hadn't been fastened to hers. He wasn't far behind, his entire body tightening against hers, his own groan sounding deep in his throat as he tumbled over the edge.

HE SHOULD HAVE let Donna sleep, but Blake couldn't seem to keep himself from touching her, sliding his fingers across the flat warmth of her belly and up to caress the underside of her full, perfect breasts.

He watched her roll over in the bed, little more than a shadow in the dark hotel room, as she wrapped her arms behind his neck.

"Hey, handsome." Her words were slurred, heavy with sleep.

"Hey, gorgeous." He pressed a kiss against the top of her head. "I'm sorry I woke you. Go back to sleep."

She yawned and pressed him onto his back, slipping her thigh over the top of his as she snuggled against him. "This is nice."

He rubbed his thumb against her nipple, delighting in how it hardened at his touch. "Yes. It certainly is."

She giggled and slapped his hand away. "I thought you were going to let me sleep. What time is it?"

"Early. Late. Take your pick. We both need to get some sleep, or we won't be able to function in the morning. But you're far too tempting. I'll go to the other bed."

He started to pull away, but she tugged him back.

"No way," she said, sounding more awake than a

moment ago. "I've got you exactly where I want you. Finally. You're not going anywhere."

Finally? Was it possible that she'd been wanting him all this time that he'd been wanting her?

She pulled herself up his body and pressed a kiss against the hollow of his throat. "Please tell me you have another condom."

He shook his head, even though she probably couldn't see him. "Sorry. I didn't plan this. I only had one."

She let her forehead drop against his chest. "You're killing me."

He feathered his hands through her hair and pulled her against him, pressing her head to his chest. "Trust me. The feeling is mutual. I really should move to the other bed."

"No. You woke me up. You have to pay the price."

"But I don't have any more protection."

"Then you'll have to pay it another way."

His body jerked against her at the thought of all the ways he could pleasure her. Eager to get started, he rolled her onto her back and began to work his way down to the very core of her. When his lips kissed her there, she bolted upright and grabbed his shoulders. She let out a shaky breath and was laughing when she pulled him up her body.

"As much as I'd love for you to do that," she said, "I'm not that selfish. I'd want you to have as much pleasure as me, and honestly, I'm just too exhausted to do that right now."

He swallowed hard just at the thought of her doing that. But, sadly, it was not to be. Not today, anyway.

"Then I guess it's goodnight." He kissed her lips this time, and then he lay back and spooned himself behind her. In spite of how hard and aching his body was right now, being this close to her, the pleasure of just being able to hold her like this was more than adequate compensation. He was in awe that she'd let him make love to her.

"You're not going to sleep just yet," she said. "You still have to make it up to me for not having enough… uh…protection with you."

He frowned. "How do you want me to make it up to you?"

"Answer some questions."

"Questions? You want to talk? At…" He leaned back to get a look at the bedside clock. "Three in the morning?"

"We just made love. The least you can do is answer some burning questions I've had for a long time."

He sighed, growing sleepy as he snuggled against her. "What do you want to know?"

"Everything. Where were you born? Where did you grow up? How many brothers and sisters do you have? Have you ever been married, had kids, pets—"

He cupped his hand over her mouth, laughing. "That's a lot of questions. If you don't draw a breath and let me answer a few, I'll forget them all."

"I'm waiting."

He chuckled again, and lightly ran his hand up and down her arm. "Let's see. Sadly, I'm not a Tennessee native. I was born in Alaska."

"That's cool." She giggled. "Literally."

"Clever girl," he teased, unable to resist pressing a kiss against her shoulder. "My family—all three brothers and two sisters of them, plus Mom and Dad—still live there, in Anchorage. They have acreage outside town. All of them built houses next to each other."

She turned toward him, even though he knew that she couldn't really see his expression in the dark.

"But you left? How old were you?"

"Eighteen."

"Then you…your family, you didn't get along with them? Did something bad happen?"

"No, not at all. I love my family very much, even visit them a couple of times a year. But I wanted to explore, see what else was out there before I settled down in one place. So I joined the navy, traveled the world and ended up in Knoxville of all places. I'm sure you'll be shocked to realize I wasn't keen on authority. I think it's because I was the middle child, with older brothers who tried—unsuccessfully—to boss me around all the time, and younger sisters I felt that I had to protect from being picked on by my brothers. I was always getting pulled one way or the other. You'd think I'd have become a peacemaker, an arbitrator between them. Instead, I just learned to fight really well. That's some of the appeal of the military—I got to fight the enemy. But I got in some pretty tight spots, so I decided not to make a long-term career of it. Went to college on the government's dime, and realized I actually missed the structure of the military. But not enough to sign up again. So I did the next best thing."

"You became a cop."

"Exactly." He slid his fingers through her hair, enjoying the silky, soft feel of it. "It's been an interesting career. Rewarding. But I've never really fit in. Dillon was right when he said I wasn't a team player. And Grant was right, too, when he told you I had…issues in Knoxville. What did he call them? Anger management problems? That's probably accurate. I punched one of my coworkers."

She surprised him by laughing. "Who hasn't? I mean, I haven't. But I'm a woman, and we tend to be smarter than men. We solve our problems without having to hit each other."

"Gee. Thanks."

She laughed again. "Maybe it's a Southern thing. I don't know. But most of the guys I grew up with, and even the ones who are adults now—like Dillon—have punched other guys at some point in their lives. I don't personally think that's a cardinal sin like some people. As long as you can move on afterward, it lets off steam. Guys can do that—get mad at each other, have a knock-down, drag-out fight, then be fine the next day. I don't know how you do it. But it works. What happened? Your boss threatened to fire you over it, like Grant said?"

"Yeah, he did. If it had been anyone else on the team, he'd have said they deserved it. The guy I punched had just shoved a woman. And I didn't personally think he should treat one with such disrespect, no matter what occupation she had."

"Prostitute."

"Yes."

"Then good for you for punching him. It's not like women in that situation do it for fun. Life has usually beaten them down, and they get in a cycle of abuse or addiction. They should be given our empathy and be helped, not criticized or made to feel worse than they already do."

"You're a kind woman, and perceptive. Most people I've met wouldn't feel that way."

"Then they're idiots. You said if it had been someone else, you wouldn't have gotten in trouble. Was it the boss's son?"

"Nephew."

She snorted. "Jerk. He should be the one who got fired."

"I didn't get fired. I quit."

"Okay, right. You quit. And Chief Thornton hired you. How did that happen?"

"He was in town to visit someone he knew, an old-timer getting ready to retire. I gather they worked together years ago. Thankfully for me, he happened to be in the squad room when the whole altercation happened. Apparently the old-timer felt the way I did about the nephew and what he'd done. He talked to Thornton about me, and the next thing I knew, he'd offered me a job. In Destiny, I'd still be a detective, in my adopted home state of Tennessee, and I'd get to become a part-time SWAT officer, something I'd wanted for years. It was a no-brainer."

He feathered his fingers through her hair again, still in awe that he was holding her like this. Holding her, loving her, had been more than he'd ever dreamed he'd get a chance to do. If he could change anything, the only thing he would change would be to keep the lights on after she'd fallen asleep in his arms in the living room and he'd carried her to the bed. He would have loved to just lie here all night staring at her beautiful face, seeing the way the light glinted off her glossy blond hair.

"Okay," he said. "I'm ready for more questions. Fire away." He smoothed her hair down and waited. "Donna?"

A soft snuffle, like a tiny cat puffing out a burst of air, sounded from her lips. Then she let out a decidedly unladylike snore.

He laughed and hugged her close. She'd accused him of snoring, when she was the one who snored. He couldn't wait to tease her about it. But for now, he'd have to wait. She really was worn out. They both were, and both needed their sleep.

As he settled down beside her and tucked the blanket around both of them, a feeling of guilt tightened his chest. Things weren't looking good for him to ever be a cop in Destiny again. Which was fine. He could go somewhere else, as long as it was in his beloved Tennessee. But Donna, well, she'd been born in Destiny and grew up there. Her family was there. He didn't have to ask her burning questions to know that. He'd been working with her for months and had simply listened. She'd freely spoken about her family, her hopes, her dreams. And all of them centered on living in Destiny. Could he ask her to give that up, to go somewhere else? The answer wasn't something he even had to think about. She'd be miserable anywhere but Destiny.

Which meant there was zero chance of them having a future together.

Worse, though, than the guilt he felt for basically having taken advantage of Donna in her sleep-deprived state was the realization of how the clock was ticking down for his fellow SWAT team members. They'd been missing for a few days. How many kidnap victims had been held that long and were returned alive and unharmed? He didn't know the statistics but imagined they were pretty dismal. Tomorrow, he and Donna needed to go full steam ahead and do everything in their power to find their friends. Because it was feeling very much like no one else was looking for them.

The clock was ticking. And it was counting down.

Chapter Thirteen

Being shy had never been in Donna's nature. Maybe being the oldest of four girls did that to a person. She'd been both friend and mother hen from a very young age, and had never had time to be shy. She was too busy making sure her younger sisters didn't kill themselves getting into something at school, or after school, before Mom and Dad came home from work. But this morning, she could barely look at Blake without feeling heat rise in her cheeks.

Not because she was embarrassed over what they'd done last night—which was probably what he thought. But because she couldn't seem to quit thinking about every kiss, every sweep of his tongue across her heated skin, every thrust of his body into hers. And she was so turned on, she was afraid that if she stared at him too long, she was going to jump him—condom or no condom.

So she showered, dressed and then ate her room-service breakfast of toast and juice on the far end of the sectional sofa while he sat at the table, poring over the files they'd brought with them. She could feel his occasional glances and questioning looks. But she was careful to pretend complete fascination with her food rather than face the elephant in the room. If he unsettled her this much after making love, how was she even going to function today? Somehow she needed to turn her thoughts. And what better way to turn them than to work on the case?

He'd spoken on the plane about possibly visiting Sanchez in prison. But she wasn't confident that talking to a drug lord was worth their time. If he'd ordered the murder and kidnapping, he had no incentive to admit it. And it could be dangerous for Blake and her if he had someone powerful pulling strings for him, and keeping tabs on his visitors.

It could even be the FBI.

On the surface, the feds being in Sanchez's pocket didn't make sense. After all, they were the ones who'd spent a couple of years infiltrating his operation to build a case against him. Why would Grant, or his direct reports, do anything to jeopardize all that hard work? And what did it have to do with Destiny's SWAT team? The connections were there, right in front of her. But she couldn't quite make them fit. Still, she knew in her bones that they really did fit somehow. She just needed the right information, that one piece of data, to make the picture come into focus. Which meant she needed information about Grant. How convenient that they were in the town where he lived?

She grabbed her phone and surfed the web. She was both shocked and pleased at how easy it was to obtain the information that she needed.

Typically, if a simple Google search didn't reveal someone's home address, then social media was the way to go to. People posted all kinds of personal details online, never realizing just how much of themselves they were exposing to strangers who might use those details against them. And Grant, surprisingly, was no exception.

Oh, he was smart enough to have an unlisted phone number and had managed to keep his address unlisted in the usual places. And he didn't have any social media accounts that Donna could find. Even his wife and kids didn't seem to have any social media accounts.

But their friends did.

Just a few advanced searches led Donna from Richard Grant to his wife and two daughters via his daughters' friends, who posted plenty on social media—including pictures the entire world could see. Pictures of birthday parties at the Grant family home, pictures of the girls leaning against a boy's car in the street out front, conveniently right by a street sign and a mailbox. That was the money shot—giving Donna the exact address of Grant's home.

She used the map feature on her web browser to zero in on the location for a street view. Her tongue almost fell out of her mouth when she got her first good look at both the property and the house itself. Holy cow.

The agent lived in west Knoxville, in a neighborhood that wound through gently rolling hills, where every home had an expansive, manicured lawn. The subdivision—if you could even call something so grand such a common name—was an eclectic mix of Craftsman bungalows, sprawling Colonial Revivals, Tudors and even ranch homes. Some were large, some were small, all were expensive. A beautiful lake—Fort Loudon Lake—sparkled in the distance. And every driveway seemed to boast a BMW, a Mercedes or some other expensive car she couldn't even name.

Grant's home wasn't mansion-sized like many of the others. But it wasn't a shack either. It was probably a little over three-thousand square feet. It was one-and-a-half stories, likely with a couple of bedrooms and a bath on the second floor. But it was the first floor that took Donna's breath away. The facade was made of stacked stone and cedar shakes, with entire walls of fancy windows with boxes overflowing with luscious pink flowers. The grass was deep green and looked as if it had been groomed with a pair of scissors.

"You look like you're ready to drool," Blake's deep voice broke into her thoughts from across the room. "What has you so fascinated?"

"SSA Grant's home. Ever heard of a neighborhood called Sequoyah Hills?"

"Sequoyah Hills? That's where he lives?"

"Yep."

"The average FBI agent makes under a hundred-thousand dollars a year. At Grant's level, he makes somewhere under two, probably closer to one-thirty or one-forty. How can he afford to live in Sequoyah Hills?"

"That's what I was wondering."

He'd crossed the room and was now sitting beside her, looking over her shoulder at the street-level picture of the agent's home. "You sure that's his?"

"Positive. It took an enormous amount of dedicated research to find it, but I did."

"Ten minutes on social media?"

She grinned. "Five. You think he's on the take? Maybe Sanchez is paying him under the table to look the other way or purposely foul up the trial."

He shook his head. "I wouldn't conclude that based on the house. The bureau knows where he lives. I guarantee they would have made sure they knew where the money came from to buy it. Is he married?"

"He has the required wife and two kids, yes. Daughters—both teenagers."

"Then either his wife has one heck of a well-paying job, or they got their money the old-fashioned way. They inherited it."

"Maybe. I'm not convinced that he isn't dirty," she said.

"I didn't say he wasn't dirty. I just don't think this is about money. He's too smart to flaunt ill-gotten gains in public." He waved toward the house on her screen. "And I've been looking into him this morning, too. He's squeaky clean, the very image of the perfect FBI agent. Literally the only thing questionable that I've been able to find is this Sanchez trial postponement and the way he's treated you and me. Something happened recently that is weighing on him, forcing him to make some questionable decisions. We need to figure out what that recent event or situation is so we can follow the trail to whoever is holding our friends."

"Our friends? Not my friends?"

He let out a deep sigh. "Our friends. I miss them, and I never thought that would happen. Even Dillon, if you can believe it."

"I believe it. I'm not even surprised. I knew we were all growing on you. It was just a matter of time until you realized it yourself. Back in the chief's office, when Grant was asking about our impressions of the ransom note, you said 'that's not how we talk.' You didn't say *I talk*. You said *we*. That's when I knew you were one of us, part of the team. You just hadn't realized it yet."

"You got all that from the word *we*?"

She shrugged.

"Maybe you're right," he admitted. "But right now, we need to focus on bringing our friends home."

"Which is why we're checking out of the hotel and taking a road trip." She turned to face him. "We're going to break into Grant's home."

THIS TIME, IT was Blake's turn to be so shocked that his mouth literally fell open, just as Donna's had done in the chief's office, when Grant basically accused them of lying.

To be fair, they were.

He cleared his throat and scrubbed his face as if the lunacy of her statement could be wiped away just as easily. Nope. She was standing in front of him, a determined look on her face, fully prepared to argue her outrageous point. And it was definitely outrageous.

"Why?" he asked. It was all he could manage at the moment.

"Because he's wrapped up in this somehow. And it's not like we can ask him any questions. A guy like that, no question he's got a home office. And where there's an office, there are files and to-do lists and calendars and any number of things that might provide a clue that will make all of this make sense."

"So you *want* to go to prison?"

She rolled her eyes. "We won't go to prison if we don't get caught."

"Sure, right. Because it would never occur to a supervisory special agent to have a security alarm at his home, with security cameras. And nosy neighbors who have to know he and his family are out of town. Yeah, sounds like a brilliant idea."

She crossed her arms. "That's the goal. Do you want to hear my plan?"

"By all means. Enlighten me. How do you propose we do this without attracting attention, getting caught on film, or getting caught, period?"

"First, stop being sarcastic. It's not helping."

"Forgive me. What was I thinking?"

Her eyes narrowed.

He held up his hands in surrender. "Okay, okay. Tell me the plan. I'll hold my snarky comments until the end."

She shook her head but continued. "One of the jobs I had while working my way through college was at a security company. They were an alarm system builder and distributor. You know how vegetable canning factories stop the lines and change the labels? Same product but they swap the outside of the cans for different brands?"

"Actually, no. I didn't realize they did that. Sounds like it should be illegal."

"I agree, but it isn't. Or, at least, it wasn't back when the security company used that example to help me understand what they did."

"They manufactured systems for other companies to sell and distribute under their own brands?"

"Exactly. I was one of their 1-800 operators who answered questions from prospective clients about the various components in the systems they sold. All the information was in the computer system, of course, so I just punched in their questions and up popped schematics and common questions and answers. But to make sure we knew the systems well enough so that we didn't sound like we were reading it off a screen, we were constantly in training. They demonstrated the systems, how to arm them, disarm them, ways to override them. Are you following?"

"Unfortunately, I am. You think you'll recognize the features of Grant's alarm system and be able to disarm it."

"I'm ninety-nine percent sure that I can, yes. The company that I worked for distributed alarms to ninety-nine percent of the market. Even if we get caught on camera, once we're inside, I can erase us from the system. No one will ever know we were there. In and out, no muss, no fuss."

"What about the neighbors?"

"It's just past typical morning rush hour. Most of them should be at work. But even if they aren't, all we have to do is act like we belong. Park in front, instead of down the block. Walk up to the front door as if we have every right to be there. As long as we don't act suspicious, no one will pay us any attention."

"Too risky. Someone could call the cops, especially if one of the neighbors is house-sitting. There are too many variables."

"We could stop at a uniform store and get some coveralls and tool belts, make it look like we're there to fix something. Everyone needs home repairs. We could walk around the outside of the house, pointing up at the roof, pretend we're figuring out the best approach to fix something. Actually, I really like that. We could get in the backyard that way without raising suspicions. And disabling the alarm out of sight of the neighbors is much less risky."

"No."

She put her hands on her hips. "No? Come on. It's a great plan. It's low risk the way I've thought it out."

"Absolutely not. We are not going to break into SSA Grant's home, and that's final."

Chapter Fourteen

"I can't believe you talked me into breaking into a federal agent's home." Blake shook his head in disgust.

"You're supposed to be pointing at the roof, not shaking your head." Donna scribbled fake notes on a clipboard as they stood by one of the pink-flowering dogwood trees about twenty feet from Grant's front door. The latex gloves they were both wearing weren't exactly work gloves to match the blue dungarees they'd worn as their disguise. But at least the gloves would ensure that they didn't leave any fingerprints. Hopefully no one would notice their hands and realize something was off.

Blake pointed. "Look. Shingles."

"It would help if you actually looked at the house when you point at it," she muttered.

His sigh could have knocked over a horse.

"We need to work on your choreography," she said. "Come on. Let's head around back and get this over with."

The hammers and screwdrivers hanging from their tool belts jangled as they walked through the deep green, well-tended grass to the garage side of the house. There was no fence, which was both good and bad. Good, because they didn't have to worry about any locks. Bad, because it meant they weren't completely hidden from view. The neighbors behind the house and to one side had high privacy fences and large back yards, which helped. But if the neighbors were home in the house on the other side, they would see everything. For that reason, she insisted they keep up the same pretense in the backyard, pointing to the roof, the gutters, various parts of the house, as if they were performing some kind of inspection. On the back porch, she peeked through the glass. A security alarm keypad was just to the left of the door inside—its red light blinking in warning.

That's when she knew they were sunk.

"What's wrong?" he asked.

She stepped back and pretended to study the window to the left of the door. "What makes you think something's wrong?"

"Donna."

Her shoulders slumped. "Remember I told you the company I worked for made ninety-nine percent of the alarms in this part of the country?"

"Yes."

"Grant bought the other one percent."

He blinked. "You can't disable the alarm."

"No. I can't."

His jaw tightened as he looked up at one of the many cameras they'd passed when they'd walked around the house.

"You might want to keep your head down," she said. "Since I won't be able to erase our existence from the recordings."

He swore. "What kind of alarm system is it?"

"Does it matter?"

He stared at her, his patience obviously wearing thin.

"Okay, okay." She gave him the information.

He pulled out his phone.

"What are you doing?" she asked.

"You're not the only one with a history." He scrolled through his contacts. "I've disarmed an alarm or two during my military days. And I have a friend who's probably dealt with that other one percent." He pressed the dial button and placed the phone to his ear.

She put her hands on her hips. "You couldn't have mentioned this at the hotel?"

"I didn't want to encourage your life of crime." He turned away from her. "Yeah, Jack. Hey. I know, I know. It's been forever. I should have called long before now."

She crossed her arms, shaking her head as he threw out alarm terminology even she had never heard before. As he spoke, he peered in windows and doors, studied the cameras, even followed what appeared to be a phone line to a utility box at the end of the house. He hung up the phone and then pried the panel open.

Donna followed him. "Just how long were you in the military?"

He ran his fingers down some cords in the box and shrugged. "Ten years. Why?"

"You said you were only in for a few years, that you didn't want to reenlist."

"No. I said I decided not to make a career out of it. You assumed I was only in for a few years." He pulled a screwdriver and wire cutters from his tool belt. His movements were sure and quick as he snipped here, re-routed there, cut the coating off some wires and twisted them together with another set.

"What exactly did you do in the military?" she asked,

in awe of his calm demeanor as he meticulously destroyed an extremely expensive alarm system, all without it going off.

He snipped one more wire, then shut the panel, before looking at her. "I'd tell you, but I'd have to kill you."

"Ha ha."

He shoved his tools back into his belt. "I bought us time, and not a whole lot of it. We need to be quick, in and out."

She followed him to the back door and reached for the screwdriver on her tool belt.

"You coming in?"

She jerked her head up. Blake was standing just inside the family room. The French door was standing wide open.

"How did you—"

He turned and headed down the hallway on the right side of the house. She shut the door and jogged to catch up to him. All the doors in the hall were open, which made finding the office easy. He disappeared into the last room on the right, and she was left to catch up yet again.

He plopped into the desk chair and scooted up to the computer sitting on the massive cherry wood desk. After turning on the monitor and tapping the keys, he shoved his chair back. "Unless you're a computer genius, we're not getting anything useful off his hard drive. It's password protected."

She pressed her hand to her heart. "You mean they didn't teach you how to break encryption algorithms in spy school?"

He pulled open a desk drawer and rummaged inside.

She stared at him, waiting for a snarky comeback. It never came. "Blake?"

"Uh-huh?" He opened another drawer.

"Were you...were you a spy?"

He pulled out his phone, checked the time. "If my calculations are right, we have approximately fifteen more minutes before we have to be out of here. Shouldn't you be searching for this amazing evidence you expected to find?"

"You and I need to talk."

"Yeah. I know. Maybe later. Like, after we rescue our friends."

His reminder of what was at stake jarred her into action. Since they didn't have enough time to study and read everything, she grabbed a book bag from one of the daughters' bedrooms, choosing a grimy, stained one that she hoped wasn't sentimental in any way. They shoved an appointment book into the bag, a calendar with handwritten notes on it, and a couple of files that seemed related to the Sanchez case.

Blake checked his phone again. "Five minutes. Anywhere else you want to check?"

"This office appears to be just for the husband. What if his wife has an office, too? There might be something useful in there."

He nodded, and they hurried down the hallway, through the living room and kitchen, to the other side of the house. Sure enough, there was a matching office on this side with decidedly more feminine decorating. Just as in the other one, they found an appointment book. She added it to her collection and headed to a set of file cabinets near the window.

"No," Blake said, motioning for her to leave. "No time."

"But I just want to—"

"Donna. If we're not out in about one minute, the

motion sensors will come back on and set the alarm off. We're out of time."

She reluctantly hurried out of the room, her fingers itching to search the files. Blake put his hand on the small of her back, urging her to run. They raced out the French doors and he shoved them closed behind them. The light on the alarm keypad, which had been green when they were inside, now switched to red. The alarm had just rearmed.

"Wow. We literally got out just in time." She drew a shuddering breath.

"Maybe, maybe not. Hurry." He grabbed her arm and yanked her with him in a dead run across the backyard to the garage side of the house, where they'd parked their car. He clicked the key fob, unlocking the doors. "Get in."

Her heart was slamming in her chest as she jumped into the passenger seat, dropping the book bag to the floor. A bead of sweat slid down the side of Blake's face as he backed the car down the driveway at a sedate pace. But he was constantly searching the mirrors, looking up and down the street. As soon as they were on the road, he accelerated to the end of the block and around the corner.

"You're going the wrong way," she said, snapping her seat belt into place.

"No. I'm going a different way. Just in case."

"In case what?"

As if on cue, sirens sounded behind them—from the direction of the street they'd just been on, zooming toward Grant's house. If they'd left the same way they'd come in, they'd have gone right past the police car, or cars, from the sound of it. There was no way of knowing if the police might have pulled them over.

Neither of them said anything as he skillfully wound his way out of the neighborhood while avoiding the police. And she didn't bother saying out loud what they both knew—they'd dodged a bullet, had almost gotten caught. If Blake hadn't forced her to leave when he had, they'd probably be in handcuffs right now. And how would that have helped their fellow SWAT team members?

"I wanted to go see Sanchez after this," he said as he headed up a ramp onto the interstate.

"Too risky. I think we should head straight to Destiny."

"My feelings exactly. My house is on the way into town, so I figure we can stop there, grab some lunch while we look over our ill-gotten gains. If we still feel the need to explore the Sanchez angle after that, I can call a friend at the Maloneyville Road detention facility and see if he has any useful information."

"Maloneyville?"

"Part of Knox County's prison system. That's most likely where Sanchez is being held for now, and it's where any visitors would go see him—assuming he's allowed visitors. As high profile as he is, they may have restricted him to visits only from his lawyer."

Chapter Fifteen

Two hours later, they were sitting at the expansive mahogany table in the kitchen section of Blake's loft-style house on the outskirts of Destiny. Their bellies were full from some sandwiches they'd grabbed at a deli along the way. And the case files and stolen appointment books and papers from Grant's house nearly covered the entire top of the table. They'd been reviewing them for the past hour.

Donna straightened in her chair, stretching, her joints popping.

Blake glanced up at the sound, then tossed his pen onto a file folder and sat back. "You okay? Can I get you anything?"

"A chiropractor would be nice. I feel like a human pretzel." She stood and stretched some more before moving to the group of couches that marked the living room area. "I've probably passed this barn a hundred times and never knew it looks like an übercool loft inside. How come I never knew you lived here?"

"You never asked."

Guilt flooded through her. "You're right. I didn't. None of us did. We should have, though. We should have worked harder to include you. All this time, I thought you were being standoffish, stubborn, refusing to be part of the team. I never tried to look at it from your side, that maybe you never felt welcomed, so you didn't try to join us. I'm sorry, Blake. I really am."

He stood and headed toward her. His long legs ate up the distance between them, and he was suddenly in front of her, tilting up her chin to look at him.

"There's plenty of blame to go around," he said. "On both sides. My background, as you've seen today, is a bit…unusual. I had a hard time fitting in at the Knoxville office because I couldn't talk about my past. That same…difficulty…pretty much transferred here to Destiny."

"Your super-secret-spy past?" She wiggled her eyebrows.

"My top-secret past. Can we leave it at that?"

She slid her hands up the front of his chest to entwine them behind his neck. Or she would have, if she could reach that far. She had to settle for letting the tips of her fingers barely touch. He was deliciously tall.

"I can live with that," she said. "And you need to stop beating yourself up. The rest of us have lived here all our lives, pretty much. There are age differences between us. We didn't all have the same classes or graduate together. But we share the experience of growing up in Destiny. And you're the first person we've ever had to welcome onto our detective squad and SWAT team who wasn't from around here, an outsider. Even though we pride ourselves on being friendly and welcoming to strangers, we pretty much sucked in the welcoming department when we brought one onto our team. I just hope we get the chance to do better—with you on our team again."

He leaned down and kissed her, a soft kiss that was over almost as soon as it began. But it was so darn sweet, it made her want to weep.

She really had it bad for this man.

She smiled up at him. "What was that for?"

He shook his head, but even though he didn't answer her with words, she saw the truth in his eyes. The mutual understanding of what had gone wrong. The desire to make it right. The relief that he'd found someone who finally "got" him. She felt the same way and hoped he read the same emotions in her eyes as she stared up at him.

He made a sound deep in his throat that reminded her of a lion. Then he was kissing her again. Really kissing her this time. Kissing her until all the clichés she'd ever heard about came true—jelly knees, the room spinning, her heart crashing against her rib cage. When he pulled back, his breathing was ragged, and there was regret in his eyes.

"Blake?"

"I want you," he whispered. "But we need to get back to work."

Once again, she'd let her fascination with him push her off course. Shame and guilt flashed inside her, making her push out of his arms.

"You're right. I need to make some phone calls to double-check some of the entries in Mrs. Grant's appointment book. Then we can compare notes."

"Sounds good. I'm a visual person. I've got a whiteboard in my closet that I haven't used in a while. I'll bring it out here so we can write out what we have and try to make sense of it. I figured I'd call Doc Brookes too, talk to him about the autopsy and any samples he took. My last call to Officer Lynch yielded nothing new. The lab still hasn't returned any results from the samples that were collected. And the private lab Lynch sent your gloves to hasn't gotten the DNA results yet. It's supposed to take a few more days. They have a backlog, like most labs. So we're back with Brookes to try to get useful information about the scene. Maybe he can talk me through what he saw, smelled, any impressions, things that might not be reflected in that sanitized version of the autopsy we got to read."

"That sounds like a great idea. Did Lynch have any reports about the team's vehicles? Were any fingerprints found that didn't trace back to the them?"

"I'll call him back and find out. I'm going to call that prison contact of mine, too, see if Sanchez has had any visitors besides his lawyer. Doubtful, but it doesn't hurt to ask."

She nodded her agreement and grabbed the appointment book. Then she headed into the other room to make her calls while Blake got the whiteboard set up on top of the table, with it leaning against the wall behind it. After they both finished their calls, they gathered their notes and took turns adding bullets to the whiteboard. Blake's notes went to the left of a vertical line he'd drawn down the center. Donna's notes went to the right.

"I think we should read them out loud, then discuss them," she said. "Want to start with yours?"

"Sure." He read each bullet on the left side of the line.

"Randy Carter, deceased, C.O.D. massive organ failure, caused by multiple gunshot wounds, all from the same gun, nine-millimeter slugs. Traces of mud with mineral deposits on clothing. No fiber evidence.

"Chief Thornton, Dillon Gray, Chris Downing, Max Remington, missing.

"All fingerprints found on the teams' vehicles had been sorted through and identified. No leads resulted from that.

"No footprint evidence, other than at the barn, one partial. Assume washed away by the rain.

"Sanchez drug trial postponed same day SWAT team went missing, per SSA Grant's request.

"Colin Lopez, one of Grant's senior agents, has driven to Knoxville every day since a week before the trial was postponed, to visit Sanchez. Visits are always approximately five minutes in duration—"

"Wait," Donna stopped him. "Your prison contact told you that, about Lopez?"

He nodded.

"Does he know why Lopez goes there? And does Sanchez's lawyer know about it?"

"From what I was able to discern, the lawyer knows about the visits and is against them. But it's Sanchez who insists he wants to see Lopez. As to what is discussed, my source assumes it's Sanchez pulling the FBI's strings, being a jerk basically, making promises he's not keeping."

"Like promising to tell them information in return for a deal, to avoid the trial continuing?"

"Maybe. We're completely guessing here. It could be any number of things. We may need to try to talk to Sanchez after all, or Lopez."

She waved toward the board. "Okay, keep going. You can read my side, too."

"Grant's family allegedly went on vacation several days before the SWAT team disappeared.

"There were zero entries in either Mrs. Grant's planner or Mr. Grant's planner about a vacation.

"Mrs. Grant missed a hair appointment.

"Both daughters missed a dance recital that had been planned for months.

"Grant's family is NOT on vacation."

He arched a brow. "Missed appointments led you to conclude that the family isn't really on vacation? That seems like a stretch. What makes you believe that?"

"Roots."

"Roots? Like tree roots?"

She laughed. "Hair roots. His wife is a bottle blonde. I saw her pictures at the house, with dark roots."

"You're not a bottle blonde." His voice was husky.

Her face flamed hot. She cleared her throat. "The salon Mrs. Grant uses is expensive, exclusive and has a long waiting list. It takes months to get an appointment. According to the owner, their clients never cancel."

"Never?"

"So she said." She rolled her eyes. "Mrs. Grant has standing appointments every three months to do her roots. She's been going there for years and has never missed an appointment. She had one the day she supposedly left on vacation. An appointment she did not keep. And she never called the salon. They're very unhappy with her."

She waved at the board again. "Plus, I may not have children of my own, but I have nieces and nephews. And I know how parents are about recitals of any kind, especially dance. Having your kid in dance classes is really expensive. The lessons alone are outrageous, but add to that the cost of outfits, and it skyrockets. It's a tremendous investment of money and time. And it all leads up to the recitals. You don't miss recitals. Period."

He stared at the board, appearing deep in thought. Donna decided to read off a few more of the bullet points herself.

"A mysterious cruise was arranged for the wives of the SWAT team. They were the only ones who 'won' tickets, even though it was supposed to be a charity for law-enforcement families. The wives left the day before the SWAT team disappeared.

"Lopez used his influence to help the one-time charity set up the cruise, to get past city permitting issues.

"The ONLY law-enforcement families on the cruise were from Destiny, even though the cruise was arranged by a charity out of Knoxville..."

She stopped. It was her turn to frown and puzzle over what she was seeing.

"What is it?" Blake asked.

"The cruise. Lopez's involvement seems to connect it with Grant, like so much of whatever is going on. And it was obviously focused on the wives of our officers. But there's a different slant to this than everything else."

He stepped beside her, as if he could see what she was thinking if he looked at the clues from the same angle. "Go on."

"Randy was murdered, which proves whoever took the rest of the team hostage means business. They're dangerous, and they want us to know that, so we give in to their demands. Only, there haven't been any."

"Which doesn't make sense in a ransom case," he added.

"Right. We've already concluded that delay, diversion, misdirection seem to be the goals. But why? Our victimology, the timelines, haven't raised any red flags. There's no one that we can point to as having any immediate grudges against our team. At least, nothing recent that we've looked at. It doesn't seem like it was personal in any way." She turned to look at him. "I'm starting to think the kidnapping of our team is random."

He stared at her a long moment, then shook his head. "Can't be. It was planned ahead of time in order for the note to be ready, and the team to have been taken so cleanly, with almost no evidence left behind."

"Well, yes," she said. "It was planned, but what I'm saying is that it could just as easily have been another group of cops, in another county, who were taken. They may have chosen Destiny because of the location alone. Lots of foothills and woods and long stretches of rural roads. Much easier to sneak up on someone out here, without witnesses, than in a city. Maybe our team was chosen because they checked off the boxes of whatever the kidnapper or kidnappers needed." She stepped to the board and wrote another bullet. *Choice of victims irrelevant—goal was to create a diversion for other law-enforcement. Diversion from what?*

She set the marker back on the tray and joined Blake again. "Other than getting lots of law-enforcement people working on the case, what did the kidnapping do? What concrete effect did it have?"

Blake slowly nodded, as if he was beginning to see her viewpoint. "The Sanchez trial. We keep coming back to that. The trial was postponed because of the kidnapping. Maybe that was the goal all along, to put the trial on hiatus. The victims, who the bad guys kidnapped, were irrelevant." His gaze shot to hers. "Not to us. I meant to the bad guys."

She gave him a sad smile. "I knew what you meant. In addition to postponing the trial, the kidnapping got the main witnesses, the FBI agents who gathered the evidence against Sanchez, out of town, and temporarily out of the picture."

"Seems like it. The dates," he said, going to the board and tapping on the dates they'd written next to several of the bullets. "They all line up. Mrs. Grant and her kids left town a little before our guys were taken. The wives of the kidnapped officers were sent out of town around that same time. What did that accomplish? It got the women and children out of harm's way. That's the only thing I can think of. But do you know of any drug lord who would care about collateral damage? I sure don't. Which leads us back to one person who seems knee deep in this thing who might have known what was going to happen ahead of time and cared enough to protect them."

"Grant," she said. "Which is double damning against him because the families were sent out of town *before* the FBI was ever called."

He nodded. "He knew our guys were going to be kidnapped, and he wanted to make sure their families, and his, were kept safe."

"Safe." She fisted her hands at her sides. "Don't expect me to thank him when this is over because he went out of his way to keep the wives safe. He knew this was going to happen and did nothing to stop it, and Randy died because of it. I'm going to tear him apart with my bare hands once we have proof."

"I'll be right there with you," he agreed. "But we need to keep our eye on our goal—bringing back our team alive. So what else do we see?" He pointed to some bullets about the evidence at the lab. "If Grant is part of this, he's doing everything he can to buy time. That means doing things to hamper the investigation. Like sending evidence to the FBI lab when the state lab could have tested it by now and had the results back. He's interfering with the investigation."

"He totally is." She put her hands on her hips. "I have to believe the FBI, in a typical kidnapping investigation where the clock is ticking and time is of the essence, would put a rush on the test results."

"Who says they didn't?" He arched a brow. "For all we know, the results could be back, and Grant isn't sharing them."

She shook her head, incensed at the very thought. A man with the coveted position of supervisory special agent had turned on his fellow law-enforcement officers. He didn't care that one had died, and four more lives were in jeopardy. She was so upset she started shaking.

Blake's arm settled around her shoulders, drawing her close against him. "We're going to find them. Then we'll focus on making sure the FBI and others know what Grant has done. But we need to focus. With Grant driving the investigation, it's going in the wrong direction. We have to figure this out. Now."

She blew out a deep breath and put her arm around his waist, drawing on his warmth and strength to try to calm down and think. They both stood there for several minutes, quietly studying the board, silently reading through the dozens of clues and theories they'd written down.

"Mineral deposits." Donna frowned at the description that Blake had written about his phone call with Doc Brookes. "What did Brookes say about the mineral deposits on Randy's pants?"

"That the lab would have to test them to identify them. There were little pieces of grit mixed in with the mud. He said if he had to guess, he'd say it was either quartz or granite. The mud sparkled when he passed a light over it. That's the only reason he even noticed it."

She blinked and drew back. "The mud sparkled? Are you sure?"

"That's what he said. Why? Is there somewhere in Destiny with mud that sparkles?"

"As a matter of fact, there is. The old quarry. It's about a mile from Hawkins Ridge. It's been closed down for years, but they used to cut slabs of granite out of those hills. Between the bad economy and local environmentalists putting every roadblock up they could to stop the company from working there, they decided it wasn't worth the trouble and left. But I don't see how anyone could hide four people there. It's an open mine, kind of like with coal strip mining. They don't cut tunnels through the mountain like the other mines around here used to do when they were open. If they were at the quarry, someone should have seen them."

"If they searched that area, yes," Blake said. "But if Grant saw that in the report, and has any kind of geological map of the area to help with the search, he could have put two and two together way before we did and directed the search parties away from the quarry. Yet another stall tactic to drag this out."

"There's only one way to know for sure," she said. "We need to see whether the quarry was searched."

"I'll call Officer Lynch and see if he knows."

While Blake made the call, Donna waited, silently praying that this was it, the clue they needed in order to find the team. If Grant had steered the team away from searching that quarry, then that could be the red flag they were looking for. Because there was no other way she could think of for those sparkling mineral deposits to be on Randy's clothes. The kidnapper, the killer, must have trekked through the forest from that direction to sneak up on the SWAT team and transferred the granite chips from his own clothes to Randy. Then he took the team back with him, somehow. She didn't have a theory yet for how he'd done that without leaving any evidence.

The team could still be at the quarry—maybe tied up, or kept in some kind of shed or small building left over from the mining operation. If no one had searched the area, it wouldn't matter that it was an open mine. Kind of like the old philosophical question—if a tree fell in a forest, and no one was there to hear it, did it make a sound? Well, if a SWAT team was kept tied up in an open quarry, but no one was there to see them, did it really matter that the quarry was open? No. It didn't.

With the phone still to his ear, Blake moved to the table to one of the maps they had of the area. They'd marked off earlier spots as searched, based on previous calls to Lynch while on the plane. Now he marked off more spots, his mouth tightening into a hard line when he circled where the quarry should be.

Then checked it off.

Donna's shoulders slumped.

"Thanks, Officer Lynch," Blake said. "We both appreciate your help. Watch your back, okay? Neither of us trusts Grant, or any of the people he brought with him." A pause, then, "Soon, hopefully. We're working on some leads. Okay, we'll keep you posted, too. Thanks."

He hung up and slid the phone into his pocket. "They searched the quarry yesterday afternoon. Not because of any evidence, and not at Grant's direction. Some volunteers, along with the state police, decided to expand the search in that direction—even though Grant never asked them to."

He stared at the board another minute, then pulled his phone out again.

"Do you have another idea to follow up?" she asked.

He shook his head and punched in a number. "Other than going into the woods and searching on our own, no. I'm drawing a blank. But if this all revolves around Sanchez, I'm going to warn my friend at the detention center to beef up security. Maybe the delay was to give

Sanchez a chance to try to escape when the focus wasn't on him and things weren't so hot. It's the only thing that I can think of at this point, even though there isn't any real evidence to back it up."

He made the call while Donna sat down and studied the map, checking all the places the teams had searched. They'd been thorough. Every building in a ten-mile radius of Hawkins Ridge had been checked. Did that mean the team had been taken somewhere else? In spite of the lack of tire tracks, had they been driven out of the county and were somewhere else entirely? If so, how were they going to find them?

"Donna."

The odd hitch in Blake's voice had her stomach dropping before she even looked at him. He'd put his phone away. And his brow was lined with worry.

"What happened?" she asked, dreading the answer.

"Sanchez attempted to escape a couple of hours ago."

She pressed a hand to her throat. "Was anyone hurt?"

"Two guards were killed."

She let out a ragged breath. "What about Sanchez?"

"They caught him. I don't have many specifics, but it seems like this must have been planned for months. It was an inside job. A group of new hires, hired when the trial first started, put everything in place to smuggle him out as one of the grounds crew members. It all hinged on him being transferred from the Knox County Jail downtown. He was at KCJ during the trial, but once it was postponed, he was transferred to the Maloneyville facility. Without that constant media attention anymore, or the extra vigilance at KCJ because of shuffling him back and forth to court, the heat died down, and guards began treating him like any other prisoner."

"Then what happened to Randy, and the others, *was* about Sanchez. The diversion was so everyone was looking the other way, so he could escape."

Her heart seemed to stutter in her chest as another thought occurred to her. "His plan failed. What does that mean for our team? If he doesn't need the diversion anymore, does that mean time has run out for our guys? Assuming he's kept them alive, now he has no need to worry about it anymore. He'll pull the plug on the operation. Or, if he can't get word out, one of his thugs will hear about the failed escape attempt on the news, and they'll know it's over. They'll cut their losses and run. We have to find our team now. It might already be too late."

He grabbed his keys from a hook on the wall and pitched them to her. "You drive while I call everyone I know and tell them our suspicions about Grant and the link to Sanchez's escape attempt. We may not have enough proof to have him arrested, but with Sanchez having tried to escape, it gives a lot more weight to our belief that he's behind this, that he and Lopez colluded to make this happen. If nothing else, they'll want to interview Grant and Lopez to see if they know anything about Sanchez—and our men. That alone means we get someone else in to run the investigation."

She hurried to catch up to him as his long strides carried him to the door much faster than her shorter ones. "Where are we going? To the FBI field office in Knoxville to plead our case?"

He paused at the door. "We're going to Hawkins Ridge to search for them ourselves. Unless you have a better idea?"

She yanked open the door. "Let's go."

Chapter Sixteen

In spite of Officer Lynch's assurance that the quarry had already been searched, that was the first place that Donna and Blake decided to check—based on the mineral deposit evidence. Unfortunately, they didn't find their missing team. What they did find were lots of footprints from the searchers. If there had been any evidence of Sanchez's men out here, it had been obliterated. That was one of the problems with getting civilian volunteers involved—they lacked the training to preserve evidence.

Blake led the way through the forest, toward Hawkins Ridge. He held up a low-hanging branch for Donna to pass under, then took the lead again. When the woods near the top of the hill they were on thinned out, she joined him, and they walked side by side, studying the ground, scanning the woods, always on the alert in case anyone else was out here who shouldn't be.

When they reached the dilapidated barn, they both stopped at the closed double doors. A notice declaring it a sealed crime scene was taped across the middle.

Blake motioned to the notice. "What do you think?"

"I think I care more about searching for clues that

might help me find my friends than preserving a crime scene."

"Exactly what I was thinking."

They both grabbed a handle and pulled the doors open, ripping the notice in half. The smell hit them immediately. Even with the body gone, the blood had soaked into the ground, and the place had been shut up without ventilation. It reeked of death.

Donna's face went pale. She blinked several times as if fighting back tears. But Blake knew it wasn't because of the odor, specifically. It was because of the memory of her friend, and what had happened to him.

"You can stay out here if you want," he said. "I'll look inside, see if there are any clues that didn't make it into the reports. You and I certainly didn't have time to properly search it ourselves when we were here last."

"No. We didn't. But I'm okay. I can handle this. The search will go faster with both of us." She stepped in past him, scanning the floor and walls off to the right with her flashlight.

Blake did the same on the left side, but he couldn't help frequently glancing back at her to see how she was doing. He couldn't imagine how hard it must be for her to be here knowing that this was the place her friend had died. Knowing that her other friends could very well be dead, as well.

No, that wasn't entirely true. He was feeling some of those same emotions himself, to a lesser degree. He'd been thinking about his former team a lot ever since he was fired and they disappeared. And he'd begun to realize that they meant far more to him than he'd ever thought they could. But more than that, his emotions were all wrapped up in Donna, and his worry and concern for how this was affecting her. He wanted to protect her from every kind of hurt, every kind of pain, physical or mental. And he hated that he seemed helpless to do that right now.

They met in the center of the barn.

"Anything?" she asked.

He swept his light toward the row of stalls that ran across the back. "There are what look like fresh scrapes across the floor over there, most of them concentrated in one stall. But there aren't any hiding places. It's all open. Maybe the crime scene techs found some blood back there, or other evidence, and the scrapes are from their boots."

"Show me."

They went to the stall, and he pointed his light at the floor along the wall. "See those scrapes right there?"

She bent down and ran her fingers over them. "You're right. They're fresh. But there are old scrapes, too. Maybe a wild animal has been nesting in here—a raccoon or possum."

"And they were spooked by the search teams. Moved their nesting material somewhere else."

She straightened. "Maybe. Whatever, or whoever, was here at one time is obviously not here now. We need to keep looking."

A couple of hours later, Blake paused in the parking area and turned in a slow circle. Donna was a good twenty feet away, slowly walking across the clearing, studying the dirt for clues. But Blake didn't think she'd find any. The lack of tire tracks and footprints from that night still baffled him. Even with all the rain, there should have been something to show that Dillon and the others had been here. No one was that good at covering their tracks—literally. Even if they'd gone back and tried to wipe them away, they'd have missed something. The area was just too large not to.

Donna crossed the clearing and stopped beside him. "What are you thinking?"

"Just…how impossible all of this is."

"Impossible? What do you mean?"

"The kidnappings. This parking area showed no tire tracks, even though we know that Dillon and the others—including you and me—were here that day. There are only two explanations that I can think of. Either the rain really did obliterate every single track, or the combination of rain and someone using, say, a rake, or something like that, purposely wiped away the tracks up here. The gravel road starts just a little farther down the mountain, so it wouldn't have been that difficult to do. There wouldn't have been an enormous area of dirt they had to worry about raking—again, assuming that's what they did to cover their tracks."

"Okay. Seems plausible not to have any tire tracks then. So where's the impossible part?" she asked.

"The road at the bottom of this mountain passes by several houses and a country store. But no one reported seeing any vehicles up here that day, other than the SWAT team's. We know they drove up here and never drove back down. But there's no evidence they were driven back down in another vehicle either. Like I said, no tire tracks of other vehicles, and no sightings by anyone who lives at the bottom of the mountain. That has to mean that the perpetrator or perpetrators didn't drive up here."

"Okay, I'm with you so far. Where does the impossible part come in?"

"The chief is a lot older and might have been easy to subdue. But the others—Dillon, Chris, Max, even Randy—were all young, in great shape. And they aren't exactly light. If someone snuck up here through the woods to surprise them, they wouldn't have been able to just carry them off somewhere, not without leaving some kind of trace. It's just not feasible. There would have been broken branches, footprints, something. So that means the team wasn't forcibly carried out of here."

He scrubbed his jaw and swept his arms out toward the woods surrounding them. "Did they walk out? Same problem exists with that scenario. Even if they'd been handcuffed, or tied up, and forced at gunpoint to walk through the woods to some other destination, they're not rookies. They'd know trackers would come in looking for them. They'd leave a trace of their passing in some way so we could follow them. I have zero doubt about that. Dillon and the others are just too smart not to have found a way. So all I can conclude is that they didn't walk down from this ridge. Which, of course, is impossible, too, because they're obviously not here."

She looked down the road, back toward the trees and then up at the sky, as if searching for answers there. "They couldn't have been lifted out by helicopter. This clearing isn't big enough to land one, and the team's vehicles were up here. There wasn't room. The trees are too thick. Could they have lifted the guys up into the chopper? Maybe it hovered?"

"No way," he said. "It was storming too bad that night. Thunder, lightning—too dangerous. Not to mention the heavy winds that blow down through these mountains in a storm like that. They didn't ride out of here in a vehicle. They didn't walk out of here. And they didn't fly out of here. So where does that leave us?"

Her eyes widened. "They're still here."

He nodded. "They have to be. But they're not anywhere that we can see. So they're—"

"Underground." Her voice rose with excitement. "The tunnels, from the old abandoned mines I mentioned earlier. They have to be in one of the tunnels."

"Tell me about those old mines. Would the openings to the shafts have been boarded up with warning signs? I don't recall seeing any during the paint ball exercise, or during our search today."

"I've never seen anything like that, and I grew up here. I remember my dad talking about the mines when I was little, and how clever the company was who created them. They were a lot more environmentally conscious than the owners of the quarry. They liked to conceal the openings with sheds that blended into the landscape and seemed as if they were a part of everyday life."

He grew still. "Sheds? What about old barns?"

They both took off running.

BLAKE SHOVED THE tire iron into the crack in the floor of the stall with the scratches they'd seen earlier, a crack that had taken him and Donna far too long to find. So long that they'd almost given up on their theory that the opening to a mine shaft might be hidden beneath the barn. Now, after searching for an opening in the floor, and then having to hike a mile to their rental car to get a tire iron and hike a mile back, they were on the verge of finding out if this was finally the end—or yet another disappointment in a long string of them.

He shoved the edge of the bar in farther, then pushed down on the other end. A loud click sounded, and a three-by-three square section of the floor popped up on one side, as if it were on springs. He dropped the tire iron and grabbed the edges, lifting to see what kind of tension might be on it. There was no tension. The floor swung up without a sound, and a dark hole was revealed below.

Donna aimed both her flashlight and her pistol down into the hole. A metal ladder was bolted into the side. There were six rungs, which led to a slightly sloping floor made of dirt. Thick timbers that were similar to old railroad ties shored up the hole. She moved her light all around. "Do you see what I see?"

"The dirt sparkles."

"It sure does. Well, partner? Obviously we're calling for backup at this point. But who do we call?"

He thought about it. "Lynch. I have no way of knowing whether the warnings I called in to my contacts have gone anywhere with the FBI. We can't risk bringing Grant in on this. And we have no way of knowing how far his corruption has gone—whether the state police are involved, too. The only people I trust to help us are the ones on our team, the Destiny police."

She grinned. "There's hope for you yet."

While Donna called Lynch and explained the need for secrecy, Blake edged forward on his stomach and leaned down into the hole. There appeared to be only one tunnel, or at least, in this part of the mine, there didn't appear to be any openings to other tunnels. And it appeared to go in a generally western direction, back toward the quarry.

"He's rounding up our guys," Donna said. "They'll

make excuses and head out one or two at a time. A mass exodus might make Grant suspicious. Lynch thinks they'll be here in about half an hour."

He pulled back out of the hole and looked up at her. "Half an hour is too long. We have no way of knowing what Sanchez's people will do now that his escape attempt failed. I don't want to wait, especially if this ends up being a wild-goose chase and the team isn't down there."

She chewed her bottom lip. "Okay, okay. But let's do this by the book. Well, without the waiting for backup part. I'm your wingman. You're mine. We're each other's backup. No running off and leaving each other no matter how tempting. Agreed?"

Her little speech stung, but he couldn't fault her. The last time he was supposed to watch her back, he'd let her down. If it had been a true SWAT situation instead of an exercise, she could have been killed.

"Agreed. But I go first."

She frowned. "Why? Because I'm a woman?"

"Yes."

Her face flushed with anger.

He pulled her face close to his. "It has nothing to do with your abilities as a police officer. And it's not because you're *a* woman. It's because you're *the* woman, the one I care about. And I couldn't bear it if you got hurt. Call me a chauvinist or whatever you want. But those are my terms. Either I go into that hole first, or we don't go at all."

He punctuated his little speech by kissing her, a quick soft kiss that he hoped conveyed just how much she mattered to him.

She let out a soft sigh. "You're ruining me. I was a badass cop before I met you."

"You still are. The biggest and baddest around."

"It's too late for flattery." She waved toward the opening. "Go. Let's get down there and see what we find."

He braced his hands on both sides of the cut-out, swung his legs into the opening and dropped down onto the dirt below. He grabbed his flashlight and pistol and trained them in front of him, watching the shadows and listening. "Clear."

"Show-off," she muttered above him. "Must be nice to have long legs." Her shoes rang out against the metal ladder as she climbed down behind him. Her flashlight clicked on, adding more light to his. "Ready."

"Donna?"

"Yes?"

He looked over his shoulder at her. "Your legs are perfect just the way they are."

Her eyes widened, and he turned around so she wouldn't see his grin. "Let's go."

They moved quickly, without pretense of stealth. There really wasn't any point. Every little sound echoed in the tunnel. If there were any bad guys up ahead, they'd hear him and Donna coming a mile off.

A few minutes in, the tunnel ended at an intersection. They stopped and studied the ground.

"Footprints," she whispered, "down both tunnels. Split up?"

"No way," he said.

"Because I'm a woman again?"

"Because we're each other's wingman—wing person, people, whatever. We're not splitting up. That's what Dillon taught me, and what you taught me. We'll check the tunnel on the left first, then come back and check the other one, if that's what it takes."

A smile curved her lips. "I think my work here is done." Then she hurried down the left tunnel before he could stop her.

He cursed, hating that he'd fallen for her trick. "Come back here," he whispered. "I'm supposed to lead."

"My turn."

He bit back what he thought of that. The ground was softer here, their footfalls more muffled. Stealth was back on the table. Donna must have realized it, too, because she seemed to be making an effort to walk more softly and she didn't talk anymore.

Blake bided his time, keeping an eye out in front of them, just as much as he checked behind. He didn't want Donna running straight into an ambush.

The tunnel turned again, a sharp turn, and a light shone from up ahead.

They both flipped off their flashlights. Blake pulled her back, pressing both of them against the wall of the tunnel. They waited. When the light up ahead didn't move, he whispered, "Keep going or wait for backup?"

"I'm not waiting," she whispered.

He hadn't figured she would. He tapped her shoulder, and they both started forward, hands touching the wall on the left to guide them. Thirty feet, twenty, fifteen. The light was coming from some kind of chamber, probably an overhead light built into the tunnel ceiling. It definitely wasn't moving like a flashlight or lantern. And it was too bright not to be from a light fixture of some kind. When they were just a few yards shy of the opening, they stopped.

There was no way to see into the chamber without anyone in it seeing them at the same time. All they could do was go for it and hope for the best.

He wrapped both hands around his pistol. Donna did the same. There was enough light for them to see each other, so he mouthed the countdown.

Three.

Two.

One.

They ran into the chamber. Everything seemed to fill Blake's vision at once: tunnels opening off to the left and right of the cavern, the gunmen about forty feet in front of them, their teammates—Dillon, Chris, Max and the chief—caged like animals behind a wall of bars in the back left corner.

"Freeze, police," Blake shouted at the gunmen.

The rest seemed to happen in slow motion, and yet all at once. The gunmen swung their weapons toward the two of them. Blake shouted a warning at Donna and fired at the gunmen. One of them screamed and fell against the man beside him, clutching his middle. Another man went down, a split second after Donna's gun boomed next to Blake. There was nowhere to hide, no cover. It was all about speed, who could outshoot whom.

Bam, bam, bam! Donna and Blake crouched together, shoulder to shoulder, firing as if they were on a gun range, but with the knowledge that every shot counted, and lives were on the line. Not just their own, but the lives of their men.

It was over as quickly as it had begun. The sudden silence was almost as shocking as the deafening gunshots had been. Blake and Donna stood together, chests heaving, staring at the carnage in front of them. Six men lay dead on the ground.

He could hear her swallow hard beside him. "Are you okay?"

He kept his pistol pointed forward, just as she did, adrenaline still pumping through his system.

"Yes," she said. "You?"

"Your three o'clock!" Dillon's voice shouted from off to their left.

Blake and Donna jerked to their right, firing as one. *Bam, Bam, Bam!* Three more gunmen fell to the ground, dead.

Footsteps sounded from the tunnel to their left. Blake swung his pistol toward the opening. Lopez ran through it, gun in hand. His eyes widened when he saw Blake.

"Freeze," Blake shouted.

But Lopez didn't freeze. He swung his weapon toward Blake.

Boom! Bam!

They both fired. Lopez went down.

"Blake!" Donna yelled.

He jerked around, expecting to see more gunmen. He did. Just one. Lying on the ground a few feet from Donna.

"Lopez shot him," she said. "He was protecting me."

He whirled back around. Lopez was writhing on the floor, clutching his chest.

Blake swore and ran to him. He kicked Lopez's pistol away from his body and dropped down on one knee. After holstering his own gun, he ran his hands across Lopez's chest, searching for the wound. Lopez's lips were turning blue, but there didn't seem to be any blood.

Blake grabbed the edges of the man's shirt and

ripped it open. Buttons went flying, pinging off the ground like pebbles.

Donna stood guard over both of them, scanning the tunnel openings with her pistol.

"He's got a vest on," Blake said. "He's just got the wind knocked out of him."

"Sit him up," Max called out. "Bend his knees."

"Like I care if the scum bucket dies," Blake grumbled. He ignored the way Lopez's eyes widened with even more panic as he struggled to draw air, like a fish gasping its last after being plucked from the water and landing on the dock.

In spite of his overwhelming desire to punch the traitor, Blake did as Max suggested and helped the agent sit up. Blake shoved the man's legs up toward his chest, and could tell exactly when air rushed back into his struggling lungs. He gulped several times, like he couldn't quite get enough of the stuff. His lips lost their bluish tinge, and he finally let out a deep, shaky breath.

"Thank you," he said, still gasping.

"Don't thank me just yet," Blake said. "Tennessee has the death penalty. And I'm going to do everything I can to see you on death row for Randy's murder." Blake jerked him up to standing and whirled him around to handcuff him.

"Wait," Lopez cried out. "I'm not the one who killed your teammate. And I'm not the one who kidnapped your team."

"He's right about one thing," Dillon called out. "He didn't kill Randy. One of the guys you shot did."

For the first time since coming into the chamber, Blake looked directly at the cage that had been set up in the corner. Relief swept through him to see all four men standing at the bars, looking dirty and tired, but other than that, unharmed.

"Are you okay?" he asked, needing to hear it for himself.

"We'll be okay as soon as you let us out of here." Dillon motioned toward the other side of the chamber. "The keys are on a hook on that wall."

Donna retrieved the keys and let them out. All of them surrounded Lopez, who cowered against the wall, his eyes round with fear. But it was Dillon who spoke.

"After we were ambushed in the barn, and brought down here," Dillon said, "Lopez came here once a day and took our picture on a cell phone. Since the guys who were guarding us let him in and out, he's obviously working with them."

Lopez shook his head back and forth. "No, I'm not. I mean, kind of, yes. But I had no choice. And I was coming here tonight to save you. All of you."

Blake gave a harsh laugh. "You and what army? There were nine armed men in here."

"This army."

Blake whirled toward the sound of the voice coming from the tunnel where Lopez had emerged moments earlier.

"Whoa, whoa, hold it." The man raised his hands high in the air. "Think carefully, son," he said. "I really don't think you want to shoot the director of the FBI."

Blake slowly lowered his gun, recognizing the man in the business suit standing there. "No, sir. I wouldn't." He holstered his gun, and motioned for Donna to do the same.

A dozen men filed out of the tunnel from behind the director.

The sound of more footsteps echoed in one of the tunnels behind them—the same tunnel from where Blake and Donna had emerged. Everyone drew their pistols, even the director, and aimed them at the opening to the tunnel.

Officer Lynch and half a dozen Destiny police officers burst from the tunnel, guns drawn.

"Hold your fire," Blake, Donna and the whole SWAT team yelled.

Everyone froze for several seconds, Lynch's eyes so wide, they looked like they might burst from his head.

"It's okay," Blake announced. "Everyone here is on the same team." He eyed Lopez. "Well, most of us." He motioned for Lynch and the other officers to holster their weapons. As soon as they did, the director's men did, too.

"Well, that was exciting." The director's voice was bland, with a hint of laughter in it. He stepped over to Blake. "Can I assume that you're Detective Blake Sullivan? The one who called Maloneyville a few hours ago and warned them that Sanchez was going to try to escape? And then called half a dozen special agents, making an outrageous claim about Supervisory Special Agent Richard Grant being a dirty agent, who may have orchestrated the kidnapping of a SWAT team and the murder of one of the members of that team?"

He swallowed and cleared his throat. "Yes, sir. Guilty."

The director offered his hand. "On behalf of the FBI, I offer you my sincere apology for whatever the hell is going on. And I promise you, we'll get to the bottom of this. Together."

Blake stared at him in surprise then shook his hand.

"I don't understand. How did you end up here? When I called, I didn't know where the team was being held."

The director motioned to Lopez. "I was in Knoxville for an FBI function, and one of the local field agents told me about your phone calls. A few minutes later, he patched a call to me from Lopez, saying he had a life and death situation on his hands and needed backup immediately—but that I couldn't tell Grant. He gave us the GPS coordinates of the entry to this tunnel, down by the quarry, and met us there."

"So there's another entrance," Donna said from beside him. "We must have missed it when we were in the quarry."

"It's well hidden," the director said. "Not sure my men would have found it if Lopez hadn't been watching for us. And now that the crisis seems to be over, I think it's time that Special Agent Lopez told all of us what exactly is going on."

As one, the chief and the SWAT team stood in front of Lopez, shoulder-to-shoulder with the director, facing a sweating, terrified-looking Lopez as his gaze darted from one to the other.

Blake waited until Lopez was staring directly up at him. "Start talking."

Chapter Seventeen

Blake and Donna were given the honor of stepping into the police station first. It was a bittersweet victory, knowing what they now knew, to see SSA Grant turn around from speaking to one of the other agents and watch them walk through the doors. Dillon and the chief followed, then Chris and Max. And finally, the director, Lopez and the small army of special agents and Destiny police officers, who'd all been in the tunnels together.

What struck Blake was how unsurprised Grant looked to see them, as if he'd known his time had run out. It wasn't until he saw the director and his entourage that he went pale and his eyes widened in shock. No, that wasn't accurate either. He'd already been pale, alarmingly so. But he did seem to blanch when the most powerful man in the bureau strode toward him. All in all, the haggard, gaunt look to his features and the lack of surprise at seeing the SWAT team went toward corroborating what Lopez had told them back in the mine.

"Director," Grant said. "What a…surprise to see you here, sir." He aimed a questioning look at Lopez. "What's going on?"

"Knock off the innocent act," the director told him.

"Lopez told us everything. How Sanchez had armed men break into your home, holding your wife and daughters hostage with the threat of killing them if you didn't do exactly as he said. Lopez was there with you at the time, so he was looped in. But he warned you that if anyone else found out, you'd come home to a dead family."

Although it didn't seem possible, even more color washed from Grant's face, leaving his skin translucent.

The director continued. "In exchange for postponing the trial, you were to look the other way and allow the Destiny SWAT team to be taken hostage."

A chorus of grumblings erupted in the room, most of it coming from the Destiny police.

Chief Thornton raised a hand, and they quieted down.

The director nodded his thanks but didn't look away from Grant. "You didn't feel you had a choice. I know that. But because of your inaction, a man died. Detective Randy Carter."

Grant swallowed, looking miserable. But he didn't say anything.

"But you did do what you could to protect their families," the director allowed. "You and Lopez created a fake charity to ensure that the SWAT team members' wives were on a cruise, out of harm's way, when the team was kidnapped. And since you had negotiated a daily proof of life from Sanchez for your own family, after the SWAT team was taken, you negotiated daily proof of life for them, as well. Lopez was the go-between. He took a picture of the SWAT team every day and took it to Sanchez at the detention facility. In return,

Sanchez would have a picture texted to Lopez's phone while he was there, a picture of your family."

Grant braced a hand on the desk closest to him, as if he was afraid he might fall without the support. "It was the only thing I knew to do, the only way to try to keep all of them safe—the Destiny SWAT team, and my family—until I could figure out how to resolve this, or find my family so I could organize their rescue. That's what I've been trying to do. But something happened. Sanchez's escape plan went wrong."

"Yes." The director's voice was harder now, no hint of the earlier empathy he'd had when talking about Grant's family being taken. "And two more police officers paid with their lives. That's unconscionable, Richard. You should have called me. You should have trusted your team to have your back before this went too far. Before good men died."

Red heat flushed Grant's cheeks, and his spine stiffened. He let the desk go, his anger appearing to give him renewed strength. "It's easy to judge me." His eyes flashed as he looked at Donna and Blake, and the rest of the SWAT team, before meeting the director's gaze again. "And it's pathetically easy to say what I should have done, looking back. I argued with Sanchez, tried to reason with him. In the end, arranging that cruise, warning Sanchez not to hurt anyone—which I did— was the only thing I felt I could do. I was buying time while Lopez and I tried to find my family without Sanchez knowing we were searching for them. I never expected anyone to get killed. I was doing everything in my power to try to ensure just the opposite."

"You should know by now," the director said, "that you can't negotiate with criminals. That was your first mistake, believing that Sanchez would follow through on the deal that you made. Three men have paid the price for your poor choices. And if it wasn't for Detectives Blake Sullivan and Donna Waters, four more men would probably be dead right now." He waved to the chief and the others. Then he motioned to one of the FBI agents beside him. "Arrest SSA Grant, please. Put him in one of the holding cells I see at the back of the room."

"No, wait. Don't." Grant struggled with the strength of desperation. It took four men to subdue him and put him in handcuffs. "My family," he yelled, as they dragged him toward the cells. "You have to find them. Sanchez will have them killed!"

"I'll do everything in my power to keep that from happening," the director called out.

Grant swore viciously, but as soon as the cell door shut behind him, he collapsed onto the bunk, put his head in his hands and wept. He'd obviously given up all hope and believed his family was doomed.

"We have to find the mole," the director whispered to Blake and Donna. "Other than Lopez, who in here are his right hands, the ones who are around him the most? Agents who would know what Grant is doing at all times and could report that to Sanchez?"

Donna turned to Blake and frowned up at him. "This room always felt big until half the county pushed its way inside. Can you see over everyone's heads? Where are Joel Lawrence and Stacy Bell?"

Blake craned his neck—for once, his height not helping a lot, since so many of the other men in the room were nearly just as tall. But then he spotted one of the agents. "There, in the back right corner. The agent talking to one of the Destiny police officers. That's Joel

Lawrence. Grant introduced him as one of his long-time core team members. Where Grant is, he is for the most part. Him and Lopez, of course. And Stacy Bell."

The director spoke softly to one of his men, who then forced his way through the crowd to Lawrence.

Blake continued his slow circle, looking for the always smiling agent who'd offered her condolences over Randy's death to both him and Donna when they first arrived.

"She isn't here, is she?" Donna said, staring up at him.

"I don't think so."

Donna immediately turned away and threaded her way through the crowd. Blake was about to ask her what she was doing, but Dillon stepped in front of him.

"What's wrong?" Dillon asked.

"Someone's missing. One of Grant's direct reports, Stacy Bell. She's Caucasian, has shoulder-length brown hair, is about five foot four, maybe 110 pounds."

Dillon motioned to Max and Chris, who immediately headed to the doors and blocked them to ensure that no one went outside. Then Dillon and Blake walked the entire room, looking in the interview room, the chief's office, his private bathroom, the squad room's bathroom.

Blake winced as he passed Grant's cell. The man looked absolutely stricken. And he had a good right to be.

They returned to the director.

"The mole has to be Stacy Bell," Blake said. "But she's gone. She must have snuck out when we were confronting Grant."

The director briefly closed his eyes as if in pain. "When I was confronting Grant, you mean. I was so angry with him that I didn't secure the scene first. I should have posted someone at the doors. I should have—" He frowned. "What's that noise?"

The distinctive squawking of someone talking through a police radio sounded from a few desks over. Dillon and Blake cleared a path. Donna was sitting at the end of the second row, her handheld radio unit sitting on top of the desk, the sound turned up. It was plugged into one of the mobile switchboards the 911 operators used.

"Go ahead, Billy," she said. "Say that again?"

The room grew silent as everyone tried to figure out what was going on.

"I said no one's been down Brook Hollow Road all day," the voice came through the speaker. "I've been out here fishing. I would have noticed. The cars scare the fish."

"Okay, Billy. That takes care of all the routes north of town. Thanks."

"Anytime, Donna."

She punched some buttons on the mobile switchboard.

"Hello?" a woman's voice came through the radio speakers.

"Molly, hey, it's Officer Waters. I've got a situation here. A missing woman, about five foot four, brunette. She's not from around here and might be lost. She's probably driving a blue Toyota Corolla, late model. Have you seen anything like that in the past hour out your way?"

The director shook his head. "What is she doing?"

Blake grinned. Leave it to Donna to get the logistics of what Stacy might be driving and get to work to try to find her while the rest of them were still standing around, pondering their next steps.

"She's initiated a call tree," Blake said, unable to keep the pride out of his voice.

"A call what?"

"A call tree. It's Donna's version of an AMBER Alert, or a BOLO. But much more effective. Trust me. I know firsthand." He crossed his arms, smiling as he watched her.

The director didn't seem impressed. He motioned to another one of his men. "Get a team together. We need to organize roadblocks and get some volunteers out here to help us look…"

Blake tuned the director out and waited for Donna to work her magic.

Dillon stood beside him. "Firsthand, huh?"

"Long story."

"You can tell me about it later. Detective."

Blake shot him a surprised look. "Does that mean what I think it means?"

"I'm sure I don't know what you're asking. I never fired anyone, no matter what you might have heard."

"What about the chief, and the mayor? Grant told me that—"

"Leave the mayor to me." It was the chief this time who spoke from behind them. "Knowledge is power, and I've been around this town long enough to have plenty of knowledge. Don't you worry about your job, Blake. It's here for you. If you want it."

Blake smiled, and couldn't help looking at Donna, and what he hoped having his job back could mean as he replied, "Thanks. I do. Very much." He cleared his throat and looked at the chief. "That is, if the rule about officers not being allowed to fraternize with each other can be lifted."

The chief followed Blake's gaze to Donna and grinned. "I'm sure I can arrange that."

Dillon clasped Blake on the shoulder. "We'll be glad to have you on the team again. From what I've seen, you've learned a heck of a lot more about teamwork over the past week than I ever tried to teach you. Great job. And thanks for sending Ashley and the others into hiding, keeping them safe. Donna told me about that while you and the director were talking during the drive here. I imagine Ashley's keeping an eye on the news. As soon as the media gets a hold of this, and she hears we're safe, they'll all be back in town. I can't wait to see her again. And my little girl. It's been way too long since I held them in my arms."

Blake wrinkled his nose. "You might want to shower first."

Dillon gave him a good-natured shove.

"I heard we're down a man," a deep voice said behind them.

Dillon and Blake turned to see their former SWAT teammate who'd moved away when he'd gotten married, Colby Vale. His eyes were red-rimmed. Max and Chris flanked his sides, having obviously relinquished their door guarding duties to someone else.

Dillon grabbed Colby's shoulder and hauled him in for a hug that should have cracked his ribs.

Colby tightened his arms around Dillon, his eyes looking suspiciously wet when they broke apart. "I'm so sorry about Randy." His voice sounded raw.

"I know." Dillon grasped his shoulder again. "We all are."

"I've got it," Donna called out, jumping to her feet

and waving a piece of paper. "I've got Stacy Bell's location." She read the address out loud.

Dillon exchanged a startled look with the rest of the team.

"What?" Blake asked. "You know that address?"

"You could say that." Dillon's face looked grim. "It was before your time, before you joined the team."

"Mind if I tag along?" Colby asked. "It would be my honor, for Randy."

Dillon nodded as Donna joined them. They all stood in a circle, and Dillon put his hand in the middle. "For Randy."

Max followed, placing his hand on top of Dillon's. "For Randy."

"For Randy," Chris said, slapping his hand down on theirs.

The chorus continued until all six of them—Dillon, Chris, Max, Colby, Blake and Donna—had joined hands in the middle. Then the chief leaned in, tears unabashedly flowing down his cheeks as he placed his hand on top. "For Randy."

"Gear up, team," Dillon ordered. "Destiny, Tennessee, SWAT has a job to do."

Chapter Eighteen

Blake crouched beside Dillon beneath the window, cradling his assault rifle. He and the rest of the six-person SWAT team waited for the green light to begin the rescue operation in the one-story office building of Gibson and Gibson Financial Services.

Once again, the team stood ready, in the same spot where they'd rescued Ashley a few years earlier at a workplace shooting. Or so they'd told Blake on the way over here. That original mission was referred to as Tennessee Takedown.

But today, they were there to rescue someone else—a mother and her two teenage daughters. And the team had a brand-new member—Blake, who finally, for the first time, felt like he really belonged. Randy was there, too, in spirit. And they were all anxious to get inside and do their job.

Beside Dillon, his friend since childhood, Chris Downing, watched the screen on his wristband, showing surveillance from the tiny scope he'd raised up to the window.

"Casualty at three o'clock," he whispered into the tiny mic attached to his helmet. "Appears to be the security guard. No sign of anyone else."

The building had been abandoned since the shooting that had nearly claimed Ashley's life. The owner of the building had told them that there was one guard who kept an eye on the place, until he could find a buyer. The chief had asked the owner to try to contact the guard to warn him. But he couldn't get through, even though he'd called a dozen times. Now they knew why.

Blake's earpiece crackled, and the chief's voice came on the line. "Witness says there might be two shooters—Special Agent Stacy Bell and one other, possibly the man assigned by Sanchez to watch the family. No descriptions of weapons. Be extra vigilant."

"Do we have the go-ahead to move in?" Blake asked, inching closer to the door.

Dillon arched a brow and spoke into the mic. "Chief?"

Thornton practically growled through the headset. "Like you're going to follow my orders either way? Just handle it, Dillon."

Dillon grinned, as did the rest of the team. Donna laughed.

Blake stared at her, wondering if she and the others had gone crazy. "Is there something I should know about?"

"Inside joke," Donna said.

Blake tightened his hold on his gun, and wondered if maybe he'd been wrong earlier in thinking he was part of the team now.

"Blake?" Donna said. "We ignored Thornton's direct orders the last time we were crouched under this very window. That's why I laughed. That's why everyone was smiling, and Thornton sounds like a grumpy bear."

"Don't push me, Officer Waters," Thornton growled again through the headset.

Donna grinned and winked at Blake.

That wink was like a jolt of electricity, shooting straight through his body, warming him from the inside out. It blasted away his doubts, and it had him wanting more than ever to finally get Donna alone and tell her all the things that had been going through his head since the moment he realized that he wasn't leaving Destiny. Or, at least, he didn't want to. But Donna was the one who would be deciding his fate.

Whether she realized it or not.

Chris tapped Dillon's shoulder. "Movement on the east corner," he whispered. "Appears to be a civilian. Belly-crawling toward the exit. I think it's one of the daughters."

"Is she hurt?" Dillon's questioning gaze drilled into Chris.

"Negative. I don't see any signs of injuries." He smiled. "Not like last time, huh?"

Relief flashed across Dillon's face. "Not so far. Let's do this. Let's bring these people home. No casualties today, team. You got that? I don't want anyone hurt but the bad guys. And not even them if we can help it." He motioned to Blake.

Blake jerked the door open, and the team rushed inside, two by two, pausing just past the doorway as they scanned the expansive rows of cubicles with their rifles.

Dillon pointed to the young girl who'd frozen in place when they ran inside, her eyes wide with hope and fear at the same time. Colby stood guard, watching over the girl while Max scooped her up in his arms and ran with her outside.

One safe. Two to go.

Dillon gave Donna and Blake a signal to search the

west side of the building while he and Chris headed east. Colby and Max would back all of them up, helping where needed and ensuring that no one but Mrs. Grant and her remaining daughter escaped their net.

The building formed a rectangle with rows of six-foot-high cubicle walls, divided in the middle by a line of glassed-in offices, bathrooms and conference rooms. Solid walls acted as firebreaks every twenty feet. The two teams would have to search and clear each section in a grid pattern before moving to the next.

Blake and Donna had just stepped down one of the aisles when a scratching sound whispered through the wall one aisle over. They both crouched down, as if the move had been choreographed. Which, if he thought about it, had been. All of their training had embedded itself as muscle memory. They worked seamlessly together, each of them knowing what the other was thinking, what they needed to do next. And everything was going like clockwork.

Until now.

Because the next logical step in the plan was for her to wait at one end of the aisle, while he crept to the other end. Then they would converge in a flanking maneuver and confront whoever was in the next aisle. That was their training. That was what they should do.

But he couldn't.

This past week, they'd shared everything a man and woman could share—their hopes, their fears, their minds…their bodies. They'd become one in every sense of the word. And then they'd run down a tunnel to save their friends, a perfect team, and had saved them all.

But he hadn't saved her. He hadn't saved Donna.

It had always been his belief that if they ever got in

a tight spot, between her skills and his, the bad guys would have no chance. And that if she ever faltered, he'd be there to protect her, to keep her safe.

But he hadn't been.

That fateful moment during the shoot-out, it had been Lopez—not Blake—who'd made the kill shot that had saved Donna's life. He'd been running on adrenaline ever since, never slowing down enough to process what had happened. But it all caught up to him now, and he knew, he couldn't do it. He couldn't let the woman he loved round that corner, run into the next aisle, into danger. Because he was no longer certain that he could protect her. And that knowledge had his hands shaking, his palms sweating inside his gloves, his vision tunneling down to dark spots.

He couldn't do this.

He couldn't send her into danger and hope that she would be okay. The very idea was insanity.

He just couldn't.

Breathe. Her lips moved, forming the silent word. Her beautiful face wavered in his vision.

Breathe.

His lungs burned.

Breathe.

Air suddenly rushed in. The darkness began to fade. He drew another gulp of air. Then another.

She smiled and gave him the thumbs-up sign.

He tried to smile back but wasn't sure he'd managed more than a grimace.

Everything came into sharp focus now. The scratching noise sounded again, from farther up the aisle. Like fabric scuffing against carpet. Whoever was in the next aisle was moving, crawling. Friend or foe? There was no way to know.

Donna motioned for him to stay. Then she signaled that she would head to the next aisle. Alone.

She crept back a step, toward the mouth of the aisle.

He grabbed her arm, stopping her.

She arched a brow in question.

I love you. He silently mouthed the words.

I know, she mouthed back. Then she grinned and gave him an outrageous wink.

The tightness in his chest eased. He wanted to laugh with joy. He wanted to grab her in his arms and crush her to him, never let her go. But that could wait. It would have to. Because this amazing, smart, strong, capable woman loved him. She'd told him that with actions, if not words. And that gave him the strength to see past his fear, to trust her, trust himself and face whatever might lie ahead.

Because he sure as hell wasn't going to let her face it alone.

He motioned for her to wait, and he crept down the long aisle to the other end. When they were both in position, he held up three fingers, counting down.

Three.

Two.

One.

They both rushed around the wall of cubicles into the next aisle. A young girl, the second daughter, backed up against the wall, her eyes wide with terror.

Blake jerked his gun to the side, while Donna hurried to her and murmured low words, soothing her.

"Second daughter located," Blake whispered into the mic, and gave the location. Moments later, Max was there, scooping the girl up in his arms, while Chris watched over them. Then they were gone, hustling her out of the building.

The mic crackled. Dillon announced that they'd taken down Sanchez's man, who'd been guarding Grant's family. Colby had him handcuffed, with leg shackles to be extra safe, and was taking him out of the building.

"One more bad guy—or bad girl—to go," Dillon announced.

"Maybe, maybe not," Blake warned, having learned from the paint ball exercise. "Be alert. There could be others."

"Noted," Dillon's voice crackled through the mic.

Donna smiled at Blake and made a rolling motion with her hand. Together, as a team, they headed into the next aisle.

In the end, it was Dillon who captured Stacy Bell, without incident. Donna and Blake were there, backing him up. As a team, they surrounded her, took her into custody with no shots fired, and escorted a nearly hysterical Mrs. Grant out of the building, unharmed. As soon as she saw her two daughters waiting near an ambulance, she let out a heartbreaking sob and ran to them. The little family huddled together, crying, but smiling through their tears, because everything was going to be okay.

Chapter Nineteen

Donna leaned against the railing of Chris Downing's back deck, unable to keep from smiling as she watched her fellow SWAT teammates and their wives, all together, once again. Minus Randy, of course. But he would always be there, in their hearts. And his mother, barely a month after Randy's funeral, was with them, too. She'd become a part of their extended family. And she was smiling and seemed to be enjoying herself, at Chris's expense, offering him tips about how to grill the perfect steak, tips Donna was quite certain he didn't want, since he considered himself a master at cooking out.

Over the top of Mrs. Carter's head, Chris gave her a suffering look, silently pleading with her to save him. She grinned and shook her head. Because she knew he didn't really want to be saved. He was a softy inside, like all the big, tough SWAT team members. Besides, if he really needed saving, his wife, Julie, would take care of it. She was inside the kitchen right now, readying some corncobs to put on the grill.

Ashley was on the other side of the grill, bouncing her toddler daughter on her hip, laughing about something Dillon had just whispered in her ear. The man was truly smitten with both his wife and his daughter.

Seeing them together always surprised and delighted Donna, because Ashley drew out the joy and laughter, the softness inside Dillon that he normally kept hidden under a tough, macho-guy exterior.

Much like Blake.

She sighed as she watched him near the deck steps, appearing to be truly fascinated by the gardening wisdom of Claire, the chief's wife, as she told him how to grow the biggest, juiciest tomatoes, and how to know if a watermelon was truly ripe and sweet. Then again, maybe he wasn't pretending. It had taken Donna months to see past that brooding, serious, intimidating persona he tended to use as his shield against the world. But now that she did, she realized just how sweet, caring and wonderful he truly was.

Blake Sullivan was a marshmallow inside.

He cared deeply about others, and what they thought. Sometimes he cared a little too much, which had led to him getting hurt too many times. So he had a habit of putting up walls to protect himself, to hide his true emotions, his fears, his insecurities. Which was why he seemed so prickly to those who didn't really get to know him. But once they did, once they were through that wall, the rewards were endless.

Oh, there'd been some rough moments between them, particularly after the rescue operation where they'd saved Grant's family. All those fears and insecurities had reared their ugly head. Blake had suffered his first-ever panic attack inside that building, and had been mortified that she'd been there to witness it. But knowing the reason for it, that he'd been terrified that she might get hurt, had pushed her over the edge she'd been clinging to—that emotional edge, wavering between an intense infatuation and full-blown love. Letting go and falling to the other side had been the best decision she'd ever made.

Of course, they'd both had to report to Dillon that Blake had suffered that panic attack. After all, if it happened once, it could happen again. Which of course could be extremely dangerous for all of them in their line of work. But Dillon was being supportive, because he too had grown to see the value in Blake, as both a member of their team and as a friend. And they would face the difficulties together, and if necessary, make some difficult decisions. Like whether the panic attack was actually part of a larger problem—PTSD—that Blake had been ignoring since his military days.

His military days.

Turned out, there was a whole lot of baggage buried in his past, baggage he'd only just begun to open up about, in little pieces. Frightening, dark little pieces that made her want to weep for what he'd endured. And gave her a whole new level of understanding for why he'd put up those walls of his and why he was consumed with wanting to protect people, especially her.

Oh, how she loved this man.

He looked over the top of Claire's head and smiled at her. Not the suffering kind of smile Chris had given her, but a true, I'm-loving-talking-to-this-wise-woman kind of smile. He was enjoying life, his new friends, his team. And her.

She smiled back, her heart nearly bursting from joy.

"Get a room, will ya?" Max's wife, Bex, joined her by the railing. "I swear, I've never seen a couple exchange more puppy dog looks between them."

"Uh-huh. Like you and Max aren't sickeningly sweet."

Bex sighed and stared off into the backyard where Max was talking animatedly with Colby and his new wife, Piper. "Love is in the air, I guess. Who'd have thought the entire SWAT team would end up head over heels in love like this? We're all turning into our parents."

"Is that such a bad thing?"

Bex smiled as she watched her own husband. "No, I guess it's not. Hey, did you ever hear the resolution of the FBI's investigation into Grant's actions?"

"I think the investigation is still ongoing. But Grant is cooperating, taking full responsibility for everything that happened. He's so happy to have his family safe and sound, that I don't think he even cares what happens to him."

"It's kind of sad, isn't it?" Bex said. "I'd like to think I wouldn't have done what he did. But, honestly, if Max was in danger, there's probably nothing I wouldn't do, no line I wouldn't cross, if it meant saving his life."

Donna nodded. "I know what you mean. But I'm still not at the forgive-and-forget stage. It still hurts too much. I miss Randy."

"We all do. But the pain will fade in time. Life must go on." Bex kissed her cheek. "I'd better go rescue Piper. She's new to our extended family and looks bored to death over whatever Colby and Max are discussing. I wouldn't want to scare her away. She might not ever come back when Colby comes to visit."

She headed off to save her new friend.

Blake caught Donna's attention and motioned for her to join him. The chief and his wife were over by the grill now, setting up mouthwatering side dishes on a little table, leaving Blake alone. Finally.

She hurried to him, delighted when he leaned down and kissed her full on the lips.

"What was that for?" she breathed, clinging to him.

"Just because."

He checked his watch, which he'd done several times this afternoon. She was about to ask him why he kept checking it when Chris called out that the steaks were ready.

Blake checked his watch again.

"Is something wrong?" she asked, as they moved to the side to let others head up on the deck to get their food.

"Yes and no. I hate to ask, but would you mind skipping the steaks? At least for now. We can come back later. I'm sure Chris will save us some leftovers. There's something I want to show you. And it really can't wait."

Disappointment slashed through her. She'd been thoroughly enjoying the cookout, seeing all her teammates and their families. But the excitement in Blake's tone told her this was important to him. So she smiled and put her hand in his.

"How long will this take?" she asked. "Should I grab my purse from inside?"

"Not long. We can come back and get it." He tugged her with him through the yard, toward the front of the house.

Everyone waved goodbye. None of them seemed surprised that they were leaving.

"Blake? What's going on?" she asked.

"You'll see."

Twenty minutes later, they were on the other side of town, sitting in Blake's truck, just off a two-lane rural highway. Tall oak trees shaded them and partially obscured them from view. A faded billboard sat opposite them on the other side of the road, advertising the best burgers in town at Eva-Marie's Diner on Magnolia Street, catty-corner from the Piggly Wiggly. A claim Donna had to admit was true. They did have the best cheeseburgers she'd ever tasted.

Blake checked his watch again.

"Blake? Will you please tell me why we're here, and why you keep checking your watch?"

"Wait one more minute. Just watch the highway."

She let out a frustrated breath and crossed her arms. The love of her life was trying to bore her to death, if she didn't die of frustration first. "I'm watching. What's going to happen next? Is a chicken going to cross the road? Are we going to find out the answer to the age-old question of why?"

He grinned, then pulled her close and kissed her so deeply, so passionately, that she practically slid into a boneless puddle when he let her go.

Maybe she should complain more often.

She was about to do that very thing, and see if it gained her another kiss, when he straightened in his seat.

"Watch," he said, sounding as excited as a little kid.

A red convertible came into view, barreling down the highway toward them with its top down, obviously going well above the speed limit. As it got closer, Donna recognized the woman at the wheel. The mayor's wife. The same woman who'd sped through a school zone, endangering children. The same woman who'd pushed the mayor into firing both her and Blake when Grant was running things.

"Where's a traffic cop when you need one?" she muttered.

"Funny you should say that."

The car sped past them.

A motorcycle cop zipped out from behind the Eva-Marie Diner billboard and raced down the highway after the little red convertible, lights flashing and siren blaring. A few seconds later, both were pulled over on the side of the road, and the motorcycle cop was walking up to the mayor's wife's car door.

Donna sat bolt upright in her seat. "You didn't."

"I did." He was grinning so hard his cheeks had to hurt. "I asked around, found out she speeds down this road every Sunday, oblivious of anyone else who might be out for a Sunday drive. I figured it might be time to teach her the perils of speeding through Blount County. We don't put up with that stuff around here."

She grinned. "Thank you."

"You're welcome."

This time, she was the one who kissed him. She held nothing back. She told him she loved him in every touch, every slide of her hands through his hair, in the way she clung to him, half on his lap. She didn't think she could ever get enough of him. And the way he kissed her back, she knew he felt the same.

When they broke apart, their breathing choppy, pulses slamming in their veins, he shakily pushed her back onto her side of the seat and fastened her seat belt. His hands were still shaking when he fastened his. He put the truck in Drive and gave her a long, lingering look.

"Do you want to go watch Officer Lynch give the mayor's wife a ticket?"

She slowly shook her head. "I think my vendetta against the mayor's wife is over. She's in my past. You're my future. Take me home, Blake. Take me home to Destiny."

"I love you," he said, his voice husky. "You know that, right?"

She took his hand in hers and rested them together on the seat between them. "I know. I love you, too. Let's get out of here before that cop has to turn around and give us a ticket for indecent exposure." She unbuttoned the top button on her shirt.

Blake's eyes widened. He slammed the gas. The truck peeled out onto the highway, in the opposite direction of the little drama playing out behind them. Donna could practically feel the mayor's wife's glare burning into the back of her head, no doubt knowing exactly who had orchestrated her getting a ticket today. But none of that mattered. Not really.

What mattered was that Donna had wonderful friends and a family that made her life whole.

What mattered was the man beside her, a brave, strong, wonderful man, who understood her, both her strengths and her weaknesses, and reveled in them.

What mattered, above all else, was that no matter how hard life got, she would never be alone. Because she had Blake, the love of her life, her destiny.

* * * * *

MAJOR CRIMES

JANIE CROUCH

This book is dedicated to Hayley, aka "Mandy". How blessed I am to still have you in my life all these years later. We may be continents apart (I move to one…you move to another) but I treasure your friendship and the memories we have. To Mandy, love Mittie. xx

Prologue

Omega Sector agent Cain Bennett sat in the back row of a Georgia courthouse waiting for the judge to come in and sentence the woman Cain had loved since he was sixteen years old.

Hayley Green, the woman Cain had arrested.

He scrubbed a hand over his face, then leaned forward to rest the weight of his forearms on his knees. Hayley currently sat ramrod straight at the table directly in front of the judge's bench, in a Fulton County orange jumpsuit, her straight blond hair in a ponytail behind her. She was obviously ignoring the whispers from the crowd that was here to see her sentenced. Press, government figures, even some people from their small Georgia hometown who wanted to be able to report the gossip live filled the room.

You would think she was about to be sentenced for murder rather than computer hacking.

He still hadn't figured out why Hayley chose to use her ninja-like computer skills illegally, to hack the College Entrance Test—CET—system. The exam, which allowed students to get their results back instantly rather than having to wait months like previous standardized tests, was supposed to be unhackable. Questions completely random.

Hayley and her cohorts had figured out not how to hack the test, but how to build false exams into the system. Ones that the system thought were real and that gave the students who "took" them real scores and credit.

Rich students were willing to pay handsomely for these false exams and scores, which would, in essence, assure their acceptance into any college they desired. A pretty nifty scam when it was all said and done. But why she had done it, Cain had no idea. The girl he'd known in high school would never have.

And Hayley sure as hell wasn't going to offer any reasons why to Cain. She was refusing to talk to him at all.

He gritted his teeth in a constant tension he'd lived with for the past several months. Yes, he'd reignited his relationship with Hayley because of the hacking case.

But because he'd thought she might be able to put him in contact with some of the hackers, not because he thought *she* was one of them.

But to her it just looked like he'd slept with her as part of some damn sting operation.

Cain looked up at Hayley's still, stiff form in the chair. God, he'd made a mess of things. She had, too. Why the hell had she been hacking? Become a criminal? She knew he'd dedicated his life to law enforcement. Choosing to break the law was like a slap in the face after what they'd once shared.

But hopefully the judge would take into consideration that Hayley had no prior convictions, no arrests. She'd pleaded no contest in order to not drag out the case and cost taxpayers thousands of dollars in a trial. Cain, as the agent who had been in charge of the investigation, had petitioned for no jail time for Hayley.

Parole with limited computer usage, definitely. But Hayley wasn't dangerous. Had no intent to harm others. Time already served would be a perfect sentence for her.

She might not like it, but Cain planned to be a lot more present in her life. He'd been wrong to let them grow so far apart as he'd gone to college, then the FBI training academy, before joining Omega Sector. They'd talked via social media and email, but he obviously had not been privy to what was really going on in her life. Aka: criminal activities.

That would stop now.

The judge would release her today, and tomorrow Cain would begin to bulldoze his way back into her life. She'd be mad—hell, so was he—but they would work through it. They had too much history, too much passion, too much *rightness* to be without each other for long. Hayley Green was his, the same way he was hers. They had been for over ten years.

Beginning tomorrow, he was going to make sure his little felon had her own law enforcement agent keeping her on the straight and narrow. Cain smiled slightly. It wouldn't be easy, but she was worth it. *They* were worth it.

The bailiff announced for all to rise as the judge entered the courtroom. Everyone sat back down as the judge asked Hayley to stand.

Cain listened as the judge spoke to Hayley about computer crimes, although not violent, not being victimless. He grew more tense as the judge pointed out that she'd stolen not just from the company that developed and ran the CET, but from students around the country who had missed out on the opportunity of college acceptance and scholarship because of the test results she had sold for money.

Bile began to burn at the back of his throat when the judge said that Hayley had not just hacked computers, she had stolen futures.

This was not good.

"Today," the judge continued, "I feel that it is important to set an example. To show that people like you, Ms. Green—young, intelligent, able to work—will be held to strict standards when you choose to break the law. To discourage others from making the same choices."

Cain wanted to stand up. Stop time. Do *something*. Because the next words to come out of the judge's mouth were going to alter Cain's entire world.

He couldn't imagine what they were going to do to Hayley's.

"Hayley Green, you have pleaded nolo contendere to a charge of first-degree computer crimes, which is a class B felony, with a sentence of up to twenty years in prison. This court hereby sentences you to ten years at the Georgia Women's Correctional Institution, Minimum Security Campus, eligible for parole not before four years."

Cain saw Hayley's body jerk as the gavel came down against the sound block on the judge's bench. The judge said a few more things and then court was dismissed.

Cain couldn't believe what he'd just heard. Feeling like all the oxygen had been sucked from the room, he stared at Hayley, still standing stiffly at the table as her lawyer murmured something in her ear. Hayley's cousin

Ariel, the only family present, was crying softly in the row behind her.

Four years. Hayley would spend at least four years in prison.

And Cain had sent her there.

People began filing out around him, but Cain couldn't force himself to move. Couldn't stop looking at Hayley. Couldn't figure out how to make this right.

Things would never be right again.

An officer came over to her and asked her to move to the other side of the table so he could handcuff her. She did, moving slowly, like she was in shock. Which she had to be.

Four years.

As the officer turned her so he could cuff her, Hayley's eyes met Cain's. He took a step toward her, unable to help himself.

He expected tears, or terror, or even hatred to light her eyes as she looked at him, skin across her cheekbones pale and drawn.

But her eyes were dead, emotionless. She looked at him as though he were a stranger.

Then she turned from him completely and was led away.

Chapter One

Four years later

Cain often dealt with the worst of humanity as part of the Omega Sector Protection and Recovery Division.

Crisis management and bodyguarding were a regular part of his job. He and his team also dealt with hijackers and kidnappers on a regular basis.

But his mission right now was to rescue not a person, but the entire Critical Response Division of Omega, which was being hijacked in its own way.

They had a psychopath on their hands, set on destroying the team one by one—by killing their loved ones. And someone on the inside was helping the madman in his quest.

Cain was currently watching a video of Damien Freihof—said psychopath—who had slit the throat of Omega psychiatrist Grace Parker last week.

Freihof and his cohort within Omega Sector had decided it would be fun to send the murder as a live feed to all active Omega Sector agents—forcing them to watch as Dr. Parker died without them being able to step in and do anything about it.

So now Cain was able to watch it over and over.

Watch as Grace's eyes dulled in death. Watch as Freihof's eyes had filled with something akin to joy as the doctor—a beautiful woman in her fifties, and an integral part of the Omega team—died sitting right in front of him.

Freihof had made it no secret that he wanted Omega Sector's Critical Response Division to pay for the death of his wife, Natalie, years ago. That he blamed the elite law enforcement task group for her untimely demise in a bank hostage situation.

He was determined they would feel the pain of losing loved ones like he had.

Grace Parker had been just one of those loved ones Freihof had gone after. For the past five months he'd been the mastermind behind attacks on nearly a dozen Omega Sector agents or their friends and family. Grace had died last week. Two other Omega agents were in the hospital after an explosion.

And Freihof was reveling in it all.

Freihof had to be stopped. But just as importantly, the mole inside Omega—the one who was feeding Freihof information that was allowing him to be so successful in his attacks—had to be stopped. Steve Drackett, director of the Critical Response team, was unsure who could be trusted.

That's why Cain was here, brought from a different division of Omega, to help catch this traitor.

Cain watched the death of Grace Parker again, hoping to notice something this time that maybe he'd missed before. He hadn't personally known the woman, which allowed him to look at the footage more objectively, see things others—people who had cared deeply about the psychiatrist—might miss.

Cain was known for his ability to separate emotion from the job. It was how he'd risen to assistant director of Omega's Protection and Recovery Division when he'd barely reached his thirtieth birthday.

Because he got the job done, no matter what.

He'd proven that four years ago.

Cain studied the footage again, pushing all thoughts of Hayley Green aside. Right now he needed to understand as much as he could about Damien Freihof. Because anything Cain could find out about him would hopefully lead to information about the mole.

In a way—as psychotic as Freihof was—he was easier to understand. The man wanted vengeance. Sure, he may want vengeance for something that Omega Sector wasn't actually responsible for, but at least his motives were clear.

What did the traitor want?

There couldn't be much money involved in helping Freihof. Maybe a little, but not the sort of big payoff someone was usually looking for in order to risk their reputation and/or life.

That left a lot of other factors. It could also be vengeance; maybe Freihof had found a kindred spirit also looking for some sort of revenge for something Omega had done. Maybe the person had a desire for control, or was some sort of political zealot, planning to bring down Omega Sector from the beginning.

Or maybe Freihof had control over the man—or woman—and was blackmailing him or her in some way.

The motive didn't really matter to Cain in terms of justifying why the traitor was behaving the way he was, but understanding motive always provided information in an unknown suspect.

Cain sat in a private conference room attached to Steve Drackett's office. It was one of the few places Steve had assured him there was no way the mole could have any type of surveillance devices.

While Cain trusted Steve completely, he wasn't leaving anything to chance. Cain had his own countersurveillance device that allowed him to know for certain that no one was recording or transmitting visual or audio data from this room.

Files of every employee—agent or not—of the Critical Response Division sat in groups on the large conference table. Cain had already been in this room for more than eight hours going through the files.

He had four distinct groups: cleared, unlikely, unknown and suspicious.

People like Steve Drackett, whom Cain had known for years and who had spent most of his life fighting people like Freihof, were in the cleared category. Other agents also, like the various members of the Omega SWAT team who had been injured or nearly killed by Freihof over the last few months. Employees who had joined Omega very recently were also cleared, as well as those who had no access to the type of information that had been given to Freihof.

But that still left a hell of a lot of people in the unlikely, unknown or suspicious categories.

Long-term operatives and agents were in the unlikely category. Cain rubbed the back of his neck as he walked around the table looking at the files. The thought of the culprit being a colleague who had been involved with Omega Sector for years churned like acid in his gut. He drowned those thoughts by taking a swig from his now-cold coffee mug, the only substance he'd had today. He wanted to move these agents to the cleared list, but he couldn't.

Emotion had no place in solving crimes. No matter how much Cain wanted someone to be innocent, he knew firsthand that wasn't always how things panned out.

He looked through all the unknown files again. People with a background in computers who would be able to get Freihof the information he wanted without being detected. The one thing they knew for sure was the traitor was highly skilled in computer usage.

But a number of people were skilled in that area. Even people who had jobs not involving computers or intel could still have the prowess needed to be the mole.

Cain picked up a file for John Carnell. The guy was a genius; his damn mind worked like a computer. Abrupt and sullen, he was often difficult to work with, but almost always the smartest person in the room.

Cain slid Carnell's file from the unknown to the suspicious pile. There it joined half a dozen others. Two from people who had filed complaints with the head Omega office in Washington, DC, when they were bypassed for promotions—maybe one of them had an ax to grind and had become the mole. SWAT wannabe Saul Poniard's file was also in the pile; he had such a perfect record that it bugged Cain.

And Lillian Muir, a member of the SWAT team. Cain didn't like putting her name in the suspicious pile, especially since she'd been one of the people injured in an explosion a few days ago at Freihof's last known place of residence. A wooden projectile had lodged itself in her shoulder. A painful but non-life-threatening injury.

But Cain could not deny that Lillian's past—and how well hidden she'd kept it—made her a suspect. Someone who had gone to the lengths she had to hide her past was someone who had something to lose.

When Steve Drackett walked in the door, Cain slid Lillian's file under another one. He knew Steve was too emotionally involved with his inner team to objectively consider the possibility that one of them was the traitor.

"How's it going in here?" Steve asked.

"I'll admit, I'd rather be out enjoying your beautiful Colorado mountains than stuck inside this window-less room."

Steve clapped him on the shoulder. "I keep saying you need to transfer from the DC office out here. Quality-of-life clause." Steve's eyes flew to the screen where Cain had paused the recording of Grace Parker's death.

Cain walked over and shut it off. Steve had seen the murder footage enough times; he didn't need to see it again. Steve gestured toward the files on the table. "Any luck?"

"I have my theories. My categories of suspects. I have to be honest with you, Steve, it's probably better if you just don't even know who I'm really looking into."

Cain wouldn't tell him anyway, but he hoped the other man wouldn't ask. Cain respected Steve, had known him for a lot of years. He didn't want to let this drive a wedge—professional or personal—between them.

But he would if it meant catching the mole.

Steve rolled tense shoulders. "I don't like it, I'll be honest. But I like even less the thought of a traitor walking among us every day. Of more of my agents getting hurt or killed."

"I know," Cain said softly. "We're going to get him, Steve. Get them. Freihof and whoever this mole is."

"Do you have any particular direction you're following?"

"Some. Based on profiling and what might be considered suspicious activities. Or even particular skill sets. But what's really going to help me catch this person is the computer stuff."

"That's why you're going to Hayley Green."

He could still see the way she'd looked at him that day in the courtroom. How dead her eyes had been. That had been the last time he'd seen her. He'd tried to visit her multiple times the first year she'd gone to prison, but she'd always refused to have anything to do with him. So then he'd stopped trying.

Although he'd never stopped thinking about her.

"I don't have the skills to find this person, but she does."

Steve's eyebrow raised. "You know Hayley is a convicted felon. You made sure of that."

His gut tightened at the thought, like it did every time. "But she's also the best at hacking a computer system."

"Are you sure she will help you?"

Hayley had been paroled four months ago. Cain knew the exact date she'd gotten out. He'd been surprised when she moved back to Gainesville, Georgia, upon release. The place she always said she wanted to get away from.

They both had wanted to get away from it. Heaven knew they had spent enough time during their relationship in high school talking about getting out. But maybe she had decided that familiar was better.

"Cain?" Steve repeated. "Are you sure that Hayley will help you? After everything that happened?"

Cain forced himself to release the tension in his shoulders. "Hayley was guilty. She's now out of prison and I'm sure she's ready to move on."

"But moving on and helping the man who put her in prison are two different things."

Helping the man who used his relationship with her to put her in prison.

Steve didn't say the words, but he didn't have to. Both of them were thinking it; Steve had known Cain when it happened. They both knew that was much more difficult to move on from.

Cain ignored it. He'd done what he had to do four years ago, even though it had gutted him. But the law had been on his side. He tried to remember that.

And he'd had no idea the judge would be so hard in his sentencing of Hayley. But that hadn't changed the fact that she was guilty.

"Don't worry, I'll handle Hayley," Cain finally said. And he would. He couldn't believe that she wouldn't help him catch a murderer, no matter what had transpired between the two of them in the past.

"If you say so." Steve wisely didn't say anything further.

"I'm going to have to go completely dark from Omega." Cain began stacking files. Many of them would be coming with him to Georgia. "Hayley can't work anywhere within the Omega system."

"Completely dark?" Steve asked. "That could be dangerous. You won't have much backup if you need it."

"Until we know how deep this goes, have a better idea of who the mole is and what sort of capacity he or she has for obtaining information? I can't work within the Omega system. If this mole is as good as we think, he'll realize it if I'm inside."

The last thing either of them wanted to do was cause the traitor to go to ground. They'd never be able to catch him then. And that would make apprehending Freihof that much harder.

"The only people who will know what I'm doing will be you, Ren McClement in the DC office and me."

Steve nodded. They both wanted to trust more people but keeping this circle as small as possible was the best scenario. McClement worked in the highest levels of Omega Sector, bringing together multiple departments when needed. The man was all but a legend. Cain trusted Ren just as much as he trusted Steve.

With his life.

"You just be careful," Steve said. "Going dark can have some hard consequences."

"I'm willing to pay that price if it means we get this traitor out of our midst."

"I know you are." Steve studied him. "But sometimes we are not the only person to pay the price. Hayley might have been guilty of whatever crime she committed years ago, but dragging her into this could be even worse."

"Don't worry, I'll protect Hayley." Believe it or not, even if she couldn't see it, he'd always been trying to protect her. From the day he met her in high school until today. "I'll make sure it's cleared through the state so that she won't be violating her parole by helping us. I won't let anybody hurt her."

Steve moved toward the door, nodding. "I hope she sees it that way."

So did Cain.

Chapter Two

Hayley loaded the dirty dishes and wiped down the booth that had just been vacated by Bluewater Grill patrons. She slid along the soft gray leather of the seat to wipe a far corner of the table. She swiped at a few strands of dirty-blond hair that had escaped her long braid with the back of her hand, then hoped the moisture left on her forehead wasn't cleaning solution.

She almost moaned in relief at how good it felt to be off her feet for just a second as she wiped. It was two o'clock in the afternoon. She'd already been working six hours and still had another eight to go. Just like yesterday.

And the day before that.

It was the only way she could make ends meet when she earned only minimum wage. Less than that, actually. But she didn't argue, because at least she had a job.

Not many people were willing to hire a convicted felon, she'd found when she left the Georgia Women's Correctional Institution four months ago. She'd been fortunate that the restaurant she worked at in high school part-time, still owned by the same family and now managed by their son, Timothy Smittle, a high school classmate of Hayley's, had been willing to take a chance on her.

They hadn't let her wait tables, explaining that they couldn't allow an ex-felon to interact with customers or handle money. But Timothy had graciously offered to allow Hayley to bus the tables, wash dishes and clean the entire restaurant.

The same Timothy who was looking over at her now, eyebrow raised, since she was no longer wiping the table, just resting. Hayley quickly jumped up, not wanting to risk another lecture about how lucky she was to have a job at such a respectable establishment.

Hayley didn't think too hard about her future. About the fact that she was twenty-eight years old, had no college degree, was an ex-felon and would probably still be working fourteen-hour days at the Bluewater twenty years from now.

Or the fact that she might have to start running for her life as soon as she was legally able to access a computer.

As she carried the bus pan back to the dishwashing area—thankful that some customer had come in and cut Timothy off from the route that had led straight to her and a lecture—she tried to count her blessings.

As a part of her parole she wasn't allowed to go anywhere near a computer. The anklet she couldn't remove ensured she had no interaction with a computer that lasted longer than two minutes every six hours. Not even social media. Although maybe she could manage a tweet in under two minutes.

It was a prototype. She should probably feel honored that she was one of the first batch of cyber criminals it was being tested on. This was what happened when you were part of a high-profile crime that even grabbed the attention of US senators. Everybody wanted to make sure you didn't do it again.

Hayley had to admit her fingers itched for a keyboard. She yearned to get back into a world that involved no dishes or people like Smittle. She had a gift. When it came to computers and coding, she knew she had a gift.

Too bad she had let those gifts get her in trouble and cut her off from what could've been a very comfortable future. No one to blame but herself for that.

Well, maybe someone else to blame. But she didn't expect she would ever see Cain Bennett again, so there was no point in targeting any anger toward him.

She rubbed at an ache in the general vicinity of her heart at the thought of Cain. Then cursed herself not only for getting her shirt damp with her wet fingers, but for even thinking about him at all.

Plus, being away from computers was what was keeping her safe right now. As long as she couldn't go near a computer, she was not a threat to the people behind the situation that had led to her arrest and going to jail. Once they knew she could get near a computer and had the ability to trace their identities, Hayley had no doubt her life would become much more complicated.

But she couldn't touch a computer for another two years at least, so she would run screaming over that bridge when she got to it. She had more than enough trouble to deal with today.

Which led to her most important blessing. She could hear him entering the restaurant right now, even from the back.

"Mama Hay-lay!"

Hayley dried her hands on her apron and ripped it off, dropping it next to the dishwasher. She walked out into the front of the restaurant, strolling by Timothy without even pausing.

"I'm taking my hour break."

Timothy didn't argue. It was the one measure Hayley had demanded when she came to work here. That she would be given a break once a day, during the lull in the afternoon, when her cousin Ariel came by with little Mason.

Mason, Hayley's three-and-a-half-year-old son.

She grabbed Mason up in a hug, tickling him, breathing in his scent that meant so much to her, that calmed her and the tight spot inside her that grew whenever they were apart.

She and her son were together. They were both healthy, they were both happy, they were both free. A piece of paper signed while Hayley was in prison had made Ariel Mason's legal guardian hours after his birth, but her cousin had made sure that Mason always knew Hayley was his mom.

Hayley wrapped her arm around Ariel also. "Hey, coz. Thanks again."

Hayley knew it had to be difficult for Ariel to get Mason here every day. They were trying to figure out exactly how to transition him back from Ariel's care to Hayley's with as little trauma as possible for Mason.

"No problem. It's the best part of our day."

Hayley's cousin had been a godsend. Hayley honestly had no idea what she would've done if it hadn't been for Ariel's willingness to care for Mason while Hayley was still incarcerated. He'd be a ward of the state otherwise.

Because there was no way in hell she would've told

Cain he had a son. He'd made it very clear how little he thought of her when he'd used sex between them just to further his career by arresting her.

"It's raining outside, so do you want to go to the mall play area, champ?"

Little Mason nodded his head vigorously. "Yeah yeah yeah."

The drive to the mall took less than five minutes and soon they were watching Mason run around the enclosed area for children, made of soft foam material shaped like cars and rocket ships. It was one of Mason's favorite places to go.

Mason took after her—slender build, sandy-blond hair, and a zest for life that unfortunately had been driven out of her in prison. Hayley loved seeing the energy in Mason, and that energy fed her soul, especially on days when work seemed never ending.

"I know I sound like a broken record," Ariel said, taking a sip of the coffee she had picked up in the food court. "But you look exhausted."

Hayley rubbed her eyes and looked at the coffee with jealousy. She'd love to have the caffeine, but food court coffee was out of her budget. She didn't want to admit how good sitting down for an hour felt. "I'm okay, no need to worry."

"You're working twelve-to fourteen-hour days, six days a week. You can't tell me that's not taking a toll."

"It's not forever. I just want to make sure I'm as financially situated as possible before you leave."

Ariel took a sip of her coffee and worked to avoid making eye contact with Hayley. "About that... I've been thinking that maybe now isn't the right time. There will be another fellowship next year."

"No!" Hayley's tone brooked no refusal. "You've given up three years of your life for Mason and me. It's time for you to go do what you really want."

That included a full scholarship to Oxford, studying medieval literature for her master's degree. It was what Ariel had dreamed about her whole life. She'd postponed that dream to take in Mason, but Hayley refused to let her cousin give up any more time than she already had.

Ariel leaned over until her head touched the side of Hayley's shoulder. "I haven't given up zilch. If anything, I've gained. Mason has been a blessing."

Hayley leaned her cheek against the top of Ariel's head. "I'm sure you didn't think that during middle-of-the-night feedings when he was a newborn."

Hayley tamped down the heartbreak she still felt at having missed that part of her son's life. The important thing was that Mason had been cared for by someone who loved him.

"You're working yourself to the bone to try to make money for when I'm gone. If I applied for next year's fellowship you'd be in a much better situation."

Hayley wasn't just trying to save up money for Ariel's absence, but she didn't want to burden her cousin with any of that.

"But we both know they're not going to offer it to you again if you turn them down this year." They both watched as Mason ran up over a foam bridge. He'd already met another little boy and girl and was giggling with them both as they ran.

"There are other places I can study. Closer to home, not across the ocean."

"Ariel, you've done your part. I don't know how I

would've survived without you. But you need to take care of yourself now. And Mason and I need to get to know each other, on our own. To become a mother and son."

Hayley had lived in the tiny apartment with Ariel and Mason since she'd gotten out of prison four months ago. Any hours she didn't spend working she spent with her son. And once Ariel left for Oxford, Hayley wouldn't be able to work these insane hours. Someone would need to be with Mason after day care, and Hayley planned to be that person.

So if she had to work herself nearly to death over the next two months to have enough money to get by while Ariel was gone, then she would damn well do that.

She would do whatever she had to in order to be able to live a normal life with her child.

"I know you don't like to talk about this, but what about contacting Mason's father?"

Hayley didn't even hesitate. "Not an option."

Ariel rolled her eyes. "You know I don't believe that nonsense about Mason's father being 'unknown' like you put on the birth certificate. There's no way you had some sort of one-night stand and didn't know the guy's name."

Hayley shrugged. "Yeah, well, we all make mistakes."

Cain Bennett had been hers.

All too soon it was time for Hayley to get back to the Bluewater. Ariel and Mason came inside to get Mason's normal scoop of Wednesday ice cream in the last few minutes Hayley had of her break.

Mason sat next to her in the booth and told about his friend he met at the play area.

"He came over and showed me his red car. Let me play with it," Mason said between bites.

Hayley reached over and kissed the top of his head. "Sounds like a pretty good friend you made there, buddy."

Mason moved on to talk about his favorite toys at preschool while Ariel and Hayley listened attentively.

Thank God Mason had taken to Hayley's presence in his life with such acceptance, that Ariel had constantly shown him pictures of Hayley and had referred to Hayley as his mom, had brought him for visitation in prison when she could. She and Ariel had done their best to make the transition natural and nondramatic. At first Hayley had just come over every day and gotten to know Mason. Two weeks later she moved in to the small apartment with them.

Hayley knew Mason loved her and that was all that mattered. When it came time for Ariel to go off to school it would be hard, but by then he would be even more comfortable with Hayley.

She saw Timothy looking over at her and then pointing at his watch. Hayley let out a sigh.

"Okeydoke guys, I've got to get back to work." Hayley stood up as Mason finished his last bite.

"I'm going to get this sugar-infested rug rat back home." Ariel smiled.

"I'll hopefully be getting off work at around seven thirty, so maybe I'll make it home in time for a bath and some book reading."

When Mason's face lit up at her words, Hayley knew she would do whatever necessary to make it happen.

"I love it when you read me books! The fire truck book! The big banana book! The green ham and eggs book!" He bounced up and down on the seat, and she knew if she'd allowed him to stand on it, he'd be jumping with his excitement.

"All of them, little man, I promise. Okay?" Hayley laughed and reached down and scooped Mason up in her arms, hugging him probably a little too tightly.

"You squeezeded me!" Mason squealed, but hugged her back.

He'd always hugged her back. Hayley was oh so grateful that he'd never turned away from her, even at the beginning. She'd like to think it was because it was his child's heart responding to her mother's heart.

But it was probably just because he was a good kid and didn't want to hurt her feelings.

Hayley set Mason on the ground after giving him a loud kiss. "Get the books out and be ready. I'll see you tonight."

She watched as Mason took Ariel's hand and they walked out the door.

"That was an hour and six minutes, Hayley." Timothy had made his way over while she watched them leave.

Hayley turned back to the table to pick up the glasses and silverware. "Don't worry, Timothy, I will make sure I get all my work done."

"I agreed to this break every day, but now I'm thinking you're trying to take advantage of it."

Hayley managed to refrain from rolling her eyes. Barely. "It was six extra minutes. There's hardly anybody in the restaurant and I have plenty of time to get everything done before the dinner rush starts."

"Well, I just don't want six extra minutes to turn into ten extra minutes to turn into thirty extra minutes. After all, we did do you a big favor by hiring you here."

Hayley didn't argue, just continued to clear off the table. Timothy Smittle was getting her labor at less cost than he would have to pay others. She was doing the work of two people and barely getting paid one person's salary.

But she didn't have any other choice, so she would keep her opinions and her arguments to herself. This was temporary. Mason was forever. Whatever she had to do to reestablish herself, to be prepared to take care of him in any situation, she would do it.

"Someone is coming in the door right now. All the waitresses are on break, so I'll seat him and you take his order. But don't do anything having to do with money. I'll give him his check after."

And keep the tip for himself, no doubt.

Hayley let out a weary sigh. "Fine, Timothy. Just let me go get my apron on and I'll take his order."

Hayley refused to let the exhaustion overwhelm her, even though she felt it much more now that Mason was gone. She would work hard, get through the shift and get home to her baby.

She grabbed a glass of water for the table where she needed to take the order. She was almost there, pulling her friendly facade over her features, when she looked up at the restaurant guest.

The water slipped out of her numb fingers and shattered as it hit the hardwood floor.

Cain Bennett.

Her eyes ran over his face. Not much had changed in the four years since she'd last seen him. His forceful chin and chiseled jaw were still completed by broad cheekbones, five-o'clock shadow already clear on them even at this early hour. His dark hair was still cut short, but with that rebellious curl that tended to fall across his forehead.

Those same green eyes with flecks of brown were now full of concern as he stood, staring at her. Cain hadn't just happened to walk into this restaurant. He was here specifically looking for her.

Under no circumstance could this possibly be good.

Chapter Three

Cain approached Hayley slowly, both arms outstretched. Not unlike how he had approached traumatized victims in the past.

Because that's exactly how Hayley looked: traumatized. Hell, she hadn't looked this drained even in court four years ago.

Now her brown eyes had shadows under them, outlining an obvious exhaustion. She looked like she could gain another ten pounds and still be a little underweight.

And she was staring at him with something akin to terror in her eyes.

Cain hadn't expected her to be happy to see him, but neither had he expected her to look like she was carrying the world's weight on her shoulders. A sort of panic itched at his gut.

He took a step closer. She took a step back.

"Hayley, what the heck happened?" The manager rushed out from the back. "Get something to clean that up."

The man turned and faced Cain. "We're so sorry about this. I'll get you another— Cain? Cain Bennett?"

Cain dragged his eyes away from Hayley to look at the man who knew his name. "Yes?"

"It's Timothy Smittle. We went to high school together, remember, man?"

"I'll go get a mop," Hayley murmured before turning and almost running into the kitchen.

Timothy hooked a thumb toward Hayley's retreating form. "And of course, you remember Hayley Green, right? You guys were all hot and heavy back in the day."

"Of course." Cain slowly sat back down in the booth, eyes fixed on the door Hayley had exited through.

Timothy slid into the booth across from Cain and lowered his voice even though there was no one else around. "And I guess you heard about the law trouble Hayley got into a few years back. That was after you had already left. She did some time at the Georgia Women's Correctional."

Cain just nodded.

"When she came back around here begging for her old job, I figured it was the least we could do. You know, since we all went to high school together." Timothy sounded very pleased with himself. Like he was collecting bonus points or something.

Cain's eyes left the door and moved to Timothy. "She helped you with your bookkeeping in high school, right? Is that what she's doing now?"

Timothy smirked. "Are you kidding? We couldn't let her near anything having to do with money."

Cain's lips pressed together although he knew he really couldn't blame Timothy. "So she's what, waiting tables?"

The thought of someone with Hayley's intelligence and skills waiting tables was difficult for Cain to swallow, but he guessed he shouldn't be surprised. Right now her job options were probably limited.

Timothy shifted a little uncomfortably in the booth across from Cain. "Um, well, that also involves money, so no. Mostly she's, you know, helping out doing other things."

Before Cain could press about exactly what those "other things" were, Hayley came back out with a broom and mop and began cleaning up the glass and water she'd spilled.

"I can help." Cain slid to the edge of the booth ready to stand.

Timothy laughed out loud. "No, Cain. You sit down. It's Hayley's job."

Hayley didn't look up from what she was doing, but Cain could see the flush spread across her cheeks. She quickly swept up the glass and mopped up the water.

"So, how have you been, man?" Timothy asked, as if they'd been best buddies in high school. Cain barely recalled talking to the other guy at all. "You went on to play ball in college, right? After leading us to the state championships?"

"Yeah, for a couple of years. Then I blew out my knee. Nothing to stop normal life, but effectively ended my football career."

Hayley had finished cleaning up and Cain could tell she was hesitating about whether to stay nearby or to leave. Timothy noticed it, too.

Timothy waved a dismissive hand in Hayley's direction. "You can go do your work in the back. I'll take Cain's order and get him what he needs."

Hayley still wasn't looking at Cain, but he didn't want her to leave. "Actually, I'm here to talk to Hayley."

Timothy stiffened. "Oh. Actually, Hayley just took

a break with Ariel and the kid, so she doesn't have another break for a few hours."

Cain looked around, noticing that Hayley became
even more tense with Timothy's words. It was three
o'clock in the afternoon and the place was nearly empty.

"It doesn't look like you really need her right at this
second. I just need to borrow her for a few minutes."

Timothy turned to glare at Hayley as if she had
planned this. "Actually, during the downtime is when
Hayley does most of the dishes and cleaning in the back.
Then she helps out in front during the rushes."

Hayley was the damned *dishwasher*?

"It's fine, Timothy. I'm not going to take another
break. I don't have anything to say to Cain anyway."
She still wouldn't look at him.

Cain had figured it would come down to this. Taking out his Omega Sector credentials, he turned back
to Timothy. "This is law enforcement business. Hayley
isn't in any trouble and isn't wanted by the law, but I
need to talk to her about a few things. I'd appreciate it
if we could have your cooperation."

He saw Hayley stiffen further out of the corner of
his eye.

Timothy stood. "Well, I don't want to get in the way
of the law, but really we don't pay Hayley to sit around
and talk to old boyfriends. I'll go get you your water."

Timothy left, shaking his head. Hayley finally looked
at Cain. "Yeah, this isn't a good time. I'm working."

She seemed genuinely nervous about being here talking to him. Maybe she was afraid she was going to lose
her job. Such as it was. "I can come to your house later
if you want." He had her address from her parole file.

"No," she immediately said. "I don't want you coming there."

"Okay." He held his hands out in a gesture of peace. "If you don't want to talk here and you don't want to talk at your home, maybe we can meet for dinner tonight?"

She shook her head again. "I can't. I'm working here until seven thirty and then I have to go straight home."

Cain refused to let himself get annoyed at her avoidance. "How about early tomorrow, then? What time does your shift start?"

"Seven a.m." She shrugged.

He felt himself stiffen. "Did you begin working today at seven a.m. also?"

She shrugged. "I'm working a lot of hours this week."

By the look of her exhausted face and the weight she'd lost, it had been more than just this week that she'd been working a lot of hours.

"What are you doing here, Hayley? Why are you working *here*?"

Her eyes narrowed at him. "Believe it or not, there's not a lot of options out there for an ex-felon with no college degree. Especially since a condition of my parole is that I'm not allowed near a computer for more than two minutes at a time."

She stuck out her ankle and pulled her khaki pants up just a little bit. Cain could see the electronic monitor strapped around her slim leg.

"It's a prototype. Lets everybody know if I'm a naughty girl. So when Timothy was nice enough to give me a job—albeit, washing dishes and cleaning the kitchen—I took it."

Even after she'd refused to see him while in prison, he'd tried to keep tabs on her from a distance. Life in a minimum security facility wasn't terribly difficult, not like a medium or maximum security facility, but it still wasn't freedom.

He had to admit he hadn't really thought about what her life would be like once she actually was released. That the agreement of her parole might stop her from using her natural abilities and skills.

And so here she was with her genius IQ and incredible computer aptitude, washing dishes and mopping floors.

Guilt started to eat at him, but Cain squashed it down. Hayley had broken the law. Cain had been doing his job when he arrested her. But allowing them to get physically involved while he was on the case had been the biggest mistake of his professional life. Something he would always regret. The one thing he couldn't blame Hayley for hating him for.

Hayley was still standing there when Timothy brought the glass of water back out. "Do you want to order anything?"

Cain turned to Timothy. "No, I'm just going to steal about five minutes of Hayley's time. I really appreciate it, Timothy. For old times and all." He smiled at the other man.

Feeling important again, Timothy grinned back. "It's no problem. Anything for Gainesville's greatest high school football star."

"That was a lot of years ago, man. And I was far from the greatest."

"Not to those of us who stuck around here." Timothy turned to Hayley. "We'll just count your break as an hour and a half today, cool?"

Hayley's lips tightened, but she nodded. Timothy walked off again.

"What do you want, Cain? Why are you here? How long have you been here?"

"Been here in town?"

"No, here at the restaurant."

"I just walked in a second ago. Why?"

Hayley studied him for a minute, looking relieved. "Never mind, it doesn't matter. But what do you want?"

"Why don't you sit down? You look like you could use a few minutes' break."

Hayley's eyebrows arched but she did what he asked.

"Do you need something to eat?" he asked. She looked like she hadn't had a solid meal in months. "I could order something for us both."

She ignored his question. "Why are you here, Cain? I know it's not to have a meal. I know you're not stupid enough to come back here for a social visit."

Cain could feel a muscle tightening in his jaw. "No, I'm here on business."

He could see her visibly tense. "I haven't done anything that violates my parole. Haven't broken any laws."

Of course that was why she would think he was here. Why wouldn't she? "No. When I said I was here on business I didn't mean to arrest you or anything like that. You're not in any trouble."

She still didn't relax. "Fine. Then what did you need to talk to me about? I need to get back to work, Cain. Some of us get paid by the hour."

"And how many hours a week do you have to work here to make ends meet? You look tired." He touched her hand lying on the table before he could think better of it.

She snatched it away as if she'd been burned.

"No." Her voice was hoarse. "You don't get to be concerned about me. Ever. You gave up that right four years ago."

"When I had you arrested? You were guilty, Hayley. Guilty of using your computer skills for hacking."

She laughed, but the sound held no amusement whatsoever. "You know what? I've had a long time to think about this. To categorize and figure out exactly how I felt about everything that happened with my arrest and incarceration. You were a federal agent, I was a criminal. It was your job to catch me—I've never blamed you for that."

She slid to the edge of the booth. "When those cops barged into my apartment to arrest me, I wasn't surprised. I think I'd always known I would eventually get caught."

Cain wanted to feel relief that she didn't blame him. That she understood he'd been doing his job. But he knew there was more.

She stared at him. He almost wished it was with fury rather than the exhaustion that seemed to blanket both her body and spirit. "Then I saw *you*. Realized you were the one in charge of the investigation. Realized you had deliberately used the feelings we had for each other, the connection we'd always had, to get close to me."

He started to interrupt, but she held out a hand to stop whatever he might say.

"You seduced me in order to arrest me, Cain. And it nearly cost me everything." Hayley stood. "So whatever business it is you want to talk to me about? Forget it. We have nothing to say to each other."

Chapter Four

The next morning before the sun was even up, Cain sat in the diner a few blocks away from the Bluewater Grill. Hayley was supposed to meet him here in twenty minutes.

She damn well better show up. When she'd walked away yesterday, he'd let her go. But he'd stayed, had lunch, even suffered through an hour of reminiscing with Timothy.

When Hayley had come out of the kitchen to refill the ice in the server's station, he'd caught her glance. He'd seen her big brown eyes widen, then narrow, from all the way across the restaurant.

Eventually she'd made her way back over to him.

"Why are you still here?"

He'd leaned back in the booth like he didn't have anywhere else in the world to be. "Because you haven't listened to what I have to say yet."

For just a second she'd looked at him as though she would like to push him into oncoming traffic. Cain didn't mind. He would take that any day over how breakable she'd looked a couple of hours before. "Fine. If I listen to you, will you leave?"

"It will take more than two sentences. You'll have to sit down. Give me a few minutes."

Hayley had looked over her shoulder at Timothy, who'd been glaring. And just like that the anger was gone. Breakable was back.

"I can't." She started loading dishes off his table and putting them in the bin she'd carried out. "I don't have any more time today."

Damn it. Cain had wanted to punch something. And it might have been Timothy if he'd started harassing Hayley again. But that would've just added to her distress.

"You're working a double tomorrow, too?" he asked.

She'd nodded and wiped down his table.

"Fine. Meet me for breakfast at the diner down the block in the morning before your shift starts."

She grimaced. "Fine. Six thirty. You'll have thirty minutes."

He'd left after that. Mostly because he couldn't bear to stay in there and watch Hayley work so hard and look so damn fragile.

Forget the mole, all he wanted to do was steal Hayley away from here, take her to a beach house somewhere and let her just sit out in the sun.

And feed her, for God's sake. Meal after meal until she finally put enough weight on to be considered *thin*. And exhaustion and fear didn't blanket her every expression.

Cain scrubbed a hand over his face. He felt like he was missing some important piece of this puzzle. He could understand why Hayley was working at the Bluewater, and even the difficulty in getting a job. But why the hell was she working herself to the bone? The cost of living in Georgia wasn't so high that she needed to work eighty hours a week to get by.

What the hell had happened to her? Had life in prison been that bad? Or adjusting back into society that difficult? Hayley was so damn smart. He'd halfway thought she would use her time incarcerated to plan a new business or get her college degree. Maybe the no-computers decree had disrupted whatever plans she'd made.

She obviously needed money in a pretty desperate way. Omega was willing to pay her a hefty consultant's fee for her help in catching the mole.

Of course, Cain was also going to have to carefully watch where that money was being spent. There weren't a lot of good reasons he could think of that would have her working herself into the ground, but there were a lot of bad ones.

Buying her way back into the den of hackers was the most obvious. Maybe she had to have a certain dollar amount by the time her computer restrictions were lifted on her parole.

Cain's hands clenched into fists. He'd be damned if he was going to let her drop back into that life again.

So maybe this mission was going to serve more than one purpose: catch the mole inside Omega and save Hayley from herself.

But first she had to show up this morning. Even if it was only so Cain could feed her.

He got a cup of coffee and put in an order for a full breakfast for both of them about ten minutes before Hayley was scheduled to arrive. He wasn't going to let not having enough time be an excuse not to eat. Although he was hoping to talk her out of going to work altogether. The consultant's fee would be at least five times what she would make busing tables and washing dishes.

He saw her instantly as she entered the diner, long blond hair pulled back in a braid. She had a large canvas bag over one shoulder and was already in her Bluewater T-shirt and khaki pants. Damn restaurant didn't even open for another four hours, so why the hell did she need to go in so early?

He knew the moment she saw him, tension shooting into her small frame like someone had fused a metal pipe to her spine. He stood as she got to their booth. She at least looked a little less tired than yesterday afternoon.

"I don't have long. I have to clock in by seven," she said by way of greeting.

"Good morning." He ignored her abrupt words as she slid into the booth across from him.

"This isn't a date, Cain. Not even a breakfast between friends. Tell me what it is you have to say."

He slid into the seat across from her. "We'll talk with breakfast."

"I don't have time for breakfast."

"Tough. I already ordered for both of us."

She glared at him, fire burning even higher in her eyes when the waitress brought their food less than a minute later.

"Presumptuous much?"

He just shrugged. "Everybody's got to eat. You more than most."

"What are you trying to say, Bennett?"

He definitely didn't want to get into a fight with her and cause her to not eat just out of spite. "I'm saying you're working a double today. So you need to eat."

He dug in to his own food, relieved a few moments later when she did the same.

"You got what I liked. Thank you," she said softly.

Fried eggs, hash browns with all the fixings, sausage, bacon. Nothing sweet. She'd always said sweet food made her coffee—which she took with a god-awful amount of cream and sugar—not taste sweet enough. He'd never forgotten, didn't think he ever would.

He nodded and kept eating, waiting until she had a huge bite of food in her mouth before asking his next questions.

"Why are you working so hard, Hayley? At the Bluewater. Why so many double shifts?"

She looked like she was going to light into him. He expected it, actually, thus the timing of his question when she couldn't easily answer.

"I know it's partially because finding a job as an ex-felon isn't easy and you took what you could get. But you shouldn't have to be working so hard that you're exhausted all the time. Timothy mentioned you work as many hours as you can every week."

The man had also said it as though he'd been doing Hayley some great favor by allowing her to work that much.

She shrugged, finally finished chewing. "That's what you have to do when you're not even making minimum wage."

Cain's eyes narrowed. "Unless you're waiting tables or something where you're making tips, he's required by law to pay you at least minimum wage."

"You stay out of it. I will handle Timothy." That pinched look was back in her eyes. Cain wasn't trying to add to her stress.

"Even if he isn't paying you quite minimum wage—" and Cain would be looking into that "—you still shouldn't need to work eighty hours a week to get by here in Gainesville. It's not like Georgia has some ridiculously high cost of living."

"Is that what you brought me here for? To remind me that I have a crappy job and pretty crappy future ahead of me?"

"Hayley—"

"I already made my feelings about the arrest clear yesterday. As for every other part of my life, including when or how long I work, it's none of your business."

He held out a hand in surrender. He didn't want this to get out of control. "Okay, fine. Just finish eating, okay?" If he had his way she would eat everything on that plate and then another whole one after that.

She took another bite and he relaxed a little. But he was running out of time.

And what did he expect, that she was just going to tell him everything going on in her life? Especially if it had to do with potentially illegal activities.

"I brought you here to offer you a job. With Omega Sector."

Her eyes narrowed in suspicion. "What kind of job could you possibly want me for?"

"We need your computer skills to catch someone providing critical information to a specific criminal."

"Doesn't Omega Sector have its own computer crimes division?"

Cain nodded. "Yes. But we have a mole inside Omega. A good one. I need someone who's even better, who's not in law enforcement. That's you."

"I'm not the only great hacker."

"You're the only one I know I can trust."

She rolled her eyes. "I can't believe you can even say that with a straight face."

He set his coffee cup back down. "When it comes to this, I do trust you. Completely. You may have made some questionable decisions four years ago, for whatever reason, but I know you wouldn't want to ever hurt anyone. The person we're trying to find is a murderer, Hayley."

He thought of Grace Parker's face as Freihof's knife slit her throat. Catching the mole inside Omega would be a direct link to putting him away for good.

"Yeah, I'm not a murderer at least."

"Of course you're not. I hope you know I never thought you would hurt somebody else. No matter what damage you might be able to do with a computer, you've always had too big a heart to hurt people."

She stirred the last of her hash browns around on her plate.

"Look, Cain." It was the most gentle tone he'd heard from her. "I don't really have time for another job. The Bluewater keeps me pretty busy. Plus, I'm not allowed near computers as part of my parole agreement."

"Actually, I'm hoping you'll be able to find the mole's movements by looking through files of code I've printed. Won't need you near a computer."

He took out the file that held the contract for the work Omega wanted her to do, including what she would be paid, and slid it over so she could see it. He felt better when her eyes got a little wide at the number. Although, damn it, that meant the Bluewater really was paying her below minimum wage.

"This amount is to complete the project. Find the

traitor inside Omega. That might take you a day, might take you three weeks. If it takes longer than either of us are thinking, then we'll renegotiate for a larger amount."

Cain knew she'd already read the contract, at least the pertinent details. Hayley could read twice as fast as the average person. But she still wasn't looking up at him, giving him any indication if she was going to say yes.

"Hays." He used his old high school nickname for her and reached out and touched her hand where it sat on the table. "I will help you. Whatever is going on, whatever reason you're working yourself to death, even if you're inching yourself back toward trouble, I'll help you. You help me catch this mole, and I'll help you with whatever it is that's weighing so heavily on you."

HAYLEY LOOKED AT where Cain's big hand rested over hers, so strong and capable.

His words, the promise behind them, were just like old times. Back when it was the two of them against the world.

God, she was so tired. She wanted to lean into his strength. She wanted to tell him about everything— about Mason, about the people she was afraid would be coming after them once she could go near a computer again, about *everything*.

But that would be the worst possible thing she could do. Might cost her all she held precious. She couldn't lose Mason again. And if Cain found out he had a son and decided he wanted custody, what judge wouldn't give it to him over a mother who was an ex-con with dubious future employment?

She slid her hand out from under his, the touch too

painful a reminder of what was never going to be again. She really didn't blame Cain for the arrest, but they were never going to go back to what they were.

She picked up the contract, glancing at it again. The money. This might really make a difference for her. For getting out of the hole, being ready to run with Mason if needed.

She couldn't turn down this amount of money, even if it would be dangerous working with Cain.

"Okay, I'll do it."

She could see relief all across his handsome features. That black curl sliding toward his forehead as it always had. He looked so comfortable sitting there in his black T-shirt and jeans. She forced herself to look away. It wasn't fair that she could still be attracted to him after all these years and after everything that had happened between them.

"You'll have to quit your job at the Bluewater," he said.

"I'm going to need that job after this project for Omega Sector is finished. It's not great but at least it's regular, dependable work."

He looked like he was going to argue. But finally just said, "Fine, but you'll have to take a leave of absence for a few weeks."

Hayley nodded although she had no plan to do that. First of all, Timothy would never go for a "leave of absence." He'd just fire her. Second, since she was going through papers, she could do that when she wasn't working. Maybe she might have to cut back on a couple of shifts, but it would be worth it.

"Can you start today? Time is of the essence in catching this guy."

"Guy?" Hayley raised an eyebrow. "You're assuming your mole is male?"

"Actually, one of my prime suspects is female. I definitely have no assumptions of gender when it comes to crime."

Was that an insult against Hayley personally? Or was it just that Cain was too good at his job to be fooled by someone just because of their gender? And Cain was an excellent agent, she had no doubt about that.

"I'll have to go in to the restaurant for at least a couple hours. I can't just leave them in a lurch. But then I'll clear off as much of my schedule as I can."

Cain nodded. "I thought we could work out of my parents' house. They moved down to Florida, but still kept the place here."

Hayley's lips tightened. She didn't necessarily want to go back to the place where they spent so much time in high school. But what choice did she have? She definitely didn't want Cain coming to her apartment and seeing Mason.

"Fine. I'll meet you there in a few hours. You know this would go much more quickly if I could scroll through a computer screen rather than have to read code on paper, right?"

Suspicion immediately shuttered his features. "Paper. That's what we're working with. No computers." His tone was final.

He thought she was going to get back into trouble if she could get online. If only he knew trouble was going to find her as soon as she did. Possibly the worst kind of trouble.

She'd worry about that another day. Right now she had to worry about how she was going to work day in and day out with one of the best agents of the most prestigious law enforcement agency in the country while keeping the biggest possible secret from him.

Chapter Five

The strands of printed code began to blur in front of her eyes and Hayley's head jerked up as it started to fall forward in sleep.

"Whoa there, girl, you all right?" asked Mara, the Bluewater's newest employee, setting a cup of coffee on the desk near the papers Hayley was going through.

The beautiful smell of it revived Hayley slightly, at least enough to pry her eyes open. "Coffee. You're a goddess, Mara. Thank you so much."

"Honey, I know we don't know each other very well, but you are looking at those papers all the dang time." Mara's thick Southern accent coated the words. "Every time you're on a break, before a shift, after a shift. Heck, I wouldn't be surprised to see you carrying in a ream of papers when you go on a bathroom break."

For four days Hayley had been scouring the computer code printouts Cain had given her. The first day she'd met Cain over at his parents' old house and, studiously forgetting that the bed in which they'd first made love was just right upstairs, they'd pored over the files together.

That afternoon he'd received a call and had to leave to go to one of the Omega Sector offices. So he'd given

Hayley the printouts of the computer code, all six huge legal file boxes of them, to work on while he was gone for two or three days.

He'd expected her to be working on them every day. And she had. She'd brought them home that night and studied them deep into the night after spending time with Mason and putting him to bed.

She'd brought a box to the Bluewater with her and, like Mara pointed out, had been going over them every spare second she had. Unfortunately that hadn't been much since she'd worked three double shifts in a row, fourteen hours a day each.

She talked to Timothy about reducing her hours, but when he'd started murmuring about hiring someone to take her place, Hayley knew she couldn't do it. His hiring Mara had scared her enough and she was mostly just a waitress. She was not going to take Hayley's job.

She needed to make more progress on the computer code, but she couldn't afford to lose the livelihood she would need once Cain was gone. Of course, if she didn't find some answers soon, Cain might fire her and try to find someone else to help.

"Honey, what is that stuff?" Mara asked as Hayley took a sip of her coffee. "I glanced at it but it didn't seem to make a bit of sense to me."

Hayley smiled at the older woman with big brassy blond hair. "Computer code."

"What are you reading computer code for? Do you do that for fun?" Mara's look placed the thought just above root canals.

"I do like computers, I have to admit. But no, this is not what I do for fun. This is actually sort of a job."

"For Timothy? Is it something to do with the restaurant?"

Hayley stood up, stretching her back. "Speaking of, I've got to get back out on the floor. Tim will be looking for me I'm sure." It was her fifteen-minute evening break, but like every break she used it to look back over the coding.

"He won't mind if you're late if you're doing something for him."

Hayley shook her head. "No, this is not for him. This is sort of a side job for me."

"Oh." Mara's eyes got big. "I didn't know you did side jobs with computer codes."

Hayley ran a hand over her tired eyes. "Only when my past comes back to haunt me."

She didn't wait to hear what Mara would say about that cryptic statement, just headed to the back of the kitchen where she could begin washing dishes. She left the box of papers there in the supply closet. Hardly anyone went in and even if they did, unless they were well versed in computer coding, none of the pages would make sense.

Weariness set heavily on her shoulders, her muscles sore, her brain tired. She needed more than the four hours of sleep she was getting each night. Needed a chance to do something else besides work here or filter through the code.

She hadn't even seen Mason in two days. She told herself it was okay as she loaded a rack of dishes into the dishwasher. She knew she had to take this opportunity while it was here to make such great money.

But she lived in constant fear that her son would forget her. That no matter how often Ariel talked to him about Hayley, he would reject her somewhere inside.

Guilt battled with exhaustion, and for the first time she was glad for all the steam that flew out of the industrial dishwasher. At least it hid her tears.

Three hours later, nearly ready to drop, Hayley had all her work finished in the kitchen. Mara and the other waitresses had left. Timothy was on his way to make the night bank deposit and had closed up the entire front of the restaurant. All Hayley needed to do was mop the floors and she could go.

The thought of dragging the mop over the entire restaurant was completely beyond her at this moment. She'd have another cup of coffee, look over a little more of the code and then mop.

And then go home for four or five hours of sleep. And then get back up and do the same thing again tomorrow.

The only light at the end of the tunnel was that for the first time today she'd seen an odd pattern in the coding. It might be nothing, but the way the data had been sent in that particular transmission had been odd, as if it possibly housed some other message.

It wasn't much but it was at least something to look for, to see if it happened again. Once she had a pattern it would be easier to find how the mole was communicating.

Of course all of this would be a hell of a lot easier if she could look at it on the screen, scrolling down as she finished each section, rather than having to physically get a new sheet of paper to look at. But she wouldn't complain. She was making money.

Cain was going to be back soon—was supposed to

have been back yesterday—and was probably going to blow a gasket when he found out she was *still* working at the Bluewater, rather than just for him full-time. She would just have to make him understand that she needed this job, too.

She made her coffee, dragging out the cream and sugar—hoping Timothy wouldn't decide this was employee theft—and made her way back to the tiny desk inside the not-much-bigger supply closet.

The coffee provided mental fortitude enough for her to confirm the first suspicious pattern she'd seen in the coding earlier today and look for it again. All she needed was to see the same loophole the mole had attempted twice and she would have what she needed.

But after another hour, pages highlighted and spread all over the stockroom, her lids were heavy again. She'd done all she could do for today. She needed to mop and go home.

The sound of the front glass breaking had Hayley bolting upright, all exhaustion gone. She jerked open the closet door and found the hallway engulfed in flames.

The building was on fire? How had it spread into the hallway so soon and why was it growing so fast?

More importantly, how the hell was she going to get out of here when the entire hall was engulfed in flames?

Going back into the supply closet, already starting to cough, she grabbed her cell and called 911. In the few moments it took for her to get connected to an operator, more smoke was seeping under the door.

"911. State your emergency."

"I'm at the Bluewater Grill." Hayley coughed out the address. "There's a fire. I'm trapped inside."

As she said the words, panic barreled through her.

Oh God, she really was trapped inside. She wasn't going to be able to get past the fire in the hall.

The operator was telling her to stay low, that help was coming. Hayley could barely hear the woman's words over her own panicked breaths and coughs.

There was no way she would survive until the fire department got here. She needed to get out of this room before the fire made it all the way in. The chemicals surrounding her would be lethal if she breathed them in, and might even explode.

She grabbed her T-shirt and yanked it over her mouth and nose before opening the door. Heat blasted her back, stealing her breath. Through narrowed eyes she saw that the flames had now encompassed the entire hall—walls, floor and ceiling. She would have to run through the hall—maybe seven or eight feet, all a blazing inferno.

"Hayley!"

Someone was calling her from the other end of the hallway.

Cain.

"Cain!" She yelled as loud as she could, but the word came out as a croak.

He would never hear her voice. Would have no idea she was back here. She rushed back into the supply room and grabbed a wrench and metal can of paint. *Please let it be enough.*

She brought it back in the hallway and began banging on it with every bit of failing strength she had left.

"Hayley, is that you?"

She banged harder.

"Hang on, I'll be right back," he yelled.

She dropped the can and wrench, falling back from the flames that were crawling closer to her. A few moments later he was back. She heard a fire extinguisher being sprayed in spurts and then could see him in the flames coming toward her. Big, strong, capable.

He yanked her into his arms. "Are you okay?"

She nodded.

"Stay close to me. We've got to move fast. Keep low."

He pulled her in front of him, wrapping his body protectively around hers, using the extinguisher he held in front of her, making a path for them. Hayley felt heat all around her as they moved, but nothing burned. Cain's arm kept her waist tucked against him, his back sheltering her from the fire that flamed behind them once they moved past.

Out of the hallway the immediate danger subsided, but the entire dining room of the restaurant was on fire. Cain pulled her through and out the front door, both desperately sucking in oxygen as they hit clean air.

"Are you okay?" he asked again once they could breathe, sitting at the far end of the parking lot, watching the fire trucks roll in.

"Yes." Her voice sounded rusty. Hoarse. But already her lungs were easing.

He yanked her into his arms again, cradling her head against his chest. She let out a little squeak but didn't try to get away. That had been way too close. Things had gone from fine to critical so quickly she wasn't even sure exactly what had happened.

And definitely didn't know what would've happened if Cain hadn't shown up when he did. She tried to ease her head back from his grasp, but he wouldn't let her.

"Why were you at the Bluewater?" she croaked out.

"I went by your apartment."

Now Hayley completely jerked away from him. Had he seen Mason? Oh God, what was she supposed to say?

"I talked to your cousin. Who, of course, wouldn't even let me in the door."

Relief flooded her. Ariel didn't know Cain was Mason's father, and even if she suspected it was him, Ariel wouldn't say anything to him. She was still mad about the whole arrest thing.

"And," he continued, glaring down at her, "imagine my surprise when Ariel told me you were at work. Here at the Bluewater. From where, if I recall, we agreed you would get time off."

"I tried, but it didn't work out and I couldn't afford to get fired. Don't worry, I've still been doing your work. I just—"

Cain's livid curse cut her off. "I don't care about the damn case, Hayley. You were already bone-weary exhausted before I got here. And now you added searching the computer codes in your *spare time*?"

Hayley looked over at the restaurant, which was now completely up in flames. All the files she had gone through over the last four days, any progress she had made, were now gone.

Maybe she would tell him that after he had calmed down about the fact that she had two jobs. Because right now she didn't have the energy to fight, or really to do anything but sit here and breathe.

But it wasn't long before the fire department had the burning building under control and everyone had questions. Cain stayed by her side, features pinched, as Hayley explained that she'd been in the back room reading. Cain confirmed that she was doing some consulting work for Omega Sector.

When the fire inspector explained that the entire back half of the restaurant had been completely destroyed, Hayley looked over at Cain.

"All my work with the computer codes is gone. It was all here with me."

"You shouldn't have even been here in the first place," he muttered. "But printouts are replaceable."

At least he didn't seem too mad about how this was going to set them back. He was much angrier about her being here at the restaurant.

Timothy joined them not long after and Hayley was definitely glad to have Cain around to calm the other man down. Timothy wanted to know exactly what had happened and Hayley had no idea.

"You must've left something on in the kitchen," Timothy screamed. "This is all your fault."

"Actually," the fire inspector cut in, "we have pretty irrefutable proof that this fire was arson related."

"Arson?" Timothy scoffed. "That's ridiculous. You're saying someone burned the restaurant on purpose?"

Timothy turned and glared at Hayley again. "Maybe some of your old prison buddies or something?"

Hayley didn't even know how to respond to that. But she didn't have to. She felt Cain's hand slide around her waist and pull her back slightly so that he could step in front of her, putting himself between her and Timothy.

Cain turned to the fire inspector. "You said you had proof?"

"Looks like three good old-fashioned Molotov cocktails. Thrown straight through the windows."

"What the hell is a Molotov cocktail?" Timothy spit out.

"Poor man's grenade," Cain muttered.

The fire inspector nodded. "Yep. They're also called bottle bombs. Basically a can of some sort of flammable liquid, with a burning wick sticking out. It gets thrown and sets everything it touches on fire."

"And if it came through the front window, then Hayley was very definitely not involved," Cain pointed out to Timothy.

"Actually, how the fire in that back hallway escalated so quickly is something we'll be checking into. So I'd appreciate it if everyone wouldn't mind staying in touch."

"I'm sure she had something to do with it." Timothy turned to point at Hayley. "She just got out of prison."

"Timmy, I know you and I went to school together, but we're going to have a problem if you keep this up," Cain said, tone hard.

The fire inspector turned to Timothy. "In my years of experience, I've found that the people who almost died in the fire are not responsible for the arson. I've also found that in many arson cases involving a business, the owner has something to do with it."

Hayley somehow managed not to laugh at Timothy's outraged look.

"Oh my gosh, Hayley honey, are you okay?" Hayley heard Mara's Southern drawl as the woman rushed up behind her. "I just heard about the fire on the news and I rushed back over here. I knew you had been the last person here."

Cain continued to talk to the fire inspector and Timothy as Hayley turned to talk to Mara.

"Yeah, it was pretty scary." Hayley really didn't want to think about how seriously close to death she'd come tonight. "If my friend Cain hadn't come by, I would've been trapped."

Mara threw her arms around Hayley. "I'm so glad you're okay. Did you lose all your stuff you've been working on so hard? All your computer papers?"

Hayley nodded. "It was all I could do to get out with my life."

Evidently the older woman was a hugger, as she threw her arms around Hayley again. "The important thing is, you're all right."

Hayley could feel exhaustion pulling at her. She needed to get home. Although it looked like nobody would have to work at the Bluewater tomorrow.

"Looks like none of us will be working here for a while," Hayley said. "We'll all have to find new jobs."

Given the fact that Timothy thought she had something to do with it, Hayley doubted she would be working there ever again.

"Yeah, that's a bummer," Mara said. "But I hope you and I can keep in touch even with new jobs."

Hayley nodded. She didn't have friends. Surviving and providing had taken up all her time since she'd gotten out of prison. "I'd like that."

Mara hugged Hayley once more and then moved on. Hayley saw Cain still talking to the fire inspector and made her way back to him.

"I'm going home. I'm tired," she whispered.

Tired didn't even come close to what she was feeling. At this point Hayley was afraid she wasn't going to be able to even walk over to her car, much less drive home.

But, like always, she would find a way.

She turned, but Cain grabbed her elbow. "No."

"Whatever needs to be talked about is going to have

to wait." Everything around her was starting to spin slightly. Crap. She needed to get to her car so she could at least sit down.

"I'll drive you," Cain said. "But we're not going to your house. I'll take you back to my place."

"No." She wanted to make a more elaborate argument, about how she just needed to be in her own bed, with her own stuff, and that she would be fine tomorrow. But the words wouldn't come.

Cain turned her so they were standing face-to-face. She focused on his green eyes, using them as a lifeline to keep her from falling.

"Hays." He trailed a finger down her cheek. She wanted to lean into the softness of the touch, to the strength he offered. "You're about to fall over. I'll drive you."

"Fine. But I want to go to my apartment."

She saw his lips tighten as he glanced over at the smoldering building. "You need to stay with me. The fire inspector thinks, based on how fast the hallway burned, that whoever did this to the Bluewater was actually targeting you."

Chapter Six

Fourteen hours later, Cain sat in the living room of the house he'd grown up in sipping a cup of coffee, trying to tamp down the toxic blend of rage that surrounded him every time he thought of Hayley trapped in that fire.

He'd already done a thorough workout with the old set of free weights his dad kept in the garage. And had run five miles on the treadmill his mother had bought for walking after she'd had knee surgery.

Neither of those had really helped.

The longer Hayley slept up in his old bedroom, the worse the feelings became.

She was so damn exhausted that she had slept for fourteen goddamn hours.

Fourteen.

She'd been working on the computer codes while still trying to work double shifts at the Bluewater? Cain could feel his teeth grind and tried to force himself to relax. If he hadn't been called back to his office in DC—for a case completely unrelated—he would've been here and never allowed that to happen. Because Hayley had already been on the verge of collapse before taking on more work.

He rubbed his jaw.

He'd had his ear singed off by Ariel when he'd answered Hayley's phone, possibly the only dumbphone left in the world used by people under the age of eighty, when Ariel had called. Hayley had been so deeply asleep she hadn't even heard it ring over and over—seriously, he wasn't going to have any enamel left on his teeth by the end of this if he didn't chill out—so finally he'd answered it.

He'd explained to Ariel what happened. About the fire and danger Hayley might be in. About how she'd fallen so dead asleep on the way to his house that she hadn't heard her phone.

Ariel had pretty much told him to keep his distance from Hayley. Except with a lot more curse words and at a volume that rivaled a screaming jet engine. Guess she hadn't forgiven him for his part in Hayley's arrest.

His coffee wasn't helping his rage, but Cain knew he was going to have to channel it. Either that or have serious dental work done.

But more than that, he knew why he was holding on to his anger so tightly. Because it was much easier to handle the anger than the fear.

That moment of abject panic last night when he pulled up at the Bluewater, knowing Hayley was inside, and saw the flames.

Now it wasn't his jaw that clenched, it was his heart.

Thank God Hayley had the sense to beat on that can, otherwise Cain wouldn't have thought to look in the storage closet area. Wouldn't have been able to get her out.

The thought of losing Hayley… Cain put his coffee cup down on the table. One thing the fire had done was force him to take a good hard look at the truth. His feelings for Hayley hadn't died, no matter what had broken between them four years ago.

Catching the mole at Omega had really just been an excuse to bring him back into her life. If it hadn't been this, he would've found something else.

Cain had been waiting four years for Hayley to do her time so they could start again. He realized now that that had always been the truth. He had never planned to let her go.

Whatever secrets she was keeping from him, and he definitely knew they were there, he was going to find out.

And now it looked like he had brought danger to her door. Did the mole know what Cain was doing? If the fire inspector was correct and the hallway leading to the storage room had burned much quicker than it should have, then it looked like someone was deliberately targeting Hayley.

Of course, the fire inspector had also mentioned that it was possible that the hallway had traces of some non-suspicious accelerants given that the storage room with its various chemicals was nearby. Just an unfortunate accident.

Either way, Cain didn't plan to be letting Hayley out of his sight. He didn't care much if Hayley or Ariel or the whole damn town didn't like that.

And keeping her safe wasn't the only reason he was going to be stuck to Hayley.

He'd received the code and key to release the ankle monitor that forced her to stay away from computers.

He'd made the decision late last night, especially since whatever she'd been working on had been lost in the fire, that Hayley was going to need access to a computer in order to discover information about the Omega mole. Going through reams of paper, especially if they had to start back at the beginning, would take too long.

Cain had submitted his request early this morning and it had been expedited to go before a local judge first thing, since a court order was needed to remove Hayley's ankle monitor.

He'd received the court order, the code needed to turn it off and the key—delivered by a state trooper— to remove the anklet all together. The condition of the court order was that Cain take responsibility for Hayley's computer activities. He was expected to know exactly what she was doing on any computer, and if she wasn't with him she would have the anklet back on.

That would not be a problem.

He was making lunch when Hayley finally woke up. She'd obviously taken a shower and slipped on a T-shirt and sweatpants of his that he'd left out for her.

The sight of her wearing his clothes did something to him. Grease popping from a piece of bacon brought his attention back to what he was doing.

"I pulled the sheets off the bed. I'm pretty sure they smelled like a flue. You should've made me take a shower before letting me sleep there."

"Believe it or not, I actually tried to wake you up. Short of dumping you in the cold shower myself, you were out."

And so damn exhausted he hadn't had it in him to force her back awake.

"I was tired."

The smallness of her voice kept him from lighting into her. He was back now. He wasn't going to let her work herself into the ground.

"Do you feel better?"

She reached her hands over her head in a giant stretch, arching her back. Thankfully bacon grease popped him again, or he might've started drooling.

"Oh my gosh, yes. I feel like my brain is working on all cylinders rather than only partial. You were right. I shouldn't have tried to do both jobs at the same time."

He took out the bacon and put on some eggs to fry. "Doesn't look like the Bluewater is even an option anymore. So let's say we just concentrate on your consultant work. Sit."

She raised an eyebrow but sat down at the table. He set a cup of coffee in front of her along with her much-needed cream and sugar.

"I was making progress before everything was lost." She rubbed her forehead as she took a sip of coffee. "I don't know how long it will take you to get another copy, but I'll try to remember where I was so I don't have to read through everything again."

When the eggs finished cooking he set a plate in front of her and sat down with his own.

"I'm going to actually do you one better. We're not going to use printouts. You're going to be on the computer."

She stuck her leg out from under the table, pointing to her ankle. "What about that?"

"Got the court order this morning that it can be turned and taken off as long as you're in my custody."

She didn't look as excited as he thought she would.

"Don't you still think this will all go much faster online rather than reading from the paper?" he asked as she nibbled on a piece of bacon.

"Yes." She nodded, but with a decided lack of enthusiasm. "Working your case from within the system will move much more quickly and intuitively for me."

"Then finish eating and let's get started."

HE BROUGHT THE laptop over to the couch where Hayley was sitting.

"You're only allowed on this while I'm sitting right next to you. And we're only going to access the electronic versions of the files I brought, and possibly some outer Omega networks. Nothing else at all. Got it?"

Amazing how he had no problem trusting her within the Omega network. He didn't worry for a second that she would do anything damaging to any secrets the law enforcement agency might be protecting.

But that didn't mean he trusted her with any other aspect of a computer.

He knew she was keeping something from him, was in some sort of trouble or heading toward it, and he was handing her the tool to get in even deeper.

"Yes, I got it."

No smart-aleck remark, no teasing at all. He was glad she took this as seriously as he was.

As a matter fact, she almost looked scared as he handed the computer to her. As scared as she looked ten minutes ago when he turned off and removed her tracking anklet.

She sat with the computer on her lap, staring down at it for long moments, not touching it.

"Everything okay?" he finally asked.

"It's been a long time. I was in the cybercrimes wing at the correctional center, so there were no computers there. Nothing. Not even closed systems."

Computers not hooked to any other system so no

damage could be done by viruses or hacks. No way in or out.

Guilt bubbled inside Cain. He had done this to her. Taking away something that had been a critical part of her.

Would he do anything differently if he could go back and change it?

He'd always thought not, because as the pithy saying went, she'd done the crime so she'd done the time. But looking at Hayley now, so awkwardly holding a computer that would've once been almost an appendage for her, hurt something inside him.

He touched her cheek with the back of his fingers. "Hays?"

She flinched and he dropped his hand. "Sorry. Yeah, let's get started."

Her fingers dropped to the keyboard and she began to work.

It didn't take long for her to get back into the flow of her talent. Hayley could write and develop and read computer code the way most people read nursery rhymes.

Cain wasn't nearly as good as Hayley, but he knew his way around coding, enough to be able to make sure she was staying within their agreed parameters.

She began her search scrolling through screen after screen of what would normally look like gibberish, stopping to follow different patterns that caught her eye.

Every time she found something suspicious she organized it into a separate folder. Once in a while she would take something out of a folder, evidently only after she'd been reassured that wasn't what she was looking for.

"Whoever is doing this is good," she said, standing

up for the first time in four hours. She wiggled her fingers out in front of her, those muscles obviously sore after having not been used in that way for a long time.

"Better than you?"

She grinned. A smart-ass smile that he hadn't even realized had been missing until now. A smile full of confidence.

"Please. Don't insult me. I'll give it twenty-four hours before I find the pattern. *If* he's extremely lucky."

"Good." He grinned back at her. "How about if we take a break for a few minutes and I'll order us some dinner."

Her smile faded. "What time is it?"

"Almost five o'clock. You're not tired again, are you?" He said it in jest but then realized maybe she was tired. Maybe she did need more rest.

"No. But I've got to go."

"Go where?"

"Home. Just for a few hours. I can come back at around nine if you want. But right now I've got to go."

"Let's just stay and keep working. You were starting to get on a roll."

Her features became more pinched. "I'll have to pick it back up later."

Damn it. This had to do with whatever she was hiding from him. Was she playing him? Had she somehow gotten a message out to someone while using the computer?

He looked down at her leg. Or maybe she thought to play him in a different way.

"That anklet is going right back on if you leave here for any reason."

She didn't get upset like he'd expected. Didn't try to talk her way out of it.

"That's fine."

He walked into the kitchen, true irritation kicking in, and snatched up the anklet. He stalked back into the living room.

"Foot," he demanded.

"Cain…" Her voice pleaded for understanding.

"Don't start. You were willing to work double shifts at that stupid restaurant and you won't even put in eight full hours of work to catch a killer?"

They both flinched as he snapped the monitor back in place around her slim ankle.

Her brown eyes stared out at him. "I just have something I need to do. I promise I'll be back in a few hours."

"You know this thing has a tracker, right? And now that I have the code, I'll be able to see where you're going?"

"I'm just going home. And yeah, if you feel like you need to track me go right ahead. You don't know me anymore. Don't know anything about my life."

He grabbed her arms, conscious not to hurt her. "Then tell me. Tell me what's happening with you."

All pleading was gone from her now. "Sorry, Cain, the great football star might be able to waltz back into the hearts of everyone else in town, but not mine. You and I are business, that's all."

She turned and left and he let her go, knowing going after her now would just make things worse.

But he damn well would use that tracker.

He grabbed the computer and began looking through the work she'd done today. Even after studying it nearly an hour he couldn't find anything at all suspicious. The only pattern he could find was the strides Hayley had made toward identifying the mole.

Maybe she just needed a break like she said. She was right—he didn't know anything about her life anymore.

That was an oversight he intended to rectify.

Chapter Seven

Hayley knew Cain was mad, and even understood his frustration, but she didn't care.

She was going home to see her son. She cursed when she got outside and realized she'd have to take a cab back to the Bluewater, where her car was still parked. But it would be worth it to have dinner with Mason, to read some of his stories he loved, to put him to bed.

She'd missed it for the last four days trying to work both jobs, but now that she had the time, she wouldn't miss it again. She'd lost too many "everydays" while she was in prison. She'd spend the rest of her life trying not to lose any more.

She told Cain she would come back at nine, and she would. She'd work all night if she needed to.

Although the thought of sitting on that couch with Cain a hair's breadth away caused heat to pool in her very core.

Maybe it was all the sleep, maybe it was working in the house that held so many memories for her, maybe it was not having sex for the last four years. But she was so aware of Cain, of the musky scent of him, of his strength and broody intelligence.

It had been all she could do most of the afternoon

to concentrate on the coding and not put the computer aside and crawl on top of him.

Her mind and her heart wanted to stay far away from him, but her body had much different ideas. She tried to remind her body that he'd used their relationship, their history, to get close to her and then arrest her.

Still hadn't seemed to make much difference.

Good thing Hayley was used to her body not getting what it wanted. She'd had four years of desperately wanting things she couldn't have. A few days with Cain Bennett shouldn't be a problem.

All thoughts of Cain melted away after she made it to her car then drove to her apartment. She let herself in and heard Mason's sweet voice chattering to Ariel.

"What's going on in here?"

"Mama Hayley! Yay!" Mason ran and launched himself at her. She snatched him up in her arms, swinging him around as she hugged him and he giggled. The sweetest sound she'd ever heard.

"Guess what?" She tapped him on the nose as she set him back down on the ground. "I got to see some real live fire trucks last night."

Mason's eyes got huge. "You did?"

The three of them made a pizza together, each of them putting on whatever toppings they wanted, as Hayley told a very tame version of the restaurant fire and the fire trucks. Mason asked all sorts of questions, stating more than once that he was going to be a fireman when he grew up. She could tell Ariel had adult questions, but neither of them would talk about that in front of Mason.

After dinner they watched an episode of Mason's favorite show together, then colored a couple of pictures. Mason drew his own version of a fire truck.

Before Hayley knew it, it was already time to get her little man ready for bed. She gave him a bath, read him his stories—all more than once—before tucking him in.

"Tomorrow's Wednesday." His grin was overpowered by a yawn.

"Hmmm. Wednesday, Wednesday." She pursed her lips to the side and tapped them. "There's something I'm supposed to remember about Wednesday, but I can't think what it is."

"Ice cream Wednesday!" Mason yelled. "We always get ice cream on Wednesday."

Hayley smiled and tickled him, but stopped before he could get wound up. "Oh yeah, that's right. Of course we're going to get ice cream tomorrow. It's Wednesday."

It had been their tradition every week since Hayley had come home. She wouldn't be breaking it tomorrow, although getting away from Cain in the middle of the afternoon would require some creative strategizing.

"I love you, little man. Sweet dreams."

"Night, Mama." His eyes were already drifting closed, which was good—he wouldn't see the tears flooding hers.

Mama, not Mama Hayley. One day that would be what he said all the time, not just as he was falling asleep.

Ariel was washing dishes when Hayley came back out. Hayley took over the drying duties.

"I'm glad you're okay. I talked to Cain Bennett twice last night, first time when he came over here looking for you, second when I called you and he finally answered.

He said you were so deeply asleep that you weren't even hearing your phone ring."

Hayley winced. She had texted Ariel from the Bluewater, not wanting her to hear about the fire on the news and worry. She'd meant to call later with more details. "Yeah, if you called I didn't hear it at all."

Hayley filled her in. Stuff they hadn't been able to say in front of Mason. By the end of it, Ariel was staring at Hayley wide-eyed.

"It's a damn good thing Cain came by to find you. You could've died!"

Hayley could still feel the heat of the fire, the suffocating smoke. "Believe me, I know."

Ariel let the dishwater out of the sink. "He was pretty mad when he found out you were trying to do both jobs."

Hayley grimaced. "It seemed like a good idea at the time. Speaking of, I've got to get back there. We're starting to make some actual progress."

Hayley dried the baking pan and put it away.

"You're going to have to tell him, Hayley," Ariel said softly.

Hayley froze midaction, but respected her cousin too much to pretend she didn't know what Ariel was talking about.

"How long have you known?"

"I didn't realize it until he showed up here yesterday, although I should have. Cain Bennett has always been the one for you."

He'd been the *only* one her whole life. The only man she'd ever been with, the only man she ever loved.

She gripped the towel in her hand, not looking at

Ariel. "I can't tell him. I'm scared. I'm scared I'll lose Mason."

"Just because you have a criminal record does not mean a judge would give Cain custody of Mason, even if he tried to take him. You have no history of violence, drug abuse or neglect. If anything, we could prove how you very methodically planned for Mason's future by making me guardian when he was born."

Hayley sighed. "It's not just that. There are some other things that are...complicated. Things that have nothing to do with Cain."

She didn't want to give Ariel too much information about the people who might come after Hayley. The more Ariel knew, the more dangerous it could be for her.

Hayley's hacking—selling fake college entrance test scores to rich kids—had been pretty benign compared to what she'd stumbled across when she'd been trying to get out.

Someone was using the CET exam to commit treason. To sell government state secrets to other countries. Someone with a lot of political power.

The only thing that had kept Hayley alive so far was that she didn't know *who* that someone was. She'd been arrested before she could dig deep enough.

But Hayley had the means of discovering who. As soon as she had free rein of a computer she would be able to access the electronic trapdoor she'd planted in the CET system before she was arrested.

But once she accessed it, whoever was behind the scheme would know she knew. If they'd already found it, they might suspect her even now.

Either way, she had to be ready to run if it came down to it.

"I know there's trouble you're not telling me about, coz," Ariel said softly. "I know that's why you've been working so hard, not just so that I could go to Oxford."

She'd done her best to protect Ariel, but she should've known her cousin was too smart not to suspect something else was going on.

"The less you know about it the better."

Ariel nodded. "I'm sure that's true. But what about Cain? Whatever trouble you're in, he can help. He has the resources."

"He was the person who arrested me in the first place."

Ariel's lips tightened. "Trust me, I'm never going to forgive what he did, especially now that I know that he must have slept with you right before he arrested you, but I also know that he will help. He will protect you from whatever it is you're afraid of. Especially if he knows about Mason."

Would he? Would Cain even believe her if she tried to explain? She wouldn't know if her computer trap had worked unless she got online. And even once she did, there was no guarantee that it would still be there. She didn't think it would've been discovered deep in the network where she'd placed it, but it was possible.

There was no way Cain was just going to take her word that there had been more involved in her hacker case than he thought. He would think she was using him to gain access to a computer.

So she would have to bide her time. Make sure there were no traces of her presence online while she did the consulting work for Cain. She would deal with the trapdoor and its ramifications once her parole was over and she had full access to computers again. And she'd be ready to take Mason and run if she needed to. Ariel would at least be across the ocean studying.

And she would make sure Cain didn't find out about Mason. At one time she would've given anything for their lives to be tied together with a child. But he'd made his choice, decided he didn't want a permanent link with her, four years ago.

Telling him about Mason would just complicate matters. And God knew everything was already complicated enough as it was.

Chapter Eight

Cain woke up on the couch with Hayley sprawled on top of him. Caught in that place between wakefulness and dreams, his mind sighed in contentment. It felt so good to hold her again.

He stretched, shifting slightly, pulling her closer. His thigh slid between hers and his arms extended more tightly around her, one hand splayed on her hip, the other arm around her shoulders.

Hayley stretched, too, rubbing against him, almost purring. Cain just pulled her closer.

They'd always slept like this, as if they couldn't get close enough in sleep, the way they always felt like they couldn't get close enough when they were awake. Of course, there hadn't been an abundance of opportunities to sleep all night together, first because of high school and parents, then because of the physical distance between them in college, and then because Hayley had gone...

Cain's eyes flew open, now completely aware of where he was and what was happening.

But he couldn't force himself to let go of Hayley.

They'd worked well into the night after she returned yesterday evening. He sat next to her on the couch as she continued her search. He'd been even more diligent to make sure she wasn't communicating with anyone else while doing this work.

He knew, like she'd said, that she had just gone home when she'd left him yesterday. But that didn't mean that someone couldn't have met her there. Cain had made a mistake in not following her, surveilling her apartment, seeing what she was up to.

He wouldn't make that mistake again.

She'd made progress in her work here, he knew she had. Had pinpointed a pattern in how the Omega traitor was communicating. And although Hayley didn't know what it meant, when she'd shown him the origin of the communications, Cain's heart had taken a dive.

It looked like the mole was someone inside the SWAT team at Omega sector. He prayed they were wrong. And he definitely wouldn't make any accusations until they had proof. Hayley would find it soon.

Somewhere around 4:00 a.m., when she'd started to nod off, he'd taken the laptop from her and laid it on the table. He planned for both of them to go to their separate rooms, separate beds, but hadn't wanted to be forced to put that damn anklet back on her.

But unless he planned to stay up all night guarding her, there was no way he could take the chance of letting her sneak by him while he slept.

He leaned back on the couch, about to explain what needed to happen, when he heard her cute little snore. He didn't have the heart to wake her up.

Instead he had pulled Hayley down on the couch and tucked her into his side. Which at some point had obviously turned into entangled limbs and Hayley on top of him.

But right now all Cain wanted to do was keep her pulled up against him. Let her body get the sleep it still obviously needed.

He dozed, too, and it was midmorning when he awoke, Hayley still in his arms. He knew the second she woke up, too. Or, at least the second she realized exactly where she was lying.

She went from soft and purring and snuggly to ramrod straight, pushing herself partway up with her hands on his chest so she could look into his eyes.

"I fell asleep." Her eyes were blinking rapidly as she tried to figure out exactly what was happening.

"I noticed."

She tried to sit up, but their limbs were so tangled she couldn't quite manage.

"Are you going to let me go?"

Cain tucked an arm under his head. "I haven't decided."

His fingers splayed more widely on her hip and almost of their own accord began rubbing gentle circles.

She eased her weight back down on top of him. "What are you doing?"

"Do you remember this couch?"

Oh, the trouble they had gotten into on this couch in high school.

"I remember always having to keep an ear out for the front door opening," she said. He could hear the smile in her voice. "And very quickly rearranging clothing."

His parents had come home more than once at an inopportune moment. "Yeah, they had impeccable timing, didn't they?"

Hayley lifted her head up to make some comment,

but he kissed her before she could. It was almost like he couldn't control his own body.

Their kisses had always been wildly passionate and engulfing. This was no different. As soon as his lips touched hers, he used his arm around her hips to pull her more fully up against him. His other hand wrapped around the back of her neck.

He kissed the side of her mouth, running his tongue over her lower lip, then drew back just a fraction of an inch before plunging back deep inside her hot, wet mouth. He felt her hands tangle into his hair, keeping him as close as he was keeping her.

He tilted her head to the side, giving his lips access to her jaw, her throat. Heard her moan as he made his way down that feminine curve with gentle bites soothed by soft flicks of his tongue.

A loud beeping noise—*that wouldn't quit, damn it*—on the computer brought Cain back to his senses.

"That's the alarm from the algorithm I set up to run while I was offline to see if we could spot a specific pattern," Hayley said against his lips.

The words threw cold water on his ardor. His hand on her nape now pulled her away rather than pulling her closer.

"You did what?"

Unease flared in her eyes. "It's just a simple pattern recognition program I set up to run. Mostly for elimination purposes. There was no point in me doing it manually. This way was much quicker."

It made sense. Was reasonable. But what pissed Cain off was that he'd had no idea she'd done it. Had no idea she'd set up a program to run.

"When did you do it?" He slid back from her.

She sat up, pulling away. "I don't know, a little while after we figured out the communication pattern I showed you last night. We agreed I needed to focus on where that pattern was occurring, so that's what I did."

"But you didn't tell me you set up a program to do it."

She shrugged. "I wasn't trying to hide it from you. I didn't plant the program within the Omega system if that's what you're worried about. It's running right here on your laptop."

"That's not the problem."

"Then what is the problem? I'm trying to do what you asked me to do in the most efficient way possible." She flung her blond hair over her shoulder and slid even farther from him on the couch.

"I just didn't know what you were doing."

He'd sat by her the entire night and hadn't recognized that she'd built the program to help her. If she could do *that* without him knowing, how much more difficult could it be for her to make contact with her hacker buddies without him knowing it?

She arched her eyebrow. "I didn't realize I needed to explain every step of what I was doing. I just thought we were trying to catch your killer as quickly as possible."

"And what else are you trying to sneak by me while you have access to a computer and I obviously have no idea what you're doing?" Cain crossed his arms over his chest, watching her closely, looking for lies.

Her eyes narrowed. "What the hell are you talking about? I haven't been doing anything. You've been peeking over my shoulder the whole time."

"Are you telling me I don't need to?"

"I'm telling you I'm doing the job you're paying me to do."

"But we both know that it wouldn't be difficult for you to squeeze in a little extra contact with someone else if I'm not watching. Hell, even if I *am* watching, as proven today."

Her lips flattened into a thin line. "I haven't done a single thing that didn't involve Omega Sector. Not one single thing."

"You'll have to excuse me if I don't believe you, given the obvious secrets you've been trying to keep."

Her face paled, and he knew he was definitely on the right track.

"Damn it, Hayley, I don't want you to get back in trouble. Didn't you learn anything the first time?"

Hayley stood up and walked toward the kitchen. "Yeah, I learned that the person I thought I could trust the most slept with me so he could make a big arrest to further his career."

He stood up. "That's not true."

"You know what? It doesn't matter." She rubbed her hand against her forehead as if a headache was forming. "Let's get something to eat and get back to work. My evil program has obviously discovered a pattern. Something that would've taken me days to find on my own."

Cain grimaced. She was right. They needed to focus. Their personal stuff could wait until they caught the traitor.

"Fine." He walked into the kitchen, started the coffeepot and made sandwiches.

"You want me to bring the computer in here to work?"

Cain grimaced. He obviously needed to watch her more closely while she was on it. He couldn't do that while he was making brunch.

"No. Just wait till after we eat."

His words were a blatant announcement of how much he didn't trust her. He saw her small shoulders go rigid before giving a stiff nod.

"Fine." Tension radiated in the word. "I've got to leave at three o'clock for a few hours, so let's hurry up and get this done."

She was leaving *again*? The evening yesterday and then the afternoon today? This was more than just time off to hang out with Ariel. He wanted to argue, demand to know where she was going, but knew she wouldn't tell him. Arguing with Hayley now would just make things more difficult between them.

And outside of using a computer or breaking any other conditions of her parole, she was free to do what she wanted. Cain couldn't stop her.

His fist clenched around the coffeepot handle. No, he couldn't stop her if she was going off somewhere to meet one of her hacker cronies.

He really couldn't stop her if she was determined to slide back into that life. He could stop her now, but soon, probably in the next couple of weeks the way she was sorting through the data concerning the mole, Cain wouldn't be here to harass her into making good choices. He didn't want to believe that she wanted the life of a criminal. The Hayley he'd known—and loved—would never have wanted that.

Maybe the Hayley he'd known in high school was well and truly gone. Something in his soul shattered at the thought.

They never had a chance to talk about why she started hacking. Why she hadn't stayed in college and gotten a real job afterward. Hayley had never been lazy, had never just wanted to take the easiest way.

But Cain didn't ask now. They just finished their meal in silence.

Afterward she brought the computer to the kitchen table, obviously wanting distance from the couch. She explained everything she was doing without him having to ask. He appreciated it, but it took a lot of time. Slowed her down significantly.

And at some point, when she was talking to him and still typing full speed at the same time, he realized the truth.

"You don't have to tell me what you're doing," he said. "I know that slows you down. Just do the work."

She relaxed just slightly. "You trust that I'm only working on the Omega Sector case?"

Cain shook his head, feeling like a jerk, even though his words were the truth.

"No. I've just realized that even while explaining something to me, you could still be slipping in or accessing something completely different if you wanted to. So trust is a moot point."

WHEN SHE LEFT at three o'clock, he followed.

He hadn't given her a hard time about leaving, which worked out well seeing as they hadn't really spoken except for work-related questions since their midmorning meal. She told him she would be back before nightfall and he just nodded.

They both flinched again as he reconnected her ankle monitor.

As soon as she walked out the door he went to the computer and turned on the tracking feature. Then got in his car with the computer.

Maybe she was just going home again. If so, fine.

But if anybody else showed up at her apartment he was going to know about it.

He refused to give in to his thoughts earlier today that Hayley was beyond saving. She wasn't. She may be on the road to trouble again, but damn it, not on his watch. Not this time. If she needed money he would help her. If she needed a job he would help her.

She wasn't on drugs; she didn't have any elaborate lifestyle. How bad off could she really be?

When the tracker showed her car had driven past her apartment his lips pursed. This didn't change anything. Just made him more determined.

When her car had stopped at what looked like a restaurant, Cain sped up. This was some sort of meeting. Anger clenched in his stomach. Fear that he wouldn't be able to take care of Hayley, to get her out of whatever mess she was getting herself into, was closing in right behind the anger.

As he arrived he saw it wasn't a restaurant but the local fast-food ice-cream joint. He pulled his car to the far side of the parking lot and watched. Hayley hadn't even gotten out of her car yet.

Maybe he should go get her now. Stop whatever was about to happen before it could even start.

He was opening his door when he saw another car pull up next to Hayley's. Then watched, somewhat dumbfounded, as Ariel got out of the other car. She opened the back seat door, reached in and pulled out a little boy.

Cain felt like the biggest jackass on the planet. Hayley was meeting her cousin and her—what? Nephew? Second cousin?—for a midafternoon ice-cream break.

He scrubbed a hand over his face. He'd been so busy

looking for nefarious reasons why Hayley would need money and be sneaking away that he hadn't taken into consideration that she truly might have *good* reasons. Like helping her cousin, who'd obviously had a baby while Hayley was in prison, with living expenses. Hayley and Ariel had always been as close as sisters. Not being there for Ariel when she needed Hayley would've weighed heavily on Hayley. Maybe she was trying to make up for that now.

The kid, who was two or maybe three years old, obviously loved both women. He gave Hayley a huge hug before she picked him up and they walked into the ice-cream place together. He watched them for a few more seconds with his binoculars.

Cain wanted to join them. Wished he had the right to join them. Maybe if he hadn't been such an ass to her today she would've invited him along.

She wasn't in trouble and in need of being rescued. She was just trying to rebuild her life after a pretty harsh blow.

He watched them much longer than he should have, even knowing he looked like a creepy stalker. But Hayley's face was so lit up and happy he couldn't stop watching. It made him aware of how tense she was around him.

He watched the kid bite a huge chunk out of the bottom of his cone and both women jump to grab napkins as ice cream started running out the bottom. Cain chuckled. He and his brother had done the same thing as kids, driving his parents crazy.

The boy sucked the ice cream out of the bottom of his cone, then wiggled and squirmed as Hayley tried to wipe his face. He said something that obviously made her laugh.

Cain was about to put his binoculars away, since there obviously was no danger to national security here, when Hayley pulled the kid in for a hug, her fingers threading in his slightly-too-long hair at the nape of his neck, lifting it.

A dark brown birthmark about an inch in diameter could be seen before she let him go and his hair fell back in place, covering it.

Cain felt like all the air had been sucked out of his car.

He had a birthmark just like that at the exact same place on his neck.

Chapter Nine

Cain started his car and drove back to his house in a daze. His brain struggled to do the math. It wasn't possible that Hayley had a child, was it?

He was on the phone to Ren McClement in the Omega DC office, the only other person besides Steve Drackett who knew what was going on, before he even got inside the house. He needed info he couldn't get himself in case it led the mole to them.

"What's up, Cain? Any progress? Didn't expect to hear from you so soon."

"Ren, I need you to do something for me personally." Cain skipped any sort of greeting.

"Yes," Ren said immediately. No stipulations, just whatever Cain needed. Sign of a true friend. "Tell me."

"I need you to check Hayley Green's medical records from the first year she was in prison."

"I'm pulling them up now. Anything in particular I'm looking for?"

"You'll know it when you see it. Trust me."

"It's running. Hayley is the same Hayley Green that we got the court order for yesterday, right? The one you're working with?"

"Yeah." Cain paced as he waited for Ren to access the info.

"Okay, I've got the records. Looks like she... Oh my gosh."

Cain closed his eyes. "Tell me."

"Baby boy was born five months after Hayley arrived at the Georgia Women's Correctional Institute. No father listed on the birth certificate. Custody given to an Ariel Green upon birth of child."

Hayley had given birth to a baby, Cain's baby. In jail. Oh dear God.

"Cain? You okay? I don't want to pry, but..."

Cain blew out a breath. "Yeah, looks like this case just got a little more complicated."

"Um, are congratulations in order?"

Cain's short bark of laughter held very little humor. "It would seem so. I haven't talked to her about it, so I don't know much more than the fact that the kid has the exact same birthmark in the exact same place I do."

"That's a pretty sure sign."

"I'll let you know if this changes anything for the case. Thanks, Ren. I owe you one."

"Nah, brother, that one's a freebie for sure."

Cain stared at nothing for a long time after he got off the phone, trying to remember all the details from four years ago.

How the hell could he have not known Hayley was pregnant?

The case had been expedited, thanks to public scrutiny of the CET exam, led mostly by Senator Ralph Nelligar. Under normal circumstances her cybercrime case might have sat for months before being heard by a jury. Hayley would've been in a county holding cell and there would've been no way she could've kept him in the dark about the baby.

But once a US senator was involved things had moved along much more quickly. Then, Hayley had pleaded no contest at her arraignment, eliminating the need for a longer trial. By the time she was at the Georgia Women's Correctional, she was probably four months pregnant. Not quite showing if someone wasn't looking for it.

Cain definitely hadn't been looking for it.

He began pacing back and forth, his fingers going to the birthmark on his neck. No wonder she'd refused to see him when he'd visited her the first year. After that he'd kept tabs on her, made sure she hadn't run into any trouble or had any health issues, but had thought it better not to try to see her.

How could she have not told him? How could he have missed this?

He was furious. With her. With himself. With the entire situation.

But part of him was relieved that he at least now knew her secret. Knew why she'd been sneaking around. Was thrilled that she wasn't falling back into hacking.

But he was still furious.

When Hayley arrived back at his house a couple hours later, Cain had gotten himself under control. Yelling wasn't going to accomplish anything.

Although exactly what Cain hoped to accomplish he wasn't sure at all.

"Cain?" Hayley called out as she entered through the door.

Most of the lights were off in the house. "I'm in the kitchen."

She looked more relaxed, looser, than she had before she left. She stopped in the hallway, not quite all the way into the eating area where he sat.

"Feeling better?" he asked. "Good break?"

"Yeah. Ready to get to it." She took a step closer. "Look, I'm sorry about before. I will explain everything more clearly. Show you what I'm doing so you don't have to be worried that it's something on the computer I'm not supposed to."

Oh, they had much different problems to worry about now.

"Sit down."

She sat opposite him, holding out her foot for him to remove the anklet. Instead he slid the photo album he'd placed on the table toward her.

Hayley smiled as she looked down at the twenty-five-year-old pictures.

"Oh my gosh, is that your mom? Look at that hair!"

His smile didn't reach his eyes. "I know. Styles have changed a lot since then."

"What's the matter, Bennett? You have so much time on your hands that you had to go reminiscing?"

He flipped the page over and pointed to a particular picture. "Actually, this was the picture I was studying. Wanted to show you."

It was one someone had taken of him when he was about three. His dad was ruffling his hair, which made the birthmark—the exact one he'd seen on the little boy today—more noticeable.

She looked back and forth between him and the picture, color leaching from her face. She slid her chair back farther from him and stood, looking like she might bolt at any second.

"Wh-why are you showing me that picture?"

He wasn't going to beat around the bush. "I know about the boy, Hayley."

All remaining color left. She gripped the back of the chair like she might fall over. "How?"

"I thought you were trying to get back in touch with your hacker friends. That's why I was so suspicious about all the work you were doing for me."

Confusion was clear on her face. "I wasn't."

"When you wanted to leave yesterday, I was convinced you were meeting someone. The same this afternoon."

"You followed me," she whispered.

He nodded. "My intentions were good. I wanted to see what I could do to help. Even had binoculars to watch you. I wanted to keep you away from whatever big baddies you were meeting. The big baddies ended up being Ariel and what I thought was her son."

Hayley stared down at the ground.

"But it wasn't Ariel's son, I realized, when I saw the birthmark. It only took a phone call to confirm that you gave birth in prison. That you are the mother of *my* son."

Hayley didn't look at him. "His name is Mason. He's three and a half."

Mason.

"How could you not have told me about him?" He slammed his fist against the table.

She looked back up at him, heat in her cheeks. "When was I supposed to do that, Cain? We weren't exactly speaking to each other at the time."

"You should've made the effort."

"You'd made it abundantly clear how little I'd meant to you."

He rolled his eyes. "Because I had you arrested for a crime you actually committed?"

"No. Because you slept with me knowing you were going to be arresting me a few days later. You used the feelings you knew I had for you to get information to put me in jail." Now she slammed her hand on the table. "So yeah, I took that to mean you didn't really care about me very much."

Her words doused his righteous fire. God, was that what she really thought? That he'd gone to bed with her four years ago because he wanted to use that to entrap her?

"Hayley." The anger had fled from his tone now. "I'll admit when we discovered the hacker network involved with selling the CET answers, I came to you. But not because I planned to arrest you."

Disbelief sat clear on her features.

"When I first contacted you, I had no idea you were involved. I'll admit I planned to use you as a source, but I didn't know you were actually one of the hackers until later. By then we were already together."

He—as always—hadn't been able to stay away from her. They'd been drawn to each other like magnets just like they had been in high school.

He'd stopped it, stayed away, when he'd realized she was one of the people his team would be arresting. But the wheels were already in motion and Cain couldn't stop it. He'd spent the night before the bust getting piss drunk, so furious that he couldn't do anything to protect Hayley without compromising everything he'd sworn to uphold as a law enforcement officer.

It had ripped his guts out.

"I was pretty damn mad at you when I found out

what you'd done. Couldn't believe you'd be that stupid."
He stared into her brown eyes. "But I never initiated
contact with you with the intent to arrest you."

The opposite. If he'd found out early enough to help
her get out of the situation completely before Omega's
cybercrime division had gotten on her trail, he probably would've done it.

She just shook her head. "Yeah, well, it didn't look
that way from where I was sitting in the handcuffs."

HE KNEW. Cain finally knew.

Anger, frustration, pain, were radiating off him from
across the table. Hayley knew she'd see the same in her
features if she looked in the mirror.

But under it all she felt relief. He *knew*.

"I was so angry," she told him. "But also afraid. I
didn't know what to do. What was going to happen to
me or the baby. I thought you had used me to further
your career, to make a name for yourself or whatever."

"You thought I would deny the baby was mine."

She turned away, couldn't even bear to look at him.
"I thought I was just a girl from your past who you discovered was doing something illegal. So you slept with
me to get close. Plus, I thought if I started making a
lot of noise about getting knocked up from one of my
arresting officers I might get in even more trouble."

She'd seen the look in his eyes that day in the courtroom. He hadn't seemed angry or even cold. He'd
seemed so *disappointed* in her. She'd been disappointed
enough in herself. So as weak as it made her seem, she
hadn't wanted to get him in trouble, either.

She heard a low curse from across the table. "Damn
it, Hayley, *why*?"

What other reason could she give him? "I—"

"Not the baby, although I want to know everything there is to know about him. Tell me why you ended up in my pathway to begin with. Why were you involved with something illegal?"

His words were so heartfelt, so desperate, she felt whatever anger she had left melt out of her.

"My dad got sick. Cancer." She sat down at the table across from Cain. "I had a year left in college when I had to come back home and take care of him. You know how it is, never enough money. His insurance was pitiful."

God, it sounded like such a cop-out. It had to, especially to Cain, the one who had grown up with such a crystal clear sense of right and wrong, black-and-white. He'd always known he wanted to work in law enforcement.

"I was working at the Bluewater, but couldn't make ends meet. A friend of mine I'd gone to school with asked if I wanted to do some freelance stuff."

"Kenneth Vargas."

She nodded. "It seemed like an answer to prayer. Jobs I could do from home and still be able to take care of my dad.

"For about six months he paid me pretty well to do some legit computer jobs." She rubbed her hands across her eyes. "Ends up those jobs were really auditions. When he realized what I could really do, how pretty desperate I was, he mentioned another possibility that would completely take care of my financial woes. Kenneth was a good salesman. Said we wouldn't be hurting anyone. Selling CET results to rich little brats."

The test itself couldn't be hacked, but the results

and reporting system could. But it involved programming and had to be done manually each time to avoid detection.

Ended up Vargas was using a dozen other people with Hayley's skills from all over the country. His greed had made the hacks much more noticeable.

"I'll be honest, I didn't need much convincing from Vargas. I liked the challenge of it and it got me the money I needed."

She looked across the table, but not directly at Cain. Didn't want to see further disappointment in his eyes.

"I don't know if you care or if you'll even believe me, but I was already getting out when the arrest went down. Had taken part in fewer and fewer hacks."

She saw Cain wipe a hand over his face and chanced a glance at him. "That's probably why you didn't show up in my initial suspects list," he said. "I knew you went to school with Vargas, knew him. But I didn't know you were a part of the group we were about to arrest."

Knowing he hadn't slept with her in order to arrest her changed a lot for Hayley. At least it didn't make her feel like he cared nothing about her, that their connection hadn't meant nothing to him.

She shrugged. "Like you said, I was guilty. Regardless of whether I was getting out of it or not, I had committed the crime."

Her father had died and the desperate need for money had passed. Once the panic had been gone, she'd realized what she was doing. Had been ashamed.

If she'd gotten out just one month earlier her life would've been totally different. One month would've probably kept her off Cain's radar. She probably never would've gone to jail.

And, maybe even more importantly, if she'd gotten out one month earlier she would've never stumbled on to the information that might one day cost her her life.

Someone was using the CET exam at international Department of Defense schools, to sell state secrets. Hayley had discovered the when, where and how, and had been in the process of finding out who when she'd been arrested and banned from computers.

Cain leaned in closer to her. "I never dreamed the judge would sentence you for as long as he did. I thought he would take into consideration your lack of criminal record. I honestly never thought you would go to prison. Especially not for four years."

She just shrugged. "It was a high-profile case. Besides, would it have really made any difference in your decision to arrest me? I was the bad guy."

He stared at her for a long moment. "Maybe. I…" He trailed off, then finally shrugged. "Maybe."

"I'm sorry I didn't tell you about Mason. I was angry and scared and honestly thought you were completely done with me. Would not want to be associated with me at all, even in this way. I was a criminal. How could you possibly want me after that?"

They stared at each other across the table for a long time, most of the truth finally open between them. She wished she could tell him the rest, but she couldn't. Not without proof.

His green eyes held her captive as he leaned closer. "I think there's one thing you better get clear. I have never stopped wanting you."

Chapter Ten

Hours later, Cain sat on the same couch where he'd woken up that morning, but this time Hayley very definitely wasn't in his arms. They'd talked more before finally reaching some sort of emotional truce and had begun working. They had finally decided to stop when Hayley announced she would probably need to access the Omega servers on-site to definitely be sure about what she was seeing.

Cain's anger had eased. It was impossible to stay mad when he forced himself to look at the situation from Hayley's point of view.

They'd both been wrong. Both made bad choices. The past couldn't be changed, but the future wasn't yet written.

He had a son.

He wanted to rush in and force himself into Mason's life. To get to know him. But Cain realized Hayley was also just getting to know the little boy. That she'd lost just as much time as Cain had. More.

He had no doubt after watching Hayley interact with Mason today that she loved the child. Wanted what was best for him. Cain did, too.

So he could wait. Ease himself into the child's life. But he would be part of it, no matter what he had to do.

He looked down at Hayley, tucked on the opposite side of the couch. He wanted to be part of her life, too. She'd always been important to him, even in the years they were separated while they were in college and then while he was pursuing his law enforcement dreams.

It was why what he'd seen as her betrayal hurt so much. How could she have broken the law when upholding it had always been so important to him? Hearing her explanation helped. Knowing she took responsibility for the choices she'd made helped even more.

But even in the tentative peace they'd made last night, both of them not knowing exactly what to do with it, Hayley seemed to have more secrets. Were the shadows in her eyes because of what had happened in the past? Because part of Cain was afraid there was something she was still hiding from him.

A hand slamming on his front door had Hayley jerking awake and Cain heading toward the door. He grabbed his sidearm on the kitchen counter out of habit.

Cain cracked open the door. Damn. The Georgia state troopers standing on his porch were not who he was expecting at all. And not who he wanted to face with a gun in his hand.

Cain nodded at them, keeping his sidearm behind the door. "Officers."

One of the officers held up a piece of paper. "We have a warrant for the arrest of Hayley Green for violation of her parole. Intel indicated that she was inside this house."

What the hell?

"There's been some mistake. I'm federal law enforcement, and I was given a court order allowing the ease-ment of Ms. Green's parole restrictions, specifically concerning her use of computers."

"Is Ms. Green in the house, sir?" the second cop asked.

"Look, just let me get my badge and the court order."

Cop One stuck his hand out to stop Cain from clos-ing the door. "Is Ms. Green in the house?"

Damn it. This was about to get out of hand.

"She is." Cain looked from one man to the other. "Also, you should be warned that I'm currently hold-ing a firearm."

The tension in the cops skyrocketed as Cain low-ered the hand holding the gun hidden behind the door. He kept it very loosely by his side, trying to show he meant no harm.

As he'd been afraid of, Cain's lack of threat didn't seem to matter to these guys. Both had their weapons drawn and pointed at him.

Cop One took a step back. "Hands up in the air. Right now."

Cain raised them, keeping his hand over the muz-zle of the gun rather than at the trigger. He hoped they could see there was no way he could shoot them like this. But tensions were high with police officers all over the country. No cop wanted to take a chance with a stranger with a gun in his hand.

"I'm going to hand this to you, all right?" Both of these troopers were young. Cain didn't want to give them any excuse to use excessive force. "Then I will get my law enforcement credentials and we can work this out."

"Cain, what's going on?"

Cop One threw the door open wide at Hayley's words and aimed his firearm at her. Guy looked a little nervous. "Get your hands up! Do you have a gun?" he demanded of Hayley, although with both hands empty it seemed obvious she didn't.

"No." Hayley raised her arms, getting paler by the second. "What's going on?"

Cop Two, a little more calm than his buddy, turned to her. "Are you Hayley Green?"

Hayley nodded.

"We have a warrant for your arrest, for violation of your parole."

Cain could feel her eyes on him. "Cain?"

Damn it, her voice sounded so scared.

He gave her the most reassuring smile he could muster. "We're going to get this worked out."

He turned to the officers. "Look, what's your name?" he said to the more calm one.

"Perowne."

"I'm Cain Bennett. I work for Omega Sector, federal law enforcement. Hayley Green is my authorized consultant for a case. Like I said, I have a court order giving her temporary freedom from her tracking anklet."

"I understand that, sir, but that's going to have to be addressed down at central booking. Our instructions were to bring her in."

The other guy strode past Cain, weapon still raised, and turned Hayley forcefully against the hallway wall. "Put your hands on the wall and spread your legs."

The guy wasn't brutal, but he definitely wasn't gentle as he pushed Hayley's chest into the wall with a hand on her shoulder blades as he put his sidearm back into its holster.

Frustration burned through Cain as he saw a tear fall down Hayley's terrified face. The cop jerked back one of her arms, then the other, cuffing them.

"Be cool, Brickman," Perowne muttered.

"You just keep your eye on supercop over there." Brickman began reading Hayley her rights as he ran his hands up her legs to make sure she wasn't hiding any weapons, then patted down her sides and chest.

Another tear fell, all color gone from her face completely. Cain was actually afraid she might faint.

"Hayley, it's okay. We're going to get this worked out. Do you hear me?"

She nodded just slightly.

Short of violently disarming the cops, which Cain might've done if it wouldn't have put Hayley at risk, there was nothing he could do. Although it went against every protective grain in his body, Cain was going to have to let them take her.

Brickman continued to use a hand on Hayley's shoulder to keep her pushed up against the wall while he turned to Cain. It was a punk move just to show his power.

It took all of Cain's considerable willpower not to show Brickman just how precious his position of power really was when he heard Hayley's soft whimper.

"Cut it out, Paul," Perowne said. "Take her to the car."

Cain touched Hayley's arm as the officer walked her by. "I'll be right behind you."

"If you can show me your credentials, I can give this back to you." Perowne holstered his own weapon and lifted Cain's.

Cain got his ID from the counter and showed it to the other man, along with the court order.

Perowne handed him back his gun. "Agent Bennett,

I'm sorry for the misunderstanding. And that court order looks official, so I don't know exactly what the problem is. Like I said, if you can come to the courthouse, hopefully you can get everything worked out."

Cain handed the man Hayley's anklet. "You'll need this."

The cop just nodded and they walked outside together. Cain could see Hayley fighting back tears from the back seat of the squad car, her arms at an awkward angle thanks to the cuffs.

He wasn't letting her return to jail. Watching her go the first time, even when he'd known she'd been guilty, had taken everything he had. There was no way he was letting it happen now.

FEAR WAS A fist in Hayley's throat, blocking her airway. She tried to think through the panic. This was just a misunderstanding. Some sort of paperwork glitch. Cain would get it worked out.

Cain, the man who had just found out she'd had his child and hadn't told him. The man who still didn't trust her.

Panic crashed over her again.

"You know, some people just never readjust to life on the outside. Will do anything to get thrown back in," the same policeman who had put the cuffs on her said, his leer evident from the front seat. "Guess you must be one of those."

The reasonable part of her brain told her to just ignore him, but the terror wouldn't let her. "Please. This is some sort of mistake. I had authorization to take off the anklet."

"Is that so? You'd be amazed at how many people

are 'authorized' to do whatever they want to, right up to the point where they get caught."

The handcuffs pulled at her shoulder blades, making sitting in the car uncomfortable and reminding her that she swore she would never be back in this position again. How long would they keep her? She needed to call Ariel and let her know what was going on. Did she need a lawyer? And where was the other officer who had his gun pointed at Cain? What was taking them so long?

Finally the other officer walked out the door with Cain behind him. Hayley's eyes devoured Cain's face, hoping to find a glimpse of good news, that he'd been able to convince these men of their official work.

"Ends up Agent Bennett is, in fact, federal law enforcement, and does have what looks like a legitimate court order for the removal of the tracking device," the nice cop—Hayley knew Cain had asked his name but she couldn't remember it—said.

Bad Cop just snickered. "Not my problem. They're going to have to fight it out downtown."

"I told him the same."

Hayley's eyes flew to Cain's again as he walked closer to the car.

"Hey, back off," Bad Cop said. "I don't care who you work for."

"Chill out, Brickman, for crying out loud," Good Cop muttered.

Cain ignored them both, his eyes on Hayley. "Six hours, okay? We'll have this worked out and you back home in six hours. Just hang on until then."

Hayley nodded. Everything in his green eyes told her she could trust him. He would handle this.

"Okay," she said softly. It was all she could do. Her life was in his hands now. She prayed trusting him wasn't the biggest mistake she'd ever made.

Chapter Eleven

Cain called Ren on the way to the courthouse.

"Cain, you know we're not dating, right? I talk to you more than I talk to some of my girlfriends."

Any other time Cain would've harassed Ren about his love life, but the look in Hayley's eyes as she had sat in that squad car had crushed all ability for humor in him.

"State troopers came and arrested Hayley a few minutes ago for violation of her parole, having to do with the anklet."

He heard Ren's muttered curse. "The court order was legit. What the hell happened?"

"That's what I'm trying to find out. Something's not right here, man."

"Damn straight. She's only had the thing off for what, thirty-six hours? That's pretty quick to pounce on a nonviolent parolee. Let me see what I can find out."

Cain could hear a keyboard clacking away. Ren's curse was quite a bit more foul when it came a few minutes later.

"What?" Cain asked.

"You still got a hard copy of that court order?"

"Yes. Why?"

"Because our entire petition and agreement from the judge has been completely erased from the system."

"What the hell? How does that happen?"

"It doesn't, Cain. Not unless someone gets inside the system and deliberately erases it."

Now it was Cain's turn to curse. "Is it the Omega mole? Does he know we're onto him? Or Damien Freihof? He's been one step ahead of us this entire time."

"It will take a while to backtrack this and figure out who did it. Ironically your gal Hayley would be the best one to do that."

"Yeah, well, I don't think they're going to let me take my laptop into her cell." Cain gritted his teeth as he changed lanes to lead him into the parking lot of the criminal courthouse. "And I can't get the help I need from the Omega office without tipping off the mole."

"Let me see what I can find from here," Ren said.

Ren McClement worked out of Washington, not the Critical Response Division office in Colorado Springs. Hopefully the mole wouldn't have knowledge of Ren's activities.

"Okay. Meanwhile I'll use this paper copy of the court order and see if it gets me anywhere." He told Hayley six hours. He wanted to make sure he kept that promise.

"There's something not right here, Cain. First the fire and now this? It might be Freihof or the mole, but they should have no knowledge of your activities whatsoever."

Cain parked his car. "So either the mole is much more powerful than we think…"

"Or we're dealing with someone else entirely."

"Someone from one of my other cases? Targeting Hayley?" That didn't make much sense.

"We'll just see what we find."

"I made her a promise to get her out," Cain said. "She's more than done her time for whatever crimes she committed in the past."

Hayley's pale face, brown eyes huge, haunted his every thought.

"I'll hurry."

Inside the courthouse things went from bad to worse.

The judge who had signed the initial court order had gone on a last-minute fishing vacation and couldn't be reached for confirmation. Nearly growling in frustration, Cain was told it would be late afternoon before he could get time in front of another judge.

He decided he would use his federal law enforcement status to see Hayley while she was held in the booking area. He could at least give her information and reassure her—and himself—that things were going to be all right.

But once he got to that section of the building, he found that Hayley had been taken to the court section, an arraignment already scheduled.

An arraignment before a judge this soon after her arrest? That was almost unheard of. Normally someone might spend an entire day or even two in a holding cell before the judge was able to hear the initial details of the case and formally charge the defendant.

It wasn't normal, but at least it wasn't bad. Hayley would've been allowed to call, or would've been given, a lawyer. She would've told the lawyer what had happened, and Cain would be able to back up her statement and provide the document.

Hopefully it would all go away from there. Lumped up as some sort of clerical error.

Cain didn't know why they hadn't called him, so immediately found the courtroom where the arraignment hearing was taking place.

Hayley sat at a table in front of the judge's bench with a lawyer. Good, maybe her attorney had found a copy of the court order allowing Hayley near a computer, and this would soon be over.

Evidently the judge had different ideas. It was like watching her sentencing four years ago all over again. Powerless to stop any of it.

"It has come to my attention that not only have you violated your parole, Ms. Green, but that you have connection to violent criminals that the court was not aware of when you were initially paroled."

"Your honor..." Hayley's attorney tried to interject, but the judge held his hand up to silence the woman.

"I'll admit I'm not certain of all the facts here, so there will be no actual ruling by me today. But I am ordering that Ms. Green be taken back into custody and will return to the Georgia Women's Correctional facility until another parole hearing can be scheduled with all the facts."

What in the hell? Cain walked into the courtroom farther, pulling out his badge as he went.

"Your honor, I'm Agent Cain Bennett, with federal law enforcement, and was the person who had requested Ms. Green's original parole conditions be released. I have the court order in hand and want to assure you that she did not break any conditions of her parole."

Cain saw Hayley's head spin around to him, but he kept his eyes on the judge.

"Be that as it may, Agent Bennett, I do not have all the information needed to make any sort of judgment right now. Ms. Green will return to custody, but I'm sure with your word and the court order this could be worked out in just a couple of weeks."

"Your honor—"

The judge brought his gavel down on his table. "That's my decision. Bailiff, take Ms. Green into custody and prepare her to return to the correctional facility."

Frustration clawed through Cain. He rushed over to the row of seats directly behind Hayley's table.

"Hayley, we're going to get this worked out."

"I have to go back to prison." Shock clouded her tone, her entire face devoid of color.

Unlike last time when her eyes had seemed so deadened at what the judge said, this time they were filled with terror.

Cain couldn't help it, he reached up and trailed his fingers down her cheek. Agony clawed at his gut. "I'm sorry, sweetheart. But I promise I'm not going to rest until I get this fixed. This is not like before. A couple of days. I promise you'll be back with me and Mason in a couple of days."

The bailiff reached Hayley and turned her around from Cain, placing handcuffs on her wrists in front of her.

Hayley glanced at him over her shoulder. "Take care of Mason." Her voice choked on the words.

"No, I won't need to. This will be less than a week and you'll be back."

Hayley didn't respond, just followed the bailiff, head down. Cain watched until she exited out the back.

He wanted to punch something, throw over the table in front of him, but knew that would just get him arrested, too. He needed to work the problem.

Cain spent the rest of the afternoon talking to whoever he could to try to find answers. He phoned Ren to provide an update, but the call went straight to voice mail.

Ren would call as soon as he had any information.

Cain caught Hayley's attorney to ask her for details as she was leaving the courthouse. He walked with her.

"Ms. Rincon, I need to talk to you about Hayley Green."

She looked over at him dressed in a crisp tailored suit. This was no court-appointed attorney, this was someone who charged hundreds of dollars an hour for her legal services. Money Hayley didn't have, even if she'd known how to obtain the lawyer's services in such a short amount of time.

"Agent Bennett, I appreciate you speaking up for my client today in court, but I'm not allowed to talk about the case with anyone without my client's permission."

"I'm just trying to figure out what's going on. She was cleared by a judge to work with me and next thing we know she's been arrested for parole violation."

Rincon shrugged. "Look, I'll level with you. This shouldn't have been my case. I basically stood in today for a colleague in the public defender's department. This arraignment took place superfast and he needed help. So I got contacted at ten o'clock this morning and was asked to volunteer some of my time. I owed a favor so I did it."

Ten o'clock this morning? That would've been about the time the state troopers had arrived to arrest Hayley.

How would a lawyer be called before Hayley was even at the courthouse?

"Ms. Rincon, there's something going on that's not right."

The woman shrugged. "I'll give you that it's all been pretty unusual, but I don't know that it's necessarily not right. But honestly, my part ends here. Someone else will be working with Hayley for her parole hearing. She can either hire her own lawyer or use a public defender."

This was a dead end. "Thanks for your time."

Rincon nodded and continued down the stairs from the courthouse.

An unknown lawyer asked to take Hayley's case before she was even arrested? An arraignment hearing in record time? Lost court orders and a judge suddenly on vacation?

Something definitely wasn't right.

Cain turned and went back into the building. He was about to cross some lines that might end up costing him his career, but he didn't care. His gut was telling him that Hayley was in danger and he damn well wasn't going to ignore that.

It took him an hour to find the circumstances he needed, as he waited for the assistant to Judge Nicolaides, who had held the arraignment hearing, to leave her desk.

Hoping this wouldn't cost him everything, but willing to pay the price if it did, Cain slid inside the judge's inner chambers without permission.

The older man looked up from what he was reading, saw Cain and raised an eyebrow.

"You lost, son?"

"I need to talk to you, Your Honor."

"You are aware that you're not supposed to be in here, correct, Agent Bennett?"

Cain was surprised the judge remembered his name. "Yes, sir."

"I will give you five minutes. Only because I was there when you led the Spartans to the state championship."

Whatever the reason the judge was listening to him, even high school football, Cain would take it.

"I was telling the truth today about having the court order for Hayley Green to assist Omega Sector on a case."

"Then you'll want to be sure to share that information when they review her parole proceedings."

Cain gritted his teeth. He was afraid Hayley might not make it to the parole hearing. "Something's not right about this entire situation."

Judge Nicolaides leaned back in his seat. "Now see, normally I would hear something like that and think that it was based off of desperation and emotion rather than actual fact. But today, it just so happens, I might agree with you."

"Can you tell me why?"

"Ends up my early-afternoon hearings were cleared off my schedule, and I was given just one. Ms. Green's case. I'm not one to complain about a lesser workload, but I must admit it did catch my attention."

"Hayley was arrested just this morning. About two hours before her hearing."

Judge Nicolaides's eyebrows seem to have found a new home in his hairline. "Two hours between arrest and her hearing? Again, normally I would say that Ms.

Green had friends in high places to get before a judge that quickly."

"She doesn't."

"What also strikes me as peculiar about the situation is the fact that I was told that the case I would be hearing involved a criminal with, wait, let me find it"—the judge riffled through some papers and found the ones he wanted to read—"*significant potential for violence and destruction* if not returned to incarceration immediately, until more details could be produced to reevaluate her parole proceedings."

Cain could hardly keep himself from gawking. "Someone said that about Hayley Green? She was arrested for cybercrimes, has no violent history and did her time in a minimum-security prison."

"Son, you either don't know your friend very well, or someone very high up in the government has some pretty incorrect information. I'm sorry I don't have a name to give you."

"How high up?"

"Pretty damn high. Washington, DC."

"I don't understand."

"Neither do I. And I hope you can get this worked out when they reevaluate her parole. All I know is, today someone wanted to make sure your Hayley Green ended up back in prison."

Chapter Twelve

Cain couldn't go back home, not knowing that Hayley was sitting in a cell. He'd tried to see her, but had been told that she was being processed for relocation. Could not be seen until after she was transferred to Georgia Women's Correctional.

Was she scared? She would have to be. This had to be her worst nightmare.

He still hadn't heard back from Ren but knew the other man would get to him as soon as he had information. Meanwhile, Cain decided to do what he had promised Hayley. He would watch over Mason.

Cain parked his car outside Hayley and Ariel's small apartment complex with no intention of going inside. Not without Hayley, not until she was ready for him to meet Mason. That was the least he could do after everything that had happened. But he would keep watch over their building from here. He wasn't going to be getting any sleep anyway.

Tomorrow would involve finding the judge who was on vacation, the one who had given the initial court order for Hayley's assistance. Cain had no intention of waiting until she had an actual parole hearing to take in proof of the court order. He'd do it as early as possible.

She'd be transferred back to Georgia Women's Correctional tomorrow afternoon. At least once she was there Cain would be able to use his law enforcement credentials to see her.

It was not quite getting dark when the door of the apartment complex opened and Ariel and Mason walked out. They were holding each other's hands as they crossed to the small park half a block away. Cain got out of the car and followed them, careful to keep his distance.

Ariel sat on a bench while Mason ran around the wooden play area with a couple of other children. He ran full steam back and forth over a bridge, across monkey bars, and up and down slides. Cain couldn't help but be enthralled with him.

"You're going to make the other parents nervous if you keep standing there like a stalker," Ariel called out.

He crossed over to her but didn't sit on the bench beside her. "How did you know I was there?"

"I saw your car before we even left the apartment. Plus, Hayley gave me a heads-up that you might be around."

"Did she tell you what happened?"

"Briefly, in a very short phone call from her holding cell, not that she knew exactly what was going on. I resisted the urge to tell her that bad things happen to her whenever you're around. She's got enough to worry about."

"I'm going to get this fixed."

"You do that." Ariel didn't seem to have much more to say to him.

"She told me about Mason. That I'm his father."

"Being a sperm donor does not make you his father."
Ariel's voice was tight.

"I plan to be his father in every way that Hayley
will let me."

Ariel turned and glared at him. "You know, you're
lucky that Hayley is a lot more forgiving than I am. Because I would've told you to go die in a hole."

Cain nodded curtly. "I get it, you're mad at me because I arrested her. And it sucked, I agree. But she did
do it, Ariel, you know that, right? Hayley was guilty."

"Yeah, I know. But I also know that Hayley paid a
much higher price than for any crime she'd actually
committed."

Cain sighed. "Four years was a long time. I never
dreamed she'd be sentenced for that long."

"You should've checked on her, Cain. What happened to her in that prison, nobody should have to bear
that. Least of all someone like Hayley. Good. Gentle."

Cain wasn't sure what Ariel was talking about. He
had checked up on her. Made sure she hadn't been hurt.
There didn't tend to be many instances of violence in
minimum security, but Ariel's words made him realize
he must've missed something.

"What happened? Was she hurt?"

"Was she *hurt*? She gave birth in a prison hospital *handcuffed* to a bed. They didn't even let her hold
Mason, did you know that? Not even one time."

"My God." He sank onto the bench next to her. He'd
had no idea, hadn't even thought to ask her about the situation surrounding Mason's birth. Not that she would've
told him if he had.

Ariel shook her head slowly. "It broke something in

her. Not just that, but losing all that time in Mason's life."

"Believe me, if I could go back and change it, I would." Cain didn't know exactly what he would do, but everything would be different. "All I can do is try to make things right going forward."

"You're doing a fine job there, Ace, considering Hayley is back in jail."

"I'll make sure she's released. I'll make sure she's safe."

"Safe? Why do you say that? There's something else going on, isn't there?"

"Why do you say that?" he asked, throwing her words right back at her.

Ariel shrugged. "Something Hayley said the other day. About why she had to be working all the time. About why she had agreed to work for you, of all people."

"I was worried about her working so hard from the beginning. She shouldn't need money that badly."

Ariel kept her eyes on Mason. "Part of it is so she won't have to work so much once I leave to study in Oxford."

That made sense. "But you think there's something else?"

"I know there is. And believe it or not I actually told her to tell you, but I guess she didn't. She's been saving up money in case she has to run with Mason."

"Did she say why?"

Ariel shook her head. "No. She said the less I knew about it the better. But I know it has to do with her hacking stuff."

That didn't tell Cain anything concrete. It could be

trouble that she might have to get away from, in which case he could help her. Or it might be trouble that she was running toward, and she wanted a safety net as she got out from underneath the law.

Cain looked over at the playground and saw that the kids seemed to be winding down. He stood up. "I'm going to go."

"Don't you want to meet Mason?"

He did. Wanted to hug him or shake his hand and ruffle his hair, whatever the kid felt comfortable with. He wanted to show him his own birthmark and how it was twins with what Mason had.

"Not without Hayley."

For the first time Ariel looked at him without utter contempt schooling her features. "Then go get our girl, Bennett. She's lost enough time with her son, she shouldn't have to lose any more."

He stood up and walked away as Mason headed toward them.

"I'll bring her home."

BY THE NEXT morning Cain was convinced Ariel was right. From his laptop in the car outside Hayley's apartment, he'd spent the night researching the CET hacking scandal. There was something much deeper going on than what appeared on the surface.

Eleven people had been arrested along with Hayley four and a half years ago for their hacker work. The judge had made an example of the hackers, largely due to Senator Nelligar's involvement; although 90 percent of them had been first-time offenders, he had given them all, including Hayley, jail time.

They'd all been getting out of jail over the last few months.

Two of the twelve hackers had died in prison. One from injuries sustained in a fight, and another who had been thought to be mentally unstable the entire time and killed himself.

Things like that happened even in minimum-security prisons.

Three more had died in the last year since they'd been released from prison. Heart attack, car accident and drug overdose.

Five out of the twelve hackers arrested in the CET scandal were dead. That was way more than coincidence.

Coupled with what had happened to Hayley yesterday, Cain knew she was in trouble. *Life-and-death* trouble.

That was confirmed a couple hours later when he finally heard from Ren.

"I'm on my way to you right now," Ren said by way of greeting.

That wasn't good. If Ren wanted to be here, then things were even worse than Cain had thought.

"Then I guess you know we've got problems."

"Funny," Ren said. "I was about to say the same thing to you."

Cain told him about the deaths of so many of the hackers who had been arrested with Hayley.

"Add another heart attack to your list," Ren responded.

"One of the hackers? Did I miss something?"

"The judge from whom you got the original court order releasing Hayley?"

"The guy on the fishing vacation?"

"Yep," Ren said. "Heart attack."

Damn it. "So the one man who could've very quickly corroborated our story just died."

"Cain, it gets worse from there."

"Worse than six people being dead?"

"I was hitting dead ends in normal channels trying to figure out what was going on with Hayley," Ren continued. "So I took to unofficial channels."

Like everyone in Omega Sector, Cain wasn't sure exactly what Ren McClement's actual job description was. The man's name was mentioned with a sort of reverence. Rumors were that McClement's specialty was undercover ops. Deep, long-term assignments. The ones no one with family or friends could take because the infiltrated groups wouldn't hesitate to kill a loved one just to see what the person would do.

McClement answered to very few people and always got his man, no matter what the cost.

If Hayley was in as much trouble as Cain was afraid she was, he wanted someone like Ren at his back.

"What did you find out from unofficial channels?"

Ren let out a breath. "There's a hit out on Hayley's life."

Cain's curse was low and foul. "Who? Why?"

"That, I haven't been able to find out. But it's someone high, Cain, really high."

Cain thought of what Judge Nicolaides had said. Almost the exact same thing.

"When? How?" Those were the questions Cain should've been asking first anyway. The who and why could wait.

"Somebody is willing to pay top dollar to kill Hayley in what looks like an escape attempt as she's transferred to the correctional facility today."

Cain knotted his fist against his kitchen counter. "Okay, I'll get on the phone and stop the transfer. Unless they've got a bus already going out there, they probably meant to transfer her in a squad car."

"That's just it. The channels I got this from contain some crooked cops. I'm not sure who we can trust."

"Then I'll go get her out of holding right now. We won't even let the transfer start." This time he wouldn't take no for an answer when it came to seeing her.

"You're not going to be able to get her out. Someone's already been changing the electronic files surrounding her. Instead of cybercrimes, Hayley's file now says that she was a violent criminal, brought in as a fugitive."

Cain was already bringing up the information on his laptop. Sure enough, after logging in to the Georgia law enforcement system, he saw everything Ren said was true. Instead of cybercrimes, she was listed as having done time for attempted murder and assault. She'd escaped from custody and had been on the run when she was caught.

There was no way the police would release Hayley to Cain.

"And even worse," Ren said, "they're not taking her back to the minimum-security prison. They're taking her to maximum security. If for some reason she lives through the transfer, whoever put out this hit has made it open season on Hayley once she arrives."

Chapter Thirteen

The hardest part about prison for Hayley had been the lack of privacy. Followed at a very close second by boredom.

Books had helped a great deal with the boredom since she hadn't been allowed near any computers while incarcerated. She'd read just about every title in the library. She'd used nonfiction books to learn about things directly related to her like child rearing, psychology, cooking and nutrition. She also learned about stuff not so related to her: climbing Mount Everest, cooking Thai food and the five-hour workweek. She'd read all sorts of fiction. Action, horror, science fiction. The only thing she hadn't been able to read was romance. Books with happily-ever-afters just didn't seem to apply to her at all.

She had no books now. And no privacy again. The county holding cell was like a twenty-four-hour diner, women coming in and out constantly. All night she'd been watching them, since sleep had been impossible.

When she had been in prison, she had pretty much been ignored. Nothing about her four years at the Georgia Women's Correctional facility had been traumatic. No one had hurt her, there hadn't been fights or people shanking others, or anything that might happen at a maximum-security prison that held the more violent offenders.

Minimum security hadn't even had barbed wire fences surrounding the facility. It had been sort of like camp, except you couldn't leave, and the counselors had guns. And they didn't really pay attention to you unless you did something bad.

None of the officers seemed to be ignoring her now. Every time one walked by, he or she glared at Hayley, anger clear in their expressions. She had no idea what she had done to warrant such hostility.

But she just kept thinking about the guards and the books and anything else except for the fact that in a couple hours they would be taking her back to prison. Maybe for a long time.

Because if she concentrated on that, the hysteria was going to bubble over. It was so close to the surface right now she could feel it.

She wanted her son. Wanted to be with Mason. He was just getting used to her being in his life and now she was gone again.

And Cain…so much of this was resting in his hands. And he had so much reason to hate her.

"Hayley Green?" An officer opened the cell door and Hayley walked over. "You're being transferred to Georgia Women's Max."

The maximum security? "No, I think there's been a mistake. I'm supposed to be transferred, but it's to the minimum-security prison."

Hayley could hear the other women in the cell snicker.

The officer placed handcuffs around her wrists. "Look, I just get the people lined up for the transfer, I don't decide who goes where." He looked her over, evidently deciding maybe she didn't look like a violent criminal. "But I'll double-check your paperwork."

The panic ratcheted up another level. Maximum security? Hayley knew only what she had heard about it from other inmates.

And that was enough to know that people like her didn't last long.

She forced herself to deliberately breathe in and out, to try to keep the anxiety tamped down. The feel of handcuffs around her wrists didn't help. Amazing how two relatively small circles of metal could make someone feel so claustrophobic.

Hayley was stopped at a desk while the guard checked the paperwork.

"Sorry, kid." He was actually nice enough to hold the papers out for her to read herself.

Sure enough, it said that she was to be transferred to the maximum-security prison, about eighty miles south of here. It had been signed by a judge.

Breathe in. Breathe out. Hayley just focused on that as she was led outside. This time she wasn't going on a bus with other inmates, she was being transferred in a squad car.

"Look," the officer said as they arrived at the car, "just keep quiet when you get there. Don't demand anything in front of other prisoners. As soon as you can, ask to see your lawyer. Your lawyer can get this straightened out."

Hayley nodded, but could barely make sense of his words in her panicked state.

Breathe in. Breathe out.

That guard left and another voice rang out. "Well,

well, well. Seems like I have the luck of being with you twice in two days."

It was Officer Brickman, who had arrested her yesterday.

"Looks like I'm your ride today."

Hayley didn't respond. The other, nicer officer who had been with Brickman yesterday didn't seem to be anywhere around. Another younger man walked up to the vehicle.

"I'm Jarod Abrams. I've been assigned to partner with you in escorting the prisoner."

Brickman didn't seem happy about that. "I let them know that I could handle the transfer by myself when my normal partner got reassigned today. Not like she's going to be a problem."

The younger man shrugged. "Just doing what I've been ordered to do. And because I don't think they want any prisoners only escorted by one person."

Brickman's jaw tensed, but he didn't argue further. "Well, let's get on the road then." He climbed into the passenger side, leaving Abrams to drive.

Hayley withdrew into herself as they drove. The metal around her wrists seemed to rub no matter how she tried to move. Brickman and Jarod Abrams talked but she paid little attention. At one point they began arguing about a shortcut when Brickman demanded Abrams pull off the highway and onto a more isolated two-lane road leading toward the countryside. Abrams didn't seem to want to, but he did it.

She was staring out the window at nothing, wondering if she might completely lose it and start bawling at any moment, when she realized Officer Brickman was talking to her.

"Is that true, Green?"

Hayley tore her eyes from the window up to him. "Is what true?"

"That you have a knack for getting out of handcuffs? That's what I heard."

Hayley had no idea what he was talking about. She no more knew how to get out of handcuffs than she knew how to do a backflip.

She held up her arms, showing they were completely secure. "I guess you heard wrong."

Brickman chuckled. "It's still what I'm going to say."

Abrams looked over from where he was driving. "Say when?"

"When they ask me how Green got out of her cuffs and tried to escape."

Before Hayley could figure out what was happening, Brickman reached over and jerked the steering wheel out of Abrams's hands, causing the car to spin around and go partially off into the small ditch that paralleled the isolated road.

Hayley was jerked painfully to the side as the car stopped, slamming her against the door, unable to catch herself easily with her cuffed hands.

"What the hell, Brickman?" Abrams yelled.

Brickman pulled his gun out and pointed it at Abrams. "Get out of the car."

"What the hell is going on?"

Brickman shook his head. "I didn't want anybody else to get hurt and went to considerable trouble to get my regular partner reassigned. Not to mention he's a Goody Two-shoes, and would've never gone along with this."

"Gone along with what?" Abrams asked.

Brickman just kept his gun trained on the other man. "Out of the car."

Hayley tried to shrink down in the back seat. Whatever was happening, she didn't want to be part of it.

Sure enough, as soon as Abrams had gotten out of the car, Brickman shot him twice in the chest.

Hayley gasped as the younger man fell to the ground.

"Kid should've been wearing his vest. I guess this will teach him." Brickman turned back to Hayley, yanking the car door open. She expected him to shoot her right there, but instead he reached for her.

"Come on, you and I have got to stage a huge escape attempt. I'm going to get fired for this, you know." He grabbed her by the hair and yanked her out of the car. Hayley couldn't stop her cry of pain. "But the half a million I'm going to get for killing you will more than make up for it.

"I'll tell them I made Abrams stop so I could take a piss. That's what will actually get me fired—breaking the rules like that. Then the kid, being a soft heart, not knowing how dangerous you were, and your ability to get out of handcuffs, let you out of the car."

Hayley had no idea what Brickman was talking about.

He pulled her toward the top of the ditch. "You guys tussled. I came over to help. You shot him with my gun."

Hayley was still trying to wrap her mind around what he was saying and totally wasn't prepared for his fist that caught her on the jaw. She fell to the ground.

Brickman stood over her, sneering. "I'd love to have a little fun, but we're kind of in the open out here. So I guess I should just get on with the killing you part."

Hayley twisted so she was on her back. He had the

gun out again, pointing it straight at her. Hayley had
no idea what his whole monologue had been about, but
damned if she was just going to lie here and let him
shoot her.

Because one of the other books she'd read while in
prison was about self-defense for women.

She swung her leg to the side and then brought it
back toward him, hooking her ankle at his knees. He
cursed as he fell to the side.

Hayley tried to scurry away, but Brickman grabbed
her by the leg and pulled her back. A punch to the stomach doubled her over, stealing her breath.

"You know, you fighting me is just adding credence
to my story."

Hayley swung out with her elbow and cracked him
in the face, glad to see when blood started gushing out
of his nose.

"Screw this." Brickman brought up his gun and Hayley knew this time it was really over.

Until a car rammed into the squad car parked just a
few yards away from them.

Not sure what was happening but knowing it was her
chance, Hayley scurried away. She heard Brickman's
ugly curse but she didn't turn around, hoping he'd be
so involved with whatever had happened at the car that
she could make her escape.

But a flying tackle had her slamming back against
the ground, air once again knocked out of her. Brickman spun her around until she was lying on top of him,
her back to his chest, then stood, arm wrapped around
her neck.

"Put the gun down or I'll kill her right now." Hayley could feel the muzzle of Brickman's gun against her head.

"It's over, Brickman. You're not going to see any of that money, so you might as well let her go."

Hayley almost sobbed with relief when she heard Cain's voice. She had no idea how he'd found them or even known she was in trouble and right now didn't care.

"We know about the contract on her, but that's not happening," Cain continued.

"I may not get the money, but I can still kill her." Brickman jerked his arm tighter around Hayley's throat. She brought up her still-cuffed hands to try to get some air.

Brickman just laughed. "You know what, Bennett? I wonder how many times I can bring her to the point of almost passing out from lack of oxygen while we stand here playing our little standoff game? That's pretty painful for her, don't you think?"

His words began to fade as black spots started overwhelming her vision. She could feel herself beginning to droop when all of a sudden the pressure released and she was able to suck in air again. She breathed the beautiful oxygen as deeply as she could.

Then before she could even fully recover, the oxygen was cut off again. She whimpered and began to struggle, desperately pulling at Brickman's arm, but couldn't get more air.

"Your choice," Brickman said from behind her.

"Fine," Cain said, his voice less calm. "Give her air. I'm putting the gun down."

After a moment, Brickman's hold loosened again. Hayley breathed, so thankful for air, but wanted to tell

Cain not to put his gun down. Surely he had to know Brickman would just kill them both.

"See?" Brickman said. "That's the problem with all you federal agents. You think everyone's going to follow your rules."

Brickman moved the gun away from her temple to point it at Cain. Before she could even react, he was forcefully thrown away from her and then knocked unconscious onto the ground with a single punch from a man who'd crept up behind them.

He'd moved so silently Hayley hadn't even known he was anywhere around. The guy took another step forward and kicked the gun out of Brickman's unconscious fingers.

"Damn well took you long enough," Cain said, rushing to Hayley.

"Didn't want to take too much of a chance of this pretty lady's head getting blown off by that bastard's gun," the big man said. He tilted his own head toward hers. "Ma'am. Ren McClement."

Hayley nodded before finding herself wrapped in Cain's arms.

"Are you all right?" Cain asked, moving his hands gently over her face and shoulders, kissing her temple.

"He was going to kill me." Her voice sounded raspy even to her own ears.

"Hey, baby cop over here is still alive. We need to call an ambulance," Ren said.

"Hayley can't be here when the police arrive." Cain was still looking her over, making sure she didn't have any serious injuries. "They'll merely take her back into custody and she'll be in just as much trouble as she was."

"I'll stay here with them," Ren said. "Pull the good

old Texas boy who wandered into trouble act. I'll say it was just the two men when I got here."

Cain nodded. "She and I will have to leave on foot. So stall them as long as possible."

Ren smiled. "You'd be amazed at how long it takes a Texan to tell a story sometimes."

"Good thing I know you're not from Texas." Cain reached down and grabbed the handcuff keys from Brickman's belt and unhooked Hayley's hands. He rubbed her wrists gently from where the metal had abused them. He took the cuffs and locked Brickman's hands behind his back, ignoring him as he moaned.

"We're going to have to run. Can you make it? Once we leave here you're going to be a fugitive. But until we figure out what's going on and how to stop it, that's safer than being in police custody."

"We have to get to Mason and Ariel. I think they're not safe, either."

Cain nodded. "I've already sent someone to pick them up."

"Who? Police? Can we trust them?" Hayley wasn't sure whom she could trust anymore.

"Actually, Brickman's partner, Perowne. We knew someone would be trying to kill you on the way to the prison, but it was him who tipped us off that Brickman used this shortcut, even though he'd been reprimanded about it before. If Perowne hadn't called me, I wouldn't have made it to you in time."

Hayley nodded, still trying to figure out exactly what was going on. She just wanted to get to her son.

"You guys better get out of here. Paramedics are on their way. I'm sure the locals won't be far behind." Ren was keeping pressure on Abrams's wounds.

They began walking across a field at a brisk pace, getting away from the road.

"Nearest town's about four miles. I can arrange a ride for us there."

She took in a deep breath through her sore throat. "Okay."

"And then you're going to tell me everything, Hayley. Every. Damn. Thing. What it is you know or have done that has someone trying to kill you. We're not going to have any more secrets between us."

Chapter Fourteen

Their escape didn't leave much time for talking. The trill of sirens filled their ears before they were more than a few minutes away, prompting them to move more quickly.

"Don't worry, Ren will buy us some time." But Cain urged her to increase her speed with a hand on the small of her back.

"Is he really not from Texas?"

"Boston, I think. But with Ren nobody knows for sure."

"But he's Omega Sector?"

"Yes. One of the best."

They picked up speed again and traveled in silence for a long while.

"Brickman was going to make half a million dollars to kill me," she finally said.

Cain glanced at her. "And do you know who was offering that money?"

She knew she was going to have to tell him everything; she just hoped she could prove it.

"I don't know the name of the person, but I think I have a way of finding out."

Cain nodded. "We'll talk about it more once we're not in the open."

Relief flooded her that he was at least willing to listen to what she had to say. Wasn't just automatically lumping her into the criminal category. Given all the secrets between them, that was the best she could hope for right now.

It didn't take long before keeping up with the slow jog pace Cain was setting became too much for her. Lack of sleep, lack of food, almost getting killed, were all taking their toll. She stumbled.

And he caught her arm and helped her right herself. "Let's slow down for just a minute."

Hayley shook her head. "No, it's all right. I know we've got to hurry."

But she could feel herself start to shake. Every time she swallowed she could feel where Brickman had choked her. When she moved she could feel where the cuffs had cut into her skin.

Cain put both hands on her shoulders, concern clear in his eyes. "Hayley…"

She couldn't fall apart right now, there was too much at stake, too far to go. But tears she couldn't control began streaming down her face.

"I'm sorry. This is stupid—"

She didn't get any other words out as she was yanked against Cain's chest, his arms surrounding her in a cocoon of safety.

"It's okay. God, Hayley, what you've been through. It's okay to cry."

He kept her against his chest as sobs erupted out of her. He murmured soft words about her strength and her spirit and how she wasn't alone in this anymore.

She could almost feel his strength seep into her. Cain

could handle anything. Knowing he was on her side made everything seem more bearable.

"Better?" he asked.

She sighed. "Except for being a blubbering idiot."

He shook his head. "You shouldn't. I've seen trained agents crack under less pressure than you've been under. And crying for all of two and a half minutes doesn't count as cracking." He pulled her close to him again.

Hayley breathed in his scent. It hadn't changed much in all these years. Deep and musky and uniquely Cain. She hadn't thought she'd ever really experience it again.

"Ready to go?" he asked, without pulling away from her.

She nodded. "Let's go get our son."

A half an hour of brisk walking later they made it to the town.

"What do we do, call a cab?" Hayley asked.

Cain shook his head. "No. We're too far south of Gainesville and it will be the first thing the cops look for."

"Do you want me to call Ariel and have her come get us?" Hayley didn't like the thought of bringing Ariel and Mason closer to the danger, but knew she and Cain had to get out of here.

"No. We're going to steal a car." Cain shrugged. "Since we're already fugitives and all."

He didn't look too worried about it, so she didn't press. He found an old truck parked near the back of the town's hardware store. After ripping out the small panel and crossing some wires, they were on their way.

She shook her head. "You know, considering I'm the ex-con, you sure do have some lawbreaking skills."

He grinned at her, that grin she hadn't seen since

high school. The one that still melted her heart, and certain intimate clothing pieces. It was all she could do to not reach over and brush that errant dark curl off his forehead.

"Sometimes to help keep the peace you have to know how to break the law."

A line she never thought she'd ever hear from Mr. Black-and-White.

A call from Officer Perowne had them going to his apartment rather than Hayley's. Cain put it on speakerphone.

"I was here with them, like you asked, when a call came over the scanner," Perowne said. "A domestic dispute call, with a child involved."

"Let me guess, it was for Hayley and Ariel's address."

"Yep," Perowne replied. "I got Ariel and the boy out quick, but almost wasn't fast enough. The squad car got there maybe twenty seconds after we made it to my car."

"Did you see who it was? Because that's probably somebody else on the killer's payroll."

"No. I just wanted to get them out of there."

Hayley's hands clenched into fists in her lap. She couldn't stand to have the danger so close to Mason. Cain talked a little bit more with Perowne, got his address and hung up.

"Were they going to kill them?" Hayley asked. "Do you think that's what the people who went to the apartment were sent to do?"

"I doubt it. It wouldn't help anyone's cause to kill Mason and Ariel outright. Domestic dispute sounded like it was a setup to be able to take Mason into custody."

"To get me back into their hands."

Cain nodded. "If I had to guess, yes. You know something or can do something that someone very powerful wants eliminated."

Hayley nodded. "It has to do with the CET case."

"I figured as much."

"Why?"

"Because of the twelve of you who were arrested, five are dead. None of the deaths individually are suspicious, but when you look at them as a whole…"

Hayley felt like the air had been sucked out of her lungs. "Someone's hunting the people involved in the case."

Cain glanced at her before turning his eyes back to the road. "Yes. And if I had to make a guess, it's because they don't know which one of you has the damaging information. But I'm assuming it's you."

She didn't know if he was going to believe her. Heck, she was the one who had discovered what was going on and still found it hard to believe.

"I know I told you the other night that about a month before I was arrested I had decided to get out of the hacking scheme."

Cain nodded, but she was at least glad to see his jaw didn't tighten the way it had all the other times they had talked about her arrest.

"I wasn't stupid," she continued. "I didn't want to go to jail, so I was going back into the CET system to cover my tracks."

She turned and looked out the window.

"Vargas was the one who banded the hackers together. I didn't know about any of the others and they didn't know me. Basically he had the contacts to sell our results. All of us individually could've hacked the system, but we wouldn't have known how to make money with what we had found."

"So he was the auctioneer. The middleman connecting the buyers with the sellers."

"Yes. The CET was pretty complicated to hack, even for us. The test is different at every testing center, and we had to crack that algorithm in order to know what set of questions would be present at any particular testing session."

"That's why CET called itself unhackable."

Hayley shrugged. "It probably is as a whole. But we weren't trying to hack it as a whole."

The CET was so popular because students could get their results immediately instead of having to wait weeks like previous college testing required. But in order to get the results so quickly, the test had to be computerized.

Anyone who said something couldn't be hacked was a liar. If it was on any sort of open system, it could be hacked.

"Okay," Cain said. "This all came out in the trial. Doesn't seem like anything out of the ordinary."

"It's not. It's when I dug much deeper to try to hide my tracks that I discovered the real problem."

"Tell me."

"Most of the CET exams are at high schools all over the country. That's where we concentrated almost all of our hacking. But there are American high schools on foreign soil at US military bases across the world. The CET system also does testing there. For both American and foreign kids."

"Okay, that seems right."

"I found out someone was using the tests to send information that had nothing to do with the exams themselves."

He glanced at her again. "What sort of information?"

She swallowed. This was where he either believed her or called her crazy. "State secrets, Cain. To be honest, some of it I didn't even understand. But in one transmission it was definitely weapon plans."

Cain's curse was low and foul. "Someone is using the CET for espionage."

Hayley let out a breath she hadn't even been aware she was holding. "Yes. I don't know how deep it goes. I was just starting to dig into it when I was arrested."

"So whoever is behind it knew someone had discovered something, but didn't know who. And is probably the one who put law enforcement on the hackers' trail to begin with."

It made sense. "They needed to flush the hackers out. And once we'd been arrested—"

"All they needed was to pick you off one by one," Cain finished for her. "Until they either found the person who knew, or had eliminated you all."

He believed her. Something inside her eased. She couldn't offer any proof yet, but he still believed her.

"I put in an electronic trapdoor before I was arrested. Once I can get back online freely I can access that. It will point me in the direction of who's behind the secret selling."

"Will it expose you?"

Hayley nodded. "Yes. Whoever it is will definitely know it's me who accessed the information."

"Then it's a race to see if you can get the information into the right hands before they find you." His hands tightened on the steering wheel. "That's why you were saving up money to run."

She nodded with a shrug. "I thought I had at least two years before I could access a computer and that would make me safe."

"But working for me gave you access early and whoever is behind this obviously has some law enforcement in their pocket."

She brought a hand up to her sore cheek where Brickman had hit her. "I don't know how high up this goes, but it has to be pretty high. They're going to be looking for me, right? So what do we do?"

"For now, we run."

Chapter Fifteen

Hayley's story explained a lot, and Cain had no reason not to believe her, especially after the contract out on her life. Ren had dealt with the situation with Brickman—he'd be going to jail, especially since the officer he'd shot had miraculously survived and would be testifying against him. But that didn't mean there wouldn't be someone else after Hayley soon.

It was time to kill two birds with one stone.

He was taking Hayley where he could protect her and she could get the information he needed about the Omega mole: inside the Critical Response Division headquarters in Colorado Springs.

Cain had already talked to Steve. Hayley would be working in a section of the building far from active agents, and therefore away from the mole. It would give her a chance to dig deeper into both the CET situation and the Omega traitor. Now he just needed to get them to Colorado. Flying wasn't an option, so they would be driving.

They hadn't gone to her apartment after picking up Ariel and Mason; it was too risky. Until everything was cleared up, Hayley was a fugitive to all law enforcement, and a huge potential paycheck for the compromised ones.

So, as they'd explained to little Mason, they were going on a road trip.

He'd met his son. Cain still could barely believe it. Mason had been excited to see "Mama Hayley" when they'd arrived, rushing into her arms. She'd held him to her, hands stroking over his little head, before letting the little wiggle-worm go. Ariel and Hayley had embraced—Ariel still giving Cain the evil eye—while Cain had explained the situation as best he could to Officer Perowne, thanking him for his help.

Then Cain had crouched down and met his son, his green eyes—a replica of his own—staring back at him.

"Mason, this is Cain." She hadn't tried to offer any more details. Mason was too young to understand family dynamics anyway.

Mason looked from Hayley to Cain. "Like candy cane?"

Cain hadn't been able to stop his big grin. "Sure, buddy. You can call me Candy Cain."

He'd held out his hand, unsure of what exactly he expected the little boy to do. Shake it?

Mason had slapped him five, smiled and run off, muttering about Candy Cain and road trips.

Cain couldn't stop looking at Mason in the rearview mirror now that they were on their way. Hayley was in the back seat of the car he'd rented, playing a color game with Mason. She'd also read him books, sung songs and played peekaboo.

"She loves him more than anything," Ariel muttered from the seat beside Cain when Hayley and Mason broke into another rendition of "The Wheels on the

Bus." "She's an excellent mother. You better not do anything to take Mason away from her."

Cain looked over at the other woman, honestly shocked. "I would never do that. Especially not now. Not seeing how much she loves him. I want to protect them both."

"Good. Because Hayley deserves that. Deserves to have time with her son as just a mom. Deserves to have someone in her life who isn't going to always lord over her the fact that she once made a mistake—"

"Ariel," Hayley said from the back seat. Cain realized the singing had stopped. Mason had fallen asleep. "That's enough."

"Why? Someone needs to say something to him."

This time it was Hayley he saw when he looked in the rearview mirror. But she was staring at the back of Ariel's head.

"Cain isn't the villain here."

"Yeah, well, I'm not sure he's the hero, either," Ariel snapped back.

"We both made mistakes in the past," Cain said. "Both have things we would take back if we could."

Now Hayley's eyes met his. She nodded. "But right now the most important thing is looking forward. There's too much at stake to bicker about the past."

She looked back at Mason.

But what Ariel said had been right. If Cain ever truly wanted to be a part of Hayley's life, he was going to have to let go of the hacking. Accept, like he'd said, that they'd both made mistakes. Not lord hers over her.

But Hayley was even more right. If they couldn't work out the problems of their present, the ones of the past weren't going to matter.

They drove as long as they could while Mason was asleep, knowing they'd have to stop and let him get some energy out once he woke up. Cain's call to Ren assured him that things seemed quiet, or that there was at least no direct word out in what direction they were heading.

Cain got to know his son. When Hayley had offered to drive so Cain could sit in the back seat, he'd refused at first, afraid it would be awkward. That he would scare the boy or make him uncomfortable. But after a little encouragement—and providing him with a secret weapon, a small toy fire truck that was sure to enthrall Mason—Cain agreed. He soon discovered that his son loved fire trucks, but like all toy vehicles he played with, he liked to pretend they were roller coasters.

Both women in the front seat groaned when Mason began to make a strange noise, bringing the fire truck up as far as his little arm, restrained in the car seat, would go. Then made a soft screaming sound as he brought it back down again quickly.

"He loves roller coasters," Ariel explained. "He's never been on one, but we've watched videos. So no matter what vehicle you give him to play with, he's going to pretty much act like it's a roller coaster."

Cain laughed. He and his brother had driven his parents crazy wanting to go to theme parks all the time as kids. "He comes by it honestly."

Cain played with Mason—seriously, the kid *really* loved to pretend his cars were on thrill rides—for hours, promising to take him to ride a roller coaster as soon as he was big enough. Cain's parents would love it, being dragged back out to a theme park once again, this time for their grandson.

He couldn't wait for them to meet Mason. Cain had been around him for only twenty-four hours and was already in love with him.

They drove through the night, taking turns. But by the second night, about eight hours outside of Colorado Springs, they decided to stop. Everyone needed to be out of the car, get a good night's rest in a bed.

Cain lent Ariel his burner phone for her to call and check her voice mail, since both women had ditched their cell phones so they couldn't be tracked. Cain offered the phone to Hayley, too, but she said no one would be calling her.

But she was wrong.

"Hayley," Ariel said after listening to her messages. "Some really Southern-sounding lady named Mara left you a message. Said she couldn't reach you on your phone and was worried maybe you were more hurt from the fire than you'd let on. Also says she has another job possibility for you both and to call her ASAP."

They watched as Ariel listened to what must've been another five or six messages from Mara, each obviously longer than the last.

"Let me just call her, okay?" Hayley finally said. "If not, she'll just keep calling. She was always looking after me at the Bluewater. I feel bad that she's so worried."

Cain nodded. "But don't give any specifics where we are. Just tell her you'll call her when you get back."

Although he had no plans to sit by and let her slave in some dead-end job where she had to work twelve hours a day washing dishes and mopping floors. He had contacts. People who would give Hayley a chance, just because he would vouch for her. Despite her past.

And he realized that was true. He would vouch for Hayley.

He heard her talking to Mara, remembered the older woman from the night of the fire.

"I'll definitely get in touch soon about the job, Mara. I've just got a couple of things to take care of." Hayley laughed. "No, I haven't been breaking my neck looking at all the papers, I promise. But thank you for checking on me."

He could hear Mara's drawl on the other end of the line but couldn't tell what she was saying.

"Thanks, Mara. I'll talk to you soon. Bye."

"Sounds like I've got a job at the local Waffle Hut if I want it," she said ruefully as she handed the phone back to Cain.

Over his dead body. "Let's finish this first, then worry about jobs."

Hayley nodded. Cain checked them into a hotel as Hayley got Mason's sleeping body out of the car. Cain had chosen a small town, well off the interstate, on purpose. The town had one main road with all the brick buildings, each two or three stories high, butting up to one another.

In a small town like this where the crime rate was low, credit cards and IDs weren't required for check-in. Cain paid with cash for two adjoining rooms, then parked the car a little way down the street, vehicle easily accessible from multiple directions. He didn't expect any trouble, but he wouldn't rest easily until they made it to the Omega Critical Response Division HQ.

Mason woke up as they got into the rooms, his internal clock off track due to their traveling. It was close to midnight, but he was wide-awake. Cain, Ariel and

Hayley took turns playing with the little boy while the others showered.

"That's no fair," Cain said as Hayley sat on the floor in front of Mason and the little boy brushed her long blond hair with a hairbrush.

Hayley laughed. "You say that until he turns the hairbrush backward accidentally and smacks my head with it."

Mason ran over to the bed where Cain sat, climbed up and started brushing his hair.

Hayley was right—it wasn't nearly as soothing as it looked.

She laughed again at the expression on his face. "Told you."

Cain would suffer all sorts of hairbrush torture to hear that laugh from Hayley. It relaxed Mason, too. He jumped down from the bed and ran back to Hayley. She distracted him this time with snacks.

Cain joined them on the floor and he and Mason pretended each cracker went over a roller coaster hill before ending up in their mouths.

Once the little boy had his belly full, he settled down, a big yawn taking over his entire face. Hayley brushed his teeth and put him in jammies, then brought him over to the bed.

"I'll just sleep in the other room," Ariel said, fresh from the shower. "You guys can stay in here."

Hayley looked concerned. "Are you sure?"

It was a balancing act between the two women, Cain knew. Ariel had been the mother figure to Mason for so long. Hayley didn't want to hurt her cousin in any way or remove her from Mason's life.

Ariel knew that, too. She rushed over to give Hayley

a hug and Mason a kiss. She didn't even glare at Cain, so he considered that a win.

Mason's eyes were already drooping.

"Let's get him into bed before he falls asleep all over you." Cain pulled the bedding back so Hayley could lay Mason down from resting in her arms.

She crawled into bed next to Mason. "I'm just going to sleep here with him."

She wrapped her arm protectively around her precious son.

Cain walked over to turn off the light, leaving the bathroom light and fan on and the door cracked. He slipped off his shoes and got into the other bed. "I'll be right here."

There was no place else on earth he'd rather be.

Chapter Sixteen

Cain's eyes flew open and he held himself motionless in the bed. Something had woken him up. What was it?

He could hear the even breathing of Hayley and Mason in the bed beside his. Was it Mason's occasional restless shifting on the bed that had woken him?

Something had him on high alert. After just a few moments he realized it was the silence that had caught his subconscious attention. The fan had cut off in the bathroom as well as the light. He looked over at the clock and it was also out. The power was out.

Cain silently shifted his weight from the bed, getting up and looking into Ariel's room. Power was out there, too.

It did happen. Hotels lost power. But he wasn't going to make the mistake of thinking it was a fluke. Not with everything that had happened in the last two days.

Cain silently stepped over to their second-floor window, keeping his body far to the side. He peeked out the farthest corner, careful not to shift the curtains.

The street outside was empty, no movement, as to be expected in the middle of the night. He allowed his vision to adjust even further. And then saw it.

A white van, halfway down the block, someone watching the building with binoculars in the driver's seat.

Cain forced himself not to make any sudden movements from the window, just gently stepped back.

They needed to get out of there.

Cain moved over to Hayley and put his lips close to her ear.

"Hays, wake up," he said softly, not wanting to wake up Mason.

Her eyes flew open. "Cain?"

"Yeah. We're in trouble. Somebody's cut the power to the building and there are people outside."

Cain had no idea how many or how rapidly and violently they would be approaching.

Hayley slid her arm out from under Mason and turned toward Cain, sitting up.

"What do we do?"

"Get your shoes on and wake up Ariel. We've got to get out of here."

Hayley nodded and got up, padding softly into the other room.

Weapon drawn, Cain stuck his head out the door and looked up and down the hall. No one was out there, which was a good sign. Whoever was after them wasn't going to come in guns blazing, or they'd already be here.

He shut the door and turned and faced Ariel and Hayley, concern evident in both their faces.

"Is there anyone out there?" Ariel asked.

"Not yet. My bet is that they have the front and rear exits guarded, and plan to pull the fire alarm and take us as we rush out."

Hayley's face lost all color. "I can't let them take Mason. I'd rather give myself up."

Cain walked to her and cupped her cheeks with his hands. "It's not going to come to that."

Her hands came up and clutched his wrists. "Promise me we get Ariel and Mason out, if it comes down to it."

Cain nodded. He understood her fear and would make sure Mason was safe. But he had no intention of losing Hayley while doing that.

He dropped his hands and moved over to the window, careful once again not to disturb the curtains.

Definitely more action outside. Whoever was after Hayley could just use her fugitive status to incorporate local law enforcement into the chase. Cain didn't know if the people about to make their move were cops just doing their job or killers who didn't care who they hurt.

Then Cain saw a uniformed police officer walk up to the white van and tap on the window.

The man on the inside rolled down the window, then, without warning, pulled out a gun with a silencer and shot the officer, point-blank.

Cain cursed under his breath. Guess that answered his question about who they were dealing with.

"Let's go. We've got to get out *right now.*"

"What happened?" Hayley asked as she slipped shoes on Mason's feet, the kid never even waking up.

He turned and looked at her. "Looks like it's some of Brickman's associates. They're going to shoot first, collect the reward later."

Hayley swept Mason's sleeping form up into her arms. "Let's go."

Cain checked the hallway once again and then led them out.

"If they're blocking both doors how are we going to get past them downstairs?" Ariel asked.

"We're not going down."

He hadn't chosen this hotel just because it didn't require credit cards. It had also been the best option in terms of multiple exit routes.

He led them to the stairs and cracked open a door. He signaled for the women to be as quiet as possible, and prayed Mason would stay asleep, as they began to climb the two stories up to the roof. He could hear the effort it was taking Hayley to carry Mason's dead weight, but couldn't afford to stop and offer to help. If Mason woke up and started crying it would all be over. After two flights they reached a small metal ladder.

"You okay?" he whispered to Hayley.

She nodded, shifting Mason slightly in her arms.

Cain climbed the five steps on the ladder leading up to the hatch going to the roof. The hatch door itself was old and rusted; he would have no problem getting it open, but there was no way he was going to do it quietly.

The next second the fire alarm began blaring. Cain didn't waste any time—noise didn't matter now. He used his shoulder to drive into the rusted hinges of the door, ignoring the pain as he felt it give way.

Ariel let Hayley up first since Mason had started crying with all the noise. She was struggling to get him up the rungs since he was now shifting his weight and trying to cover his ears. If she wasn't careful the boy was going to cause both of them to fall.

Cain reached down and grabbed Hayley under her armpits, hoisting both her and Mason up and onto the roof.

"Thank you," she muttered. Ariel climbed up right behind them and Cain put the door back in place.

"Where do we go now?" Hayley asked.

She wasn't going to like it. Hell, he didn't even like it.

He led them over to the east side of the building that was connected to the next one. They ran together onto the roof of the third building. Cain was thankful for the older design of the town, which caused the stores and shops to be built connected together to save money.

The next building had an outdoor fire escape. They could use it to get down, but they would need to jump the five-foot gap between the buildings.

He saw Hayley's face as she realized what was going to happen. She began shaking her head.

Cain crossed to her. "We have to hurry. It won't take them long to figure out we are not in our room and the only way we could've gone was up."

"I can't make it with him," she said, features pinched.

"I can."

She nodded. Cain turned to Mason. "Hey, buddy. Want to play a game?"

The youngster looked skeptical. Cain couldn't blame him. "You and I are going to pretend to go on a roller coaster ride. Sound fun?"

Mason's eyes lit up and his little arms reached for Cain. Cain took his son for the first time and held him in his arms.

He just wished it wasn't because someone might burst onto the roof at any moment and try to kill them all.

"I'll go first in case you need help." Ariel backed up and ran, clearing the gap easily. She motioned for Cain to jump with Mason.

He felt Hayley's hand on his arm. He reached his hand under her nape and pulled her in for a quick kiss. "We'll make it."

Mason giggled. "You kissed Mama Hayley."

"Hang on, buddy," he whispered in the little boy's ear. "Time for our roller coaster ride."

Keeping one arm firmly planted around Mason's tiny middle, Cain pushed into a run, gathering more speed than he needed, just in case. A few moments later he was airborne, Mason's giggles in his ears.

Cain's feet hit the roof of the other building without any problem. He squeezed Mason quickly, then handed him to Ariel, who began leading him to the fire escape. "Be as quiet as possible."

Ariel nodded and Cain turned back to Hayley, who was already backing up to run.

The hatch door to the roof opened behind her, but it was too late to signal—she was already running. Cain pulled his firearm at the same time the man made it through and drew his own gun. The man shot at Cain first, causing Cain to dive to the side. He got off two rounds as he flew, killing the man.

But the man also got off a shot. At Hayley.

He heard Hayley's cry as the bullet hit her just as she left the safety of the roof. Instead of a smooth jump across like he and Ariel had, Hayley's body jerked, throwing her weight to the side.

She wasn't going to clear the ledge.

Her chest hit the corner and fingers pressed for a grip as she slid toward the edge. In his periphery, he could see Ariel pick up Mason and keep his head averted.

Cain dived for the ledge, grunting at the hard impact, his fingers grasping Hayley's just as she was falling.

"Got you." There was no way he was letting go.

She used her other hand to reach up and grab his wrist, even though he could tell it was painful for her.

"I'm okay."

Cain pulled her up and wrapped one arm around her, easing her to the ground.

"Where are you hit?"

"My side."

He lifted up her shirt and immediately saw the wound. It hit the fleshy part of the very outer edge of her waist, through and through. In terms of a torso shot, that was almost the best spot someone could hope for. It was bleeding, but obviously hadn't hit any critical organs.

"I know it has to hurt, baby, but we've got to get off this rooftop. As soon as the guy who shot you doesn't check in, they're going to know where we are."

Hayley nodded. "I can make it."

Keeping as much pressure on her wound as he could, he helped her off the ground and led her quickly over to the fire escape. Ariel continued her downward path with Mason.

"Do you want me to carry you?" He'd have to do a fireman's carry, which would probably be more painful for her, but the narrow stairs of the fire escape wouldn't allow him to carry her in his arms.

"No, I'll be all right."

He kept his arm around her as they made their way quickly down to the ground. Hayley made it, true to her word.

They kept to the shadows as they hurried down the block to the car. Fortunately all the chaos at the hotel meant no one's attention was on them.

"You ride in the back with little man," Cain said to Ariel. Blood was already soaking through Hayley's shirt. Cain didn't want to scare him.

Ariel nodded and got Mason into his car seat while Cain got Hayley in the passenger seat.

"We need to get you to a hospital."

Hayley shook her head. "No. Once they realize one of us was wounded, they will be checking the hospitals. We can't take the chance."

The wound wasn't life-threatening, but that didn't mean it didn't hurt like hell. Hayley was sweating, her face pale.

"I can make it, Cain."

"You keep saying that."

He gritted his teeth, biting off a curse. They had to get out of here before they were noticed. Ariel passed up a clean T-shirt from the back seat and Cain gave it to Hayley.

"Keep pressure on your wound."

She nodded and he jogged around to the driver's side.

He started the car without turning on the lights, and drove down the side street. He didn't turn on the headlights until they were a mile outside of town. Soon they were speeding back toward the highway.

"What are we going to do?" Ariel asked, her hand reaching up from the back seat to wipe Hayley's sweat-soaked hair away from her brow.

"Do they have some sort of medical facility at Omega headquarters?" Hayley asked. "Enough to patch me up?"

Cain looked over at her. Pain bracketed her mouth, but she didn't look like she was in danger of going into shock.

"Yes, we have excellent field medics." And it would be safe. "But we're six hours from Colorado Springs, and that's if I drive like hell."

Hayley's brown eyes pinned him. "Then drive like hell."

Chapter Seventeen

Hayley felt like her whole body ached. They'd been in the car for three hours, and she tried to console herself with the fact that they were more than halfway.

They'd stopped two hours ago at an all-night drugstore where Cain had bought hydrogen peroxide and gauze.

That had hurt.

But Cain had some basic medical training and he hadn't insisted on a hospital after seeing her wound more clearly. If it was that bad he would've insisted on a hospital despite the possible danger.

She grimaced as she shifted.

"How are you holding up?" He didn't glance over at her; he was going too fast to take his eyes from the road.

"How come people on TV and in movies who get shot jump up and run a marathon or something while looking gorgeous?"

"Because those people have stuntmen. They don't even *pretend* to get shot."

"I think I want to hire a stuntman for my next adventure."

She shifted to try to get more comfortable. But she couldn't. Physically or mentally.

The people chasing her had found them. Had found them and shot at them.

What if the man who had shot her had shown up fifteen seconds earlier? What if he had burst out when Cain had been jumping with Mason in his arms?

Hayley would've had no way to stop him. Cain and Mason would have plummeted to their deaths.

Hayley's heart turned icy at the thought.

Moreover, a truth had become clear to her.

She turned to Cain. "I can't run. I have to fight."

Cain gave a half shrug. "It's hard to fight when you don't know who your enemy is."

"My plan had been to buy myself some time. To stay off computers until I had enough money to run if I needed to. But that won't work. Look at how fast they found us."

"You're never going to have enough money to run from someone with this much power. Whoever found us this quickly is highly connected."

Hayley nodded. That much she already knew.

"What I said in the hotel is the truth to me." She glanced over her shoulder to where both Mason and Ariel were sleeping in the back seat. "Mason's safety is the most important thing. Ariel's, too. They are both innocent in all this."

"You're not guilty of these crimes, either, Hayley."

"I know. But it was my mistakes that led me down this path to begin with. I need to get Mason and Ariel somewhere safe so that I can figure out what to do."

"So *we* can figure out what to do. You're not alone anymore."

Hayley wasn't going to let Cain risk his life for this.

This was her fault and her fight. But she needed him. Needed his help.

Wanted to rely on the strength he offered. And once she figured out who was behind this, and how to catch them, then she would hand it over to him, let him do what he did best. Enforce the law.

But she wouldn't let him take a bullet for her, literally or figuratively.

The weight of it all bore down on her. She stared out the window wondering how the straight-A student she'd been in high school had become a fugitive ex-con with a bullet wound.

She felt his hand reach out and touch just above her knee. "Hey, did you hear me? You're not in this alone. I mean it."

His fingers left her leg and moved up to her cheek, making a gentle trail. Hayley couldn't help it; she leaned into his touch.

"All right," she said softly.

"I know a place where Mason and Ariel can stay and be safe. A friend from Omega Sector."

"How can you be sure this friend isn't the traitor we're searching for?"

Hayley didn't want to insult the bond of friendship, but she couldn't take a chance with Mason's life.

"Because the traitor and his partner, Damien Freihof, nearly killed my friend and his fiancée a few months ago."

That seemed like proof enough indeed.

"Ashton and Summer have a daughter, around Mason's age, so their house will be ready for kids and he'll have toys and stuff."

"Do you think they'll mind?"

"I think they are both willing to do anything, particularly something as easy as opening their home to Ariel and Mason, to help bring these criminals to justice."

She couldn't help but smile. "Bring criminals to justice," she repeated in a deep voice, obviously mocking him. "I feel like you should be wearing a cape or something."

"I've got my cape in my closet at home. Maybe if you're good I'll let you see it."

It had been so long since she'd flirted she couldn't even remember how. She tried to think of something clever to say, but just smiled instead.

His hand reached over and squeezed her leg once more before returning to the steering wheel. She could swear she felt heat through her clothes where his fingers had been.

"Rest now," he said gently. "Capes and catching criminals in a few hours."

Hayley turned and looked back out the window. Sleep was a long time in coming.

"WHAT SHE CAN do is pretty amazing," Steve Drackett, head of the Omega Sector Critical Response Division, said to Cain thirty-six hours later. "And after a bullet wound? Even more incredible."

They were in a small set of rooms, not much bigger than closets really, in the corner of the headquarters building. This area, used for data entry and analysis, got neither much traffic nor much scrutiny from regular agents. The people in this section of the building definitely did not have the clearance, or inside information, to be the mole.

Steve had set them up with the computer resources

Hayley needed to do both the tasks she was currently concentrating on. She had two full computers in front of her, each with its own keyboard. One system had two screens she could toggle between. Her fingers flew over the keys faster than Cain could even tap his on a table.

This was Hayley in her element.

"She's definitely impressive. And motivated."

They were watching her through a window, which allowed her to work without being distracted but also allowed Cain to be able to see what she was working on.

He hadn't asked for Steve to set them up like this, but he had to admit it made him feel a little better. Did he still not trust her completely?

"Someone coming after their young will cause even the most nonaggressive animals to fight. So I don't blame her for being motivated," Steve said. "And, by the way, congratulations. I hear you are a dad."

Cain knew the information would get around Omega as soon as Ashton and Summer saw Mason, when Cain and Hayley dropped him and Ariel off at their house. And of course Cain hadn't denied the truth when they had asked if the boy was his son.

"Yeah," Cain said to Steve. "Pretty big surprise."

Steve chuckled. "I can only imagine. Hell, I was shocked when Rosalyn showed back up in my life six months pregnant. Surprise child has to be a lot more jarring than surprise pregnancy."

"It caught me off guard, that's for sure."

"But she's a good mother?"

No matter what mistakes Hayley might've made in her past there could be no misinterpreting how much she loved Mason. "I couldn't ask for anything more for the mother of my child. She loves him completely and unconditionally."

Steve slapped him on the shoulder. "I'm glad to hear that. And I hope you won't make some of the same mistakes I did with my Rosalyn."

"And what would those be? I doubt you could have made as many mistakes as I have."

"I know that after Rosalyn hurt me once—well, didn't hurt *me*, hurt my *pride*—it was hard for me to let it go. I kept refusing to think she changed. Almost lost her because of it."

Cain watched Hayley. He wasn't studying the screens to make sure she was doing what she was supposed to, he was studying her.

"I trust her."

"Good. That's definitely important." Steve took a step back. "You'll let me know anything you find?"

"First thing. But I'll want to do it face-to-face. I don't trust any communication device in this building."

Steve nodded. "I agree."

As Steve opened the door he turned back. "Can an old man give you a word of personal advice?"

Now it was Cain's turn to chuckle. "You have a three-month-old at home and a gorgeous wife in her twenties. Plus, I don't think forty-one counts as old."

"Fair enough."

"But I'll still take your advice, especially if it has anything to do with this case."

"No, it has to do with your Hayley."

Cain just raised an eyebrow. *His* Hayley?

"I'm glad you guys worked out your trust issues. That you don't feel like you have to look over her shoulder all the time." Steve pointed in Hayley's direction.

"But that woman in there needs more than just trust. She needs someone to care for her."

"I do care about her. Hell, I've cared about her since she was fifteen years old."

"Right now she needs the sort of care that shows action. She knows you'll fight beside her, particularly against anyone who will harm your child. But I think she needs to know that you're willing to fight *for* her, even if it's against her own inclinations and fears."

Steve didn't explain any further, just nodded and left.

Cain watched Hayley for a long time after the other man departed. Her hands continued to fly over the keyboards, one screen sorting through code like something out of *The Matrix*, another screen cross-referencing communication channels at Omega Sector. Every once in a while she would slide one section of code onto the other screen.

She shifted in her chair, stretching out her side. He knew it had to hurt. Even though the medic had agreed that no major damage had been done by her bullet wound and stitched the openings at the edge of her waist, it still had to be causing her great pain.

But here she was thirty-six hours later working, having only slept for about six hours the entire time.

She leaned closer to one of the screens, which she had done a few times in the last five minutes. Cain thought it was because she was studying something interesting on the screen, until he saw her rub her eyes.

The screen was blurry for her. Probably because of exhaustion. But she just kept soldiering on.

And she would continue to do that until she fell over from exhaustion.

Fighting for her against even her own inclinations.
Steve was right.

Cain opened the door. "Time for a break."

Hayley didn't even turn to look at him. "I'm okay. I ate a couple hours ago."

He walked straight up to her chair and wheeled it back from the desk.

"Hey." Her brown eyes peered up at him.

"Time for a break."

She let out a sigh. "A break is not going to help me. Finding out who's trying to kill me and attacking our son…that will help me."

Cain crouched down so that he was directly in front of Hayley's line of sight. "Mason is very well protected right now. You were shot a day and a half ago and haven't gotten much rest. The nights before that you were either in a car or in a cell about to be sent back to prison. I know you didn't get much sleep in, either."

Her small hand came up and rubbed the back of her neck. "That's true, but—"

He reached over and kissed her forehead. "Six hours of sleep, that's what I'm asking of you. You and I both know that what you're doing now—trying to work without all your cylinders firing—might cause you to miss something." Not to mention collapse on the floor.

"But—"

"Work's over for today."

"Just one more hour…"

Cain bent down, sliding his arms under her knees and around her back, and picked her up bodily from the chair. She let out a surprised squeak before her arms flew around his neck.

"No 'one more hour.' Because in an hour, you'll want another one. You need rest."

This close to her he was able to see the dark circles under her eyes, the exhaustion bracketing her mouth.

He should've made her rest long before now. Steve was right. Cain didn't need to tell Hayley she was important to him, he needed to *show* her.

"I'm really not that tired—" Her words were cut off by the huge yawn that overtook her.

Cain raised an eyebrow. "You were saying?"

"Fine." Her pout was adorable. "Just get me to a couch. I'm sure I'll be able to crash there just fine."

He gently set her on her feet in front of him at the door, wrapped an arm around her waist and led her out into the hall. The door automatically locked behind them.

"There's a studio apartment here in the complex especially for situations like this. Steve got it set up for us."

She was almost asleep on her feet by the time he got them to the room. He led her over to the bed and sat her down so he could bend to untie her shoes and slip them off. Then his hands moved to the snap of her jeans.

"Let's get these off you, too. You'll be more comfortable."

It took every ounce of control Cain had to just peel Hayley's jeans off, not touching any of the smooth skin of her legs. He got them off and was setting them to the side when he felt Hayley's fingers on his arm.

"Stay with me," she whispered.

He wanted to. More than anything he wanted to. "If I get in that bed right now, you are not going to get the sleep you need."

The corners of her lips rose in a temptress's smile, blond hair spilling on the pillow all around her. Beguiling. Enchanting. His heart thundered in his chest.

"Hayley…" His voice was husky even to his own ears. He sat down on the bed beside her.

Her hand reached out for him again. "I'll get the sleep I need. It just won't be right away."

Cain stared at her. He wanted to do what was right in this situation, but damned if he knew what that was. "I didn't bring you here for this. For sex. You're exhausted."

"And you don't want to take advantage of me."

"Yes, exactly."

She sat up and hooked an arm around the back of his neck, pulling him closer. "Then how about if I take advantage of you. Multiple times."

Her lips met his. Hot, wet, open. Cain didn't even try to resist. His hands slipped into her hair and he pushed her back against the pillows, mindful of her wound, and devoured her. He couldn't hide the affect she had on him. Didn't even try.

He'd waited so long for this. *They'd* waited.

Pleasure arced through him. He swallowed her sigh as their tongues dueled, mated. He felt her fingers gripping his hair, keeping him close.

As if he were going anywhere else.

Cain eased his weight more fully on top of her, keeping off her injured side. He moaned as he felt one of her legs move up to wrap around his hips. Everything about this was right. This was Hayley. He'd been so empty without her.

He pulled back from their kiss, just needing to look at her face.

Eyes hooded, lips swollen from his kisses, hair tousled. He wasn't sure he'd ever seen anything as beautiful as how she looked right now.

"Everything okay?" she asked.

"Perfect," he said.

And he proceeded to show her.

Chapter Eighteen

"I'm such an idiot."

Cain responded from where he sat in the other room. "You have the highest IQ of anyone I know. You're very definitely not an idiot, and you're going to lose a couple more hours of work if I have to drag you back to bed and prove that to you."

She was glad he couldn't see her face since she could feel the heat rising in her cheeks.

She could feel heat rising in other places, too. Especially after last night.

The lovemaking between them had always been passionate, burning hot through them both. Last night they'd had a much different perspective than they'd had when they were teenagers. Both aware of how easily love could be lost. And how precious it was when it was in your grasp.

And although the passion had still burned just as hot, it had been undergirded with a tenderness and sense of being cherished. Nothing taken for granted.

"No, I think that got proven plenty last night," she said. And this morning. "But I said that because I think I've figured out how to draw out whoever is trying to kill me, and it's so simple. I've just been looking at it the wrong way."

Cain came and sat down next to her. He'd been doing that on and off all day. She wasn't sure if it was to provide moral support or to double-check what she was doing because even after last night a part of him still didn't trust her.

She was afraid to ask which.

"Since the trapdoor I set before I was arrested didn't gather much useful information, I've been trying other algorithms to see if I could figure out the pattern of the people using the CET exams for espionage."

"But no luck."

"Nothing. If they were smart they stopped once they found out someone was onto them. Or they may have just changed their patterns altogether. In that case, my finding them again the same way I did the first time would be a matter of sheer blind luck."

"But you figured out another way."

Hayley nodded, then brought a new set of figures up on the screen. "I don't need to find the seller. I can find the buyers."

"In the foreign countries."

"Yes. There have to be people allowed in to take these tests who are unusual in some way. I highly doubt they've recruited high school students from US Department of Defense schools on foreign soil."

Cain leaned forward to look more clearly at the screen and data she'd pulled up. "Maybe in a couple of the schools, but definitely not in all of them."

"The computer will filter out most of the kids and will pull files based on the criteria I've set for red-flagging—not being a US citizen, over eighteen years old or any ties to criminals in any country. We should have a list of people by the end of the day."

"You have access to that information?"

Maybe she should've asked him before pulling in all the law enforcement systems for her algorithms.

"Not me personally." She hesitated. "But Omega Sector, combined with the FBI and Interpol, do."

His face turned grim. "Did you just hack law enforcement databases from all over the world?"

She shrugged, not looking at him. "Technically I only had to open myself a window into the Omega system. You guys already had access to the other law enforcement and I could run it through you."

Cain ran a hand over his face.

"I'm not going to apologize for using every available resource I can access. Not when it comes to keeping my son safe."

"*Our* son."

She looked at him now. "Our son. Even more so. I would think you would understand that."

He rubbed his face again. "I do. It's just…"

"It's just you don't know if you can fully trust me."

He didn't say anything for a long moment. Finally he sat back in his chair. "You're right. I want to do whatever has to be done to keep you and Mason safe."

But that still didn't address the issue of trust. Which stung considering what they'd shared last night.

They worked in silence for the next few hours while the computer was running her program to sort out suspects. Hayley moved her attention to the Omega mole. Cain didn't put pressure on her to explain anything she was working on or justify any methods, but she noticed he never wandered far from where she was working.

Trust again?

The pressure of it seemed to crash down on her. Cain had never spoken about the future—with her or Mason—not even last night in the midst of their physical intimacy. Maybe he didn't plan on a real future.

And if he did, how could they even consider it when he was never going to be able to trust her again?

Hayley took her hands off the keyboard and put them in her lap.

"What's wrong?" Cain asked immediately.

"I want to see Mason." She hadn't seen her son in two days. Heaven knew she had gone much longer than that without seeing him, but right now with everything that was going on, and the world spiraling out of control, she wanted to see her son.

"Right now?" Cain asked.

She nodded, preparing herself for all the arguments he was going to make. That the work she was doing was more important than spending time with her child. That every minute not spent trying to catch the people selling secrets of the United States, the more dangerous it was for everyone, including Mason.

But instead Cain just nodded. "Okay. Give me a few minutes to set it up."

Tears pricked her eyes. His willingness to understand her need to see Mason meant a lot. She touched Cain on his arm as he was grabbing his cell phone. "I—thank you."

His fingers trailed down her cheeks. "Your needs matter, too. God knows you spent long enough without him."

Just when she thought there could be no future for them, he went and said something like that.

Gathering Mason into her arms an hour later, Hayley felt like she could breathe again. Just seeing his little face, feeling the fierceness of his hug, reassured the mother's heart in her.

He hadn't forgotten her. She always worried that he would. Intellectually she knew he wouldn't, but it was still hard to convince herself of that when her fears began to press in all around her.

But when she held him, all the fear melted away and the truth couldn't be denied: Mason loved her.

He squeezed her and gave her a wet kiss on the cheek until he saw Cain.

"Candy Cain!" Mason climbed from her over to Cain and began chattering about riding the roller coaster again. It took her a minute to realize what Mason meant.

Cain still hadn't quite figured it out, even though Mason kept pressing him. He looked questioningly at Hayley.

"He wants to ride the roller coaster again. You know, leap across a rooftop at full speed."

Cain threw back his head and laughed. "I don't know about that, buddy," he said to Mason. "But I'll bet we can find some other roller coasters to go on."

Cain flipped Mason onto his belly in his arms and flew him around the room. Mason's giggles could be heard all over the house. Hayley gave a quick hug to Ariel and shook the hands of Summer and Ashton, thanking them once again for allowing Mason to stay with them.

"It's really no problem. Chloe loves him and he's very gentle with her."

Hayley looked over to where Cain now had Mason tucked up under one arm and Chloe, who evidently hadn't wanted to be left out of the action, tucked under the other, flying them around the living room.

Cain would make such an amazing father. No matter what happened between the two of them—whether her heart ended in a bloody, broken state as she was afraid it would—Hayley would never try to keep Cain from Mason's life. She would be doing both of them a grave injustice.

"I understand you're trying to help bring down the mole inside Omega Sector." Summer came to stand next to Hayley as she watched Cain play with the children.

"Yes. I'm trying."

"Whoever the traitor is almost killed me, Ashton *and* Chloe. So when I say that we will make sure your family is safe so you can do your job, I mean it. Nothing is more important to us than catching whoever is behind these attacks."

"We're getting closer every day."

Summer slid an arm around Hayley's back and gave a little squeeze. Her smile was as bright as her name. "You don't strike me as the hugging type, but I wanted to do that anyway. I know it must be hard being away from Mason. And nothing makes up for Mommy not being here, but I promise we will protect him."

"Thank you."

Summer's words were enough, were everything to Hayley. This woman knew what it was like to have the ones she loved most targeted. Hayley could go back to Omega now, secure in the knowledge that Mason and Ariel were truly out of harm's way.

It was time to catch a killer.

Chapter Nineteen

"Cain, I've got something."

It was the next morning. Hayley had insisted on working all night after they'd returned from seeing Mason. He'd tried to talk her into stopping for rest, or even other things, but she was moving forward with a purpose now.

He could only admire it.

Her program was still narrowing CET exam takers in foreign countries. The first round of results had given them a group of suspects too broad, so she'd had to reset the parameters and run it again.

"CET case or the mole?" he asked.

"Mole. I've got a name."

"What?" Cain rushed to her side now.

She grimaced. "Not a real name, unfortunately. I've just discovered he calls himself Fawkes."

"Fawkes? As in Guy Fawkes, the British guy who attempted to blow up the government a couple hundred years ago?"

"I would assume so, especially based on what I found."

He sat down next to her. "Show me."

"It doesn't help with identification, but it's definitely

something set up by him. Or her. And it wasn't meant to be found. At least not this early."

"What is it?"

She brought up a picture on a screen, with the name of a file.

Manifesto of Change.

"What the hell?" Hayley opened the file and Cain began to read.

"'On my honor, I will never betray my badge, my integrity, my character or the public trust.

"'I will always have the courage to hold myself and others accountable for our actions.

"'I will always uphold the constitution, my community and the agency I serve.'"

Cain looked over at her. "That's the Oath of Honor law enforcement officers take at their swearing-in ceremony." He continued reading out loud.

"'We all took an oath to uphold the law, but instead we have allowed the public to make a mockery of it. Where is the honor, the integrity, the character in not using the privilege and power given to us by our training and station to wipe clean those who would infect our society? We were meant to rise up, to be an example to the people, to control them when needed in order to make a more perfect civilization.

"'But we are weak. Afraid of popular opinion whenever force must be used. So now we have changed the configuration of law enforcement forever.

"'And now, only now, will you truly understand what it means to hold yourselves accountable for your actions. Only with death is life truly appreciated. Only with violence can true change be propagated. As we build anew, let us not make the same mistakes. Let the badge mean something again.

"'Let the badge rule as it was meant to do.'"

Cain stared at the screen, reading the manifesto again silently before whistling through his teeth. "That's some pretty extreme stuff. Calling for a police state. For a law enforcement ruling class."

Hayley nodded. "And history wasn't my best subject, but it's pretty ironic that the mole chose the name Fawkes. Fawkes was trying to destroy the government to give the *people* more power."

"This guy is doing the exact opposite." Cain read the words again. "Can you tell when it's set to release?"

"I'm trying to nail down the date, but I can't. But it's for soon, Cain." Her brows knitted. "Maybe even in the next couple of weeks."

Cain cursed under his breath. "Who will it release to?"

"Everyone at Omega Sector, for sure." She typed a few commands into the keyboard and a flowchart came up on the second screen. "And it looks like it is set to then automatically forward to every other law enforcement agency Omega Sector is connected to."

"After some huge, violent event that we don't know."

"That obviously targets law enforcement in some way." She bit her lip. "And worse, because I know you're close with Ashton and some of the others, but this message is linked to someone on the Omega SWAT team."

Cain's curse was even more foul. "How certain are you?"

"Given the fact that the mole doesn't know I'm in the system? Almost completely."

"Do you know who?"

"No, because the mole routed the information

through almost every login ID on the SWAT team. Which was smart. Implicates everyone."

Cain thought of John Carnell and Saul Poniard, both of whom had caught his attention when he'd first been brought in for investigation. Carnell was a genius and definitely had the ability to do the computer dirty work Hayley was suggesting. Poniard was a power-hungry SWAT wannabe who had been reprimanded more than once for unnecessary use of force.

"There's only one SWAT team member whose ID wasn't used in the routing," Hayley said. "Someone named Muir. I don't know why. He might've just been overlooked or it's possible that Muir was skipped on purpose. Given that we accessed this information before the traitor meant to send it, I would start investigating this guy Muir as soon as possible."

"Gal."

"What?"

"Lillian Muir is a woman. The only female on the SWAT team."

And another one who'd been on top of Cain's *suspicious* pile. Given her history that she'd gone through so much trouble to hide, this Manifesto of Change could definitely be her brainchild.

Cain stood. "I've got to get this information to Steve so we can run it against upcoming events and possible terrorist attacks."

"Okay. I'll just keep working here. I should be able to manually eliminate some of these CET suspects my program is red-flagging."

Cain hesitated for just a second. He would be leaving her here, unprotected, knowing that the mole—

Fawkes—was also in this building and would kill her if given a chance.

Also knowing he would be leaving her here with full, unfettered access to a computer.

But damn it, he needed to get this info to Steve, so he could begin making contingencies. That couldn't be done here.

"Okay," he said. "I'll be back soon. Stay in here and keep the door locked."

Hayley's look was shuttered as she turned back to her computer. Obviously his hesitation hadn't been lost on her. Tension knotted Cain's shoulders as he walked to the outer door. There never seemed to be any easy solutions when he was with Hayley.

He turned back before he left. "It's your safety I'm concerned about, too. Okay?"

"But it's also about what you're afraid I might do while you're gone."

"I'm leaving you here so I'm obviously not that afraid." And he realized it was true. He would prefer it if he could stay by her side every time she was at a computer, since that's what he'd agreed to in the original parole easement agreement. But it was more because he wanted to be able to say he'd lived up to his end of the agreement than it was because he thought she was going to do something bad if left unsupervised.

She nodded, looking back at him. "Fair enough."

Fair enough.

That was just it, wasn't it? He and Hayley had to figure out their balance together. What was fair. What they wanted. How they fit together.

Cain walked back over to Hayley and leaned down to her. He cupped her face and brought his lips to the generous curves of her mouth. What he'd meant as a light kiss turned deeper. A fire licked at them both, and when he pulled away they both were breathing heavily.

"We have things to work out. And we will," he said.

"Everything feels so shaky sometimes."

He nipped at her bottom lip. "That kiss didn't feel shaky."

Her soft, sweet laugh wrapped its way around his heart. "No, it sure didn't."

He straightened and turned back toward the door. He really did need to get this Manifesto of Change info to Steve immediately.

"I'll be back soon. Stay out of trouble."

HAYLEY BROKE THE order to stay out of trouble in the worst possible way. Fortified with another mug of coffee, she dived into the CET case. She found a pattern an hour later. Confirmed it long after that.

Ran it one more time to be sure.

She shot back from her computer as if that would protect her from the information. She'd known it was someone pretty powerful who was selling the secrets. But she'd had no idea the link between the buyers would be a US senator.

Not only that, Senator Ralph Nelligar had been one of most vocal detractors of the CET exam system over the years. He was one of the people who had called for a speedy trial of the hackers, arguing that this sort of electronic exposure was what he'd been afraid of from the beginning.

Proving that Senator Nelligar was the one selling state secrets by using the test would be almost impossible. All Hayley had right now were vague links between his office and questionable people who'd taken the CET on foreign soil. Definitely not enough to convict the senator. Hayley was lucky she had someone like Cain who believed her at all.

Even worse, the senator had the resources to find Hayley and Mason, no matter where they hid. He was obviously the one behind making her parole documents disappear from the system and her rapid rearrest and arraignment. Hayley wouldn't be able to outrun him and his resources.

Maybe—*maybe*—Hayley might be able to build up enough evidence of the situation to scare the senator into stopping his actions. But she doubted she'd ever be able to prove it was him. Especially now that he knew she was the one who knew his secret. Cain wouldn't be able to help, either.

She was still just staring blankly at the screen, trying to figure out what in the world she was going to do, when Cain returned. She had no idea how long he'd been gone.

He took one look at her face and sat in the chair beside her. "What?"

She told him what she'd discovered. That all the paths were leading back to Senator Nelligar.

His low curse pretty much echoed everything she felt about the situation.

"I know," she whispered. "I know this is a lot and your plate is already full with what we found out about Fawkes. I just don't know what to do."

Cain rubbed the back of his neck. "We'll see if we can figure out some way to set a trap."

Hayley nodded, but she doubted the senator would

be dumb enough to fall for one. Not knowing she was looking for him.

"Meanwhile," Cain continued, "we're going to need to put you and Mason into protective custody."

"Last I checked, law enforcement wouldn't put a known fugitive in protective custody."

"Yeah, we'll have to work around that. I'll talk to Steve. We can work something out, even if it's temporary. But for right now, at least for a few days, you, Mason and Ariel are safe at Ashton and Summer's place. You have no ties to them and there's no official record of it."

"Yeah, we definitely need to remember that whoever is doing Senator Nelligar's electronic dirty work is good. Very good."

"As good as you?"

"Maybe." She shrugged a shoulder wearily. "The point is, we should work under the assumption that nearly any information put into a networked computer can be hacked by Senator Nelligar."

Cain nodded. "Got it."

"I should do more work now, but it seems pointless until I come up with some sort of plan."

He slipped an arm around her shoulders and kissed her temple. "We know who the bad guy is. That gives us a huge upper hand. Now we just need to wait for him to make a mistake, or even better, do something to cause him to rush into one."

"But I don't know what that is." Her brain was tired. She needed to get away from screens and keyboards. "Let me go rest in the apartment. That will help."

"How about if I take you to Summer and Ashton's. Be with Mason and Ariel. Get rest there." He held out a hand. "And before you even think it, this is not about not trusting you. You need a break from this."

She reached her hand up to twine her fingers with his. "What about you? You need a break, too."

"And I'll get one. Just not yet. Not with what you found about Fawkes and his damned manifesto."

"What did Steve think?"

"Same as us. That Fawkes has a big explosion planned and that this is his love letter regarding it. Problem is, without knowing who Fawkes is, we can't get as many agents focused on this as we normally would."

"Too big a chance of us tipping him off that we're onto him. I'm sorry I couldn't get a positive ID. He, or she, is pretty clever."

Cain trailed his fingers down her cheek and she couldn't help but lean into the touch slightly. "What you found is going to save a lot of lives. You take a break. Let Steve and me do some work. You can come back tomorrow and look at it all with fresh eyes."

Hayley prayed it would make a difference.

Chapter Twenty

Cain had been right: everything seemed not so over-whelming when she woke the next day, after ten hours of sleep, Mason running in to ask if she wanted pancakes.

"Kiss first," she said.

He scrunched up his little face, but then kissed her before running back into the kitchen. Hayley could hear Ariel and Summer in there with him and Chloe.

She got dressed and ran a brush through her hair—good thing about prison had been the elimination of a lot of unnecessary beauty habits—checked the dressing on her wound, and made her way out to help.

"There she is, just in time!" Ariel gave her a huge smile. "You look so much better."

"Thanks. I feel it. Looks like a feast in here."

Summer grinned. "We had two aspiring chefs." She set out a tray of pancakes and put Chloe into her high chair. Hayley helped Mason into his booster seat.

"Ashton's not here?" she asked.

"No, he got called in to work." Summer gave her a direct look. "A project only certain people can work on."

So he was helping Steve and Cain with the info about

Fawkes. Good. They needed all the people they could trust working on this.

It was only a few minutes later when Summer's cell phone rang. After talking into it for just a minute she handed it to Hayley.

"Cain wants to talk to you."

She took it. "Hello?"

"We've got to get you your own phone. I've got to get a new one, too. This burner has outlived its purpose."

"Yeah. There's a lot I need to start thinking about if we're going to be here long-term."

"I know you're supposed to have a full twenty-four hours off, but we think we might be onto something and I was wondering if you could come in."

"Sure."

"Okay," he said. "I'll be there to get you in about forty-five minutes."

"Why don't I just drive if Summer doesn't mind my borrowing her car?" Summer nodded from across the table, giving her an okay sign with her fingers. "It's a waste of time for you to come all the way out here just to go all the way back. Nobody knows I'm here, so it's got to be safe."

She heard Cain say something to someone else before talking to her again. "Yeah, that would be good. Evidently I have someone here to see me anyway."

"I'll call you as soon as I'm in the building."

Hayley hated to leave Mason again, but Summer assured her he was fine and welcome. Hayley provided a bit of information about what was going on, and the possibility of witness protection for her and Mason. To be honest, Hayley wasn't exactly sure what it would mean for Ariel and her upcoming plans for Oxford.

But as always, her cousin hugged her and told her they would figure it out.

As Hayley pulled out of the subdivision she tried to work through what this new change was really going to mean. Would Ariel be safe to go to Oxford? Would Senator Nelligar go after her to try to get to Hayley?

If she could take it all back, never accidentally stumble upon those dark activities, she would do it. She would do just about anything to keep her loved ones safe.

And she had to admit to herself that now included Cain.

She stopped at a red light, trying to come to grips with those feelings—

When the passenger door was flung open and someone got inside her car.

"Oh God." It took Hayley a second to realize what was going on. But before she could unbuckle her seat belt and fling herself out the door, she saw the gun pointed at her.

"Light just turned green. I need you to drive, Hayley."

Hayley's eyes flew to the woman holding the gun, her voice familiar yet different.

She did a double take. *"Mara?"*

The woman looked different, her hair no longer as teased and poufy as when she'd worked at the Bluewater. Her voice was different, Southern accent gone. Even her posture had changed—more domineering, self-assured.

"Drive, Hayley."

Somebody honked behind them, but Hayley still couldn't make herself move the vehicle. What was Mara doing in the car pointing a gun at her?

"Hayley." Mara gave a big sigh. "If you don't move the car my next call is going to be to have someone go point a gun at your son."

That got her driving immediately. She took off through the intersection.

"What are you doing here?"

"I know for a fact you're not that dumb, Hayley. Figure it out."

Hayley knew that the woman was obviously here due to one of the cases. What she didn't know was which one.

"Senator Nelligar sent you?"

"Actually, no."

"Fawkes?" She just kept driving straight, no idea where she was going.

"What the hell is Fawkes?"

So not the traitor inside Omega. "So the senator did send you."

"No, the senator has no idea I'm here. Has no idea anything is going on at all."

Hayley wanted to bang her head against the steering wheel. All the clues had led her to Senator Nelligar's office, so she'd assumed the man himself was behind the crimes of treason. But really it could've been any of his close assistants. Anyone who had access to the information and his computer network.

"You work in his office." It wasn't a question.

"Yep. I've been his aide for eight years now, although I'm on a temporary leave of absence to take care of some 'family issues.'" Mara used her fingers to make air quotes for the last two words.

"How did you find me?"

"You were nice enough to call me back a few days

ago. Once I had the details from that phone I was able to track it. It was used again today. I couldn't get inside Omega Sector, but it was easy to track where the call went. Turn left here."

Hayley did what she said, not wanting to take a chance that Mara would send someone after Mason, especially since Ashton wasn't home.

"Having to chase you across the country wasn't what I had planned. I still haven't figured out how you got out of the fire at the restaurant."

"Cain," Hayley muttered.

"Of course. Big Omega agent swooped in to your rescue."

"He wasn't even there for you or anything to do with the CET. He needed my help with another case."

Mara blew out an irritated breath. "We couldn't take that chance. As soon as your name showed up for a court order to get your computer privileges reinstated we knew you had to go. Although honestly I didn't think it was you who had figured out our little scheme."

Which was why so many of the other hackers had died and Hayley was still alive.

"Turn right at the next light."

Mara was leading her toward the outskirts of town, Hayley realized. Somewhere she could get rid of her quietly.

"I'm not just going to let you drive me somewhere so you can shoot me and dump my body, Mara."

"Oh, trust me, I'm not going to shoot you. That would be way too suspicious. Besides, we need you and Agent Bennett to die together in order for this story to work."

Mara had Hayley turn again, this time into a parking

lot for a three-story office building. A huge sign hanging on the front said the building was for rent.

"What is this?" Hayley said after Mara made her get out of the car with the gun.

"An empty office building," Mara said as if that explained everything. "This is where we're going to wait for Agent Bennett to show up."

Mara led Hayley through the door and up the elevator to the third floor. She opened a set of doors and pushed Hayley through. The space was wide and empty except for a desk with a computer that sat over near the window.

Hayley didn't know why Mara had brought her here, but it couldn't be good. She did know this might be her only chance to get away, so Hayley was going to take it.

She waited until she could feel Mara close behind her, then spun and knocked the gun out of the other woman's hands. Then it became a fight to see who could reach the weapon first. Mara dived for it but Hayley plowed into her, gasping as she felt her stitches tear from the wound at her waist.

Hayley elbowed Mara in the midsection and scrambled for the gun when the other woman doubled over, and had her finger on the tip of it, but Mara caught her leg and pulled her back. A second later Hayley cried out through the starburst of agony as Mara dug her knee into Hayley's wound. Hayley fell to the ground, gasping for air, and Mara was able to get to the weapon.

Blood was already soaking Hayley's shirt as Mara turned the gun on her again from where she sat breathing heavily on the floor.

"You know, you're really starting to piss me off.

You're lucky we need you and Bennett to be here when you both die or else you'd be dead already."

Careful to keep her distance this time, Mara gestured to the office chair by the desk and computer. "Sit there and don't give me any grief or you'll know what it's like to be shot twice in one week."

Hayley got off the ground, trying to resituate the bandage over her wound to help stop the bleeding. Handcuffs with one metal circle already linked around the chair's armrest handle hung to the side.

"Cuff yourself to the chair."

"I need my arm to be able to deal with my wound."

Mara laughed, an ugly, bitter sound that filled Hayley with dread. "Believe me, that wound is going to be the least of your problems." She pointed the gun at Hayley's kneecap. "Cuffs, or I make sure you can't run."

Hayley clinked the metal band around her wrist. Mara lowered the gun and tightened it, then fastened her other wrist with a second set of cuffs.

"Now what?" Hayley asked.

"Now we wait for Agent Bennett to show up. Shouldn't take very long."

"I won't call him. I won't lead him into a trap." Hayley prayed they wouldn't use Mason against her to make her lead Cain to his death.

Mara leaned back against the desk and stretched her legs out in front of her. "Oh, you won't have to call him. He'll come on his own."

"To rescue me? Do you really think that's a good idea? Cain works with one of the greatest law enforcement groups on the planet. You really think they won't be able to rescue me when they figure out I've been kidnapped?"

"Oh, sweetheart." Mara tsked and Hayley wondered how she could've ever liked the woman. "He won't be coming here to rescue you, he'll be coming here to arrest you."

"What?"

"Even right now Agent Bennett is being notified of this location. Where you and a couple of your hacker buddies have been participating in a few extracurricular actives of the illegal variety."

"Oh my God."

"Yeah. We knew we wouldn't be able to get Agent Bennett here alone by kidnapping you. Like you said, we'd be no match for Omega Sector. But how do you think he's going to feel when he's given irrefutable proof that you've been lying to him?"

Hayley jerked against the handcuffs and Mara laughed.

"Been lying to him about the boy. About the hacking. About the CET. Proof that you were just using Bennett as the fool who could get you unlimited computer access, so you could continue your espionage and blame it on poor Senator Nelligar."

Mara turned and walked closer, grinning. Hayley wanted to claw the other woman's eyes out.

"A representative from Senator Nelligar's office fortunately became aware of your dirty deeds and has brought the info to Bennett. He's hoping Cain will be willing to take you in without a huge scene. Nobody wants this to get into the press's hands."

"So Cain will come here to arrest me." Bile itched at the back of Hayley's throat.

"And won't it be a shame when you both die in the process of that arrest?"

Chapter Twenty-One

Cain wasn't particularly interested in meeting whoever was waiting for him in the lobby of the Omega HQ. The name—Joshua Lawson—had not rung any bells, nor had the man stated why he was here when he had someone call for Cain.

Cain had a ton of stuff to do, not the least of which was helping Ashton and Steve sort through the possible targets Fawkes might be considering. Plus, Hayley would be back in a few minutes and he needed to be with her as she ran down some possibilities for where Fawkes might be planning his—or her—attack.

When the lobby guard pointed Lawson out, Cain walked briskly over to the man dressed in a suit that was probably more expensive than all of Cain's combined.

"Mr. Lawson. I'm Agent Bennett. What can I do for you?"

Lawson shook Cain's outstretched hand. "I was wondering if I might have a few moments of your time to discuss a case you were the lead agent for a few years ago."

Cain very definitely did not have time to discuss old cases right now.

"Mr. Lawson, I am really very sorry, but today I am

totally swamped with something that is of a critical and timely nature."

Cain didn't want to dismiss the other man's concerns, whatever they were. But he couldn't deal with them today. "Would it be possible for you to come back next week? Plus I can give you the number of my office assistant and she can go ahead and pull the files for me so I can be better prepared to answer any questions you might have."

Lawson didn't look like he was going anywhere. "The case I need to speak with you about involves Hayley Green."

Cain's eyes narrowed. "I'm sorry, I didn't get who you represented or what this was about."

"I work for Senator Ralph Nelligar. We've gotten hold of some very interesting information that I think you will want to see. Preferably not here in the lobby."

The man who had offered a reward to have Hayley killed, who was committing treason by selling state secrets to foreign countries, was sending someone to talk to Cain *inside his own headquarters*?

Cain didn't know where the hell this was going, but he was definitely going to ride it out. Maybe Hayley wouldn't need to set a trap for Senator Nelligar. Maybe he was setting one for himself right now.

But it was definitely important that she not come waltzing through the door in case Mr. Lawson wasn't here alone. She could be arrested immediately.

"Can you wait here for a minute while I get us a conference room?" Lawson nodded and Cain grabbed the phone at the guard's desk to call Steve.

"Drackett."

"Steve, it's Cain. I'm in the lobby with a representative from Senator Nelligar's office."

Cain had already filled Steve in on what Hayley had found with the CET situation. "That seems pretty risky for someone in danger of being arrested for treason."

"I'm going to hear what the guy has to say. See if we can get Nelligar to hang himself. Hayley's on her way in, actually should've already been in by now. I'll need you to waylay her while I'm meeting with this guy in case this is a fishing expedition."

If Cain had to guess why Lawson was here, it was to figure out where Hayley was, so they could take her out.

"Will do. I'll set up conference room two for you."

Cain led Lawson to the conference room after his briefcase and person were scanned for any dangers. He shut the door behind them and sat down at the table.

"I know you said you are busy, so I won't waste your time, Agent Bennett. I need to talk to you about Hayley Green."

"What about her?"

"You are aware that Ms. Green is a fugitive, correct? She was last seen at your family's home when she was arrested."

Looked like this *was* a fishing expedition. "Yes, I am, and yes, she was. But she was brought into custody by Georgia law enforcement."

"And escaped," Lawson said. "But really that's not my point. We know Ms. Green has been…working with you."

"If the question you're ultimately asking is if Hayley Green is here, then the answer is no, she's not. Omega Sector and their agents do not make a practice of harboring fugitives."

All true, technically speaking.

Lawson smiled, and something about it made Cain's gut clench.

"We know where Ms. Green is. We also know there's a connection between the two of you that is very strong."

Cain wanted to stop and call Steve, see if Hayley had arrived yet. Because he very definitely did not like Lawson's assuredness about Hayley's location.

Cain leaned back in his chair, not giving away the panic itching at his throat. "Well, sounds like you know a lot of stuff. Which also probably means you know that someone is trying to kill Hayley. That a hit has been put out on her life." Cain watched the other man closely as he said it. Would Lawson try to deny it?

He didn't. "Yes, it would seem that way, especially to you."

"To me?"

"Agent Bennett, we have reason to believe that Hayley Green is the one who put the 'hit' on her own life."

Cain rolled his eyes. "So you're saying she wanted to pay someone to kill her."

"I'm saying she wanted to pay someone to make *you* think someone was trying to kill her."

"Is that so? And the fact that Hayley was *shot* by the would-be assassins at one point?" Cain knew he was giving away a little information, but knew he could cover if needed.

"A life-threatening wound?" Lawson asked.

Cain grit his teeth. "No." As a matter of fact he remembered thinking that as far as getting shot went, Hayley couldn't have possibly taken a bullet in a better place.

Lawson raised an eyebrow. "Let me ask you this. Did getting shot cause you to trust Hayley more or less?"

Cain didn't respond. He hadn't thought of her wound in terms of trust level.

Lawson took a different tack when Cain didn't answer. "You arrested Ms. Green nearly four and a half years ago with the CET hacking case."

"That's correct."

"What if I told you that I have proof that she was using the hacking to hide even more nefarious activities? And now that she's out of prison she's interested in resuming those activities—using you to gain early access to a computer without bringing law enforcement down on her."

Cain could feel tension creeping into his body at the other man's words. "I would say that sounds pretty far-fetched."

Lawson took sets of printouts from his briefcase. "I think this will provide proof of Ms. Green's questionable activities."

Cain sat as Lawson explained each paper. Showing him how someone had accessed the CET system again, for certain foreign countries like Hayley had been studying, but through a back door.

"Just like someone would do if they were going to say, sell secrets, using the exam."

"I agree it's suspicious." Cain now held the paper in his hands. "But this doesn't prove anything about Hayley."

Lawson pointed out numbers on each set of papers. "These are the Internet protocol addresses—or as you and I would call them, IP addresses—for the actions. I think if you looked it up, the first set are for your laptop computer and the second set are for a computer here within Omega Sector."

Cain wasn't sure what the IP address was for the computer here, but he did know his laptop. It was the same number.

And the dates and times recorded in the printouts were the very ones when Cain had felt like Hayley had been trying to sneak something by him. That her actions seemed suspicious. He'd wondered if she'd been trying to reconnect with the hackers she'd worked with. Then he'd decided it was just her nervousness concerning Cain finding out about Mason.

But looking at it now, it seemed like very damning evidence indeed.

The other dates and times were definitely at points where she'd been working at Omega HQ, sometimes completely unsupervised.

Cain wanted to rip the papers into shreds and throw Lawson bodily from the building. Wanted to pummel the other man. But that wouldn't solve the problem.

He couldn't believe this was happening again. Worse.

"Agent Bennett, we know you and Ms. Green had— *have*—a personal relationship. I can certainly understand how you would not want to believe that someone you've been intimate with could betray you and your country in such a way. Treason."

His personal feelings for Hayley had nothing to do with the situation at hand. He was about to tell Lawson when he slid across another set of papers.

"As you know, Ms. Green gave birth to a child while at the Georgia Women's Correctional Institute about four years ago."

Cain definitely did not want to talk about Mason with

this man. Especially not with what he'd just told Cain about Hayley. But he finally looked down at the papers Lawson continued to slide across the table at him.

Every ounce of blood drained from his face when he saw what they were.

"Complete blood work and DNA testing is done on any child born within the prison system of Georgia. For insurance purposes."

Cain couldn't believe what Lawson had given him to read.

"So, as you can see. Your DNA and the child's do not match. So you could not be biologically related to that child. I don't know that Ms. Green would've implied that you were. But in hopes that this makes your decision easier, we wanted to make sure you knew the truth."

Cain didn't want to look at the papers anymore. He folded them. "Do you mind if I keep these?"

Lawson gave a sympathetic nod. "Certainly. You might want to look it over more closely later."

The more compassionate Lawson looked the more Cain wanted to punch him. But it wouldn't do any good. Wouldn't change the past or anything that needed to happen now.

Cain could see exactly where he fell as a player in a very elaborate game.

It was time to end it.

"Why are you coming to me with this? What do you want me to do?"

"I'm not in law enforcement," Lawson said. "So I can't make an arrest. I don't want to lead regular police to where she is in case it gives Green a chance to warn the people she's been in contact with. And I certainly don't want the press involved."

Cain just nodded.

"These are very dangerous secrets she's been selling. Weapon and gun schematics as well as other valuable intel. Items that will give enemies of the United States the upper hand. Cost the lives of American soldiers."

Cain just wanted this to be over. "Where is she?"

"I'll take you to her. Right now, if that works for you. Then you can make sure she's put away for good."

Cain wiped a hand over his face and nodded. This was his chance to take control. To end this once and for all. He hardened himself against any thoughts of gentleness for Hayley. This wasn't going to be easy for either of them.

"I just need five minutes to line up a few things." Cain rubbed the back of his neck. "And to pull myself together." Cain felt like the papers with Mason's DNA results were burning a hole in his pocket.

Lawson nodded with understanding. "Sure. This is all pretty difficult to digest."

Cain just nodded. It didn't matter how difficult it was. He had a job to do.

Chapter Twenty-Two

Hayley sat handcuffed to the chair, desperate to try to find a way to contact Cain. He was going to walk into a trap and they were both going to die.

Mara had delighted in telling Hayley all the "evidence" her colleague was showing Cain right now. They were so clever, printing documents to make it look like Hayley had been the one selling state secrets. Making it look just real enough to be possible.

Once Cain was presented with this proof, Hayley wouldn't blame him for believing them. They'd done a damn good job of making it seem like Hayley had strung Cain along just to get access to a computer.

Mara and whoever else she was working with obviously knew their way around a computer. They were good. Their evidence was nearly flawless. Especially when Cain had never been able to get past his innate mistrust of Hayley to begin with.

Mara and Company had basically just given Cain a push in the direction his brain and instincts already had wanted to take him anyway.

"What if he doesn't buy it?" Hayley asked, hoping beyond all hope it would be true. She didn't want both of them to die here in this empty set of offices.

She didn't want to die here alone, either. But would take that over both of them dying.

Mara grinned at her, nothing friendly about the expression. "Oh, he bought it. Just got word. Your boyfriend was so distraught it took him twenty minutes to pull himself together, but now he's on his way. To arrest you."

Hayley pulled violently on the handcuffs holding her wrists, wanting desperately to get out of this chair and throw Mara across the room. Mara just laughed.

Mara read another text. "Joshua says Bennett is in 'full agent mode.'"

Of course he was. He wouldn't let the fact that they had a history, or even that she was the mother of his child, stop him if they'd convinced him she was guilty of treason.

"You know what I think sealed the deal?" Mara walked closer, still smiling. "I think it was the fake DNA and blood records we showed Bennett of your son. Records that showed the kid and he had no blood relation whatsoever."

Hayley kicked out with her leg hoping to catch Mara, but she just stepped back.

"So it is true! Ha! That was just a lucky guess on my part, thinking the kid might be his, since I couldn't find any record of you ever dating anyone else, even in the years you were both at different colleges. But I can just imagine handsome Agent Bennett's face when he found out little Mason wasn't his."

Hayley wilted in the chair, the last of her hope deflating. It wouldn't have taken much for them to falsify a medical record for Mason. Unless Cain took the time to truly authenticate it—which he clearly hadn't if he was on his way here—then it would look like Hayley had lied to him about their son.

Just another lie he thought she told him.

He probably couldn't wait to get here to arrest her.

Hayley just stared out the window at the offices across the street. Even if she could get up and wave her arms they probably wouldn't notice her. This building was fully empty, but that one had looked pretty deserted, also.

But trying to figure out a way to get the attention of people who may or may not be across the street was better than sitting here waiting for Cain to arrive and the mistrust between them to sign both of their death warrants.

When she heard the elevator ding she knew it was too late.

Mara came to stand right behind Hayley, her gun pointed directly at her temple. Cain would realize he'd been fooled, but he wouldn't be able to do anything about it.

The door opened and a young man walked in with Cain right in front of him. She could see shock blanket his features as he took in the situation. When he turned to face the man behind him, the guy had already pulled out his own weapon and had it pointed at Cain.

The man gestured to Cain's shoulder holster with his gun. "Take your weapon out, very slowly. Put it on the ground. If you try any daring heroics I'm going to be forced to shoot you and Mara will shoot Hayley."

Cain's eyes narrowed to slits but he did what the other man asked, putting his gun on the ground and sliding it away with his foot.

"What the hell is going on, Lawson?"

The man laughed. "Oh sorry, there's been a change of plans. We don't really need you here to arrest Hayley. We needed you here so we could make it look like you were *going* to arrest Hayley and then the two of you killed each other in the process."

Hayley watched as realization dawned on Cain's face.

"All that stuff you told me at Omega headquarters…"

"Yeah." Lawson shook his head ruefully. "False. Ends up your girl is not the only person good with the computer."

"You made all of it up?"

Lawson shrugged. "No. We did what any good con man does. We took elements of the truth and blended them with what we needed them to say."

Hayley had never seen Cain look so defeated. It crushed something inside her. She pulled at her handcuffs again. Cain looked over at them.

"You're the lady who worked at the Bluewater. You were there the night of the fire," he said to Mara.

"We tried to get rid of her that night, but you were too quick. Got her out of the building."

Cain took a few steps toward them, his hand held out almost as an apology to Hayley.

"And the hotel?" he asked. "Someone really was trying to kill Hayley. She didn't set that up."

"Ms. Green has proven exceptionally difficult to kill," Lawson answered. "Unlike her other hacker cohorts, who we were able to eliminate so easily."

Mara pushed at the back of Hayley's head with her gun. "We thought we had more time with you since you were actually following the rules of your parole and not accessing any computers. FYI, your fellow cocriminals accessed them as soon as they could manage it."

Hayley turned her head so she could look at Mara. "So you killed them because you couldn't figure out which one of us had set that trapdoor inside the CET system."

Cain took another few steps toward the window. Maybe he was thinking, like Hayley had, that there was someone across the street he could try to signal. Hayley needed to keep Mara's and Lawson's attention on her.

"We knew it had to be one of the top tier." Lawson followed Cain, keeping his gun pointed at him. "Some of the hackers weren't capable of that sort of maneuver. Mara never thought it was you, but I did." The man leered at her and Hayley couldn't help but cringe.

"You accessing a computer came at a very inconvenient time. We've made millions in our sales, but our biggest one yet is scheduled for next week," Mara said. "Normally we would just lie low for a few years, let this all blow over. But that sale is too big."

Lawson pushed Cain in the back with his gun. "In the billions with a *b* not an *m*. So even though this is going to bring down some definite heat on the situation, we still had to get rid of both of you. Because we know whatever you know, Hayley, you've told Agent Bennett here."

"You won't hurt Mason?" Hayley didn't even want to bring up her son, but if Cain was going to make a move she wanted to give him every opportunity she could.

Mara tsked at her. "We are not monsters. The baby doesn't have anything to do with this."

"Great." Cain rolled his eyes. "Criminals with a conscience. What is it you're going to sell with your billion-dollar sale? Is that going to cost any lives?"

Lawson just shrugged. "You mean plans for the newest stealth drones? Yeah, I'm sure that's going to come back to cost a few lives. But we're not actually pulling the trigger on those like we would be with the kid."

Cain took another step toward the window.

"Just in case you're thinking you might get some-one's attention from the other building, we made sure that was empty, too." Lawson gave them both a big grin.

Hayley deflated into her chair. That had been her last hope, that someone across the street would at least see what was going on, even if they couldn't stop it.

They were going to die here. Her eyes met Cain's. There was so much she wanted to say to him. Even to tell him that she understood how he could've believed the proof they'd given about her guilt. She would never expect him to trust her when what seemed like cold, hard facts of her guilt were laid out in front of him.

She wished she could just hold him one last time. Kiss him. But she knew they weren't going to let her, so she wasn't even going to ask.

Maybe she could take out Mara if they unshackled her before killing her. Hayley had no doubt Cain could disarm Lawson. It was Mara's gun at Hayley's head that was holding him back.

Hayley tried to get Cain's attention without the other two people seeing, to give him some sort of signal to take out the woman. Maybe Hayley would die, but it was better than both of them dying. It was at least a chance.

"Let's get this over with," Mara said to Lawson. "I'm sure the Omega people will be looking for these two soon."

Cain walked all the way over to the window to look out. "Is the senator even in on this at all?"

Both Mara and Lawson laughed. "No. His comput-ers are, but the man himself has nothing to do with it,"

Mara scoffed. "Although he gave us the perfect platform, didn't he?"

"To be the most vocal opponent of the CET because of the danger of it being hacked? And he really helped us out by making sure all you hackers went to prison so quickly and for so long. Gave us time to figure out who might be onto us." Lawson walked over and picked up Cain's gun from near the door.

Hayley shook her head. "The funny thing is I had just realized that since you'd found the trapdoor I wasn't going to be able to prove anything. We thought it was the senator himself committing the crimes, but would never be able to prove it unless he made a mistake."

Mara reached down and unbuckled one of Hayley's wrists. "Sorry. We couldn't take the chance. Although, had we known that, we might've given you a few more months to live."

"Especially since you're a fugitive," Lawson said. "We could've just let the law do our dirty work for us."

Cain turned from the window as Mara unshackled Hayley's other wrist. Now both of them kept their weapons pointed directly at Hayley's and Cain's heads.

"So let me make sure I understand this," Cain said, shoulders drooping more than Hayley had ever seen them. "You almost killed Hayley in the fire, then hacked law enforcement computers to make it look like she violated her parole, put a contract out on her life, which almost got her killed first by Officer Brickman, then again at the hotel. You kidnapped Hayley, then falsified documents again to make me think Hayley was behind all of this. And then you planned to kill us both."

Lawson looked over at Mara, chuckling. "Damn, it reads like a grocery list of badassery, doesn't it?"

Mara laughed, too. "And don't forget making billions of dollars selling classified documents. I think that should top the list."

Cain glared at her. "I do, too."

"And now we're going to make it look like you two killed each other in an arrest gone wrong." Mara pushed Hayley over toward the windows. "You both have got to have gunpowder residue on your hands for this to be believable for forensic purposes. We know enough to know that."

Hayley tried to catch Cain's eye as Mara put a gun in her hand. Maybe he could dive to the side or something.

Anything.

Finally he looked at her. But instead of trying to communicate, he just winked.

Winked.

What the hell?

"Ready?" Cain said.

Was he talking to her? Was she ready to shoot him? Ready to run? Dive? What was he saying?

Even Lawson was looking at him funny.

"Now," Cain said.

The word was barely out of his mouth before the glass of the window shattered and Hayley screamed, covering her face before she felt arms come around her and she fell to the ground.

Seconds later she peeked up as half a dozen people with guns and full tactical gear stormed into the deserted office. Mara and Lawson were both moaning on the ground, shot but alive.

Cain was lying over her, his body protecting her with his own, his arms covering her head.

"Are you okay?" he asked.

She realized she was. Except for a few cuts from the glass, she was uninjured.

"Yes. Wh-what just happened?"

"Cain, you bastard," someone on the SWAT team called out from across the room after they made sure it was secure. "You got them to admit to every damn thing. That was unbelievable."

Cain sat up and began carefully brushing pieces of glass off her and then himself, ignoring the SWAT team who were now handcuffing Mara and Lawson.

"How did they get here?" Hayley asked, pointing at the SWAT team, still trying to process what had just happened. "Were you able to signal them in some way? Did the team track your cell phone?"

But if so, why would he have *winked* at her just before Mara and Lawson were taken down?

Cain pulled a tiny earpiece out of his ear and showed it to her. "They've been with us the whole time. I was trying to buy them time to get set up and to see what we could get those two—" he gestured toward the criminals, who were now being treated for their gunshot wounds until the ambulance arrived "—to admit. Which, as it turns out, was pretty much everything."

Hayley felt like she was in some sort of daze. Couldn't quite figure out what was going on.

"But he showed you proof that I was selling the secrets."

"Yep. Pretty impressive proof, too."

"If you believed him, then why would you have SWAT here with you?"

Cain reached up and picked a small piece of glass out of her hair, then scooted closer so they were almost chest to chest.

"I never believed for one single second that you were the one committing the treason," he said, running the backs of his fingers down her cheek. "People were *dying* due to the secrets being sold. I knew you would never do that. It didn't matter how many printouts showed me otherwise."

"But what about the DNA testing with Mason?"

Cain rolled his eyes. "At that point I was just trying to keep from pummeling Lawson into the ground. I didn't even so much as read that piece of fiction. Not to mention a certain birthmark that had sealed the truth for me from the first time I saw Mason."

"So the time Lawson said you needed to pull yourself together?"

Cain's lips brushed against hers. "Time needed to get the *team* together. I knew this would be our best chance to end this once and for all. You're safe now. No one will ever be coming after you or Mason."

Hayley felt a tear leak out from the corner of her eye. She couldn't help it.

"Hey," he said, catching it with his fingertip. "It all worked out. Don't cry."

She wasn't crying because of what had happened all around her.

"You trusted me." Even when presented with overwhelming evidence of why he shouldn't. And they were alive because of it.

He pulled her closer. "You're worth trusting. And I hope I can convince you I'm worth trusting, too. The past is past. You and Mason are my future."

She launched herself into his arms, trying to find words, but having to settle for clinging to him instead. His arms folded around her, arms she knew would keep her safe, lend her strength, protect her and Mason from anything that would attempt to harm them. She would do the same for Cain.

She pulled him closer, desperate to feel him against her. Then suddenly the words she needed to say were so clear. Had been since they were teenagers.

"I love you," she whispered.

He kissed her with a reverence that brought tears back to her eyes.

"Me, too. Always have," he murmured. "Always will."

Chapter Twenty-Three

One month later, Hayley stood back before Judge Nicolaides in his Georgia courtroom. Brandon Han, Omega Sector agent and fully licensed attorney, sat at her side as representation.

Although this time she really shouldn't need it. She'd already been cleared of the fugitive charges, the correct information placed back in the law enforcement computer system. This was to revisit her parole.

Cain sat in the row immediately behind Hayley's table. Ariel had Mason outside in the hall running around.

"I'm glad to see you back here unharmed," the judge said from his seat. "And I understand there's been a change in some of your circumstances? Particularly in your last name?"

Hayley glanced over at Brandon, who just held out his hand for her to answer. After the last two times she'd gone before a judge, Cain could understand her nervousness.

"Yes, your honor. My full name is now Hayley Green Bennett."

"Did your husband ever tell you about the time he burst into my chambers and almost got himself arrested?"

Hayley spun around to him before returning to face the judge. "No, Your Honor."

"No matter. I forgave him seeing as I was once a big high school football fan." Judge Nicolaides looked down at the papers on his desk. "Interesting to me that the arresting officer in your original case was also named Cain Bennett."

"Yes, Your Honor."

Cain could tell Hayley was getting a little nervous.

"Ah, well, if you can get past being married to a man with the same name as your arresting officer, then I guess that's all that matters." The judge's smile said he knew exactly what was going on.

"Yes, sir," Hayley said softly. "I think I can manage."

"What I have in front of me is a petition for the complete repeal of your parole conditions. That, according to multiple agents in federal law enforcement, you have provided critical assistance in stopping terrorists from selling state secrets."

Both of whom would be spending their lives in prison if they didn't end up getting the death penalty. Mara and Lawson had been more than willing to provide details about their upcoming "billions with a *b*" deal in order to get whatever leverage they could for themselves, which hadn't been much.

Hayley nodded. "Yes, Your Honor."

"I trust that any hacking you do in the future will be on behalf of the United States government, not for any nefarious purposes of your own?"

"Your Honor, I am out of the hacking business altogether. I'd like to take the next few years and just concentrate on being a wife and mother."

Judge Nicolaides chuckled. "A job not without its own risks."

"And its own rewards."

The judge nodded. "I once assisted your husband because I told him I was there when he led the high school team to the state championships." He smiled at Hayley. "I was also there long after the hoopla died down and there were very few people left in the stands. You were one of them, waiting for Agent Bennett, very much out of the limelight. He came up to you and wrapped his arms around you like you were his lifeline. I've never forgotten that."

Cain had never forgotten that, either. Everyone had been running around the locker room and school, celebrating, making plans for the victory party. All Cain wanted to do was get to Hayley, who had never been comfortable around crowds or as the center of attention. When he saw her in the stands waiting for him, he'd felt relief, more, course through his whole body.

He had no idea how he'd let something as precious as Hayley get away from him, but he knew he'd never make that same mistake twice.

Judge Nicolaides looked at Cain and then back at Hayley. "Hayley Green Bennett, you are hereby released from the previous conditions of your parole. According to the State of Georgia, all time for your previous crimes has been served and you are free to go with no restrictions." The judge brought his gavel down on his desk. Everyone stood as the judge turned to exit.

Brandon hugged Hayley. "That's it, it's all over."

Cain saw the judge hand something to the bailiff before finding himself wrapped in Hayley's arms. He squeezed her to him in a way that left no room for either of them to doubt his joy in this outcome.

"It's time to move on to today's important events, like getting some ice cream," he whispered.

Her smile was radiant. Breathtaking. "No kidding. Mason will have our heads if we don't get him there soon."

The bailiff walked over and handed a small postcard to Hayley.

"Judge Nicolaides asked me to give this to you and Agent Bennett."

Cain looked up at the judge's bench, but he'd already retired to his chambers.

Hayley turned the card over so they could read it. It was a quote from Zig Ziglar.

We cannot start over, but we can begin now, and make a new ending.

Cain wrapped his arm around Hayley as they walked out the door. Omega Sector would continue their search for the person behind the manifesto and threat of attack, and he would help. But Hayley, like she'd said, was just going to spend as much time as she wanted being a wife and mother. If that was forever, that was fine with him.

They both were free to begin their new—and perfect—ending.

* * * * *

COMING SOON!

We really hope you enjoyed reading this book. If you're looking for more romance, be sure to head to the shops when new books are available on

Thursday
12th July

LET'S TALK
Romance

For exclusive extracts, competitions
and special offers, find us online:

f facebook.com/millsandboon

◉ @millsandboonuk

𝕏 @millsandboon

Or get in touch on 0844 844 1351*

For all the latest titles coming soon, visit
millsandboon.co.uk/nextmonth